BROWN EYED
Girl

La Fleur de Love: Book Three

By
LORI LEGER

CAJUNFLAIR
PUBLISHING

Copyright © 2012 Lori Leger

Cajunflair Publishing

www.lorilegerauthor.com

ISBN-10:194030525X
ISBN-13:978-1-940305-25-7
(New ISBN's for 6X9 version)

Edition 2

Cover art by Lori Leger

DEDICATION

To my sister, Carla Hebert Roemer—the caboose.
This one's for you. I love you, Sis!

ACKNOWLEDGMENTS

Thanks to my husband, Michael, for preventing the house from falling down around me as I write.
Thank you, Joan Granger, of Simple Memories Photography for the awesome photo of the author.

CAJUN FRENCH
words and phrases used in this story

Beau – Handsome
cher ami – dear friend
Comment ca va? – How goes it?
se beausir – to become more handsome
mon vieux monde – my old folks
mon pere – my father
ma mere – my mother
allons danser! – let's dance!
Non, non, non – No, no, no
Allons piquer, oui? – Let's make love, yes?
Arret ca – Stop that
Cher – dear
Moi? – Me
Je connais pas – I don't know
 putaine – prostitute, hooker, whore
gros betaille – big scary creature
oui – yes
I feel *ti peu* (a little) sick to my stomach, but *beaucoup* (a lot or very much) sick at heart.

Map of South Louisiana
Real and *Fictional* towns in book

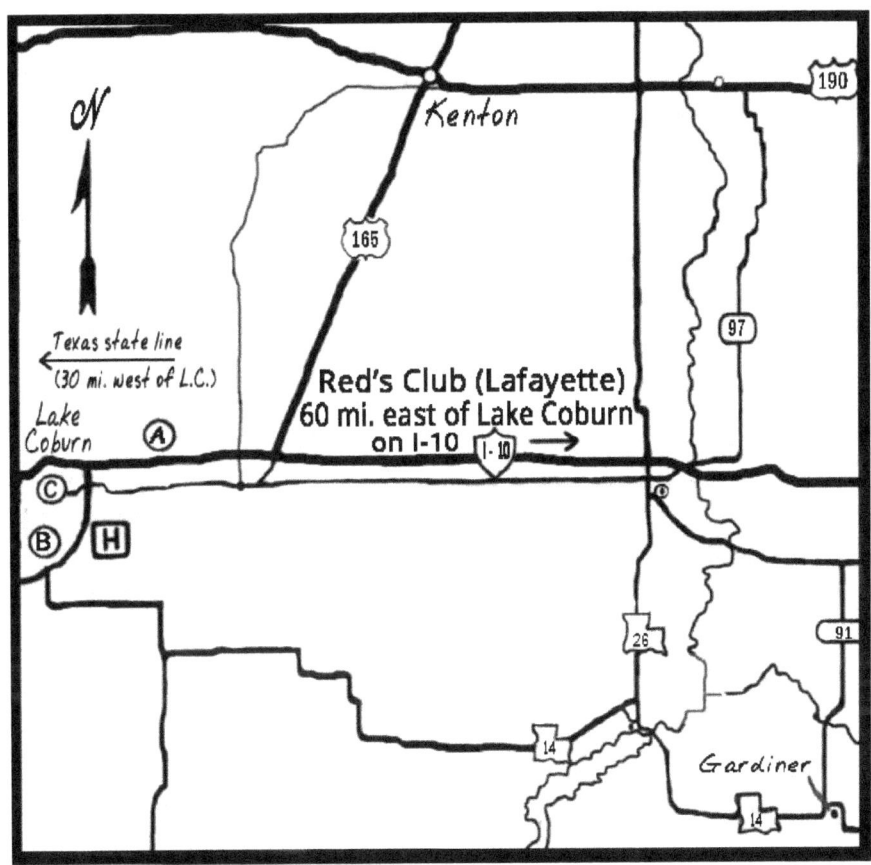

N

Kenton

165

190

97

Texas state line
(30 mi. west of L.C.)

Lake
Coburn   Ⓐ

Red's Club (Lafayette)
60 mi. east of Lake Coburn
on I-10   I-10 →

Ⓒ

Ⓑ   Ⓗ

26

91

14

Gardiner

14

LEGEND:

Ⓐ Red's new home
Ⓑ Tiffany's home
Ⓒ Site of Red's new L.C. Club

Ⓗ St. Luke's Hospital, Tiffany's workplace
(Red & Doc's 1st encounter in Last First Kiss)

Red's Club (Lafayette) is located 60 miles
east of Lake Coburn along I-10
Gardiner: Red's hometown

Houston, TX is 140 miles west of Lake Coburn

Prologue

Late August

He waited until the coffin had been lowered into the ground before tossing a single shovel full of dirt onto its surface. The rose he'd plucked from someone else's fresh flower arrangement went next, landing with a soft thud on the dirt. He stayed a moment longer, not to pray, but to make a promise: a solemn vow that the bastard responsible for this boy's death would pay, with his life, either six feet under or behind bars for the rest of his sorry-ass days.

He took a step back and turned away from the coffin, contemplating his options. This obviously called for a little research and a lot of patience, both of which he was adept at pulling off. He slipped a toothpick from his pocket and popped it into his mouth, using his tongue to flick it from one side to the other. By the time he reached his truck, he'd already mapped out a plan for revenge. He slipped the key into the ignition and his V-8's engine rumbled to life. One last glance at the gravesite and he shook his head. The little shit had been a worthless piece of crap for the most part, but he'd been the only family he had left in this world. No way would he let one asshole off the hook without paying—and paying dearly for what he'd taken from him.

He had no idea it would take two long years for his mission to ripen into execution mode.

Chapter One

October 25th
Bill Broussard's ranch
Giselle & Jackson Broussard's wedding reception

Damn, but he'd kill for a smoke right now. He flicked a toothpick from one side of his mouth to the other, trying to stave off the urge. Number one rule of surveillance—never do a damn thing to call attention to your position.

He watched as the groom's best man, Scott "Red" McAllister, laughed and carried on with the other wedding party revelers like he didn't have a care in the world.

"If only you knew your world is about to come crashing down, you son of a bitch," he growled. "I can't wait until you're wondering what the hell hit you, and where it came from."

Satisfied, for now, with visions of the future pain he'd cause McAllister, he relaxed in the shadow of the century old oak and watched the man whose life he was about to ruin. He slid another toothpick between his teeth and grinned, anxious for the kill, wishing today was the day to execute his plan.

He'd observed Red's gaze continuously shooting over to a particular blonde. She'd arrived with another guy, but that wouldn't stop McAllister if he wanted her. Up until now, McAllister hadn't paid any particular attention to one woman. He gave a satisfied grunt. If this bitch turned out to be someone special in Red's life, it would make his mission so much easier—one more thing to use against the self-righteous bastard. He studied the woman carefully for future reference and flicked the toothpick over his tongue before turning his back on the crowd. He made his way, almost certainly unnoticed, back to his vehicle, already itching to get his plan started.

He'd had to play it safe, had stretched his patience to the limit; and it was finally beginning to pay off. Everything was in place, and soon, very soon. McAllister would begin to pay the price for what he'd taken.

Tiffany LeBlanc skirted the edge of the dance floor while scanning the group of wedding guests for her missing fiancé.

"Come on, Tanner. Where the hell are you?"

Her grumble was spurred more from disappointment than anger. After a month of taking on an injured colleague's patient load in addition to her own, she was ready to relax and have some fun. She hadn't intended on spending the entire reception watching everyone else dance while she warmed the chair seat.

A moment after she muttered another low curse, she heard the masculine clearing of a throat from behind her. She swung around and stared up into the captivating blue eyes of Red McAllister, the groom's best man. The man she'd taken to calling "Sir Hunkalot" in the private confines of her mind's vivid imagination.

"Dr. LeBlanc, would you like to dance?"

His voice, deep and alluring—the black designer tux elevated his already buff good looks at least a notch or two up the sexy as hell ladder.

She faltered a bit at first before reaching out to his extended fingertips. He took her hand as she stood, led her to the dance floor. His large hand on the small of her back caused an immediate sense of awareness, sending chills up her spine. By the time they reached a clear spot on the floor she had to force herself to *breathe*. He captured her in his strong embrace and led her masterfully to the soulful crooning of Percy Sledge singing *When a Man Loves a Woman*. She took a deep breath, releasing it slowly.

Relax, Tiffany. He's just a man—one who's not your fiancé.

"The doctor can dance."

Somewhat startled by his words, Tiffany gave him what she hoped was a nonchalant nod. "She can, when she has the opportunity. You'd think as few chances as we get to cut loose, Tanner would be by my side." It amazed her how easily they fell into step. Despite her and Scott McAllister's sketchy first meeting back in August, she couldn't deny the pull she'd felt in his presence since then. She'd thought about him often over the last few months. Every instance had resulted in her feeling, in turn, guilty—then determined to try even harder with Tanner.

Not that it had done any good. Despite Tanner's constant urging, she was no closer to setting a wedding date today than she had been two years ago when they'd become engaged. When anyone, including herself, asked what she was waiting for, she drew a complete blank.

She supposed the *Cindy Lou Who* in her was hoping Tanner would stop chasing other women before they built their life together. Her inner *Grinch* suspected he never would. Living with Tanner had proved to be an extreme challenge without the marriage license. She couldn't see life with him getting any easier. What she wouldn't give for a peek into a Gypsy's crystal ball right now.

Red moved Tiffany smoothly around the dance floor, showing off his skills. If nothing else stayed with her about this evening, he wanted her to remember how well they danced together. He'd thought about her often over the last few months, although he'd only had the opportunity to see her a few times since Jackson's hospital release. Her image had invaded his thoughts no less than several times a day, not to mention the nights.

He passed his right index finger lightly over the huge diamond she wore on her left hand. He hoped to make enough of an impression on her today to have her question her engagement to Tanner. No way did he want to see her married to that asshole.

As though thinking of him conjured the devil himself, he suddenly spied her missing fiancé walking toward the barn and stable area. Something about Tanner's body language caught his attention—kept him from mentioning his presence to Tiffany. He moved stealthily, casting furtive glances around as if to make sure nobody followed him. Red scanned the area around the stables, caught sight of his youngest sister, Annie, disappearing into the structure. She'd always been an animal lover, so of course she'd want to check out Bill's livestock. He suspected Tanner's trip to the barn was for completely different reasons. By the time the song ended, Tanner had already reached his destination.

Itching to interfere, Red walked Tiffany back to her seat. "Thanks for the dance, Doc, but there's a little something I need to tend to." He rushed to the stables, still reeling over how good it felt to hold Dr. LeBlanc in his arms.

He hit the entrance just in time to hear his younger sister's angry objections.

"Stop it, asshole!"

Red homed in on her voice and turned into the last stall. Just in time to see Annie throw every ounce of her tiny, plus or minus one hundred pounds into a slap to Tanner's face. Before the man had a chance to recover she tripped him and shoved him down into a pile of hay.

"Don't you have a fiancée?" she snarled.

"Yes he does, and she's been looking for him." Red stepped forward surprising both Annie and her would-be-molester.

Annie spoke up, her voice calm, unruffled. "I can take care of myself, big brother."

Red nodded at his sister. "I can see that, but I have a vested interest in this. Tanner here is the reason I wasn't invited to Jackson's first wedding fifteen years ago."

Annie turned on the man still on his butt in the hay. "You're that asshole? If I'd known, I'd have done some *real* damage to that pampered face."

Red walked slowly toward Tanner. "Please, Sis, allow me."

Tanner scrambled to his feet and backed up to the rear wall of the stall, He raised his hands, clearly concerned. "If you damage my hands, I'll sue!"

Red shook his head slowly. "I won't touch your hands." He swung with his left fist and connected with Tanner's jaw.

"Crap, Scott!" Tanner gingerly felt his jaw as though feeling if it was broken. Satisfied that it wasn't, he looked up. "Okay, I'd say that evens things up, wouldn't you?"

Red smiled. "You wish, asshole. That was for Annie. I've waited fifteen long years for this one." He hit him square in the nose with a powerful right.

Tanner swore as blood gushed from his nose. "Son of a bitch! You broke my nose!"

Red looked down his nose at Tanner. "You deserve worse than that, but I don't want to ruin the wedding. If you go out there and make a scene, I may reconsider."

Tanner pressed a handkerchief to his nose, as Red took Annie's arm gently and turned her toward the exit.

"Oh, one more thing," Annie said, pulling out of Red's grasp. She stepped in front of Tanner and with one lightening quick move, had him on his ass again—this time in a pile of fresh horse manure.

Red burst into laughter. "Damn girl, that was cold."

"Hmm, I don't know." Annie stared at the man struggling to rise from the 'muddy' surface. "It looks kind of warm to me."

Red smiled as he watched his sister's approach. "Somebody's kept up with her self-defense classes."

"Religiously." Annie flashed her brother a grin as they headed out the stall and towards the door.

"Could you at least get Tiffany?" Tanner called out in a muffled, nasally voice.

"That's the plan, asshole." Too late, Red realized he'd spoken loud enough for Annie to hear. His youngest sister's head whipped around to face him.

"You really like her, don't you?"

He shrugged, trying to make light of the situation. "I don't think she deserves to be saddled with a fool like Tanner, that's all." He cringed at her next words.

"Bullshit! You're crazy about her."

Hoping to sway her, he tried to change the subject. "Did you see any new foals in the stable?"

"Are you in love with Tiffany, Red?"

He stopped to glare down at the diminutive clone of his mother. "No, I'm not, and quit trying to make more of this than what it is. I want Tanner to suffer, that's all." He snorted, disgusted at his sister's knowing grin, all too aware of what it would mean for him. He walked away from her then shook his head at the sound of her reciting an old jump rope song from when she was a kid.

"Scottie and Tiffany sitting in tree—K-I-S-S-I-N-G."

He lifted his head to call back at her raucous laughter. "You're such an infant."

Back at the reception, a word to his club DJ assured immediate play of two specific songs. That done, he turned to where Tiffany still sat, scanning the crowd for her missing fiancé. He approached, extending his hand. "Dance with me, Dr. LeBlanc?"

Her eyes softened, crinkling at the corners. "I will if you call me Tiffany."

"I will if you call me Red." She nodded as he took her hand and led her to the dance floor. He wanted to make the best impression possible on this woman before she discovered what he'd done to her man.

"Jackson's made a remarkable recovery since his bike accident in August."

He smiled. "I told you he would, didn't I?"

"Yes, you did. You were very—" She cleared her throat. "—opinionated about the matter."

He chuckled. "You can say it. I was a hard ass when you talked about amputating his leg."

"Yes, well. You said he would come back from that and you were right."

He lifted one shoulder. "Yes, I was."

Her laughter rang out between them. "Humble to the very last."

"I had the advantage of knowing the man for twenty years. You couldn't have known how determined he'd be to recover. Still . . ." This time he cleared his throat. "I shouldn't have insulted you the way I did. You were concerned for your patient."

"And you were concerned for your friend. Truce?"

"Absolutely." He took her around the perimeter, forced himself to breathe as he molded his hand to fit her lower back. It took a monumental effort to keep his dance steps smooth and fluid, when all he wanted to do was pull her closer, find out how her mouth would taste if he kissed her.

He couldn't help but marvel at how good she felt in his arms.

She'd have had to be dead not to realize how well they fit together, moved together on the dance floor. She would have had to be blind not to see how good he looked tonight. As a woman who ran every day to keep in shape, she could well appreciate the lengths he must go to keep up his athletic build.

Red possessed a wealth of physical qualities—each one equally attractive in and of itself. When combined, oh so perfectly, on his muscular sex foot plus—uh—make that *six* foot plus frame—he was damn near irresistible.

Think about the dance, Tiffany. Nothing else, just the dance.

She tried, but their movements were so well matched, so perfectly synchronized, that she found herself wondering what else they'd do well together.

Really? Time to get a grip.

Her hand tightened involuntarily on the well-developed trap muscles. Her heart kicked it up a notch or two.

Not that kind of grip. You're engaged to Tanner. You remember Tanner, don't you? That guy who spouts excuses, lies, and alibis like Mount St. Helens spouts ash?

The thought of her wandering fiancé should have been enough to give her overheated thoughts an ice water bath. She closed her eyes, resisting the urge to loop her arms around Red's neck, and waited for the gradual return of sexual sanity. It didn't.

She opened her eyes—found his crystal blue gaze locked on hers.

Damn, but they moved well together.

Doc opened her eyes, caught him studying her. The real shock came when she didn't look away. They had obvious sexual attraction—strong—evident in the pull between them—difficult to resist. Like opposite poles of two magnets. Somehow, he found the strength to avert his gaze, break the eye contact that held him hostage.

Red applied pressure on her back, her slim waist, pulled her closer, tried not to think about other things he'd like to do with her besides dance.

She didn't speak again. Probably for the best, since the less he spoke, the better off he seemed to be when it came to Dr. LeBlanc. But God almighty, he'd never felt so comfortable with a dance partner before. Two words—*perfect fit*—kept flashing across his mind. As soon as the first song ended, he whisked Tiffany right into the second dance before she had a chance to protest.

He watched her head fall back, her eyes drift closed in surrender, as John Michael Montgomery crooned an old song called *Hold on to Me.*

"Oh God, I adore this song." She spoke in a low groan.

I adore you. He stared at her exposed throat, wishing he could bury his mouth on the smooth expanse of delicate skin. His breath hitched as she smiled, lifting her head slowly to open her eyes. "It's an old favorite of mine, too," he confessed.

"You're a fabulous dancer, Red."

He shook his head. "I'm a good dancer. If I'm fabulous, it must be due to my partner." He gazed down at her beautiful face. How the hell could Tanner look at another woman when he had this? Maybe it was the beer responsible for his loose tongue. Maybe it was simply wanting better for Tiffany. But he couldn't stop himself from asking the one thing he'd wondered since meeting her.

"Why do you put up with him, Doc?"

Her body language shifted immediately, a slight stiffening of her spine at his invasive curiosity.

"We have things in common—and five years together."

The senseless answer set his teeth on edge. "Neither of which is good enough reason to marry him. You've got to know what a jerk he is."

She shrugged in his arms. "He can be at times. At other times he can be very charming and sweet."

Red emitted a barely audible snort then pushed all thoughts of Tanner aside, and tried his best to enjoy the feel of Tiffany in his arms before he'd have to let her go. He wasn't completely delusional. He knew exactly what her reaction would be once she found out what he'd done. She'd be good and pissed at him, but what the hell—If victory was fleeting, he'd enjoy it while he could.

He rubbed his thumb gently on the small of her back—she shivered through her silk blouse. Lowering his head slightly toward the crook of her neck, he inhaled. A fragrantly soft floral aroma combined with her unique scent to tantalize his senses. He'd fantasized about holding her in his arms this way. Red pulled her even closer, held her tight for the duration of the dance. Neither of them spoke again until the last faded notes. He kept her at the edge of the floor for a moment after the music ended, reluctant to let go of her.

The damage done, he released her, gave her a somber look. "Thank you, Tiffany. Try to remember these last few minutes, would you?" He pointed toward the stables. "You'll find Tanner over in that building. He may need your assistance." He left her there. Walked away, knowing good and well she watched his departure.

⚜

Try to remember? What the hell was that about? She stepped off the platform, and headed in the direction he'd pointed. Even then, she was drawn to him. She studied Red's retreating form, noting the grace and ease of his movements. The man looked every bit as comfortable in that classy black tux as he did in a pair of boot cut jeans and a polo shirt.

And his smell—God, he smelled divine. It had been all she could do not to bury her nose in his solid, broad chest during that dance. Red McAllister was a man whose persona oozed with confidence and masculinity. He was obviously intelligent, but she sensed other qualities as well. Pushing the thought from her mind, she turned her attention to her trek to the stables. Her childhood nanny, Melinda Dawson, had always said wondering 'what if' never did her any good.

Tiffany walked at her leisure, observing the lovely grounds of the ranch. She'd always longed for country living. On more than one occasion she'd tried to convince Tanner to find something outside the city. It was one of many reasons she resented him—he said he wouldn't be stuck like some bumpkin when he could be close to everything he enjoyed right there in the condo. She suspected he just didn't want to drive so far to sleep around on her.

So, why *did* she put up with him?

Because, according to her mother, all men cheated, that's why. In the upper class household in Houston, Texas, where she and her brother were raised, their parents both had open affairs. Her father had mistresses, and her mother had her kept men.

The thought brought her back to Red and how both Jackson and Giselle always gushed about him. He didn't seem the type to take anything lightly, especially marriage vows. She dismissed the thought as irrelevant. She had five years invested in Tanner, and at thirty-six years old, she was too old and emotionally exhausted to start over with anyone new.

Tiffany finally reached the stables, entered the shaded area and saw her fiancé leaning against the wall with his handkerchief over his nose.

Noticing her approach, he removed the cloth to speak. "You took your sweet time getting here."

"I was just told where I could find you. What happened?" She checked out his nose. "Ugh. It's broken."

He pushed her hand away. "I know that. You may be the great Dr. Leblanc, but I'm a surgeon too."

Ignoring his attitude and his brush off, she reached out again to examine his nose. "How about an explanation. Did you fall off a horse or something?"

"You really think I'd ride a horse dressed in an Armani tux? That cretin, Scott McAllister hit me in the nose."

Tiffany froze, trying to comprehend his accusation. "Red hit you?"

"Red? You call him *Red?*"

"Everyone calls him that."

"Not everyone, Tiffy—only his low class family and white trash friends. His betters would call him Mr. McAllister, or Scott, or better yet, how about asshole?"

She shook her head. "That's real classy, sweetheart. Besides, he just asked me to call him that when he . . . before he . . . he . . . aaah, now I see." She squeezed her eyes shut as it all came together. Not one dance. *Two* dances. She swore under her breath then eyed her fiancé suspiciously. "Why did he hit you?"

"Over something that happened fifteen years ago. It was nothing. *Less* than nothing."

She reached out her hand. "Give me the keys." He fished in his pocket and threw them at her. "I'll bring the car around." She headed back toward the parking area, wondering why she was even surprised. Of course her image of Red McAllister was too good to be true. He was just a man. This was more proof that not a single one of them could be trusted.

Sons of bitches. Every. Last. One of them.

Red followed Doc's trudge to the silver Mercedes and decided to enact some damage control. He approached as she opened the car door. "Did he tell you why I hit him?"

She rounded on him, her brown eyes flashing furiously. "Does it matter? Does it ever matter why somebody feels it necessary to break someone else's nose? Really, *Mister* McAllister," she sneered. "I didn't think you were such a brute. I thought after thousands of years of walking upright, surely your people would have found a way of resolving issues other than with their fists—especially issues that are fifteen years old!"

"Fifteen years?" Slack-jawed, he thought about explaining the situation. Then he recalled the phone conversation he'd overheard outside the hospital the day he met her. The moment he discovered she was Tanner's girl. His mind conjured an image of her crying silently because her fiancé was with another woman, obviously not the first time. Instead, he took a deep breath and released it slowly. "Well, Doc. Sometimes there's no other way to resolve a conflict."

WHAP!

The slap came out of nowhere, fast and furious, the sound resonating in the open air.

"*That's* for not telling me about Tanner until after those two dances," she hissed. "I despise being used to make someone else suffer."

His hand on his stinging cheek, Red stood speechless as she got into the car. He kept vigil as she drove to the stables to collect her poor, pitiful fiancé. His gaze followed the car as it continued on out the driveway and onto the paved road that led back into the city.

He whistled, rubbed his still stinging cheek. Despite everything Tanner had put her through—was still putting her through—he'd yet to put that fire out in the good doctor. He turned as Jackson called out to him.

"Hey, did ya hear the big news?" Jackson grinned from ear to ear. "We're pregnant."

"No shit? Well, damn that was quick! Congratulations." He gave his friend a quick hug and slapped him on the shoulder.

"Thanks, man." He scanned the area. "Do you know where Doc is? Giselle wanted me to find her—she said she wanted to tell her personally."

"She had to bring Tanner to get some medical attention. His nose got broken."

"By what?"

Red raised his right fist and flashed Jackson a smug grin.

"No kidding?"

He nodded then related the story in its entirety to his friend. "I wasn't trying to break the damn thing. That was a bonus, or *lagniappe* as my mother says."

Jackson reached up to adjust the angle of Red's chin. "She left a hell of a mark on you. I hope she didn't hurt herself."

Red frowned. "Thanks for the concern, buddy."

"Hey, she heals people with those hands."

Red rubbed his cheek. "I assure you, her hands are fine," he said, wondering to himself what else she could do with those hands of hers.

Jackson started to chuckle. "Oh, man."

Red stared at his friend. "What's wrong with you?"

"Now I know how Carrie and Uncle Bill knew I was in love with Giselle."

"What are you talking about?"

Jackson poked Red's shoulder. "You've got a serious hard-on for Doc."

Red stuck a finger in his friend's face. "I'll let that one slide because it's your wedding day and all. But don't you talk that shit in reference to her again, man. She's better than that."

Jackson stopped, stared at him long enough for Red to wonder what the hell was going on. "Oh, man. You didn't tell her what he tried. This is serious."

"How do you figure that? My mom taught me to be a gentleman, you know. Besides, she doesn't think I'm good enough for her."

"What did you say to make you think that?"

"For one thing, her 'your people' comment." He pointed at his cheek. "And let's not forget this."

Jackson chuckled. "I think she was making a comment about men in general, Red, not your fine Scottish-Cajun heritage. Damn, you're sensitive when you're in love."

"Your ass!" Despite his annoyance at his friend, Red followed Jackson back to Giselle's side.

"Hey hon, you're going to love this. It seems my best man, here, is crazy about my doctor."

Giselle sent Red a sly grin. "You mean you've finally admitted it to yourself?"

Jackson gawked at his wife. "Wait, how could you possibly know that already?"

Giselle laughed "How could you not? He asked about her every time we saw him. Really Red, why do you think I asked you to drive Jackson to some of his appointments? You're probably already in love with her."

He slung an arm casually across her shoulders. "I figured it was so you could get some time away from the patient from hell, here. You're wrong," he said, into her ear. "But, it's the thought that counts, so thanks, anyway. Congratulations, by the way. I hear you're *en famille*."

The smile she sent him was all-knowing, bordering on downright gleeful. "Thanks, but honestly—you guys are so clueless sometimes."

Red waved off her comment and headed toward his parents, who stood a few feet away, talking to Carrie Langley, an old family friend.

Carrie looked up at his approach. "Speaking of the red-haired, blue-eyed devil, here he is. I was just remembering how cute you were when I used to babysit for you, all those years ago."

"And I was your favorite, right?"

"You're still my favorite, but what the hell happened to you?" Carrie placed a hand to his left cheek.

Red raised his hand self-consciously to his face and reached desperately for a change of subject. "I'm looking for a dance partner. Are you game?" His effort was wasted apparently, because once his mother got a good look at his face, there was no way around her.

"Son!" Vivienne McAllister's voice rose in outrage. "Have you been fighting?"

"No, someone slapped me."

"What did you do to make a woman slap you that hard? Did your father and I not teach you to be a gentleman?"

Red stared down at the tiny woman who'd raised him and his siblings with a firm hand. The silver mixed in with her naturally blonde hair sparkled under the artificial lighting of the outdoor reception area. The short, sassy style of cut complimented the clear blue eyes and smooth skin of the sixty-four year old woman. She was fit, healthy, and blessed with good metabolism, weighing maybe ten pounds over the weight she was on her wedding day. Vivienne Broussard McAllister was a beautiful woman, and when she was anywhere near her husband, Pete, anyone could tell they were still in love.

"It's not what you're thinking," Red added quickly. "Do you remember when I got kicked out of Jackson's first wedding?"

"Vaguely." She gave him a suspicious glare.

"Well, Tiffany's fiancé, Tanner, was the reason, and all I can say is, payback's hell."

"Oh, Red, what did you do?" Vivienne groaned.

Annie walked up to the group and joined the conversation. "Take it easy on him, Mom. He was defending my honor."

"How's that?" Pete McAllister, a taller, older looking version of Red spoke up, his voice an ominous growl. At sixty-eight years old and well over six feet tall, with big, broad shoulders, a barrel chest, and a bit more belly than in previous years, he still commanded attention. He had a head full of dark auburn hair, peppered with silver, with a mustache and trimmed goatee to match. His blue eyes, normally sparkling with laughter, now flashed with anger, hinting at the damage he would do to anyone who tried to harm a hair on the head of his youngest daughter.

"I went to the stables to check out the animals, and didn't realize Tanner was following me," Annie explained. "When I turned around he was there and started pawing at me, so I slapped him, and then knocked him on his butt. Red came running in, hit him in the jaw then punched him in the nose. It was beautiful!"

Red threw an arm around his baby sister. "Thanks sis, it's nice to have a cheering section."

"I'm still confused," Vivienne commented. "Who slapped Red?"

"Tanner's fiancée did after she saw what I did to him."

"It seems like she should have slapped this Tanner fellow for trying something with Annie."

"I didn't tell her that part."

Annie's mouth gaped open. "Why the hell not?"

Red gave the group of onlookers a shrug. "I didn't want to hurt her. I let her think I hit him because of getting me kicked out of Jackson's first wedding."

His mother clucked her tongue in distaste. "Honestly, you men and your fists. Can't you settle anything without fighting?"

Pete grunted. "Don't listen to your mother, Scott. As far as I'm concerned, you could have broken a rib or two along with the nose. Really give him something to think about next time he wants to go poking where he shouldn't."

"Pete! Carrie, *you* tell him how foolish they're being."

"Sorry Vivi, I have no sympathy for Tanner Collins. When Jackson was still in surgery, even knowing Giselle was his girlfriend, that slimy son of a gun still tried to play touchy-feely with her. A few broken ribs would have served him right."

Vivienne turned to Red. "He tried something with Giselle while poor Jackson was in surgery?"

Red nodded. "Giselle said he was the pretty boy type that couldn't be trusted."

"Oh, well—I can understand that." Vivienne gazed up at her husband and smiled. "Your father saved me from marrying someone like that." She touched Pete's face tenderly and he leaned over to give her an indulgent kiss.

Annie groaned and rolled her eyes. "Oh, good Lord! Somebody stop them before they cause a scene."

Red gaped in disbelief at his sister. "Are you ever going to accept that you weren't the product of a virgin birth? You're the last of eight children, Annie. They *did it*, okay? You should be thankful our parents still show affection for each other."

"I know that, but must they *do it* in public? It's embarrassing," she hissed.

"Infant," Red pushed playfully at her.

"Bully," she shot back, shoving him.

"Was I a bully when I rescued you from Tanner?"

"I didn't need rescuing. I'd already put him on his butt once. If he'd tried anything else I would have kicked him in the bal…"

"Annie Nicole!" Vivienne's bark had Annie's mouth snapping shut, any and all remaining commentary cut short. "Surely you two can find a better topic of conversation."

"Yes ma'am," Red mumbled, knowing better than to argue with her. He caught the look of amusement in Carrie's eyes. "Where's Sam, Carrie?"

She pointed at her approaching husband. "Here he comes, now." She waved him over and linked her arm through his.

"Hey, Sam," Vivienne said. "You know, it's obvious how happy you've made Carrie the past fifteen years."

Sam nodded. "Thank you, ma'am. I appreciate that. She's the reason I've been so happy for the last fifteen years, too." He smiled down at his wife as she touched his face lovingly.

Red nudged his sister. "Hey Annie, I bet Carrie and Sam still do it, too."

Annie looked at her brother in disgust. "Oh, you are such an ass!" She stormed off as the group dissolved into laughter. Before she got too far, she stopped and turned. "Hey Red!"

The smirk on her face gave him fair warning. All he could do was suck in his breath and wait for it.

"Did you ask Mom to start planning your wedding yet? It's only a matter of time."

Red watched his imp of a sister spin about and dart off, cackling like a little bantam hen. He turned slowly, seeing four sets of eyes boring into him.

He raised his hands and started backing away slowly.

"She doesn't know what the hell she's talking about, I swear she doesn't." He turned on his heel and hauled his butt out of there before either of the two salivating women could fire any questions at him.

Red joined the groom and his Uncle Bill, already deep in conversation. "Hey, Bill, is it true you're thinking about selling this ranch?"

Bill Broussard nodded brusquely. "Yep, my new wife and I bought a pretty little spread just west of Kenton so our daughter wouldn't have to switch schools. You know somebody who's interested?"

"I sure do. I want it."

Bill gave him a curious gaze. "I thought you liked living in downtown Lafayette."

"I love Lafayette, but I'd like to be close to the club I'm building in Lake Coburn."

"Not to mention a certain doctor," Jackson mumbled.

Red punched Jackson playfully on the shoulder. "Keep your opinions to yourself, Jack."

Bill chuckled. "Well, make me an offer and I'll see what we can work out. I'd love for you to have this place. It'd almost be like keeping it in the family."

"I'll have one for you by Monday." His DJ kicked off another oldie-goldie-belly-rubber and Gwen and Giselle walked up to claim dances with their husbands. Red watched the two couples blend into the crowded dance floor and couldn't help remembering the feel of having Doc in his arms. He rubbed his cheek, wishing she'd parted with a somewhat better impression of him.

Once more, he couldn't help but consider that Tanner Collins must be the biggest fool in the world.

Chapter Two

Late November – Wednesday before Thanksgiving Day

Red barely had time to set the huge turkey on the counter before his landline began ringing. He grabbed for it, wondering which family member needed directions to the ranch. "Where are you?"

"Closer than you think."

He pulled back the phone and checked the screen. No info, other than a number he didn't recognize. "Who is this?"

Nothing.

"Look, I don't have time for this."

"One of these days you'll have all the time in the world to think about what you did."

"What I did? Look buddy, I think you have the wrong number."

The deeply masculine voice, muffled and unrecognizable, continued. "No mistake, McAllister."

The use of his name shocked him. "What is it I'm supposed to have done?" The low chuckle that followed had the hair on the back of his neck standing.

"Like I said, one day."

"Bring it on. I'm not afraid of you."

"Your mistake, asshole."

The line went dead. Red stared at the phone, jumped slightly at the sound of the doorbell. He set the phone down, already determined to dismiss any and all signs of negative energy. This was his first holiday in his new home, the ranch he'd coveted for years. His family had decided the day before Thanksgiving was preferable, so his siblings could spend time at their in-laws this year. It worked out well for everyone.

He approached the door and pulled it open to greet the first arrival for Thanksgiving lunch. He opened his arms to Giselle, only to have her rush past him. Red stared after her. "Hey, where's the love?" He turned at the sound of her two little girls giggling.

"It's not you, Uncle Red," Lexie explained. "Momma needs to pee really bad 'cause she's preganunt and the babies pressing on her bratter."

Red's brow furrowed. "She needs to pee—because she's pregnant—and the baby is pressing on her bladder, right?"

Jackson followed the girls inside, hefting a large roaster, and grinning like he got the last platter of boiled crawfish in the batch. "You're pretty good at deciphering five year old," Jackson said.

"Put that on the stove top." Red nodded toward the kitchen before hefting both little girls in his arms. He kissed his honorary 'nieces' until they giggled, then released them. He followed Jackson outside to help him unload the car.

Jackson grabbed the last bag and slammed the hatchback. "We definitely need a bigger vehicle, something with more cargo area."

"And a third row of seats for that infant car seat you'll be hauling around by next summer."

Jackson smiled mysteriously as he nodded. "Are you settled in the ranch house yet?"

"Yep, I closed two weeks ago and started moving in the next day. I sold the house in Lafayette, at a good profit, too. That pool really raised the value. The new owners love the grotto."

Jackson placed the box he carried onto the floor and stared at him, his mouth agape. "You mean a *couple* bought it?"

Red nodded. "A family with two kids, and don't look so shocked."

"I thought for sure it would go to some other playboy type, like you."

"Your ass!" Red snorted. "I told Giselle once that the closest that grotto's ever come to seeing any action was you and her. I like it in a bed."

Jackson groaned. "That wasn't action—that was agony."

Red elbowed his friend in the ribs. "I guess you're getting it pretty regular now, huh?"

Jackson's eyes rolled back in his head. "Aw man, you have no idea. I never dreamed I could be this happy. I love going home every day to my three girls."

Red moved the roaster to the center island and turned to hug Giselle as she re-entered the kitchen. "Hello, beautiful, how's that baby doing?"

She beamed up at Red. "Just fine, and the due date's been narrowed down to June twenty-fifth, but my doctor thinks I may deliver earlier."

"I guess that's always a possibility," Red agreed.

"More like a probability—with twins," Jackson added. He pulled out an ultrasound picture showing two distinct fetuses.

Red studied the snapshot then embraced Giselle in a hug. "Twins!" He kissed her on the forehead then shook Jackson's hand and slapped him on the back. "Way to go, stud."

Jackson flexed his arm and grinned. "Who's the man now?"

"I can't wait to see those kids," Red exclaimed.

"Me either. I can hardly wait till June."

Giselle shook her head and chuckled. "That's because you don't know what it's like to be sleep deprived for months at a time. Carrie said to put them on the same feeding schedule immediately, or we'll never get any sleep."

"She should know," Red commented, referring to Carrie's set of fully grown twin girls.

Jackson pulled his wife into his arms. "Hell, I'm already sleep deprived, what with my wife waking me up for sex in the middle of the night."

Giselle slapped his arm and blushed. "It won't happen again if you're going to tell everyone about it."

Red shook his head in disgust. "Yeah, and quit bragging."

"I'm just basking in the glow of marital bliss, my friend." He wrapped his arms around Giselle's abdomen. "It sure is nice to be loved." He cocked his head as if he suddenly remembered something. "And speaking of loves, I hope you don't mind, but I invited someone extra for today."

"Not at all, who'd you invite?" Red took a swig of water.

"Tiffany LeBlanc."

Water spewed from Red's mouth as he broke into a fit of coughing. Eyes watering, he finally caught his breath. "How the hell did you manage that?"

Jackson grinned. "She loves this place, so I invited her. I may have left out the fact that you bought it from Uncle Bill."

Red shook his head, exasperated with his friend. "You know how pissed she'll be when she sees me here, right?"

"Maybe, but she was depressed about not having any other plans. Tanner left last night to spend a couple of days with his parents. She has to work Thanksgiving Day and Friday. I told her we were coming to the ranch, and she was welcome to come along. She's bringing dessert, by the way."

Red sighed, accepting the inevitable. "Is she still mad at me?"

Jackson shrugged. "Ask her when she gets here."

"I'm not bringing it up if she doesn't. Has she said anything to you about me since then? Do you know how it's going with her and Tanner?"

"Not a word and I have no idea. Sounds like a question for you to ask her. Is all of your family coming?"

"Yeah, they should be getting here any minute. All except for Chad, he's got a flight. Enjoy the peace and quiet while you can, bro, because the noise factor is about to multiply tenfold." He went to answer his doorbell, expecting to see one of the twenty or so of his family members scheduled to attend his first holiday celebration in his new home. His breath hitched as he opened the door to see Tiffany standing there, dressed in what was a far cry from scrubs. Her short black skirt made from some kind of suede material hugged slim hips, and he prayed she'd leave its matching jacket draped over her arm. It'd be a damn shame if she covered up any part of that red, form-fitting sweater. He could have done without the black leather boots, knowing they covered far too much of her shapely legs. Damn if she didn't look hot, anyway.

She wore her silky blonde hair down around her shoulders. Red finally managed to speak. "Happy day before Thanksgiving, Tif—Dr. LeBlanc." He reached out to take a large casserole dish from her hands before she had the chance to run. "Come on inside. Giselle and Jackson are already in the kitchen."

Her breath caught at first sight of him. Handsome as ever, but wearing a mysterious smile that seemed a little on the resolute side, if anything. Did he know something she didn't? "Happy Thanksgiving, Mr. McAllister." She stepped inside, supposed she should at least act surprised to see Red here, although she wasn't. The truth is, when Jackson invited her, a small part of her wondered if his best friend would be present.

Nor was she surprised by the fact that she still found him extremely attractive. If she were to be honest with herself, she'd hoped to see him here. Then again, she was lousy at being honest with herself. She tried to look casual as she studied the way he carried himself. The rugged good looks, along with his beautiful blue eyes, still commanded her attention. He didn't have the pretty boy good looks that Tanner did, but he was far more appealing to her in other ways—unfortunately.

Red lifted the glass lid of the only extra-large casserole dish she owned. "Oh, man. Is this banana pudding?"

She nodded. "Yes it is. It's kind of my favorite thing to make since I got the recipe from a nurse at the hospital. I love it."

"I know you had no idea, but this happens to be my all-time favorite dessert." He replaced the cover.

"Seriously?"

"Oh yeah—so serious I'm thinking about shoving this to the back of the refrigerator until everyone leaves. This won't go far."

She frowned. "Well, I made a double batch. Jackson said something about a large crowd." She had to wonder at the look he sent her. "What?"

"Something tells me you're about to be overwhelmed."

Giselle broke into their conversation. "Hey Tiff, Happy Thanksgiving. I'm glad you could make it."

Tiffany gave both Giselle and Jackson hugs.

Giselle stared at the dish, her eyes round with expectation. "Ooh, what is that?"

Red lifted the dish out of her grasp. "It's banana pudding, and just because you're eating for two doesn't mean you can hog it all."

Giselle pushed him playfully. "Hey big boy, I'm eating for three, and I can't believe you'd deprive your Godchildren of their mother's favorite dessert."

Tiffany set her purse on the barstool. "Eating for three?"

"Yep, look here." Jackson whipped out the snapshot again.

Tiffany studied the ultrasound. "Look at those twins. You two sure work fast. Congratulations." Tiffany scanned her surroundings, looking for their host and hostess. "Am I too early? Where are Bill and Gwen?"

Jackson cleared his throat as Red placed the dish in a huge custom installed refrigerator. "They should be getting here soon. They actually live just west of Kenton now."

"Oh. I didn't know that." She surveyed her surroundings. *Someone* obviously lived here. "So, who lives here?"

"Um . . ." Red cleared his throat, passed a hand through his hair, obviously nervous. "I do. I bought the place from Bill and moved in two weeks ago."

Tiffany leveled a gaze on Red, to Jackson, then back to Red. Red's house . . . for an early Thanksgiving celebration. Oh. *Hell* no. "I see." She reached for her purse, got her keys, and spun around toward the door.

Jackson attempted to explain. "Come on, Doc—It wasn't like that, I swear." He quieted suddenly, as Red fired a stony glare in his direction before following Tiffany out of the kitchen.

He caught up with her at the front entrance and followed her outside. Closing the door behind them, he restrained her gently by placing a hand on her arm.

"Look, Doc, I didn't know until five minutes ago that he'd invited you but we can be adults about this, can't we?"

Tiffany turned on him. "You're kidding, right? I'd never hear the end of it if Tanner found out I spent Thanksgiving at *your* house. You broke his 'precious' nose! You have no idea what I've had to put up with since then. The swelling, the black eyes, and nosebleeds—the endless bitching, whining, and complaining—Jesus, Red, you didn't just break his nose. You made my life a living hell, too."

Red grunted, surprisingly pleased at the extent of Tanner's discomfort. "I guess I messed up that aristocratic profile of his, but whether you want to believe this or not, he had it coming. I am sorry if he took it out on you. Maybe you should have moved out for the duration."

The narrow-eyed glare she fixed on him had all six foot four inches of Red taking a step back—just in case she decided to take a swing at him.

She shook her head. "Are you still playing that old fiddle? You hit him for something that happened fifteen years ago! Come on, Red, how old are you?"

'Red' instead of 'Mr. McAllister'—that's progress, anyway. "Haven't we already exhausted this discussion, Doc?"

She spun haughtily away from him.

Undaunted, Red followed, pulling her to a halt by the arm. "Look, you can leave *after* I've had my say, but you need to know what kind of asshole you're engaged to," he sneered.

"I know everything there is to know about Tanner. He's not perfect, but at least he's not a *Neanderthal* like you. He doesn't believe in using his fists to settle ancient arguments."

Tiffany jerked her arm free and disappeared around the corner of the house. He followed, and unexpectedly plowed into her backside. She stood frozen in place, giving as good an impression of Lot's wife as he'd ever seen in his life—as the dozen or so men, women, and children of clan McAllister blocked her escape route to her car.

"Jesus, Mary, and Joseph!" He realized immediately, as she obviously did, that his family had heard every word of their argument. Tiffany chose the lesser of two humiliations and turned to face him rather than the curious hoard of onlookers. His gaze locked onto her flushed face and he placed his hands protectively on her shoulders. "Aw, Doc," he murmured, feeling the mortification roll off of her rigid body in waves.

Red sent tight-jawed glances at the various members of his family. "Y'all go on into the house, please. Giselle and Jackson are in there already." He released a loud sigh as his mother reached up to pat his cheek. "Hi Mom." She gave him an encouraging wink before urging the others into his home.

Annie paused next to him just long enough to punch Red in the shoulder. "Good job, big brother."

He winced as someone else snickered before agreeing about the Neanderthal crack.

He watched as Tiffany kept her gaze riveted to her boots, understandably too embarrassed to move. When the last McAllister finally meandered past and disappeared into the house, she covered her eyes with one hand.

"Oh. My. God. Could I *possibly* be any more humiliated than I am at this moment?"

Red's snort of amusement had her pivoting to face him.

"This is *not* funny." Her tone was short, and clipped with annoyance.

He shook his head and grinned at her. "Doc, I know you don't want to hear this right now, but one day you'll look back on this and laugh."

She shook her head vehemently. "Not in this lifetime." She picked nervously at her jacket.

"Look, if you want to know what the old argument between me and Tanner was about, I'll tell you."

She raised large, liquid, brown eyes to his, and nodded. "I think I have a right to know."

Red took a deep breath. "He and Chloe, Jackson's ex, got me banned from the wedding. I was supposed to be his best man, but she got Tanner to substitute."

"What did you do to make her want you out?"

"She threw herself at me and I turned her down. She and Tanner became close after that. Would you care to guess why?"

"If you're trying to tell me he slept with Chloe before the wedding, that's ancient history. She's dead, and Jackson's remarried already."

Red took a deep breath. "Are you aware that he had sex with her before the wedding, during the reception, or so I've been told, and long after they were married?" He shook his head as she closed her eyes and nodded, telling him she'd long-suffered through her fiancés indiscretions. "Unbelievable . . . you knew and still kept him around." He wasn't quite able to hide his disgust.

Tiffany's eyes narrowed angrily before she turned to her car. "I sure as hell don't have to stand here so you can judge and insult me."

Red reached out and grabbed hold of her arm, bringing her to a jerking halt. When she turned, her right hand clenched like she was ready to swing at him, he grabbed that hand too. "Stop!" He was determined she'd hear him out.

"Let me go, McAllister," she hissed at him. "Or you'll be damned sorry!"

He released her quickly, raised both hands. "I will—I am. But I'm asking you to listen." She lowered her hands, as though relenting. "I didn't want to tell you this at the wedding because I didn't want you to be humiliated in front of everyone, but in light of the situation." He lifted one hand toward his house and dropped it. "I guess it's pointless to keep it from you now. Did your fiancé tell you he made a pass at Annie in the stables?"

Tiffany turned an astonished gaze toward him.

"It's true. He followed her there and threw himself at her. She slapped him. Knocked him into a pile of horse sh. . . manure."

She growled. "He blamed that on you, too."

Red shook his head, a low chuckle escaping. "Nope. That was all Annie."

Tiffany lowered her head as though she were somehow to blame. "But, no. He didn't tell me any of that. Of course he didn't." Her eyes closed as she shook her head. "It's no wonder you hit him."

"That was the last straw. It was time he paid."

She scuffed her boots on the brick walk and crossed her arms tightly across her chest. "He's threatening to sue, you know."

"Let him try. I've got a good lawyer and a sister who'll testify that he attacked her. Besides, it didn't stop him from performing any surgeries."

She sent him a curious look. "How do you know?"

"I did my homework. The proof is in my lawyer's office. I'm a businessman. I know how to protect my ass—sets."

She lifted a brow in his direction. "I'm impressed, I guess." A ringtone of Linda Ronstadt singing *You're no Good* cut through the following moment of awkwardness.

Red grunted as Tanner's name flashed on her screen. "Speak of the devil—"

She ignored him and answered, her voice tight and controlled. "Yes, Tanner."

"Where the hell are you, Tiffy? I called the condo and you didn't answer. Did you get called to the hospital?"

"I told you several times that Jackson invited me to the ranch for Thanksgiving dinner."

"Did you?"

"Yes, I did," she said blandly. "How are your parents?"

"They're wonderful, and they send their love."

"Give them mine, too. I have to go."

"All right, but don't eat too much. You know you have a tendency to overeat around the holidays."

"I do not."

"You're getting older and it gets harder to keep off those unwanted pounds."

Tiffany clenched her jaw. "You and I are having a talk when you get back, Tanner." She gave the button a hard press to end the call.

"Tiffy?" Red grimaced, having heard every word of their phone call. He lifted one shoulder carelessly at her glare. "I can't help it if I have excellent hearing, and I can't believe you let him call you that."

"I hate it," she growled. "And he knows I hate it." She sighed and rolled her neck as if to release tension. "I have to go. Just keep the dessert."

"Don't go, Doc. Melissa and Bailey will be here soon. They'd be thrilled to see you."

"Red, there's no way in hell I can face everyone again." She pointed toward his front door. "Do *they* all know what Tanner tried with Annie?"

"My parents do. I don't know about the rest." He could practically see her wheels turning, could see her working through her emotions, hoped she'd find it in her to stay. "Come on, Doc. Stay for lunch, at least."

She waved off his plea. "No. I'm going." Her voice was clipped, determined, as she turned and walked toward her car.

When he started to follow, she paused and lifted a hand to stop him. "Go. Tend to your guests, Red. I'm fine, really."

He sighed. "I'm sorry it turned out this way, Doc." Resigned for the moment, but not totally defeated, he walked inside, bypassed his family, and went straight for his office. He closed the door and watched from the window that looked out over the parking area. She rested her elbow on her door while making a call from her mobile phone.

Who are you calling, Doc? Tanner? A co-worker? Who's that call about, huh? Damn, but he'd like to hear both sides of that conversation. She ended the call and slammed her hand on the steering wheel. A slow smile stretched across Red's face. "Tanner. Definitely Tanner," he whispered. "Come on, Doc, you *know* that son of a bitch isn't worth wasting a day off."

His heart pounded as he watched her get out of her car and stand there, as if trying to build up her nerve. Her first determined steps back to his front door had him pumping his fists victoriously. He spun around to rush back to the front door, stopping at the kitchen just long enough to issue a desperate plea to his family members.

"I'm begging y'all. Please. Keep all comments to yourselves." He continued to the front entrance, taking a moment to wipe his slightly dampened palms on the front of his jeans. He opened the door and stepped out as Tiffany's booted foot hit the first step.

She stopped to look up at him—adjusted the strap of her purse over her shoulder. "I think I will stay for lunch."

"Want to tell me about it?"

Her mouth twisted in a tortured smile. "I checked in with his parents. He called them last night to say he couldn't make it."

He released one long sigh, silently thanking Tanner for being such a world class fool, before stepping aside.

"Come on in, Doc. Forget about him for one day. I guarantee you'll have some fun. Probably at my expense, but you'll enjoy yourself."

Tiffany adjusted her purse strap higher on her shoulder. "It sounds good, Red. I could use some fun." She approached him and stopped. "Particularly if it's at your expense." She shrugged. "You kinda owe me."

He gave a low chuckle and nodded. "I kinda do."

He held the door open for her and she stepped inside. The noise coming from the large home had increased dramatically with his family's arrival. She counted at least seven children scattered around Red's den, varying in ages from mid-teens to one adorable toddler with strawberry blonde hair and blue eyes. The chubby baby boy waddled closer and raised his arms to her.

"Oh my goodness, he's adorable!" She didn't hesitate, but immediately lifted him into her arms. "Hello there, handsome boy." The toddler cracked a big grin at her.

Red chuckled. "That's Conner, and he's never met a stranger. He's my sister, Kathleen's boy."

Tiffany settled the child on her hip and stroked his silken curls. Conner gave her another cheesy grin then turned to face his uncle.

"Unca Wed!" Conner cried, as he reached out for Red.

Red took his nephew from Tiffany and held him. "Hey buddy, how's it going?" The toddler patted Red's cheeks as they butted foreheads.

Somehow she managed to hide her shock at his ease with children. She had to wonder if there was anything else about this man that would surprise her.

He cocked his head toward the kitchen. "Come on, I'll introduce you to the family you haven't met yet."

Tiffany already knew Annie and his parents, but it took several minutes to go through the rest of his family.

A tall, red-haired young woman stepped forward. "You were Jackson's surgeon, weren't you?"

"Yes, I was."

"I'm Rebecca. Annie told me what a great job you did on his leg. It's very impressive that there were no complications, considering the seriousness of his injuries."

"That's just diligence after the surgery. I try to do as much of that myself, as I can. Our nurses are excellent, but so overworked and understaffed they just can't catch everything," Tiffany explained.

"Your work is highly respected in this area."

"Well thank you, I try. Where do you practice? I remember Red telling me that his sisters were all in the medical profession."

"I'm a pediatric nurse at St. Gabriel's in Lafayette," Rebecca said. "Understaffing is one reason I switched to Pediatrics a year ago. I get to spend a lot more one on one time with my patients. Annie said you make a real effort to get to know yours." She nodded approvingly. "That's admirable. So many surgeons don't these days."

Tiffany smiled. "Sometimes I get to know them so well I'm asked to be a witness for their wedding—and then get invited to Thanksgiving dinners."

"That's right. Both she and Red witnessed for us when we got married at the courthouse," Giselle piped up.

Tiffany reached up to run her fingers through Conner's silky locks. "So, who does this adorable child belong to?"

"That would be me and his daddy here," said a tiny, younger version of Vivienne McAllister with strawberry blonde hair. "I'm Kathleen, and that young man is the older brother to his baby sister," she said, patting her large belly. "She's due to make an appearance a couple of days before Christmas, if I make it that far." When she propped her feet up onto her husband's knees, he removed her shoes and began to massage her feet tenderly. "Thanks, Babe," she groaned. "That feels so good."

Tiffany wondered what it must be like to be included in the McAllister family. They didn't seem ashamed to show affection for one another in front of others. This family actually cared for each other. She knew it all had to start with the parents. She glanced up and caught a look from Red's mother, who smiled warmly at her. She smiled shyly back at Vivienne, feeling her face heat with a blush.

Red released the wriggling toddler and stepped in front of her, blocking out his family to whisper his concern. "Is everything okay, Doc?"

She nodded, just a little shocked at his concern. "I'll live. You have a great family Red." She nodded at Vivienne and Pete McAllister. "Your parents look like they're still so much in love." She smiled as Pete McAllister wrapped his arms around his diminutive wife.

"They are, and most of us realize how lucky we are that they show it. It drives Annie crazy though. Watch her reaction. She can't stand it." He pointed out his sister who was steadily rolling her eyes at the sight of the older couple sharing a kiss. "Hey Annie!" he called out. When she turned to meet his gaze, he jerked his head in the direction of their parents as he grinned, nodding gleefully.

"You're. An. Asssss," Annie mouthed to her big brother before turning her back on him.

Red laughed. "The last of eight children and she can't accept that they 'did it'—it's unbelievable."

Tiffany burst into laughter at Red's interaction with his youngest sibling. He turned to face her suddenly.

"You have a great laugh, Doc."

She smiled shyly. "Thank you."

He glanced at the door as more guests rang the bell. "It's too bad it took this long to hear it." He gave her a sad smile before excusing himself.

Tiffany watched in fascination as he walked to the door, his arms swinging in rhythm to his long easy strides. Her mouth watered at the sight of the broad shoulders and back, the long waist tapering down to trim hips, accentuated more so by the tailored fit of his shirt. She dropped her gaze even further to the firm butt and muscular thighs covered in just tight enough jeans.

Red opened the door to two women, followed by men she supposed were their husbands, and even more beautiful children. She approached the group, immediately recognizing her old college buddies.

Melissa saw her first, screamed before grabbing her in a hug. "Oh my God. Tiffany? What are you *doing* here?" She turned to her sister. "Bailey, do you remember Tiffany LeBlanc?"

The second woman beamed up at her. "Sure, I do. We did some partying together my freshman year. Your hair is different but you look wonderful." She took her turn hugging Tiffany. "Damn, girl. If I'd have known you were coming, I would have dug out my college scrapbook—brought it along for a little reminiscing."

Red cleared his throat. "Just what kind of stuff is in that scrapbook?"

"Well, I can't give away all our secrets, big brother. Suffice it to say the three of us had *a lot* of fun that year."

Red cocked an eyebrow in Tiffany's direction as he spoke to Bailey. "I'd pay good money to see that book, Sis."

Tiffany stepped forward and pointed up at Red. "Bailey, don't you dare give that man any incriminating evidence against me."

Bailey laughed. "I wouldn't dare. I couldn't believe it when he told me you were the one that saved Jackson's leg."

"Sure did, and my favorite patient felt sorry for me and invited me to this shindig. I had no idea I'd be seeing any of you here." She aimed her gaze at Red. "It came as a complete surprise."

Red shrugged his shoulders sheepishly. "And if I'd known, I would have let you girls know sooner."

They introduced her to their husbands and then their daughters, two seven year olds with more curly auburn hair like their mom's, and what must be the trademark blue eyes of the McAllister clan. As several more grandchildren walked into the room, Tiffany turned to Bailey again. "Is there any member of this family that doesn't have those gorgeous blue eyes?"

Bailey shook her head and grinned. "Not yet, but I'm going to keep trying. One day I hope to have a child with big brown eyes like my husband's."

The statement seemed to jar Red's memory as he palmed his phone. "Hey, Sis, come here and watch this video. See if you can figure out who this little girl belongs to." He pulled up the pictures and video he'd taken of Carrie's granddaughter, Ava, when Jackson was still in the hospital.

Bailey groaned as she watched the video of Ava telling her mom she was going to the hospital to see Jackson.

"You see? Isn't she precious with those big brown eyes? Wait, that's one of the Jeansonne twins. I can't tell if it's Lauren or Gretchen, though. It's been too many years since I've seen them."

"Yep," Red agreed. "That's Lauren and her little girl, Ava Grace. She looks like Shirley Temple with all those curls. She's adorable, and talk about a character."

Tiffany watched the video again, smiling as Ava kissed Red on the face and waved to her mama. She wasn't watching the child as much as she was watching Red's reaction to her. She wanted children so badly. Tanner didn't seem interested at all, other than one son to carry on the family name. He already said he didn't plan to participate much in raising the child. That wasn't exactly her idea of the kind of family she wanted.

She jumped slightly as Red spoke from just over her shoulder. "There's something about girls with big brown eyes and a head full of curls, isn't there?"

Tiffany's gaze clashed with his, and just for a moment, she wondered if he was talking about the child in the video.

Chapter Three

Once more, Red's doorbell rang. He opened it for Jackson's Uncle Bill, his new wife, Gwen, and their daughter, Alyssa.

Red shook Bill's hand and hugged Gwen. "It's about time you three got here. I was wondering if I'd have to send out a search party."

Bill Broussard smiled and looked around at the place he'd sold to Red. "Does it feel like home yet?"

"Today it does, with the family all here. How about yours?"

"Just like you, any place I'm with my family feels like home." Bill pulled Tiffany close for a hug. "And you are an unexpected surprise, little lady. It sure is good to see you here, Doc."

"You too, Bill. How've you been?"

"Never better." He smiled as his gaze followed Gwen and Alyssa. "I've got a new wife and step-daughter, and maybe one day we'll add one or two. Life doesn't get any better than this."

The crowd inside the home suddenly got a lot louder with several different conversations going on at one time. Tiffany laughed as Jackson, once again, took the snapshot of the ultrasound out of his pocket to show it off to anyone who'd look. She felt her face flush with heat as Red lifted his gaze during another conversation to send her an encouraging smile.

The noise seemed to reach a crescendo, and she suddenly remembered Red's statement from earlier. *Something tells me you're about to be overwhelmed.*

The unaccustomed chaos of this many family members under one roof was a little overwhelming for someone with her upbringing. She headed for the patio doors, thinking she needed to catch her breath for a minute. Tiffany closed the door on the noise, and crossed her arms to ward off a chill. The humidity had dropped overnight, leaving brisk, dry air in its wake.

Closing her eyes, she lifted her face, inhaling the sweet, smoky scent of the oak logs burning in Red's fireplace. She loved the smell, had yearned for a fireplace for years. Of course, Tanner didn't care for them. It seemed to be a far more common occurrence for them to disagree than agree on any matter, whether it was his love life or preferences in apartment living.

Tiffany ran her hands through her straight blond hair. The act reminded her of one more reason to resent Tanner. She could still hear Red as he spoke about girls with brown eyes and curly hair. There's no way he could know—could he? Surely, it was only wishful thinking on her part. Tiffany pushed the thought away as quickly as it came up. She was engaged to Tanner, and this infatuation with Red was curiosity—plain and simple—manifesting itself in the form of temporary physical attraction. She'd get over it.

She approached the large building lined with windows at the opposite end of the large patio. Tiffany peered through a window, but couldn't see anything. She tested the doorknob, slightly surprised when it turned in her hand. She nudged the door open and peeked inside, gasping in appreciation at the huge indoor swimming pool. She walked over, squatting to dip her hand in the water.

"It's heated, you know."

Tiffany swiveled to see Vivienne McAllister standing at one of the windows. "Oh, I'm sorry, I didn't see you there." She stood, shaking off the water.

Vivienne smiled and handed her a towel. "I guess this is what people do when they have more money than they know what to do with. I've never had that particular affliction." Vivienne smiled, not sounding particularly upset about it.

Tiffany shrugged. "I was raised with money."

"You don't seem all that pleased."

"I don't mind having money, but I'd rather work for what I have, not marry into it like my mother and grandmother did."

"Red told me you have a brother. Is he a surgeon also?"

"No ma'am, an attorney."

"A doctor *and* a lawyer—your parents must be proud."

Tiffany gazed down at Vivienne McAllister, blinking several times at the sudden surfacing of tears. "Red said the same thing to me about three months ago."

Vivienne placed a hand on her arm. "What's wrong, dear?"

"Nothing." Tiffany braced herself against the sudden urge to cry. She didn't cry. She never cried. Who would she have cried to? She and Drake had only ever had Melinda, the Nanny and housekeeper who'd raised them. Something about Vivienne McAllister—some motherly nurturing quality— radiated trust. She brushed away the moisture at one corner of her eye. "Nothing. And everything."

Vivienne led her to a comfy looking glider for two. "Sit." She sat beside Tiffany and stroked her hair. "Now talk to me."

Tiffany took one shaky breath before starting. "I'm engaged to a man I don't love. My parents want me to marry him because his family has money."

"Surely, you're intelligent enough to know that money can't replace happiness, Tiffany."

"I do know that, Ms. Vivienne. My mother wants me to stop practicing medicine—just get married, pop out a couple of children and stay home, while my cheating husband does whatever he wants. I don't think I can live like that."

"And you shouldn't have to," Vivienne agreed.

"I know all men cheat, but—"

"Whoa!" Vivienne held up one hand. "Hold on a minute, honey. Not all men. If your fiancé cheats, maybe it's time to cut him loose. Or at least let him know you won't put up with it anymore. Why should he stop if you won't make him?"

"You obviously don't know Tanner."

Vivienne nodded. "I've heard of him. And as for your mother—hasn't she heard of maternity leave? I was a stay at home mother and I loved it, but my husband and I are very proud of our daughters who handle their careers and families beautifully. You're too talented a surgeon to walk away from your career. People need you."

Tiffany shook her head. "You make it sound so simple, but I have a difficult time standing up to my parents."

Vivienne chuckled. "I've seen the handprint you left on my son's face. You're obviously stronger than you think."

Tiffany looked mortified. "You know about that?"

"Yes, but I'd love to hear your version of the story."

Tiffany filled Vivienne in on how Red had taken his sweet time to tell her about Tanner's broken nose. "Red just wanted him to suffer. Of course, if he'd told me that Tanner had come on to Annie, I wouldn't have slapped him." Tiffany clenched both her hands into fists. "The thing is, I have all this pent up resentment for Tanner, you know?"

"I'll know if you tell me."

She looked at Vivienne. "For one thing, I'm so angry about my hair."

"What about your hair, Tiffany? You have lovely hair. It's very—polished—and—sophisticated."

Tiffany shook her head. "It's not me. I do this for Tanner. He's got this idea that any woman who doesn't have straight, blonde hair is beneath him. So, I go every two weeks to have my roots done, and I waste an hour every morning straightening my hair. An hour I could be doing other things that I want to do. I resent it. And I resent him the entire time I'm doing it. It makes me so sad that the man I'm supposed to marry doesn't think I'm good enough the way I am."

Vivienne stared at her, her mouth gaped open in obvious shock. "Are you telling me you have naturally, curly hair?"

"Yes ma'am—I do. Mousy brown, naturally curly hair." She pointed with both hands to her hair. "*This* is not me."

Vivienne shook her head. "Why would you go to so much trouble for a man who shows so little respect for you?"

Tiffany shrugged. "I thought if I tried my hardest, one day we could find a way to be happy with each other. You know, he even tried to convince me to wear blue tinted contacts once to change the color of my eyes. I don't even need contacts."

Vivienne's voice rose in obvious anger. "Blonde hair and blue eyes— Who does he think he is, Adolf Hitler?" She leaned forward. "Find yourself, Tiffany. Not who anyone else wants you to be, but the person you're meant to be. If the people who supposedly love you can't accept that, then *c'est la vie*—that's life."

"So, you think I should call off my engagement?"

Vivienne lifted one hand. "I can't tell you what you should or shouldn't do. I don't know Tanner. Do you think he'd change for you if you asked him to?"

Tiffany sighed. "I think even if he could, it's too late. I'd never be able to trust him."

"Well, I'm old enough to know that time is precious, dear. It's foolish to waste it on something that can't be."

Tiffany shook her head. "My parents would have a fit."

"They'll accept it, eventually. I know this because my mother tried to marry me off to another man. Her 'good catch' was Marshall Baker. Good looking, conceited, and a perfectly awful dancer. But worse by far, was the fact that he loved flaunting his wealth. I've never been impressed by money."

"I'm not either, Mrs. Vivienne."

"Marshall asked me to go to a dance in town and I accepted because no one else asked me. I was seventeen years old, and I'll never forget that night. Marshall had been stepping on my feet all night long. So I was glad to see him go outside with his buddies. I sat on a bench with my shoes off. When Pete McAllister walked up and asked me to dance, I nearly turned him down. I honestly didn't think my toes could take anymore punishment."

Vivienne smiled, as though reliving the moment. "Pete was four years older than I was, but we were both raised in the same small town. I knew who he was, but I'd never been that close to him before. I looked up into those blue eyes as he held his hand out to me. He said, 'Come on, Vivi, give me a chance. I won't hurt you, and I promise not to step on your toes.' It turned out he was a wonderful dancer, and by the end of the song, I was head over heels."

"What song was it?"

"*All I Have to Do is Dream* by the Everly Brothers. He told me later that he'd waited all night long for Marshall to leave me alone. As soon as he did, Pete went to the guy playing the records and paid him two dollars to play that song. Two bucks was a pretty good tip back then."

Tiffany's hand flew to her heart. "That is the sweetest thing I've ever heard."

"It is, isn't it? You see, Pete used to come to our farm to help my dad, because I didn't have any brothers. One day dad asked him his opinion of Marshall Baker and Pete said he didn't like him much. Dad told him he'd hate to see me end up with Marshall because Pete was too scared to do anything about it. Up until then Pete thought my father wanted me with Marshall."

"How did your mother take the news?"

"Oh, she fussed awhile then let it go. She knew the McAllister's were good people. She just didn't want to see me struggle as a farmer's wife like she had. The first time I ever went to Pete's house, and I saw how his parents treated each other, I knew he'd be a wonderful husband. Those old people were crazy about each other. That's just how Pete and I feel. I've told all my children never to settle for less, and so far, they've chosen well." She smiled and placed her hand over Tiffany's. "Are you feeling better now?"

"Yes, ma'am, I'm okay," Tiffany answered.

"Good, I'm getting hungry and it's time to eat."

They were talking amiably as they re-entered the kitchen. Tiffany met Red's gaze as he walked over to meet them.

"Where'd you two go off to?"

"We had to check out that pool of yours, son. It's impressive, I must say," Vivienne said.

"It is." He shrugged. "It came with the house. But, I love it. I swim every day now, when my other pool only got used half the year."

"It seems like I remember someone saying you built your own pool. Is that true?"

"It is. I like to relieve stress by working with my hands."

"I like to garden and run," Tiffany said.

Red's brow lifted, as though he were shocked at her admission. "You're a jogger?"

"I don't jog, I run. I have *a lot* of stress in my life."

"So, you *run* away from it?" he asked.

She eyed him warily. "I wouldn't say that."

Vivienne cleared her throat. "I'm starving! Is it time to eat?" She took Tiffany's arm and whisked her away from Red, but not before she aimed a glare in her son's direction.

Within seconds, everyone broke into action, setting the massive dining room table Red had purchased for family gatherings such as this one. Between the table, breakfast table, and island, he had seating for thirty people. Red waited for his sisters to serve and seat the children first, before asking his dad to give the blessing.

He watched Tiffany bow her head in silent prayer, slightly surprised when she crossed herself afterwards. He had no idea she was Catholic.

As the formal dining table filled with adults, Red realized he was lacking one chair. He grabbed one from the breakfast table and placed it between his mom and Tiffany, winking at her curious look. "It's kind of funny—this table *looked* plenty big enough in that furniture showroom."

Tiffany gave a low chuckle. "My parents throw dinner parties all the time and I think their table only seats sixteen."

"What if someone shows up unexpectedly?" Red asked.

She plastered an appalled look on her face. "That doesn't happen at *those* kinds of dinner parties."

Red laughed. "I guess not. Did you go to many of them?"

"My brother and I were forced to attend many as we got older. They weren't much fun, I assure you."

He leaned close to her. "And, are you having fun today?"

She gave him a shy smile. "I'm beginning to."

"Good."

Tiffany served herself a portion of turkey and took a bite. "Who baked the bird, Red? It's perfect."

He smiled. "That would be me."

"You cook?" she asked.

Red gazed at her over his fork. "You seem surprised. What, I'm not the Neanderthal you thought I was, Tiffy?"

Her words belied her sugary sweet tone. "If you call me that again I might have to hurt you."

He gave her a sly smile. "I'd like to see you try."

"You know, someone just told me I'm a lot tougher than I look." She sent his mother a secretive smile.

"I don't doubt that for one bit, but I'd still like to see you try." Red forced his gaze from her before she'd see just how serious he was.

Red and his guests spent the next forty-five minutes dining on the delicious array of foods as laughter and discussions about everything from politics to sports filled the air.

"Do you watch football?" Red asked her.

"Of course I watch football," she replied.

"But when the Saints play the Texans or the Cowboys—who do you pull for?" Conversation came to a dead stop as all heads turned toward her.

Tiffany's jaw dropped as she faced off with him. "That was low, Red— even for you."

"Hey, you being from Texas and all, I thought maybe you have allegiances to teams from your home state." He smothered a grin as she balled her napkin in one hand.

"You know," she said, her tone hard and serious, "I've got roots in this state, too. My father was born and raised in Louisiana, and I've been a resident for half my life. That was totally uncalled for."

He grinned smugly. "Just answer the question . . . Tiffy."

She wiped her mouth on the cloth napkin then threw it deliberately on the table as though challenging him. "Of course I pull for the Saints, and when I'm not pulling for the Saints I *bleed* LSU purple and gold." Everyone broke into applause.

"She must have roots in Louisiana, because we're seeing a little of that Ragin' Cajun right now," Pete commented.

"It's Red's rudeness that brought it out," Bailey added.

Red met the glares of his family members and raised a hand in self-defense. "I had to ask!" He was met with a chorus of boos and hisses.

Tiffany leaned closer to speak lowly into his ear. "They don't like you much right now."

"Easy fix." He stood and addressed the rowdy gang. "Who wants dessert?" He sent her a wink as the jeers turned to cheers. Hands flew up around the table. "You see? All you have to do is satisfy their sweet tooth and they're your best friend." Everyone got up to check out the array of pies, cookies, candies, and other desserts that were set out on the huge buffet.

"Oh, where's that pudding?" Giselle asked, reminding Red to get it out of the fridge. "My babies want pudding!"

"What kind of pudding is this?" Kathleen asked, as she eyed the luscious looking concoction covered with whipped cream.

"Ba-na-na...Our favorite, isn't it twins?" Giselle patted her belly.

Jackson came back with a dessert bowl filled with it and handed it to her. She took a bite and her eyes widened. "This isn't pudding from a box is it?" She licked her spoon. "It's fantastic."

Tiffany shook her head. "No, it's homemade. I got the recipe from one of the nurses I work with. I made a double recipe, but I clearly underestimated the guest list. I should have quadrupled it."

After a few minutes of everyone scrambling to get pudding, Red began to worry. "Now, look here. This is my house, and I don't mind having to squeeze a chair in from the kid's table, but I'm telling y'all now, I want some of that pudding."

"Here, pass this to him." Annie handed down the casserole dish and it eventually made its way to Red.

"Yeah, that's what I'm talking about," he said, reaching for the now *empty* dish. "Oh, come on." He turned to his mother. "Mom, remind these people. What do I ask for every year instead of birthday cake?"

"You ask for banana pudding," she said.

"You see? Y'all know it's my favorite."

"Here—you big baby." Bailey passed him a dessert bowl containing some pudding. "We dished it out so everyone would have some."

"Thank you." He took a bite and closed his eyes to savor it. "Doc, this is excellent."

"Tiffany, anytime you come to our house for a meal, you're designated to bring this for dessert," Giselle added.

"I can do that." Tiffany sat down with a saucer laden with homemade fudge, divinity and pralines.

"Didn't you want pudding?" Red asked.

"I can make more of that," she answered. "I don't know how to make this stuff.*"*

He leaned in closer. "Can I have your share?"

She turned slowly to face him, their noses nearly touching. "I don't know, Red. What's it worth to you?"

Their gazes locked and Red caught his breath at the look in her eyes. "Name your price. I *really* love—your—banana pudding."

Tiffany bit her lower lip and looked away. "Take it."

He laughed and got up to get the last remaining bowl of pudding. He sat down again, grinning at the look on her face as she bit into a praline. "Good, huh?"

"Sugar is my only vice."

"I can think of one other vice." He leaned over and whispered in her ear, "Careful, Tiffy. You're getting older and it only gets harder to take off those unwanted pounds."

"I guess I need to lower the speaker volume of my phone when you're around," she said dryly. "Who made these?"

"Mom makes the candy. I'm sure she could give you some recipes."

"Is it difficult?"

"I have no idea, but I'm thinking you could handle it."

After dessert, everyone got up collectively to clean the kitchen. The adults were sitting in Red's huge living room filling every spare seat including dining chairs brought in from around the table. Others chose to lounge on the thickly carpeted floor as the large group visited and drank coffee.

Before long, several of the men rose to get various instruments, including the fiddle and two guitars. Red went to his room and returned with one acoustical guitar and a banjo. He handed the latter to his dad then sat in a chair next to Tiffany.

"You play?" she asked.

"I can do lots of things you don't know about . . . yet." He sent her a look that suggested she was in for a treat of another kind.

She sat, fascinated, as Red began to play skillfully, his long fingers picking, strumming, and warming up until the rest of the men were ready.

Red addressed his sisters. "What are we singing today, ladies?"

"Something we can sing harmony to," Melissa suggested.

Tiffany suggested Little Big Town, her favorite mixed gender country group and Red kicked off *Boondocks*, a snappy tune with lots of harmony parts. By the end of the song, nearly everyone in the room was singing along, including Giselle and Jackson. With Melissa's encouragement, even Tiffany had joined in.

She'd always had a decent voice, although she'd never felt comfortable singing around other people. Somehow, in the midst of this family, it didn't seem to bother her.

For the second selection, Brandon and Bailey treated everyone to a duet, a stirring rendition of their favorite Michael Buble song, *Home*. Tiffany watched the muscles in Red's forearms strain and bulge as he rhythmically picked, plucked, and strummed the strings of the guitar. She watched his long fingers as they moved gracefully from string to string—chord to chord— nearly embarrassed herself wondering what other talents those fingers held. She'd moved to the floor in front of him with her head leaned back against the arm of the sofa. Sated from the food, and relaxed from the swell of music, her lids drifted closed of their own accord. As he strummed the last chords, Tiffany opened her eyes to find him watching her. She sucked in her breath, surprised at the intensity of Red's gaze from just a few feet away.

"That was beautiful," Vivienne said, of her daughter and son-in-law's performance.

"It was," Tiffany agreed, brushing aside her self-consciousness long enough to address Red. "I've never seen a family this large where everyone is so musically inclined. Does everyone sing or play an instrument?"

He looked around the room and nodded, lowering his guitar for the moment. "Pretty much. Annie plays the piano, but I don't have one yet. Chad plays the drums, and has a good voice, but he's got a terrible case of stage fright." He cocked his head at her. "Speaking of singing, I heard some pretty sweet sounds coming out of those pipes of yours. Is there anything in particular you'd care to perform for us today?"

She thought on it for several seconds. "I'm not—"

"Unless you're too intimidated to sing solo," he said, loud enough for everyone else to hear.

She narrowed her eyes to slits at the obvious challenge. "I was just going to say I'm not sure if you can handle the guitar part in the song I had in mind. It seems pretty *complicated.*" A few 'burn' comments made their way around the room.

"You just call it, Doc," he said, beaming as she applauded when he began to play her choice.

Tiffany stood in front of him and turned to her audience. "I'd like to dedicate this song to my missing in action fiancé, Tanner Collins." The room erupted in boos and hisses.

Red's voice rose above the jeers. "Hmmm—he may be missing in action, but I doubt seriously he's missing *any* action."

She shot him an icy glare.

"What?" he asked, all too innocently.

Deciding the best revenge would be to show him what she could do, she belted out the song about a doomed relationship. If Red seemed impressed with her delivery of lyrics, she was equally impressed with his guitar skills.

At the end of the song, she took an exaggerated bow before turning to Red. "You play that thing pretty well."

Red bowed his head. "Thank you. You have a nice voice. That was real good for a 'bitter bitch' sing along, but can you sing something with substance?"

"Excuse me?" She fisted her hands on her hips.

"I said, can you sing something like—oh—I don't know—a ballad? Can you, Tiffy?"

Tiffany knew he was goading her, hoping she'd accept the challenge. She suspected it was so he could hear her range, which she didn't particularly mind. Wanting to show him he wasn't entirely in control of the situation, she leaned forward, resting her hands on his knees so she could look him in the eye. To the man's credit, his eyes never dipped lower to the hint of cleavage created from her position, but remained on her own gaze—steadfast in its commitment—unwavering from its target. "Red McAllister," she breathed, inches from his face. "Are you picking on me?"

Red stared into the depths of luminous brown eyes sparkling with amusement. Eyes that only hinted at the fire they hid. His heart thudded heavily in his chest as he made an effort to swallow. "Maybe."

"I'll tell your mother."

He frowned. "Mom can't abide tattle tales. Besides, you think she'd take your side over mine?"

"In a second." A sweet smile accompanied her quick comeback.

"She only just met you," he snorted. "I've been her favorite for thirty-eight years."

"Spoiled brat."

"Look who's talking." He swallowed audibly.

She took a deep breath and stepped back. "So you want a ballad, huh?"

He cleared his throat nervously. "Only because I think you're capable of more."

Tiffany laughed softly. "Oh, is that what this is?" Once more, she leaned in, getting nose to nose with him. "And here I thought you were just being . . . you." She breathed the last word seductively at him.

Red froze, transfixed by this confident, sexy as hell lady before him, and uncomfortably aware of an inherent heat stirring in his lower regions. The sudden image of two giant chess pieces, alone on a board, came to mind. Her queen approached expectantly, looking satisfied with the check mate as his king fell forward with a resounding *thud*. Damn.

She straightened, wearing a 'don't mess with me' expression, obviously pleased with herself.

"So, is there anything in particular you'd like to hear, Mr. McAllister?"

Red cleared his throat again, feeling the heat as he stammered like a teenager. "No—no ma'am—um—entirely your choice."

"What if I choose a song you don't know?"

He stopped, suddenly fully confident in *this* particular challenge, and stared her down. "Don't you worry, Doc. I'll know it."

She flipped her hair casually behind her shoulder. "Mighty sure of yourself, aren't you?"

He shrugged and gave her what he hoped was a cocky grin. For some reason, once he heard a song, it stuck with him. But, if truth be told, there was something about this woman that instantly deflated all the cockiness right out of him. Hell, he'd be following her around like a puppy if it wouldn't completely null and void his 'man-card' into a useless scrap of paper. He took a deep breath and steeled himself against her understated, though totally effective signals. "Name your tune, Ms. LeBlanc."

Tiffany's eyes narrowed the slightest bit as she pursed her lips at him. He knew instinctively that she was out to prove something. He also recognized her look of determination to wipe any and all traces of smug cockiness from his face.

"There's a song from LeAnn Rimes that means a lot to me. It's older and never got any radio play, so I doubt you've ever heard of it. It's called *What I Cannot Change.*"

He grinned at his extreme luck—Angelique, an old girlfriend, had loved the cut from her CD years back. He nodded as melody and lyrics flooded his mind. "As a matter of fact, I do know that one, Doc. It's pretty deep. Are you—uh—are you *sure* you can handle it?" As it happened, he chose a particularly quiet moment to voice his challenge, resulting in the complete halt of commotion in the room. Its occupants seemed to hold their collective breaths.

Tiffany took it all in stride, sending him a single wink as she nodded. "Bring it on, McAllister."

The room buzzed with excitement and sounds of approval as everyone settled down for Tiffany's ballad.

Red plucked his strings softly until he found the chord she could live with, then sat back and waited. At her nod, he closed his eyes and began picking the intro, practically seeing notes and haunting melody float through the air waves. Everything was visual with him, especially music. She skipped the first intro as though needing a little more time. He continued without pausing, replayed the intro. He heard her deep intake of breath and braced for impact.

His head fell forward as Doc's voice filled the room. In an instant he knew he was in big—really big—trouble.

It was agony, hearing the heart wrenching lyrics crooned by that angelic voice. He lifted his gaze once during her soul stirring rendition, and paid for his foolishness. He nearly lost control as she gazed tearfully at his mom while singing of the heartbreak of not being able to talk to her own parents.

Red succumbed to the feelings of sadness her tortured words evoked in him. He lowered his head again, listening as she lamented over not being able to change what was wrong in her life. His heart broke for her as she sang of letting go, forgiving, loving what she could not change, and changing what she could.

Her sweet voice, perfectly pitched, and in turns, strong, then soft as an infant's coo, stirred a part of him deep inside. A place he didn't allow others.

His sisters and mother sang well, and so did Giselle, but there was a pureness and clarity to Tiffany's voice that the others didn't possess.

He'd not lost many challenges in his lifetime, but this day she would claim victory over an epic failure on his part—the failure to recognize the seriousness of a challenge that had completely blown up in his face.

She finally ended his torture, singing the last of the lyrics, and he struggled to close out the song he knew he'd always think of as *her* song.

Red took a deep breath and met her gaze. She stood, her eyes glistening with the slightest hint of tears, proof that the words truly meant something to her. His heart ached for her, longed to reach out to her as she wiped at one corner of her eye. He sensed his family waiting for him to speak—to say or do something other than sit there, zombie-like and silent.

Red finally managed to blink several times before giving her a slow nod in the heavy silence of the room. He cleared his throat, felt like a fool when the only thing he could think to say was a lame one-liner.

"Well done, Doc."

His family seemed to come to life suddenly, moving as one to surround her, lavishing her with praise. The commotion cut through the mind-numbing trance that had taken hold of him. He stared at Tiffany, members of his family surrounding her. His chest tightened with the wild thudding of his heartbeat. He rose from his chair, laid his guitar across the seat. He wiped sweaty palms on his jeans, fisted both hands afterwards to hide the shaking. She meshed so well, fit easily into his large family. Having her here felt . . .

It hit home then. Just that quickly.

Chapter Four

Red turned and walked—no, he *ran* from the situation. Maybe not in the literal sense of the word, he forced himself to walk slowly, steadily, with purpose, into his kitchen. Metaphorically, he ran his ass off.

He grabbed two bottles of beer from his fridge and hit the back door. By the time he'd closed himself up in his pool house, he was in full panic mode. He sucked downed the first beer in a few gulps, slamming the empty bottle on one of the tables. He wiped the sweat from his brow and opened the second beer. He downed half the bottle before the creaking door drew his attention. He swung around, mentally unprepared for speech of any kind, most certainly not to Doc. His father stood there, wearing a sympathetic grin.

Red spun away from him, his frustrated groan a clear indication of his take on the matter. Just once, he wished the members of his family would leave him the hell alone. At least until he could sort out his own freaking feelings. Unfortunately, alone time in a family this size had never been an option. Not now. Not ever.

A calming touch on his shoulder was first indication that his father had crossed the room to meet him.

"It's overwhelming, isn't it, Son? When you first realize you're head over heels in love?"

Red swung around, fully prepared to deny it; to defend his actions. Or at the very least, glower at the man for making fun of him. But his father stood steady and solemn, no trace of laughter in his voice, no hint of it on his features. Just more proof of the seriousness of his situation.

Red released the huge breath he'd been holding and shook his head several times. "I don't know what the hell's happening here." He lifted one clammy hand and clenched it to stop the shaking. When that didn't work he downed the rest of the beer, wiping his mouth on his shirt sleeve. "I've never been afraid of a damn thing, Pop, but I'm not gonna lie to you. *This* scares the ever-loving shit out of me."

Pete nodded, crossed his arms across his barrel chest, and finally chuckled. "That's a common reaction for most men."

Red shook his head. "I'm not ready for this."

"Scott, you're thirty-eight years old. Besides, from what I see, you don't have much choice in the matter."

Red clapped his palms over his eyes and groaned, then froze as another thought overtook him. "Do you think I have a chance with her?"

Pete McAllister laughed and slapped him on the back. "I don't know, Son, but I'd sure hate to see you lose a chance because you're too scared to ask."

"Isn't that what Paw Paw told you?"

"Yep, now come on back inside. Your mother sent me to remind you that you're the host of this party. Besides," he said, nodding at the two empty beer bottles. "Two beers won't change a damn thing. Hell, I stayed drunk for a week, and when I sobered up, I was still in love with your mother."

Red tailed his father back into the kitchen, where his attention was immediately dominated by the beauty his family still surrounded.

His gaze clashed with Tiffany's. Her initial smile turned into a look of worry. After addressing Bailey they both turned in his direction, as though studying him.

"Oh, great," Red mumbled to no one in particular. He tried to shake it off and busied himself strapping his guitar onto his shoulders. He made small talk with Jackson, wiped his sweaty palms on his jeans several times, all the while praying his act was convincing enough to throw his nosy sisters off the scent. The women in this family were like a pack of wolves—one sign of weakness and they pounced, determined to discover the cause.

Within seconds Red knew his half-assed attempt to hide his discomfort lacked the ability to keep said wolves at bay. He turned to his left and nearly ran over Bailey, who immediately tried to put a hand to his sweaty brow.

"Scottie, are you okay? You look a little pale, and you're sweating." Her brow furrowed with concern.

He batted her hand away irritably. "I'm fine. I just ate too much."

She didn't look convinced. "Do you need something? I practically travel with a pharmacy."

He pushed her hand away as she tried to feel his forehead again. "For crying out loud, would you stop? I don't have a temperature, Miss Nurse Practitioner."

Jackson leaned in close to Bailey so that only she and Red could hear him. "Besides, why would he settle for a nurse practitioner when can have a bona fide doctor?"

Red glared at his friend, who was, at that very second, sharing a meaningful look with his sister. He grunted, indicating his disgust with the two of them, and reseated himself. "Are there any requests?" He kept his head lowered, feeling a heated flush suffuse his face. He glanced up, just in time to see Bailey and Melissa, their heads together, whispering and staring at him. He watched, horrified, as one by one, the women in his family gathered, the veritable pack of she-wolves in one corner of the room. Tiffany stood at his left elbow, talking animatedly to Jackson and Giselle, seemingly oblivious to his sister's actions, thank God.

"Any more requests?" Red repeated, more to escape his sisters' scrutiny, than anything else. He knew better. There would be *no* escape, this day, or any other.

Annie looked up with a wicked gleam in her eye. "I'd like to hear *When a Man Loves a Woman*."

Red sent her a dark look. "No, pick something else."

"Gary Allan's *Loving You Against My Will*," Melissa threw in, chuckling.

He shook his head. "Something else."

"*The One* by Gary Allan?" Bailey asked as he continued to shake his head and send his sisters looks that could kill.

"Jake Owen's *Don't Think I Can't Love You*," Rebecca added.

"Or maybe James Otto's *Just Got Started Loving You*," Kathleen chimed in.

Red glared at his sisters, thinking he'd like to throttle every last one of them the first chance he got. He shook his head in disgust, and started up a quick paced tune by a popular country artist. It was a safe tune about a guy with no commitments, and it was something with no female vocalization, so he wouldn't have to hear Tiffany sing.

Afterwards, Jackson sang a favorite of his wife's then he and Giselle performed a duet by Josh Turner and Trisha Yearwood, prompting a standing ovation.

"What else?" His heart clenched in dread as his mom raised a hand, her eyes sparkling with amusement. "Red, I'd like to hear something Christmassy to ring in the season."

He could feel the tension ease from his shoulders, so relieved at her request. He knew her favorite Christmas carol and it was safe, to say the least. His relief was short lived as his mother voiced her request.

"I'd love to hear a duet. *Baby, It's Cold Outside*. Please?"

"I thought *The Little Drummer Boy* was your favorite Christmas song." A distinct uneasiness crept into his bones.

"It is, but your dad and I watched that *Elf* movie last night and the duet those two characters sang was lovely."

He watched his mother weave her way through the crowd, stopping in front of Tiffany, just as he suspected she would.

Here it comes—the ultimate act of treachery—betrayal by the one person he thought would never throw him under the figurative bus. His sisters came by it honestly.

"Do you know it, Tiffany?" Vivienne McAllister's question seemed innocent enough.

Tiffany nodded. "Yes, ma'am, I surely do."

Red was already shaking his head no as Vivienne turned to him. "Mom, are you sure you wouldn't rather hear *The Little Drummer Boy?*"

"No, I'm sure I'd rather hear this one, dear." She sounded convincingly innocent to everyone but him.

"He looks too *scared* to sing that with Tiffany." Annie's comment had everyone in the room snickering.

"Probably thinks he can't keep up with her. She's that good." Bailey sent him a wicked grin.

He shook his head. *Traitors—every last one of them.* Red glared at his sister then chanced a cautious glance in Tiffany's direction. She stood beside his chair, arms crossed, her face a study of smug amusement.

"Bok. Bok."

Red stared at her. "Excuse me?"

"You heard me. I *said* Bok—Bok—Ba-cawk!" Soon, everyone in the room had joined in with their own poultry imitations.

Red snorted then shook his head as he cursed under his breath. He looked back at Tiffany. "Are you ready to sing?"

The roomful of clucking and crowing sounds were immediately replaced by whistles and applause.

Tiffany's eyes crinkled with laughter. "I don't know, McAllister—did I pass your test?"

"Your. Ass." He turned to his family. "And you all are nothing but a bunch of turncoats! Now, get on up here—*Tiffy.*"

Tiffany approached and poked her finger into his chest. "Keep it up, *chicken man.*"

Red repositioned himself and started playing the mellow guitar opening as Brandon and the rest of the musicians joined along. Tiffany sang the first lines of each stanza with Red picking up the back-up lines. During the guitar solos she entertained both him and their audience by placing a finger on the top of his head as she pirouetted playfully around him. As their voices blended, ending the song in perfect harmony the room exploded in cat calls and cheering.

Red laid down his guitar and stood. He grabbed hold of his duet partner's hand and together, they took their bows. Tiffany's delighted laughter reached him and he couldn't help but pull her close for a big hug. He released her and leaned forward. "Are you having fun yet, Doc?"

She gave him an enthusiastic nod. "I haven't had this much fun since college."

Almost immediately, Tanner's tell-tale ringtone rang out in the room. Red groaned, wondering if that son of a bitch could somehow sense the subtle lift of Tiffany's spirits.

Melissa stepped forward, her head cocked curiously. "Why am I hearing Linda Ronstadt?"

Red snorted, but resisted revealing the ringtone's owner as he caught

Tiffany's glare of warning.

She hit the answer button. "Yes?" It took all of three seconds for her to end the call and turn to Red. "Do you have a landline here, Red?"

"I sure do."

"Would you mind if I gave it to the hospital? I'm on call, but if I leave my cell phone on, he'll just keep calling."

"He knows you caught him in the lie?" he whispered.

"Of course, and he's crawfishing—trying to get out of it. I don't have the stomach for it today."

Red fought the urge to smile at the sound of pure disgust in her voice. Instead, he handed her one of his business cards with his number on it.

"Thanks." She disappeared through the patio door.

He watched her from the window, turning when he heard Jackson's voice at his elbow.

"What the hell was that about?"

"She's giving the hospital this number so she doesn't have to hear any more of Tanner's lies. Apparently he's not where he's supposed to be."

"Imagine that," Jackson said. "I think someone needs to tell that prick he's about to be replaced."

Red shook his head. "I don't know about all that."

"Are you up for it—are you willing?"

"I'm not sure," Red murmured. He caught sight of Tiffany outside on his patio and suddenly knew nothing was further from the truth. "Yeah, I am."

Jackson gave him a playful punch on the shoulder. "Tread carefully, my friend. Your mom's gonna kill you if you screw this up. You know that, right?"

Red grinned at Jackson. "Failure is not an option."

Tiffany hugged herself, wishing she'd grabbed her jacket before coming outside. She heard the door open, but didn't bother to turn around. She'd expected Red to follow her out here. She thanked him with a smile as he slipped her jacket over her shoulders.

"You okay, Doc?"

She turned back to stare out at a pasture, knee deep with winter grass. "It's so beautiful out here. So peaceful. The condo Tanner and I live in is . . . well . . . not like this."

"That's an easy fix," he said. "Just move."

"I'd never get Tanner to move out to the country. He loves being in the middle of things."

"Don't you have any say?"

"Sure I do. I tell him I hate it and he says we're staying put."

"Why does he have to be the one to get his way? Have you ever heard of compromising?"

"I have, but Tanner hasn't." She shrugged and turned, mentally bracing herself for the sight of him. Even though, her breath caught, as it always did when he appeared in her line of vision. Red always stood tall and straight backed, confident masculinity pouring off of him, with no trace of pompousness.

When, if ever, was the last time Tanner had this effect on her?

"It doesn't matter. I let it happen, and it's just like your mom said; why should he stop if I don't make him?"

He shoved his hands into his pocket and looked down, scuffing his boots on the brick pavers. "My mom?"

"Yeah, we had a talk in your pool house earlier."

"What about?"

"Me, Tanner," after a pause she added, "—my parents." She blinked several times and cleared her throat. "You're a very gifted musician—nice singing voice."

"Thanks, but yours is better. Who does it come from?"

She answered with a careless lift of shoulder.

"Don't you know? It must come from one of your parents."

"We didn't hear any singing in my family. I honestly don't know where it comes from," she said.

He ran his right thumb and fingers lightly over his five o'clock shadow and seemed to contemplate her answer. "Do you play any kind of instrument?"

"Mother forced me to take piano lessons, but I never took to it. I can play enough to bang out a few Christmas carols in the children's ward for parties but that's about it. Now my brother, Drake, on the other hand, is truly gifted. I guess he still plays." She finished in a low murmur.

"Don't you know?"

"I see him twice a year, when we go to our parents for the two parties they require us to attend. One is for Christmas and the other is an annual fundraiser."

"So, you'll be in Houston for Christmas," Red commented.

"The Christmas party is always the weekend before." She crossed her arms and looked down at her shoes. "God, we both hate it."

"Then don't go."

"I have to."

"Why?"

"Good or bad, they're still my parents."

"Will you be disinherited if you don't go, or something?"

She turned to him. "Now, why would you ask that?"

He readjusted his stance under her scrutiny. "I'm wondering how important money is to you."

Her brow furrowed in annoyance. "I don't need an inheritance. I make out well enough on my own."

He shrugged. "Me too."

"What exactly do you do?"

"I've owned a string of businesses over the years, but I currently own a club in Lafayette. I've got another one in the works here in Lake Coburn."

"What club?"

"Oh, you may have difficulty remembering the name." He grinned. "It's called *Red's*."

She stared up at him, unable to hide her shock. "You're *that* Red?"

He laughed. "I believe I'm the same Red I've always been."

"Some co-workers are regulars. They're always going on about how nice it is. No smoking right?"

"That's right."

"What made you do that when Louisiana still hasn't banned it from clubs?"

Red walked over to a flower bed and bent over to pull a stray weed. "My Uncle Ben, dad's brother, died from lung cancer due to smoking. It's the one thing I can do."

Tiffany followed him to the bed of pansies and leaned over to pluck some winter grass from between the bright purple and gold blooms. "Doesn't it hurt business?"

"There are a lot more non-smokers out there than smokers. I have four rules. No cigarettes, no drugs, no fighting, and no drunk drivers—we'll call them a cab. We ask for a decent sized cover charge, and in return people have a nice time. So far, we have a lot of repeat customers."

"You said you went to LSU, right?"

"Yes. I had a baseball scholarship and got my business degree."

"Bachelors?"

"Initially—I got my degree summa cum laude. I got a job after graduation and went to night school for my Masters."

"Top honors while playing Tiger baseball?"

"You sound skeptical." He flashed that devilishly handsome grin of his. "Would you like to see my degree? It's framed and everything."

"How would I know it's real?" she teased.

He grinned down at her. "I've got the documentation to back it up. We had several Magna cum Laude graduates in my family, but you are looking at the one and only Summa cum Laude of the McAllister family, honey, and don't think my mom wasn't above throwing *that* around at the Garden Club meetings."

Tiffany smiled, imagining Mrs. Vivienne doing just that. "Did you study harder? Did you do less partying than the rest of your siblings?" She found herself curious to know more about this man.

He chuckled. "I partied plenty—the truth is I have this ability to retain and recall information. Facts, numbers, notes, quotes, music, and lyrics, it all comes easily to me. If I read or hear something once, I remember it."

She snorted. "That's the kind of thing that can annoy the living hell out of a roommate."

"Yeah, it used to irk the crap out of Jackson. We bunked together during my sophomore year when he was a freshman. Then he got hurt and transferred out of the athletic dorm. You know about the shoulder injury, right?" When she nodded, he continued. "It didn't matter though. By then we were best friends." He looked down at his watch. "You know we missed the kick-off, right?"

Not wanting to end the conversation with him, she met his gaze. "You ready to go inside?" The slight shift of his head let her know he felt the same way.

"So . . ." he said, walking casually toward the pool house. "Did mom give you any advice you could live with?"

"She absolutely did. You and your siblings are lucky, you know."

"We realize that."

Tiffany turned toward the patio doors. "I was watching your parents in there and I realized that I don't have one single memory of mine showing affection for each other. Their marriage was always more like a business arrangement. My dad has always had his mistresses and mother has her men."

Red's voice betrayed genuine sadness at her confession. "I'm sorry for you."

She met his gaze again, letting him know with a look instead of words that she appreciated his concern. She started to say something then thought better of it.

"What?"

She smiled, wondering why she wasn't surprised that he could tell she was holding back. "It's just that it worries me—maybe they warped Drake and me. That's one reason I've stayed with Tanner. If I hook up with someone decent, I'm afraid I wouldn't know how to act. I'd probably scare him off." Red emitted a low chuckle that caused a fluttering in her stomach.

"I seriously doubt you could scare *me* off, Doc."

Tiffany cleared her throat and turned, hoping he'd miss her reaction.

She turned away from him, but not before he caught the slight flush of her skin. He smiled, pleased that his statement had that effect on her. "Besides, look at Jackson. Fifteen years with Chloe, the wife from hell, only made him appreciate Giselle more."

"Maybe you're right."

"But, you'll never know unless you cut him loose. It's not likely Tanner will make as sudden an exit as Chloe did."

"I should hope not," she said, tapping the heel of her boot on the pavers.

"Hey, if you want to keep talking and watch some TV got a big screen in the pool house. Interested?"

She rocked back and forth balancing on her heels, and gave him a brief nod. "I'd like that."

He led her inside to two chairs and a table in front of the large screen set hanging on the wall. "Do you want a soft drink or a beer?"

"I'll take water since I'm on call." She rubbed her belly and grimaced. "Besides, if I drink a beer after all that food I'll be down for the count."

Red turned the set on and found the game. "So, did my mom reveal any family secrets?"

"She told me the sweetest story about when your dad rescued her and her sore toes."

He handed her a bottle of water and sat next to her. "Ah, the Everly Brothers. My old man could work it, couldn't he?"

"Your maternal grandfather helped him out a little."

"Yeah, gave him the all clear. Did she tell you about how my dad's parents met?"

"No, were they both Irish?"

"We're Scottish. My grandfather came over from Scotland after World War II, but my grandmother was an Hebert (*A-bear*) from Gardiner. My mom was a Broussard (*Broo-sard*) and she was from there, also. Those names are common in south Louisiana. So, I've got strong Cajun roots with a Scottish last name."

"How'd your grandfather end up in Gardiner?"

Red sat forward and rested his elbows on his knees. "He came to the states looking for a place to work as a farm hand. Gardiner, being a huge exporter of rice at the time, was the ideal place for him. He didn't know anything about rice farming, but he told the man who hired him that he was a quick learner."

"How did he meet your grandmother?"

"She and her sisters had gone to a dance and she saw him standing alone in a corner. My grandmother decided to be polite and introduced herself. Pops had been in town less than a week, and spoke with a Scottish accent so thick my Maw Maw could barely understand him. But they danced together all night long. She taught him all the Cajun dances, and by the end of the night he was an expert."

"Now I know where you get your dancing skills," she teased.

"Maw Maw told me when she got home, her older sister asked if she didn't mind all of that carrot red hair. Maw Maw told her she'd never noticed the color of his hair—all she'd seen were his blue eyes. She called him her red-haired, blue-eyed devil from Scotland—said he had just enough mischief in him to make life interesting. That's who we have to blame for the red hair and freckles."

Tiffany's eyes sparkled with laughter. "Don't forget to give him credit for those beautiful blue eyes of yours. Besides, I don't see any freckles on you."

Red groaned. "I outgrew them, thank God."

"Do you remember your grandparents?"

"I remember my grandfather a little—he died when I was four. Maw Maw Bess was the sweetest lady. She passed away just after I graduated from college." Red's eyes misted over at the memory. "She missed that old man until the day she died."

"Is that possible anymore, Red? Do people still have marriages like that?"

"Sure they do. Look at my parents."

"I mean people who get married today. Are there any marriages like that for couples just starting out?"

Red leveled a serious gaze on her. "Mine will be—I'm counting on it."

"Good luck with that. It doesn't seem possible with today's lifestyle and divorce rate," she added.

"That's because too many people settle." He laughed at her smirk. "What? It's true. People today always settle for less than what they think they deserve." He crossed his arms. "Case in point—you, settling for Tanner."

She nodded. "I'll give you that one, but I've already explained my warped family. So what's your excuse? You're a thirty-eight year old bachelor."

He shrugged again. "I don't want to settle."

"Maybe you're afraid of commitment."

Red gazed straight into Tiffany's eyes. "I'm not afraid of anything." *Not anymore.*

"We-ell," she murmured, getting past the hitch in her breath. "Maybe you should be."

He held her gaze in a silent game of chicken, wanting to prove how ready he was to take this on—to take *her* on.

Tiffany conceded and tore her gaze from his. She circled the room slowly, checking out his photograph collection. She stopped in front of a grouped collection of LSU baseball shots. "I've seen these before. I'd forgotten you and Tanner played the same years. What position did you play?"

Red gradually closed the gap between them, and stood with his mouth near her ear. "First base," he said, near enough to disturb her hair with his breath. He studied her delicate ear, fighting off the sudden urge to nibble on the velvety lobe. He wanted to get her back on subject. "What about you, Doc? You're thirty-six and unmarried, so does that mean you're afraid of commitment?"

She twisted a lock of her hair around one finger. "I definitely have a problem with commitment, but at least I'm engaged."

"For how long?"

"Um—Two years now."

"Set a date yet?"

"No."

"Why not?"

"Problem with commitment, remember?"

He stepped closer. "Could be you have a problem with Tanner."

She took one step away from. "Could be." She continued to look at pictures until she stopped at a large leather bound book with the name *Scott Brendan McAllister* and the date *January 28th* stamped in gold on its cover.

She turned to Red. "May I?"

"Sure."

She sat on the double lounger with the book, turned to the first page and gasped.

"I didn't realize it was a photo album."

"My mom went online to a company and had one made for each of us for Christmas last year."

"I can't imagine my mother going through that kind of trouble for Drake and me. You were a beautiful baby," she said, referring to his first studio portrait.

He cleared his throat. "I believe the word 'handsome' is a better description."

Her eyes sparkled as she touched the photo. "Babies are beautiful, and contrary to belief, not all babies are beautiful, but you definitely were."

"I was kind of cute, huh?" He sat next to her, enjoying the nearness, wishing it would last, hoping she didn't find some excuse to distance herself from him.

She flipped through pages as he answered her questions about the photos. She laughed at the photo of him in fifth grade, the year he seemed to have an abundance of freckles, and groaned at the eighth grade pictures of him with braces. "That brings back bad memories," she said. "I hated the metal mouth years."

Tiffany saw pictures of him playing t-ball at five and six, on through little league baseball clear through high school. One page had his high school graduation photo with the words *Gardiner High School Valedictorian – 4.0 GPA* underneath. There were several photos of him with the Tiger baseball team and shots of him in action, as well as a few good shots of him and Jackson together. There were college graduation photos with the words "*Our own Summa Cum Laude graduate!"* in a bold font.

She glanced at him with one brow lifted, clearly amused.

"I told you so," he said, flashing a confident grin.

She smiled back at him. "I believed you." She returned to the book, chuckling at the last several snapshots of him wearing nothing but a pair of swimming trunks and a cheesy grin while flexing his muscles for the photographer. "Who took these?"

"Mom," he said, seeing the caption under the photos that said, *"It would be such a waste if these genes weren't passed along. . ."*

He explained at the look Tiffany sent his way. "She's always telling me if I don't procreate before she dies, she's going to haunt my ass."

She laughed nervously, but didn't stop staring at the photos. "When were these taken?"

"That was—" he stopped to do the mental calculation. "That was the summer before last, after I finished my pool at the place in Lafayette. We had a huge birthday bash for mom and I was playing around." He shook his head, a little embarrassed. "I can't believe she put those in there."

"You're lucky they didn't end up on the internet."

Red removed a pack of snapshots from an envelope and handed them to her. "Here's some of the club I opened up about three years ago. That's my oldest brother, Chad and his wife, Julia." He pointed to a smiling couple sitting at the end of the table. "He's the only one you haven't met here today. They're separated, but we're all hoping they'll work it out. Julia was offered the chance to work in England for two years and Chad decided to go all macho jerk about it. He told her he wouldn't move."

"You're not upset with your sister-in-law?"

"Nah, Julia's the best. Chad's being a stubborn ass." He handed her a stack of snapshots taken when his latest club opened up. "You might recognize a few of these faces. This is opening night at the newest place in Lafayette."

"I sure do." She studied the snapshots of Jackson and Giselle. "Your club looks very classy and tastefully done."

"That's what I wanted. The one in Lake Coburn won't be as large as this, but just as nice, and the same rules will apply."

"When will you be opening?"

"Doors open on New Year's Eve. Think you'll be able to make it? Jackson and Giselle will be there." Tiffany closed the book, and stood. She set it on her seat and walked over to the window. He wished he could read her mind.

"I don't know. How difficult is it to get in?"

"Not difficult at all if you're in good with the owner."

"I'd have to ask Tanner if he wants to go," she said quietly, crossing her arms and staring at her feet.

Tiffany's body language told him what he needed to know. Hell, everybody could see she was miserable with Tanner, so why couldn't she?

"Doc, you can't tell me you're happy with him."

She shrugged, but the ringing phone saved her from commenting any further. Red picked up the pool house extension, checking out the caller ID. "It's for you," he said, handing it to her.

"This is Dr. LeBlanc."

Red's heart sank as she checked her watch and said she'd be there in twenty minutes. There was some comfort in knowing that at least she wasn't leaving him to go to Tanner.

"I've got to go," she mumbled, handing him the phone.

He held the door open for her before accompanying her back into his home. As she collected her things and stepped into the living room, all heads turned in their direction.

"Happy Thanksgiving, everybody—thanks for letting me crash your party," she said.

"Where are you off to?" Vivienne asked, as she, Melissa, and Bailey approached.

"The hospital called, I have to go in. It was lovely seeing you again, Mrs. McAllister." She held out her hand to Vivienne.

"Call me Vivienne, please. It was wonderful seeing you again, Tiffany. I enjoyed the talk earlier."

Red watched his mother bypass Tiffany's hand and pull her into a hug. He overheard Vivienne's quiet message whispered hurriedly into her ear.

"And I hope the next time we meet, I'll see the *real* you."

"You just may, Vivienne," Tiffany whispered back before turning to Bailey and Melissa. "It was great seeing the two of you." She reached into her purse and pulled out two business cards. "Both my numbers are on here—call me." She hugged the two women. "I *wish* I could stay longer. Bye everyone," she said again, smiling as Jackson and Giselle both blew her kisses.

Red held the front door open for her and moved to follow her outside. At the last second, he aimed a warning glare in his sisters' direction. "Don't even think about it," he spoke in a low murmur before shutting the door. He knew full well how pointless it was to expect them not to spy.

Red walked Tiffany to her car. "So, how about it Doc, are you glad you came?"

She nodded enthusiastically. "I am. It felt good to let go and have some fun. Thanks for talking me into staying."

"You're welcome here anytime—I hope you know that."

She gazed up at him, her face a study in curiosity. "What about Tanner?"

He bowed gallantly. "If you must," he said with an exaggerated sigh. "I'd be civil for your sake, and I promise not to break his nose, Tiffy."

She poked him playfully in the chest. "Don't call me that again."

"If it's good enough for Tanner, it should be good enough for me—Tiffy," he taunted.

"Stop it," she said, this time with more conviction.

"Aw, but Tiffy is such a cute little nickname…like Buffy or—"

"I'm warning you, Red!" Her voice rose in anger.

"You don't stop Tanner from saying it, why should you stop me, huh Tiffy?"

"Stop it!" she snapped.

Before he knew it, she'd popped him good on the mouth.

He grabbed her wrist in one swift movement. "You know, Doc, that's the second time you slap me in less th—" His accusation trailed off as he witnessed something else, something just as heated, replace the fury in her eyes. His heart pumped furiously as he stepped closer, pressing her back firmly up against the car. His breath quickened, matching her own rapid panting as she gazed up at him with eyes the color of rich, melted chocolate.

Without a doubt, he'd never wanted someone so badly in his life.

"Doc . . ." Not wanting to scare her off, he lowered his mouth to hers agonizingly slow. In a perfect world that would have been enough and she'd have let him kiss her. But this was reality, and a second before their lips would have met, her whispered plea stopped him.

"Don't Red, please."

He paused, pulling back enough to watch her long eyelashes flutter closed. He let go of her wrist and slowly, gently, moved that hand behind her head to pull her up against his chest.

Stiff with tension, she clenched the sides of his shirt until the tension eased slowly from her body. Her hands slid to his back as she finally settled comfortably against him.

Red brought his right arm around to pull her closer and they stood, holding each other, surrounded by the quiet sounds of late autumn. The north wind whipped through the yard full of pecans, oaks, and silver leaf maple trees, sending the dry leaves skittering across the ground around their feet.

"You feel so damn good," he whispered. "Like you belong here."

"Oh, God. Don't say that," she murmured into his shirt.

He moved his hand to the back of her neck, gently massaging, as he pressed the softest of kisses upon her crown. "Doc. Please don't marry Tanner," he whispered, not caring if his plea sounded desperate. He *was* desperate—desperate to make her see how good they'd be together—desperate for her to give him a chance to prove it to her.

She buried her face in his shirt and spoke through a muffled half-sob. "Don't say anything more, Red. I have to go."

He took a deep breath to fortify himself. "I know," he said. He reluctantly released her and backed away so she could get into her car.

She started the engine, avoiding eye contact with him as she shifted into drive. Keeping her head lowered, she sat there with her foot on the brake, the steering wheel tightly clenched in both hands. He tapped lightly on her window with his knuckle then flattened his palm on the glass.

Tiffany looked up, her eyes wide with agonized longing. Red's breath caught painfully in his chest as he caught the hint of tears on her long lashes, certain it was a rarity. Just as he reached for the door handle, she released the brakes. He stood, hands shoved deep in his pockets, watching the slow progression of her car, every second taking her further out of reach.

He took his time walking back to the house, not quite ready to replace the memory of having her in his arms. Once inside, he leaned against the door jamb, observing the couples in the room. Whether they held hands, curled a foot or leg around the other or lightly touched an arm or shoulder, there was some form of contact. Red met Jackson's gaze and shrugged at the unspoken message of understanding from his friend.

He turned to meet his parents as they entered the kitchen through the patio door. He returned his mom's smile and accepted a hug from her.

"Now, tell me the truth," he said in a low voice. "How big of an audience did we have while we were out there?"

"Oh, about what you'd expect after being raised in this family." Her eyes sparkled with laughter. "All your sisters, Sienna, and Giselle—it's been reported you handled yourself very well—even though you didn't kiss her."

Red felt the heavy, but comforting weight of his dad's hand on his shoulder.

"That call from the hospital sure was lousy timing, wasn't it, Son?"

"It's sucked all the fun out of this day for me," he told his father. "But, that's her career, and I'd sure as hell put up with it for one chance with her."

"Only one?" Vivienne smiled and gave his cheek a reassuring pat.

He turned his gaze on his mother. "One chance, Mom, I swear that's all it'll take. But I won't get it unless she finds the strength to walk away from Tanner."

Chapter Five

Thursday, Thanksgiving night

Tiffany entered the condo the next evening, both mentally and physically exhausted. Although she'd put in a grueling fourteen hours at the hospital, she knew her exhaustion was due more to unresolved feelings floating around in her head and heart. As soon as she'd left Red's presence the previous day, a distinct sadness had settled upon her, leaving her feeling desolate and alone.

She thought of the ballad she'd sung at his request. Could she learn to let go, to forgive, to love those things in her life that she couldn't change—one of those things being Tanner? Could she love him the way he was? Was it time to let him go and change her life? Her head was spinning from all the questions. If she just had someone she could talk to.

Tiffany stepped out of her shoes, left them at the door. She attempted to shake off her exhaustion, no easy thing when an act as simple as returning home depressed her to no end. She freed her hair from its ponytail and pulled her phone from her purse.

She finally bothered to check her messages. There were six, all from Tanner. Ignoring them, she went straight to her bathroom, turned the taps on in the tub, and poured in her favorite bath salts.

She grabbed a bottle of wine from the cooler, along with a glass and her cell phone. She placed the items on the wide tile ledge of her whirlpool tub, the one thing she truly enjoyed about this place.

After powering on the wall mounted radio system and tuning it to her favorite country station, she eased herself into the steaming water. A low groan accompanied the settling of tired limbs into the water, and she allowed herself a few quiet minutes of soak time. Without lifting her head, Tiffany used her toe to turn on the jets. She had just poured herself a glass of wine and laid her head back when her phone rang. She let it ring several times, suspecting the caller was Tanner. She clenched her jaw, imagining the sound of his pompous, excuse-making voice, knew she was in no mood to hear his crap tonight. He could damn well leave message number seven.

But, it could be the hospital. She lifted her head to check the phone, didn't recognize the number.

Groaning, she hit the answer button. "Tanner, if this is you, I've got nothing to say to you."

She waited expectantly. There was a pause from the caller then the one word that had her head snapping to attention.

"Doc?"

"Red?"

"Hey Doc, I just wanted to tell you-uh-that you left your casserole dish here."

"Oh."

"And, well, I really wanted to see if you were okay. I hope I didn't say or do anything to upset you before you left for the hospital."

"No, I was okay."

"Are you home?"

"Yes, but only about five minutes ago."

"Oh, if you need to rest or get something done, I can hang up, or call back."

"No! This is a good time for me to talk, believe it or not."

"Did you get a chance to watch the game this afternoon?"

"I caught part of it during my breaks. I heard the Tigers pulled it off."

"What's that noise I'm hearing in the background?"

"Oh, hang on." She reached over and turned off the jets. "Is that better?" She sat back in the tub.

Silence greeted her.

"Red, are you still there?"

"I'm here. Are—are you in a tub?"

"Yep, it's been a long day." After another long pause she cleared her throat. "What are you doing, Red?"

"I'm trying my damnedest to conjure up a mental image of you in that tub."

She laughed softly, knowing he was smiling on his end. "Knock yourself out, McAllister."

"What happened at the hospital yesterday afternoon—for the call-out, I mean?"

"A four wheeler collision—typical grown men and their toys. The guy had a few broken bones, but no internal injuries."

"Glad it wasn't too serious. How about today?"

"Car accident and an emergency surgery, other than my normal rounds. Another typical day, it just started unusually early."

"Right. So, everyone said to tell you again how good the dessert was, and they all want the recipe."

"I'll get it to you, and thanks again for having me. I had a blast until I got the call." She twirled a lock of hair around her finger and waited. There was silence on the other end of the line then she heard the words that she'd somehow known were coming.

"Why are you still with Tanner, Doc? Can you tell me that?"

She closed her eyes and took a deep breath.

"Never mind," he said in a rush. "It's none of my business and I had no right to ask."

"It's okay, Red. On my way home from the hospital I was thinking it's time to end this mess and move back into my own place."

"You have a place of your own?"

"I lease a house on Fleur de Lis Avenue. When Tanner asked me to move in with him four months ago, I hoped it would improve things between us, but it hasn't."

"Knowing Tanner as I do, I can't say I'm too surprised."

"No, me either. That's why I didn't give up my lease. I kept the utilities turned on with the central running so it doesn't get musty. Most of my stuff is still there."

"That showed some foresight on your part."

She smiled, remembering the phone call with her brother when he'd urged her to keep her place. "It was Drake's idea."

"It sounds like he knows Tanner."

"He's not a fan. I've been thinking about what your mom told me. How I need to find myself again. I think I need to be alone for a while."

"Sometimes being alone isn't all it's cracked up to be." Red's voice barely registered above a whisper.

Tiffany drank the last sip of wine from her glass. "It can't be worse than living like this."

"Well, hell, I can't argue with you. I don't know how you took it this long."

She let the comment pass and sat up to reach for the radio.

"Are you getting out of the tub now?"

"No, just switched to the classic rock station. Oh, I love this song! I haven't heard this in years." She raised the volume so Red could hear the mellow sounds of Led Zeppelin's Stairway to Heaven. She refilled her glass and eased back into the water, groaning as the warmth enveloped her. "I used to be putty in the hands of any guy who could play that acoustical guitar part for me."

"Are you still?"

She heard the hint of mischief in his question and smiled to herself, already feeling the effects of the wine. "Maybe."

"Want me to play it for you?"

She sat up. Was he serious? "Don't tease me, Red."

"I'm serious. I'll get my guitar and play it for you right now, if you want me to."

"Now what girl could say no to that?" she cooed.

"Hang on."

She heard him put the phone down. While he was gone, she reached over and turned off the radio then refilled her wine glass. A minute later he came back to the phone.

"Are you ready?"

"Absolutely." She heard him warming up, pictured his deft fingers manipulating the taut strings into what turned into the well-known guitar solo.

Tiffany turned the phone's speaker on and raised the volume. She set it on the ledge and settled back, eyes closed, enjoying the music she loved. Her enjoyment grew as Red began to sing to her in rich dulcet tones, and she wondered if—no—she hoped he'd repeat the performance for her one day, face to face. Several wonderful minutes later, she released a long, low sigh of satisfaction.

"I haven't had anyone do that for me since spring break my freshman year of college. I'm not sure, but I think his name was Eric." She tried to jog her own memory.

"His performance couldn't have been that good if you're not sure of his name."

After a slight pause she asked, "Are you referring to his musical performance?"

"I was, but if either of his performances had been worth a damn, you'd remember his name."

Tiffany chuckled. "Have you ever been to Panama City Beach during spring break? There's a hell of a lot I don't remember."

"As a matter of fact, I went four years in a row and I remember the names of every girl I met there."

"Ah, but do they remember your name?"

Red's deep chuckle rumbled over the line. "I'm sure they do, they repeated it enough during the throes of passion."

Tiffany snorted. "How do you know they weren't faking it?"

"A guy knows those things, Doc."

"Hmmm—I'm remembering a scene from a particular Meg Ryan movie."

"Well, in all honesty, I've learned a lot since then, but I call those years my learning period."

"What did you learn?"

"How to please women in bed, or on the beach, or the back seat of a car, or the kitchen tab—"

"Enough! Honestly, you are such a guy."

"What else would I be? And what else would I do there? Why did you go to Panama City during Spring Break? Wait, no, don't tell me—to get a tan?"

Tiffany sipped from her wine glass. "Certainly, among other things. I went especially to shock my parents. I wanted three things. To get a tattoo, any form of body piercing, and have unprotected sex with the first guy I met."

"That's a hell of a bucket list. How many of those things did you get to cross off?"

"Let's see—I nearly passed out while I was watching some guy's nipple being pierced."

"But . . . you're a surgeon."

"I know, but I don't perform surgery after five margaritas and as many shots of tequila."

"I sure as hell hope not," he snorted. "Anything else?"

"Uh—well, the only guy I ever had sex with over there wore a condom, so I guess I wasn't the type after all."

"Was it the Stairway to Heaven guy?"

"Yes, actually, it was."

"Damn, if I'd known that, I would have saved it for a live performance."

She chuckled. "It's too late now, stud."

"Maybe next time, but, I think you left something out."

"Mm, I don't think so."

"Give it up Tiff-a-ny," he drawled. "What kind of tattoo did you get?"

"I'm not telling."

"Come on, where did you get it, Doc?"

"I got it—at a parlor on that Front Beach Road."

"That's not what I meant, and you know it. Where is it?"

"On a place that never sees the sunshine."

"Fine, I'll ask Tanner."

"Right." She giggled. "Like he'd tell you."

"I'll sing to you again if you tell me."

"What will I get to hear?"

"Anything you want, if I know it."

She thought awhile and said, "Two songs—one of my choice and one of your own. I love that old song New Orleans Ladies. Can you handle it?"

"Sure I do. I have to admit, though, I never would have taken you for a classic rock kind of girl."

She laughed at his remark. "My brother used to tell me I was born fifteen years too late."

"Nah, you were born at just the right time."

Tiffany bit her lower lip, wondering if this was all just harmless flirting or something a little more substantial.

Red cleared his throat. "I'll play it for you, but I want the location first and what it is. Either that, or a promise to let me see it for myself."

"It's a yellow rose and it's just above my right butt cheek," she said quickly. "Now where's my song?"

"Hang on now. I need a minute or two for the visual to take shape. First you're in the tub and now you have a yellow rose on your right butt cheek. This could take a while."

Tiffany cleared her throat. "Since we're visually imaging, I think it's only fair you tell me what you're wearing."

"My oldest, most comfortable faded jeans," he told her.

"What else?"

"Nada."

She sucked in her breath, recalling the pictures she'd seen of his fabulous body. "Nothing?"

"That's right. When I got out of the shower, I realized I'd worn my last pair of clean undershorts today."

"Sounds like it's time to do some laundry"

"Hmph. Past time. It's been a hectic week."

"Boxers or briefs?" As soon as she uttered the words, she gasped and slapped her hand over her mouth.

A shocked laugh burst from Red. "Why, Doc, I didn't know you cared!"

She squeezed her eyes shut, deciding it was useless to apologize. "It's the wine," she groaned.

"Don't worry about it." He began strumming the notes of the song.

Tiffany laid back and relaxed as he sang his own beautiful version of her second favorite song, New Orleans Ladies. Afterward, he paused for several moments before making his choice.

"I've got it," he said, finally. "I'm switching to country. Do you remember Doug Stone?"

"Sure do," she said, relaxing as he began to play another old favorite of hers, *Come In Out Of The Pain*. Red's version was soulful and sexy, and she easily conjured up her own image of him sitting with his guitar propped comfortably on his leg, wearing an old pair of jeans—and absolutely nothing else. Tiffany thought of the near kiss situation earlier today. She'd been tempted, but wouldn't make a move with any man until she had ended the relationship with Tanner.

She blinked several times as the song came to an end. "That was beautiful," she whispered. "I love the way you sing."

"Enough to let me have a look at that tattoo one of these days, Doc?"

She giggled. "You know, I have a tendency to show it off when I shoot tequila—"

"Good to know," he interrupted. "What brand so I'll know what to stock?"

"—and that's why I don't shoot tequila anymore," she finished.

"Bummer," he groaned. "What does Tanner think of the old yellow rose?"

Tiffany lifted her head. Just the mention of Tanner's name sobered her. "He doesn't like it."

"It's a flower and it's on your butt. What's not to like?"

She adjusted the clip in her hair. "He's always wanted me to have it removed."

"Don't you dare!"

"Why do you care?" she asked. "You'll never see it."

"Never is a long time, Doc."

"Red . . ." Damn, she was glad he couldn't see her blush. Judging by his low chuckle, no doubt he'd suspect she was doing just that.

"Hey, what were you like as a kid? I bet you were a prissy little thing."

"Shows how much you know. My brother, Drake, can verify how wrong you are. I beat up a kid who picked on him once, and got myself in a lot of trouble at school."

"I bet that upset your mother."

Tiffany mulled that over before answering. "She didn't care what I did, as long as she didn't have to look at me." She waited through another prolonged silence.

"You want to talk about it?"

"Nope, but thanks for asking."

"Anytime, but I guess I need to let you go. You're probably pruning."

She stopped herself from telling him she'd like to keep talking. "I guess so."

"Listen, I know you don't like the name Tiffy, and I can understand that, but does it bother you when I call you Doc? I'll stop if you don't like it."

"Strangely enough, I find it comforting."

"Oh. Good." He sounded pleased. "Then I'll talk to you later."

"Goodnight Red."

"Hey, one more thing."

"What's that?" She froze, waiting for his final words.

"Boxer briefs. G'night Doc."

Tiffany foraged through her fridge for something to eat, wishing she'd taken up Red's offer to bring home leftovers yesterday. Settling on a personal pizza from the freezer, she'd just popped it into the microwave when her phone rang.

She checked the caller ID and answered with a bland, "Hello Tanner."

"Who the hell have you been talking to for an hour?" he demanded.

"What do you care, and where's the bimbo of the week?"

"There you go with your paranoia again, Tiffy."

The sound of the hated nickname grated on her nerves to no end. "Where are you Tanner? What's her name?"

"Hmph! It must be that time of the month again," he said. "For a couple of days you have no control over your emotions, and your imagination runs rampant for an entire week."

Tiffany cursed lowly. "Why don't you for once, in your pathetic life tell me the truth? I'm not stupid, you know. I've just chosen to look the other direction for the past five years."

"I'm not with anyone else."

"Last chance, Tanner. If I don't get the truth right now, I'm out of here." She fumed internally at the impatient sigh he released.

"You know, this attitude of yours gets to be so boring."

Tiffany let out a long sigh, but remained calm. "Aren't you as sick of this as I am?"

"Stop being so dramat—"

"I'm done with this, Tanner. I'll be gone by the time you get back," she said, cutting him off quickly. "Don't waste your time calling me again. I won't answer if it's you." She hung up without giving him a chance to respond.

When he didn't call back, she breathed a sigh of relief. She added Red's name and number into her cell phone's contact list then sat on the couch to call him back. "Hey," she said after he'd picked up on the third ring. "Are you busy?"

"I'm never too busy for you, Doc."

She smiled at his answer. "Tanner called, demanding to know who I was speaking to for so long."

"What happened?"

"I asked him to come clean and he accused me of being paranoid, of course. I told him by the time he comes back I won't be here. We're over."

"Good for you. He won't come back and bother you tonight, will he?"

"Tanner would never go through that much trouble." Her phone beeped and she checked it. "Hang on, Red. It's the hospital." She switched to the other call. "This is Dr. LeBlanc." Sally from the switchboard answered.

"Hey, honey, your nine a.m. knee replacement just got cancelled—that's a Mr. Mouton. His pre-admit blood work showed a high white blood cell count. It turns out he's got a bacterial infection, so Dr. Trahan put him on antibiotics. Looks like that one will be put off for a while."

"Okay Sal. That was my last surgery scheduled, so I won't see you until Monday." She switched back to Red's call.

"Looks like I'm free until Monday. So, I guess I'll be moving some things back into my house tomorrow."

"Do you need help?"

"I could probably use a big strong man to help me move a couple of heavy items. Do you have any idea where I could find someone that fits that description?"

"You have no idea how much I'm looking forward to that."

She crossed her ankles and laughed. "Oh, I think I do, but thanks. It shouldn't take long. I left most of my stuff in the house. I only have my desk and a couple of chairs to move. Everything else is clothing and personals. I'll need to find packing boxes, though."

"You're in luck, Doc. I didn't finish unpacking until Tuesday, so my garage is full of 'em. I'll bring some when I go."

Tiffany's phone beeped again. She checked it to see her mother's name flashing across the screen. "Oh God. He called my mother. I can't believe it."

"Do you need to take this?"

"Yeah, I do."

"Be strong, Doc."

She hit the button to switch to her mother's call. "Hello mother. Did you call to say Happy Thanksgiving?"

"Tiffany Danielle, you know very well why I called. Poor Tanner just called me, so distressed about you dumping him during the holidays."

"Poor Tanner was supposed to be spending it with his parents, but never made it that far. He called you from some other woman's bed."

"Why didn't you go with him?"

"I'm on call. I can barely leave the city much less the state, Mother. I've been at the hospital all day."

"And whose fault is that? You know how I feel about you working once you're married. A woman who doesn't need to work, shouldn't. Marry

Tanner, quit your job at that awful hospital, have a child or two, and join a few clubs to keep you busy."

"And endure a loveless marriage like yours and fathers."

"We both have our forms of entertainment."

"No kidding."

"Don't be rude, Tiffany."

"Don't be obtuse, mother. Entertainment is just a polite way to say you both sleep around."

"Your father and I are satisfied with the arrangement."

Tiffany shook her head in disgust. "You shouldn't be. I want a better life, a better marriage than that."

"This is a good life, dear. We've raised you and your brother to have the best of everything."

Tiffany couldn't stop the bitterness from seeping into her reply. "You didn't have a damn thing to do with raising Drake and me, mother. Melinda took care of us, thank God. Don't you ever wonder why we only go there twice a year?"

"I don't need to wonder. It's because you're both selfish, ungrateful children."

"It's because it's not a home. It never was! I'll be damned if I raise children in a place like that. If I marry, it will be for love, and to a good man who'd rather die than hurt me the way Tanner has." She cringed at the sound of her mother's hysterical laughter.

"Oh, listen to you, so full of hope that there's still a decent man out there waiting for you. You always did live in a fantasy world, Tiffany. Now, you listen to me. The phrase 'good man' is an oxymoron, and there is no such thing as a faithful marriage. The sooner you accept it, the better off you'll be."

Tiffany closed her eyes and sighed. "Mother, I feel so sorry for you. I've seen how other people live, and it's not how you and father live. Other people are happy. Not all, of course, but I can name dozens of couples right now who are truly happy together."

"Pah! Newlywed love fades. Trust me."

Tiffany ran a hand through her straightened locks and let her head fall back. "You're wasting your breath, Mother. I will not marry Tanner. He's selfish, vindictive, spoiled, and weak."

"Yes, you will." Her mother spoke in an icy tone. "You will do what your father and I have groomed you to do, to make a good match."

"Groomed me? Why not just call it what it is? You want to whore me out. Sell me to the highest bidder!"

"Don't be ridiculous!"

"You know, most parents would be thrilled their daughter is a successful surgeon, but not you and father. Neither of you give a damn about that. I've got money, Mother—money I earned myself. All you care about is how much I can add to the family coffer by marrying a rich husband."

"Money can bring comfort to a woman that a husband won't."

Tiffany placed her hand over her eyes. "Don't you love Drake and me enough to want us happy? Have you *ever* loved us?"

"How dare you say such a thing to me? You have no idea how many sacrifices I've made for you and your brother! We've given you everything you ever wanted. We paid to send you both to the finest schools. The least you could do is to show us gratitude."

Tiffany laughed. "Do you even know which college I attended, mother?"

"I'm sure it was the finest money could buy."

"Louisiana State University in Baton Rouge. I went on a full scholarship because of my grades. My counselor and I filled out all of the papers ourselves because you said father wouldn't pay for my college unless I went to law school."

"We'd have paid to send you to Harvard."

"I didn't want to be a lawyer."

"You always were too obstinate for your own good."

"I graduated at the top of my class in med school."

"What has that got to do with anything?"

"I don't owe you and father a damn thing for my education! I took out school loans and paid every dime of it back. Two years later you sent Drake to Harvard when he wanted to be with me at LSU. I convinced him to go to Harvard because it was the best education money could buy."

Tiffany stood up to pace the floor as she continued to rant. "So, if you think I'm going to give up everything to marry a spoiled, self-centered, cheating ass-hole like Tanner, you're wrong. I'll choose my own husband or I'll choose not to marry at all. But I will do the choosing, do you understand me? And don't you dare send father over here, because I'll tell him the same thing!"

"Tiffany, you will be shaming me in front of our entire circle of friends," her mother screeched. "I'll be a social outcast after this."

"Oh mother, for crying out loud, you act as if this is the nineteenth century."

"Tiffany Danielle, don't you trivialize this situation!"

Tiffany couldn't have stopped the short burst of laughter if she'd wanted to. "Everything about this situation is trivial, Mother!" The ensuing icy silence reigned supreme.

"Well," her mother finally huffed into the phone. "I have no need of ungrateful children."

One single click of the phone and it went dead. Tiffany dropped to the couch, and threw the phone on the cushion. Her laughter began as a quiet chuckle, gaining strength, until it bordered on hysteria. The journey from hysteria to tears proved to be short and very unexpected.

Sniveling and needing to talk to someone who gave a damn about her, she attempted to call Drake. By the time his voicemail picked up, she was crying too hard to leave a message.

What had she ever done to deserve getting so little love from either of her parents? Red's last words telling her to be strong rang through her head, and she threw her shoulders back, straightening her spine. She'd learned to be independent and strong at an early age, had always taken immense pride in her strength. She had friends and co-workers who relied heavily on their partners in times of trouble. What must it be like, just for once, to rely on someone else's strength?

Her phone rang, flashing Red's name across the screen. She answered, sniffling into a tissue.

"I couldn't stand it, Doc. I had to call. Are you okay?"

Red's voice, saturated with concern for her, turned into her undoing. Within seconds, she was blubbering uncontrollably, totally incapable of intelligent speech.

Nothing could have prepared Red for the sound of Tiffany's heartbroken sobs.

"What happened?" he said, ready to kill, or at least cripple the person responsible for her tears.

"Red," she sputtered.

"Are you alone?"

"Y-y-yes."

"Can you talk to me?"

She choked out a tortured sob. "No."

Red waited only a moment before making a decision. "Pack a bag. Whatever you need to hold you over until tomorrow. I'm picking you up."

He grabbed the keys to his car and his cell phone on his way out the door. Thanks to Giselle, he knew exactly where Tiffany lived, and floored it until he stood in front of the condo she shared with Tanner.

His breath caught in his throat as Tiffany opened the door. He took in the puffy, tearstained face, her faded jeans and tee shirt, and longed to hold her close. She covered her face, sobbing quietly into her hands. He suspected that by tomorrow she'd be embarrassed over breaking down in front of him, but right now she seemed too upset to care.

He lifted the overnight bag at her feet, looped the strap over his shoulder. He picked up her purse and keys from a table near the door then placed his arm around her. "Come on, Doc, I'm taking you away from here."

She nodded and stepped out into the frosty night air. As Red leaned in to shut the door, she lifted one hand to stop him. He watched with a strange mixture of sadness and delight, as she slipped the multi-carat emerald cut diamond from her left hand. She stepped inside to hang it on a key hook next to the door then left the apartment. He pulled the door shut behind her and walked her to his car.

Enveloped by the decked out Camaro's warm interior, and heated leather seats, Tiffany's head lolled back on the headrest. Her eyes drifted closed as silent tears streamed down her face. A fresh round of heart-wrenching sobs had him reaching out to cover her hand with his. She clutched his hand tightly throughout the drive home, giving him a whole new appreciation for automatic transmission packages.

Less than ten minutes later, he dropped her bags at the door and led a shivering Tiffany to the still blazing fireplace. He positioned her back to the fire and rubbed her arms and hands briskly for a minute.

"What's going on, Doc?" He stopped to gently tilt her chin up as her tears continued to flow.

She shook her head. "I d-don't know. I n-never c-cry, but I c-can't s-stop."

He clenched his jaw, angry at the people in her life who'd brought her to this state of sadness—her parents and Tanner. He pulled her into his arms, allowing her to cry out her misery and sorrow onto his chest. He held her tightly, rubbing his hands over her back, occasionally placing his hand on the back of her head to massage her scalp. After a full ten minutes, the tears slowed, and eventually stopped.

"Better now?"

She nodded.

"Want something to drink? Water? A glass of wine?" He lifted one finger. "You'll notice I didn't offer tequila. I'm trying to be a gentleman."

She nodded. "B-beer?"

He smiled and walked around to his bar area. He opened a bottle of beer and brought it to her.

She took a sip. "Thank you."

"Now, tell me what happened."

She closed her eyes, bit her bottom lip to keep from crying, and shook her head.

"Don't cry again," he groaned. "I can't take it when you cry." He placed his hands gently on both sides of her face. "Just take a big breath and try to tell me what happened."

She looked up with puffy sad eyes. "You happened, Red; you and your family."

He frowned. "I don't understand."

"Seeing you and your family together—the way you interact with each other—it made me realize how empty my life is. After seeing that, I know now. There's no way I can live in a loveless marriage." She squeezed her eyes shut.

Red reached out to place his hands on her shoulders. "You shouldn't have to. Nobody should have to live like that."

"I know," she said miserably.

"With a man who refuses to be faithful to you."

"I know."

"No one should ask that of you, not even your parents. Hell, *especially* not your parents."

"I know that." Her voice broke with another sob.

"Then why are you crying?"

She hugged her waist as she turned toward the fireplace. "Because I just now realized that in my thirty-six years, I've never had one single person in my life, other than my little brother and our nanny, who's ever truly loved me. Not my parents, not my grandmother, and not the man I just wasted five years of my life with." She turned back to face Red. "That's pretty damned sad, don't you think?"

Red grabbed a tissue to gently pat the tears from her cheeks, sorely tempted to tell her there was someone right here who loved her. "Please don't cry anymore."

"Even after I told my mother what Tanner had done, she still wants me to marry him. It's all about money—she doesn't care about me. She never has." Her tortured groan revealed frustration laced with pain.

Red spent the next half hour listening as she spoke about the years she and Drake spent in that loveless house—watching their parents grow colder to each other and their children. He shook his head in amazement as she told him the circumstances of her and Drake's college educations. She told him everything she could about her life in that cold, forbidding place she'd never considered a home. She ended by telling him the last thing her mother had said to her.

"I know it's just a ploy to try to make me feel guilty, but it's having the opposite effect. I almost wish I never had to see her again, and that's what's so sad, Red. Other than Drake, she and my father are the only family I have."

Red watched as a tear trailed down her face to fall from her chin. He didn't know how he'd managed to remain silent through it all, but he had. He longed to pull her into his arms and tell her how much he loved her—that he wanted nothing more than for her to be a part of his family. But this wasn't the time. She'd made a choice, a choice to cut someone out of her life—someone who'd been a part of it for five years. She would probably need time to grieve. Maybe need the time to restructure—to rearrange her life around the loss.

Besides, according to Tiffany, there *was* one person in her family who gave a damn about her. "Maybe it's time to call your brother."

"I tried calling him after mother hung up on me, but he wasn't home." She wiped her nose and sniffed softly.

"Did you leave a message?"

She shook her head. "I couldn't."

"I want you to call him again, and if he's not home, leave him a message. Make sure he knows it's urgent you speak to him."

Tiffany nodded, making a quick search of her purse before she realized she didn't have her phone.

Red handed her his cordless landline. "Here, use this." He went into the kitchen, leaving her alone to make the call.

Tiffany took a deep breath and called Drake's number. His voicemail picked up and her brother's baritone, familiar and soothing, asked her to leave a message. "Hey, little brother, I just broke off my engagement and had it out with mother on the phone. I really need to talk to you, Drake. I'm spending the night at a friend's house, and I'd appreciate it if you'd give me a call at this number. Love you," she finished quietly, before ending the call. She stood alone in the living room and wiped the tears from her eyes.

Red approached her and took the phone. "Why don't you go rinse your face in cold water; it'll make you feel better."

"I believe I will," she said, nodding. "Where's my bag?"

He picked it up and held it out to her.

"I feel bad for imposing on you like this, Red. I could have stayed at the condo. For that matter, I could have gone back to my own house."

He shook his head. "You didn't need to be behind the wheel in that shape, and you sure as hell didn't need to be alone. This house is big enough for the two of us, believe me. Come here, I'll show you your room for the night." He walked her down the hall and opened the guest room door for her.

"This is very nice," she said, admiring the room.

"You have your own private bath through that door."

"Thanks again for all of this, Red."

"Anytime." The silence between them was suddenly broken by the sound of Tiffany's stomach growling in hunger. He grinned at her. "I'm guessing you didn't have a chance to eat."

"No. Remind me to take that personal pizza out of the microwave tomorrow," she said, sheepishly.

"Can I heat up a plate of leftovers for you?"

"That would be great. This is really nice of you, Red."

"That's what friends are for." He left the room, closing the door behind him.

Tiffany stepped into the bathroom to admire the huge whirlpool tub, walk in shower with multiple showerheads, and the deep granite sink. She cringed at her reflection—splashed ice cold water from the faucet over her red puffy face. While patting her face dry, she ran the fingers of one hand through her straightened, blonde locks, all the while staring at the stranger in the mirror. *No more.* She was done changing herself for Tanner or anyone else.

Chapter Six

He flipped his toothpick from one side of his mouth to the other and punched Red's number into a cheap ass disposable phone. He couldn't wait to see the self-righteous bastard's head on a platter. Too bad the time wasn't right to let McAllister know exactly what he had planned for him. He smiled evilly, stewing, as he waited for Red to answer. He'd planted the seed of unrest in Red McAllister's safe, secure world on Thanksgiving Day. Now, it was time to reinforce that feeling of unease. Keep the bastard looking over his shoulder, and wondering.

Red placed some leftovers in the oven to reheat for Tiffany, and reached for his ringing cell phone. He didn't recognize the number. It couldn't be Tiffany's brother. He only had the landline number. "Hello."

"McAllister."

Red's brow furrowed at the same deep, gravelly growl he'd first heard on Thanksgiving Day, again muffled, as though the caller were trying to disguise it.

"Who the hell is this?" An immediate sense of unease flooded through his system.

"All in good time. You have it all, don't you?"

Red straightened to his full height. "Whatever I have, I've busted my ass to get, and I've come by it honestly."

"The holier than thou attitude is still intact. We'll see how long that lasts when you're rotting in prison."

"Prison? For what? What the hell do you want?"

No answer.

He checked the screen. Just like that, the call ended.

He placed the phone on the counter, more than a little curious. He checked on Tiffany's food reheating in the Viking oven, and his landline rang, showing a number with a Texas area code. Tiffany's brother, no doubt. Regardless, he answered somewhat cautiously.

"Excuse me," drawled a deep voice with an east Texas accent. "I received a call from this number earlier. Is there a Tiffany LeBlanc there?"

"She's here, but let me see if she's available." Red carried the phone down the hall and knocked on the guest room door. When he didn't get an answer, he put the phone to his ear and addressed the caller. "She's not available right now. Is this her brother?"

"Yes, I'm Drake LeBlanc. Who am I speaking to?"

"Scott McAllister, I'm a friend of hers."

"So what exactly is going on over there? Is Tiffany all right?"

Red took his time walking back into the kitchen. "She's better now, but when I called her apartment earlier, she was crying so hard she couldn't speak, so I picked her up and brought her to my place. I didn't think she needed to be alone tonight."

"Where's Golden Boy?"

"Who?"

"Tanner Collins, her ex," Drake growled, revealing his clear disdain for the man.

"Off with another woman, I imagine. He was supposed to be at his parents, and he wasn't."

"So, she finally gave him the old heave ho? It's about damn time," Drake drawled. "I don't know if you know him or not, but he's not exactly husband material."

Red paced a slow path in front of his fireplace, the same spot he'd occupied while comforting Tiffany a short while ago. "I've known him for twenty years and he may be someone's husband material, but he's definitely not for Doc." The following prolonged phone silence told him Drake LeBlanc was analyzing every word he heard. He got the feeling that Tiff's brother was sharp at judging people—the practicing attorney in him, no doubt.

"And where exactly do you fit in, Mr. McAllister?"

"I'm just a friend of hers."

"But you'd like to be more."

The man was blunt, to the point. He couldn't help but be impressed with Drake's astute grasp of the situation. "Yes I would."

"Maybe you're a little in love with her already?"

It wouldn't do to hedge with this guy. "Yes I am, actually."

"What does my sister think about that?"

"She doesn't know yet."

"You plan on telling her tonight?"

"No, she's not ready. She said she needs to be alone for a while and it would probably do her some good."

"Do you happen to know if she kept her rent house?"

"She did. I'm going to help her move her things back tomorrow."

"Good girl, she took my advice."

"Excellent advice from someone who knows Tanner."

"Never bet against a stacked deck. Okay, McAllister, I know Tanner spends his days in surgery and his nights sleeping around on my sister. What do you do for a living?"

"I own a club in Lafayette, and will be opening up a second one in Lake Coburn next month."

"What's the name of the club?"

"Red's—that's what my friends call me."

"I've heard of it, believe it or not. It's nice, I hear."

"I wouldn't run one that wasn't."

"I have friends and business associates over there who've been several times. So, when I ask them about Scott "Red" McAllister—and you can be sure I will—am I going to hear anything that will make me urge my sister to slap a restraining order against you?"

Red rubbed his chin. "I guess it depends on who your friends are. I've owned businesses in and around the Lafayette area for fifteen years and I've made a couple of enemies. As a matter of fact, I think one of them called me just a minute before you did. I'm still trying to figure that one out."

"What kind of enemies?" Drake asked, sounding understandably concerned.

"I had one guy in particular who tried to hold back my liquor license unless he got a significant kickback. It seems dishonesty is a lucrative business here in Louisiana."

"Though lacking in exclusivity. We also get our fair share in the great state of Texas, unfortunately."

"When I get shoved, I normally shove back."

"As you should."

"I think so, too, Mr. LeBlanc, but by all means, ask around. You'll find my friends are top shelf."

"That's good to know."

"Is this interrogation over now, counselor?"

Drake chuckled. "She told you I was a lawyer?"

Red hesitated. "She told me your parents *paid* to send you to Harvard. I only assumed you passed the bar."

There was an uncomfortable silence on the other end of the phone. Finally Drake spoke in a tight voice. "I didn't want to go to Harvard. I wanted to be with Tiff, but she talked me into going. Our parent's treatment of her is deplorable."

"It turned out she didn't need anything from them. The only thing she wants, they can't seem to give her—and that's love. I guess that's why she called you. She said you were close once."

"We are close. We just don't get to see each other enough."

"You should make time for family, in my opinion."

"You sound like a family man, McAllister. Ever been married?" Drake asked, sounding more protective than curious.

"No, I've never been interested, before now. I come from a large family and we're all very close. So, how about you? Are you married?"

"Hell, no! The women I tote around aren't the marrying kind. I'm a hopeless bachelor."

"Yeah, well, all that can change in a heartbeat. Take it from me."

"I wouldn't hold my breath if I were you. Tell Tiff I'll be here for the rest of the night—I'll be waiting for her call."

"I'll do that."

Drake ended the call and stared at his cell, hoping Red McAllister proved to be as decent a guy as his gut told him he was. He contemplated less than a minute before calling his commissioned private investigator. "Sorry for the wake-up call, buddy," he said, after Dan answered in a sleepy voice. He gave him the information he'd gleaned from the conversation with Red.

"When do you need the scoop on this guy?"

"As soon as possible," Drake said, knowing full well he paid Dan enough to expect immediate results.

"I'll get right on it. Happy Thanksgiving, Boss."

Drake hesitated, taken back by the comment. "You too, Dan," he said before disconnecting and consulting his calendar. He sat back, shaking his head. Damned if he hadn't missed Thanksgiving. With no family around, or anyone close, for that matter, he'd worked in his downtown Houston apartment all day long. He'd gone out once to grab some Chinese takeout from the place around the corner. He thought it had been quiet, even for a Thursday night.

How pathetic is that?

Red had just removed the reheated leftovers from the oven when he heard the door of the guest room open. "Hey, Doc, I didn't know if you had a preference for white or dark meat so I heated up some of both for you." He set her plate on the counter beside the platter of food.

"Your brother called, and he wants you to call him back at that number. He said he'll be there all night," He turned toward her. "And he'll be waiting—for—your—call . . ." His voice faltered. "What did you do to your hair?"

Tiffany's chin lifted. "This is my hair. Tanner liked it straight."

"You're kidding." Her tight mouth and slow shake of her head said she wasn't. Unable to resist, he reached out to touch the silky tendrils with one hand, watching in awe as they looped and twisted, curling around his fingers. Fighting the nearly irresistible urge to burrow his fingers in the glorious mass, he shook his head. "How the hell could he *not* like it like this?"

"I have brown hair."

Distracted by the sight before him, her comment barely registered. "What did you say?"

"My natural hair color is brown, and as soon as I can get to that, I will. I'm tired of seeing a stranger in the mirror."

Red nodded, as full understanding dawned on him. Tanner. What a prick.

"I'd guess you are," he whispered, unable to tear his gaze from her. A low rumbling from her stomach finally did the trick.

He turned away as she laughed nervously, pressing her hand to her stomach. Red filled a plate with her favorites and placed it on the island. "What do you want to drink?"

She climbed onto the barstool and grinned. "I'll have another beer. I'm celebrating."

He pushed the phone to her. "Before you celebrate too much, call your brother. He sounded concerned."

"Thanks," she said, hitting the redial button.

Red could tell from the smile on her face the instant her brother answered the phone.

"Hey, little brother."

They *are* close. He left the room so she could talk in private.

Drake settled down for the long overdue heart to heart between siblings. "Hey, Sis. Word is you're having a rough night."

"Yep, Mother's not pleased, of course."

"You called her?" Her snort brought a smile to his face.

"Surely you know me better than that. She called me after 'Poor Tanner's' anguished phone call about our broken engagement."

"Collins always was a pussy." He smiled at her outburst of laughter.

"Mother wants me to take him back because he's such a good catch. Oh, she also wants me to quit my job."

"So you can be just like her? Pop out a namesake or two, let a nanny raise them, and live out your days playing bridge and sleeping with the tennis pro and anything else that moves?"

"Can you imagine me living that kind of life, Drake?"

"Hell no, and you shouldn't have to. I never could understand the way they treated you."

"They treated both of us badly."

Drake rubbed a hand over his eyes. "You worse, Tiff, at least they paid for my education. I'll always feel guilty as hell about that."

"It doesn't matter. I got the education and the career I wanted. There's not a damn thing they can do to take that away from me. I spend my days helping people."

Drake opened his mouth to reply, but couldn't find the words.

"Are you still there?"

Drake gave the back of his neck a one handed massage. "I'm here, but I've been thinking lately that I don't."

"Don't what?"

"Help people. I practice corporate law, and I don't help anybody but big business." He flipped a silver swivel photo frame, sending it spinning on its stand. It stopped, the shiny side reflecting his haggard face back at him. "Most of the time I'm helping to take over some company which results in putting hundreds of people out of work. I haven't been sleeping well lately. Maybe I'm developing a conscience."

"You've always had a conscience, Drake. You just wouldn't listen to it. Open your private practice. Do what you want to do."

He pinched the bridge of his nose, feeling a headache coming on. "I think it's too late for me. I'm probably already permanently corrupted."

"If that were true, you'd be able to sleep at night. You *do* have the right to walk away, you know, despite what they tell you."

He nodded, surprised by his sister's sudden change. He had to wonder if McAllister had something to do with it. "They did a number on us, didn't they?"

"I'd begun to wonder if I'd ever be able to feel again, but I know damn well I can't live the way they do. Not after seeing what I saw yesterday."

"What's that?" He was curious to know what finally brought her to her senses about Tanner.

"A real family. It seems not everyone was raised in a household like ours."

"Whose family?"

"Red McAllister's, the friend I'm staying with tonight. He had a big dinner here. His entire family came—his parents, six of his brothers and sisters, their spouses, and children. Plus other friends of ours were here. His parents have been married almost fifty years and they're still so much in love with each other. I've never seen anything like it. They all sing or play instruments. Our own parents don't even know that you and I can sing, Drake. Who do we even get that from? How is it that we don't know things like about our own parents?"

"Beats me," he admitted. "So, Red told me a little of what happened tonight. He rescued the damsel in distress. Okay, so what's in it for him? Should I be concerned?"

"No, he's a good friend."

Who happens to be in love with you. "Where'd you meet him?"

"I performed surgery on a friend of his back in August and he was at the hospital. We—uh—actually we got off on the wrong foot, but we eventually straightened it out."

"What do you mean, the wrong foot?"

"He assumed I was a nurse."

"And you jumped on him for being a sexist chauvinist, of course."

"Of course I did, but he claimed I looked too young to be a doctor. How can a girl feel bad about that?"

Her laughter sparked a feeling of pride for his sister.

"I had a good Thanksgiving, Drake. I wish you could have been here. His parents are wonderful, especially his mom. You know, it's sad, but I spoke more to her yesterday than I have to our mother in my entire life."

Extremely sad but not one bit of a shock. "And I bet she didn't mention once how your selfish act would ruin her reputation, did she?"

"Has someone been running around with the wrong type of woman again, little brother?"

Drake's living room filled with his own raucous laughter. "Always, Sis. You know that." They both quieted suddenly.

"I wish you could meet Red's family. If you ever do, I'm warning you now, it'll change you. You'll know you can't go back to living the way you were."

"Maybe one day I will," he murmured.

"Maybe I can get us invitations for Christmas. I'm eating Thanksgiving leftovers right now—turkey, cornbread dressing, and some kind of yummy veggie casserole his mom made."

Drake groaned. "Rub my face in it, why don't you?"

"She also makes pecan pralines, fudge, and divinity just like Melinda used to make us, remember?"

"Man, I'd kill for some of Melin's pralines. And those tart or pie things with the strawberry preserves. Man those things were good."

"How'd you spend Thanksgiving?"

"I had work to do. It was just me and my Chinese take-out." He waited, through Tiffany's prolonged silence.

She finally spoke. "Promise me something, Drake."

"What, Sis?"

"Promise me you'll be here with me for Christmas. I won't be making any Christmas party in Houston this year."

"Where will you be?"

"I have no idea. It doesn't matter where I'll be. I just want to make sure you'll be with me. Please, Drake, we're all we've got."

"I'll plan for it, if it means that much to you."

"It does," she said.

He heard her try to stifle a yawn. "Are you tired?"

"Yeah, it's been a long day, and I'm beat."

"Go get some rest. I promise I'll be there for Christmas. I love you, Tiff."

"I love you too, Drake. Thanks."

Tiffany ended the call and got up to put her empty plate in the dishwasher. She heard Red's bedroom door open and looked up. He walked into the kitchen wearing soft faded jeans and a clean, white T-shirt, his hair still damp from the shower.

As their gazes met, he stopped and shook his head. "I still can't get over the difference your hair has made. How'd it go with Drake?"

She smiled brightly. "I made him promise to be with me for Christmas. I'm not going to Houston this year."

"You know, after you left, my family decided they wanted to have Christmas here too, so if you and Drake want to join us, we'd love to have you."

Tiffany grinned. "I'm accepting for the both of us. How much banana pudding should I bring?"

"At least double what you brought here today so I have leftovers. It's a family rule: Whoever's house gets used and abused gets to keep the leftovers."

"That sounds fair."

He nodded. "That's why I volunteered my place again. I won't have to cook for days. Did you get enough to eat?"

"Yes, and it was even better the second time around." She patted her belly with one hand and covered a yawn with the other. "Excuse me. Two beers and a belly full of food, and I'm not very good company."

"Why don't you go on to bed, Doc? We can start moving your things first thing in the morning."

"Are you sure it's not too much of an inconvenience for you?"

He waved off her concerns. "It's worth it to get you out of that place. Besides, I don't sleep much."

Tiffany sent him a sideways glance. "You too? I hardly ever sleep past four a.m., whether I have to go to work or not. It drives me crazy."

"My magic number is 3:15. I can't tell you how many times I open my eyes to see that time on my clock or my phone."

"That's crazy, right?" She covered another yawn with her hand. "I think I will go to bed." She let Red walk her to her bedroom.

"That mattress is brand new. It's got the memory foam pillow top like mine. You should be really comfortable."

Tiffany turned at the door. "I'm sure it'll be fine." She reached up to give him a hug. "Thanks for everything, Red."

He hugged her back tightly. "Good night, Doc."

She changed into flannel lounger pants and a T-shirt before crawling under the down comforter. She made sure her cell phone was silenced, thinking it seemed much later than 11:15—she supposed due to the drama-filled day. She stretched out on the luxuriously comfortable bed, and was asleep within minutes.

Tiffany blinked several times in the darkened room to get her bearings. She stretched out on the soft bed, trying to remember why she wasn't in her own. It all came back to her in a rush of warm memories.

Red.

The digital clock flashed 4:02 AM in bright blue led lights. She groaned, frustrated that even here, in Red McAllister's oh-so-damned-comfortable guest bed, she couldn't get a full night's sleep. She functioned well on five or six hours but couldn't help but wonder how much better she'd feel with a full eight hours.

Tiffany washed her face and rinsed her mouth. She stared at her reflection in the mirror, taking the time to fluff her curls. Amazing how quickly the change made her feel a little more like her old self.

Regretting she hadn't remembered to pack her latest medical journal, she slipped her robe over her lounger set. She stepped into her slippers, setting off in search of reading material. Tiffany tiptoed into the living room and picked up a Forbes magazine on an end table. She cringed at the articles in it, and put it back. As she walked over to the kitchen to get a drink of water, she noticed a glow of light shining out from under a door at the opposite end of the hallway.

Tiffany tiptoed over and stood listening to the soft strumming of a guitar. She gave the door a gentle push and peeked inside. Red sat in his office chair, jean clad legs propped on his desk and crossed at the ankles, his chest bared and brawny, as he strummed a somewhat familiar melody. John Michael Montgomery's *Hold on to Me*. She smiled, recognizing one of the songs they'd danced to at Jackson and Giselle's wedding.

Tiffany shivered, remembering how good Red had looked in his classy black tux—how good it had felt to dance with him. She stared long and hard at his bare upper torso, thinking she liked the half-dressed version of him even better. Clearly, he'd retained all physical attributes since Vivienne had snapped those photos of him posing at his pool. She hadn't seen anyone that buff since she and some co-workers saw the Chippendale dancers last year.

Tiffany watched his fingers skillfully manipulate the strings of the guitar, listening as long as she dared, before making her presence known to him. Reluctantly, she took a deep breath and spoke.

"Red?"

He jumped slightly before grinning up at her. "Well, hell, Doc. I thought for sure you'd sleep longer than this, considering the night you had."

She lifted her hands, dropped them to her sides. "This is what I do."

He chuckled. "Just look at us—Sleepless in Lake Coburn."

"How long have you been up?" she asked.

Red propped his guitar against the desk and stood. "Since around three."

She nodded. "I was looking for some reading material, but I don't need it now. Is this what you do when you can't sleep?" She nearly groaned in protest when he slipped on his T-shirt.

"Among other things."

Tiffany leaned over his desk, picked up a tablet covered with lyrics in a masculine handwriting. "Are you writing a song?"

"I've been trying to write something for my mom and dad's forty-sixth wedding anniversary next month. I'm no poet, or lyricist, that's for damn sure. I'm better at the melody. Two weeks I've been working on this thing, and that's as far as I've gotten."

She read the words to herself. "This is pretty good. Who's composing the music?"

"I've already got the tune down," he said.

"Could I hear it, please?"

He nodded and began strumming a beautiful melody on his guitar then began to sing the words he'd written.

I was alone once, no hope for love in sight
Until your love saved me from the lonely night
My heart stops beating; my world could rip in two

When I think how close I came to never having you.

"This is the chorus," he said.

A love like ours doesn't happen every day
Written in the stars, perfect in every way
I thank the Lord for the lifeline that he threw
The day he heard my prayer, and led me straight to you.

Tiffany waited until he'd finished, then released the breath she'd been holding. "That's really beautiful."

Red shrugged. "Thanks, but I can't seem to think of anything else. I keep trying to imagine what my dad would say to her, or about her, but—my dad's a man of few words."

"Maybe that's the problem. This is not just his story, it's hers too. You should have a verse from her point of view now and have it sung as a duet."

"Did you take song writing in college or something?"

"No, but I'm a closet romantic. Now that I've heard their story, it's a little more personal for me." She took a few minutes to jot down a few more lines then smiled. "Play that melody for me again." As he strummed, she began to sing:

I can't imagine the kind of world this would be
If your sweet love had never rescued me.
The man they chose for me – no kind of man at all
I can't be happy without your love's sweet call.

Red looked at her in amazement. "I can't believe you just wrote that in under five minutes."

Tiffany smiled then pulled up a chair next to him. "You've already done the hard part. Now you have them grow old together and it should be sung in harmony."

He nodded and began experimenting with a few words. He came up with half of a line and Tiffany finished it for him. They continued to work together until they had the final verse for the song. Putting their heads together, they harmonized the last verse.

We're growing older, our lives are now entwined,
Our hearts so joined, can't tell what's yours or mine.
With lives so rich, so full of laughter and love
It had to come straight from heaven up above.

A love like ours doesn't happen every day
Written in the stars, perfect in every way
I thank the Lord for the lifeline that he threw

For the day he heard my prayer and led me straight to you.
Thank God he heard our prayer and led me home to you.

He strummed the last notes and grinned at her. "Hey Doc, we just co-wrote a song."

She smiled. "I believe we did. Think it's any good?"

"It's for Mom and Dad's anniversary. They won't be expecting anything professional. I know they'll love it."

Tiffany tapped one long fingernail on the top of Red's mahogany desk. "You know, it would be wonderful if all of your siblings could have a part in it. Can you write scores for other instruments? You'd need the piano, a fiddle, and the bass guitar. Are there any other musical instruments lurking around in your family?"

Red took a swig from a glass of water. "That's about it. Kenneth and Brandon don't need my help for their parts – they can hear it once and play along just fine. It's really the piano part I'd have to come up with and I don't play the piano."

Tiffany shook her head. "I can't help you there, but I bet your sister Annie could come up with something. I know Drake could."

Red stood beside her. "But the difficult part is finished. You have no idea how relieved I am to have this done."

She pushed her hair back from her face and smiled again. "I'm glad to be of service. It's the least I can do for you, helping me out the way you did. What time is it, anyway?"

He checked his watch and grimaced. "Almost five."

Tiffany grabbed her head and groaned. "God, it makes me *crazy* not being able to sleep through the night."

Red leaned his guitar against his desk. "I know what you mean. I thought about taking something to sleep, but some of those products have some scary side effects. I'm afraid I'd get up and cook a meal while I'm asleep, or something."

Tiffany laughed. "I'm afraid I'd go shopping for the ingredients. With my luck, I'd wake up naked in the middle of the street."

"Showing off that yellow rose tattoo of yours," he added, with a chuckle.

She cleared her throat, avoiding his gaze. "I knew it was a mistake telling you about that."

He burst into laughter. "Don't worry, Doc. Your secret's safe with me."

"It'd better be. I know where you live now." She re-directed the conversation quickly. "Seriously, when it comes to my insomnia, I keep hoping something will kick in one day. Hopefully, I'll catch up on all the years of sleep I've lost."

"Maybe it's the stressful situation with Tanner, and when you're back in your own place it'll be better."

Tiffany shook her head vigorously. "I can't blame it on Tanner. I've been like this since college."

Red sat forward in his chair. "Me too. The only time I got enough sleep in college was when I was hung over. Jackson thought I drank because I liked beer, but hell, I just needed the sleep."

Tiffany collapsed in laughter on the small couch. "That is the most pitiful excuse for drinking I've ever heard."

Red grinned. "You know, you have the greatest laugh, Doc. It sure would be nice to hear it more often." He reached out to touch her curls. "And I still can't believe the difference your hair has made."

Tiffany fluffed her hair with both hands. "It'll be nice not to waste an hour straightening my hair every morning."

He lifted a finger as though just thinking of something. "Does this mean you'll be coming to the club opening?"

"I don't see why not. Will your family be there?"

Red placed his guitar back in its case. "I'm sure a few of them will be. My folks don't usually do grand openings. They don't like the crowds."

Tiffany leaned back, her head resting against the cushions. "What was it like, Red? Growing up with parents like yours? I can't even imagine."

Red smiled as though lost in the past. "I knew by the age of seven or so that we had it better than our friends. I'd get home from school and there were warm cookies, or donuts, or something like that waiting for us. What still amazes me is that my parents hardly ever argued. They would disagree about things, don't get me wrong. Every now and then things would get icy between them for a few days, but they never yelled or called each other names. They tried their best to compromise."

Tiffany stood and pulled her robe tighter. "My parents never yelled at each other. They'd have had to be in the same room for that to happen. Drake and I were raised by our nanny. Now *she* would have warm cookies waiting for us when we got home from school. Melinda—we called her Melin, was more of a mom to us than our own mother was."

"At least you had someone. Do you ever see her?"

"No, she moved back up to Washington state after Drake went off to college. Once she got there, she met up with an old flame from high school who was a widower, and they got married. His first wife died of cancer and they'd never had children." Tiffany shook her head slowly. "Melinda never had kids, either, and it's so sad because she's a natural mother. We speak at least once a month and we email back and forth. But, she has her own life now." She released a long sigh. "There are times I miss her so much."

"Sounds like the two of you are due for a long talk." Red stood and stretched, flexing his back. "You ready for some coffee? I set the timer earlier."

"I'd love some."

They headed to the kitchen. "Since moving here, I've started swimming when I can't sleep. You didn't happen to bring a swimsuit did you?"

"Not exactly something I thought about when you told me to pack a bag."

He poured a cup of coffee for her and let her prepare it, then grabbed his black.

She sipped at her coffee and pursed her lips. "You know, I won't know what to do with myself after today. Catch up on some reading, I guess."

"Romance novels?" he asked, sending her a grin.

"Medical journals. Have to keep up with the changing times. Today's new procedure is tomorrow's old news."

"Blech! Sounds interesting."

"About as interesting to you as the articles in that Forbes magazine looked to me," she added.

Red laughed as he sat down across from her. "I guess you're right. I'm impressed with your medical skills, Doc. You're young to have the excellent reputation you have."

Tiffany sipped her coffee. "I love learning about new procedures in orthopedic surgery. It's exciting when someone develops a way to change people's lives for the better. Twenty years ago, Jackson's leg would have been amputated and fit with a less than perfect prosthesis. Today, he's walking around fit and healthy because of a device that someone took a chance at developing. It's fascinating."

Red placed his cup on the table. "That's how I feel about investment opportunities. I love the research involved—studying the demographics of each particular area—knowing what it takes to create a successful business before you even think about opening one. The kind of club that may work in Lafayette may not work here in Lake Coburn, so adjustments have to be made."

Red brought the paper inside and they sipped their coffee while scanning different sections of the paper.

Tiffany lifted one corner of the curtain to stare out into the darkness of the stark, winter morning. "It sure is dark out there. I don't think I'll be running anytime soon."

"You sure you don't want to go for a swim instead of a run?"

"Not without a suit. My skinny dipping days are over."

He snorted. "You've never skinny dipped in your life."

"I have so," she shot back.

"Was that before or after the tattoo?"

She frowned, trying to remember. "Both."

Red's mouth fell open. "I'm shocked."

"Don't be, I was alone before the tattoo and with a bunch of girls after the tattoo. It wasn't that big of a deal."

Red gasped "A girl orgy? Tell me more."

Tiffany laughed. "So you can conjure up an image?"

"Absolutely."

"Well, sorry to bust your bubble again, but it was a bachelorette party when I was in college and I believe both your sisters were there, too."

"Nuh-uh! My sisters would *never* do anything like *that*!" He grinned at her. "Did they see the tattoo?"

Tiffany chuckled. "Maybe they were with me when I got it. Ask *them*, if you have the nerve."

Red shot her a look over his shoulder on the way to the pool house. "Oh, I've got the nerve."

She laughed as he opened the door. "I believe you do."

Chapter Seven

Lured by the promise of seeing Red in swimming trunks and nothing else, Tiffany's resistance lasted a full ten minutes before she walked quietly into the warm air of the building. She watched him swim for a minute, appreciating the athleticism of his long, smooth strokes.

She curled up on a lounge chair with her cup of coffee, and began to flip through the photograph album. She stopped at the photos of him as a toddler, amazed at the resemblance between him and his nephew, Conner. Conner's hair was a little lighter, but the facial features were so alike it was uncanny.

A little bit of McAllister apparently goes a long way.

She skimmed over the photos, and soon she was ogling the 'Mr. Universe' poses of him again. She peeked over the top of the book and closed it. Why admire a photo when she had the real thing in front of her? After moving to a spot where she could observe him, Tiffany discovered that Red moved as gracefully in the water as he did on the dance floor. She watched his upper torso muscles flex as muscular arms sliced through the water with graceful precision, while powerful legs propelled him forward.

He finally noticed her sitting there and treaded water for a few seconds before swimming to the edge to rest his arms on the pool's ledge.

"I didn't mean to interrupt," she said, unable to tear her gaze from the bulk of shoulders protruding from the pool's edge.

"It's too late. I've already lost track of my laps."

"I'll go back in the house so you can finish," she said.

"Don't go. I've done enough for today." He pulled himself out of the pool by his powerful arms.

"I'm impressed, McAllister; you're not even that winded."

He grabbed his towel. "You should've seen me two weeks ago. I've adjusted."

She gazed, entranced, as he dried himself with the towel. "Are you glad you moved here?"

"Oh yeah," he said, grinning at her. "I love it here."

Tiffany tore her gaze from the alluring sight of him, and forced herself to walk away. "What about the club in Lafayette? Isn't it going to be a hassle driving back and forth?"

"I hired good people to manage it, but I still go every day. When this club opens, I'll divide my time equally between the two."

Tiffany walked leisurely around the room. "Lake Coburn's half the size of Lafayette. Won't you miss all that action?"

Red snorted, "What action? I went to the club then I went home. I spent most of my day stuck in traffic."

Tiffany cringed. "I hated driving in Houston. Drake is the only reason I'll have to go, now."

"What kind of law does your brother practice?"

"Corporate, but he was telling me he hasn't been feeling very satisfied with it the last year or so. His conscience has been bothering him lately."

"What does he do for that to happen?"

"Nothing illegal, but his firm works mainly for a large corporation that buys out companies. People sometimes lose their jobs."

"Takeovers," he said.

"What?"

"You said his firm 'buys out' companies, but in truth, what they probably do is 'take over' the company by secretly buying stock when it goes public. Your brother's a corporate shark."

"No, he's not," she said defensively.

"I'm not judging him, Doc. That's just another name for lawyers. Haven't you ever heard that old joke "Why don't sharks bite lawyers?""

"Apparently not, what's the punch line?"

"Professional courtesy." He chuckled as she rolled her eyes. "It's a testament to his good character that he's got a guilty conscience about it."

"He said he's been having trouble sleeping lately. Imagine that," she said.

"Yeah, imagine that."

Around six-thirty the eastern sky began to show a little pink on the horizon and Tiffany told him she was ready for her run.

"Are you going to want breakfast when you get back?"

"It depends. What will you feed me?"

"Oatmeal." He laughed at the face she made. "Eggs and bacon?"

"Much better," she said.

"Grits or toast?" he asked.

"Grits, cheese grits."

"You're going to make me work, aren't you?"

She chuckled. "I'll help you if you wait until I get back."

"Oh, no," he insisted. "You're the guest here. My mom would skin me alive if she found out I made you do any of the cooking."

"But I like to cook, and I won't tell her."

"Next time." He hoped there'd be plenty of next times.

"Okay, I'm going to change into my running gear; I did think to pack that." They walked back into the house.

Red changed quickly and went into the kitchen to start preparing breakfast, glancing up as Tiffany walked by wearing her *gear*—faded jogging pants, an old L.S.U. sweatshirt, and some running shoes. His surprise at her get up must have shown on his face.

"What?" she demanded. "I don't need to look good to run. I'm about to get all sweaty."

He laughed at her. "You won't sweat, it's too cold out there."

"It's *cool* out there, and believe me, I'll sweat." She gathered her curls in a ponytail holder.

"See, when your hair is pulled up away from your face you look like a teenager. *That's* why I thought you couldn't have been a doctor."

She adjusted her hair, tsking at his comment. "Let it go, Red—I've forgiven you."

He narrowed his eyes at her. "Go run, smart ass! Get all stinky and sweaty."

"I said sweaty, I didn't say anything about stinky," she said, making a face at him. "Do you happen to know how far it is to the end of the driveway?"

"No, but I know it's a mile and a half from the house to the intersection of highway 101. How far do you usually run?"

"Three miles, so that's perfect. By the way, I'll be famished when I get back." She winked at him on her way out the door.

Red watched her from the window as she did some serious stretching to warm up. She inserted her earbuds, checked her watch, then began running at a quick pace. He watched her until she got about half way down his driveway before losing sight of her.

"You're pathetic, McAllister," he mumbled as he hurried to his kitchen, wanting to make sure she came back to a good breakfast.

Twenty minutes later, he found himself perched in front of the same window, watching as she neared the house, still running at the same quick pace. She ran into the yard, slowing, and eventually jogging in place to cool down. He made sure he was standing at the stove by the time she re-entered the kitchen.

"What is that, about a seven minute mile?" he asked, when she joined him. "Not bad. Are you training for a five-k race?"

"No. I just run. To relieve stress." She breathed deeply, released them slowly. She poured herself a glass of tap water, took a long swig before stripping off her sweatshirt to reveal a bright pink tank top underneath.

"Breakfast is ready." He handed her a plate then showed her various pans filled with scrambled eggs, grits, and crispy bacon. "Want more coffee? I also have orange juice."

"Got milk?" She grinned as she filled her plate.

"Sure do." He poured a glass and handed it to her.

Red served himself and sat down next to her as they ate for a few seconds in silence. Finally he said, "I have to admit, Doc, knowing that you came from money, you surprise me."

"Yeah, but you know the rest of the story too. Drake and I would gladly have given up the money to grow up with parents like yours. Please don't fault me for that."

"Oh, I believe you; and I can't fault you for anything except waiting as long as you did to cut Tanner loose."

She shrugged, but remained silent and continued to eat.

Red cringed. "I'm sorry, Doc. That was rude of me."

"It's no big deal," Tiffany admitted. "It's the truth. I never thought I was the kind of woman that felt like she had to have a man around to be happy, but maybe I am."

"Having Tanner didn't make you happy, obviously. Maybe it's a matter of having the *right* man."

"Well sure," she agreed. "But how are you going to know who's right unless you go out there and take a chance? When's the last time *you* took a chance on a relationship, Mr. 'night club owner'?"

"It's been a while," he admitted.

"Have you ever been in love?"

"The closest I've ever come was Katrina Boudreaux in the tenth grade." *Until now.* "A year and a half ago, an old friend and I tried to date exclusively. It only took three months to figure out that wasn't going anywhere. We ended it mutually and went our separate ways. Since then, just a couple of . . " His voice trailed off.

"One night stands?"

"Not exactly that," he said, hoping Tiffany would let it go. She didn't.

"Well, I can't imagine you having to *pay* for it."

He studied her features, suddenly tight with—what was that? Anger? Blame? She expected him to disappoint her. "Why don't you just come out and ask me if I've hired a prostitute? I know you're dying to."

She met his gaze and held it. "Have you ever hired a prostitute for sex?"

"Of course not, but I've had a couple of women friends that I shared *mutual* benefits with." The relief on her face spoke volumes about what that son of a bitch, Tanner, had put her through. "Not for a while, though. I'm not a big fan of casual sex, and I'm getting too old to play games."

"What do you mean?"

He pushed his plate to the side and rested his elbows on the table. "I'm ready to settle down."

"But you have to commit to someone for that to happen."

He sighed heavily. "Okay Doc, ask yourself something. If you'd grown up having my parent's marriage as an example, do you think you'd have been so willing to settle for Tanner?"

Tiffany's brow furrowed in concentration. "I guess not."

"They set the bar pretty high for us," Red commented. "They taught us not to settle for less than what we wanted."

She frowned thoughtfully. "But, what if that person doesn't exist? What if women of today can't reach that bar that your mother has raised so high?"

Red ran his hand through his hair in exasperation. "You're missing the point, Doc. My parents aren't perfect—they have flaws just like everyone else. But they're perfect for each other—they're a match. I'm waiting for my match."

"But how will you know when you find her?"

"My dad always told me I'd know when I met her." He didn't flinch under her unwavering gaze, waiting—*hoping* she'd ask if he already had. He'd waited too damn long for it to happen to deny it. He was ready to get it started.

Obviously, she wasn't. He could tell the instant she decided to let it go.

She pushed away from the table and stood. "Thanks for the breakfast, it was delicious. Can I help you clean up the kitchen?"

"Nah, go on and take your shower. I've got this. I'll load the boxes in the truck. When you're done we can head over to the condo."

By nine a.m., they had already filled several large boxes with Tiffany's personal items. True to her word, she'd left most of her things at her rent house. The only furniture she'd moved into Tanner's condo was her computer desk and chair, along with a few end tables, lamps, and one chair for the bedroom. Tiffany packed up her hanging clothes in garment carriers while Red loaded most of the other items. Between the two of them they got the desk loaded into Red's truck and filled the rest of the space with boxes.

An hour and a half after their arrival, Tiffany made one last run through the place. Before leaving, she hung her condo key on the same hook that she'd hung her ring, locked the door and walked out.

They pulled up in front of Tiffany's bungalow on Fleur de Lis Avenue. The house and neatly trimmed yard, with its flower beds bursting with purple and gold pansies, seemed to transform Tiffany instantly. The welcoming eight foot deep front porch with its wide decking and tall windows beckoned guests to stay for a visit.

"First thing's first." Red handed Tiffany the hanging baskets she'd brought from the condo. "I'll let you do the honors," he said, smiling as she hung them carefully on strategically located hooks around the sunny porch. He followed her inside, carrying two lamps and a shoulder bag then helped her move all her outdoor furniture back to its positions on the front porch and back deck.

Red stood on the deck, staring out at the medium sized, but beautifully landscaped back yard, and whistled. "You must have felt stifled in that condo after living here for—how long?" He turned to face her.

She adjusted the position of a lounger. "About five years."

"I don't know how you lasted as long as you did."

"I don't either, Red." She stretched her arms out and turned in a slow circle. "I feel like I can breathe again."

He threw an arm casually across her shoulders. "Come on, Doc. Let's get the rest of your stuff moved in."

They moved the boxes into the designated rooms and began to systematically unpack them. By noon every box was unpacked, every item back in place. Red checked his cell phone and grinned, seeing his Wifi had picked up TLeblanc501. "I see you kept your phone and internet service going, too."

"Uh huh," she said, passing a dust cloth over her end tables. "There's that fear to commit thing again. Hey, I'm ordering pizza, is that okay?"

"Sure. I want the meat lover's special," he said.

She called in one medium meat lovers for Red and a small extra veggie for herself, along with an order of dessert turnovers, and a jug of sweet tea.

Red swiveled in her desk chair to face her. "Am I correct in assuming Drake had something to do with you keeping the utilities going?"

She nodded. "Absolutely, and just what kind of conversation did you have with my brother last night, anyway?"

"What did he tell you?" He hoped Drake had kept quiet about his intentions.

"He hardly mentioned you at all."

Red allowed himself to relax before answering her. "He said it was time you cut Tanner loose. Then he asked if you'd taken his advice and hung on to this place."

"He warned me not to get rid of it—turns out he knew what he was talking about," Tiffany admitted.

Red looked around and admired the bungalow. "This place suits you, Doc." He left out the obvious, of course. That his ranch suited her better, but this sure beat the hell out of her sharing a bed with Collins.

Tiffany smiled and lovingly ran her hand over the front door. "I fell in love with this house the second I saw it. It needed a paint job and a little TLC, but I saw the potential. They don't build homes like this anymore."

"Yeah, these old houses have a lot of character. My place in Lafayette was a 1950's Craftsman style that I refurbished."

"Your mom told me about the pool, but she didn't say anything about the house. How could you bear to sell it?"

"I made a huge profit on the sale and the benefits of moving on this end were too tempting to pass up."

"What benefits?"

"Being near my friends and future Godchildren was a plus."

"And the new club," she added.

He nodded. "That, too. But, I've always loved Bill's ranch, and I was ready for country living. As soon as I heard he was selling I made him an offer."

Tiffany rearranged some items on a built in bookshelf then stopped. "I just thought of something. I know your parents' anniversary is next month, but what day?"

"The 25th."

"They got married on Christmas Day?"

"Yeah, that's when we'll all perform it for them. It's a good thing you and your brother will be there. The co-writer has to help me sing the lead vocals."

"We'll need to rehearse with your sisters; it takes time to come up with all those harmony parts you'll need."

"Do you think Drake will be able to make it?"

"I made him promise to be with me for Christmas, no matter where I am. He's never broken a promise to me yet."

"I like your brother already."

Tiffany smiled. "My brother's a good man. He's excellent at reading people."

Red thought about the conversation he'd had with Drake and knew that for a fact. He respected the man, even without having met him. Sometimes a phone conversation could be just as revealing as a face to face meeting.

They were deep in conversation when the doorbell rang, signaling the pizza's arrival. They listened to classic rock radio while they ate and laughed at each other's childhood antics. Red finished off the last of his tea and stood up to stretch. "This is nice, but I've got to get to my club."

"Have fun in that Black Friday traffic," Tiffany said, cringing visibly.

"You want to come? Marc Broussard's playing."

"No, I'm going to have to pass tonight. I want to stay home and savor having my own space again. But I want to invite you over for a home cooked meal soon. As thanks for helping me move in today."

"I'm always up for that." *It can't be soon enough.*

"How about Sunday afternoon?"

He nodded, his outward appearance cool and collected, despite being thrilled at the thought of seeing her again. "That's good for me. Give me a time and I'll be here."

"The Saints play at three o'clock and I hate screaming at the TV alone. How about you get here by three and we can eat around six?"

"Will you give me banana pudding for dessert?" Red adopted what his mom called his deprived puppy expression.

"Somehow I never took you for the begging kind, McAllister."

"Next time I come I'll wear my WILL BEG FOR BANANA PUDDING T-shirt."

Her eyes crinkled with laughter. "So, who'll be playing in the club tomorrow night?"

"It's a band called 'Country Rhodes' as in R-H-O-D-E-S. It's Brandon Rhode's band."

"Bailey's Brandon?"

Red slipped his jacket on. "The same, and they're a local favorite. Bailey will be there, as well as Melissa and her husband. Annie was undecided when she left yesterday."

"Sounds fun. Count me in for tomorrow night."

Swallowing the urge to release a big ole *Ai-Yee*, the Cajun equivalent of a *Yee-Haw*, he simply nodded. "You're welcome to come with me if you're willing to go early and stay late."

She followed him as far as the front porch. "Can I let you know later?"

"Sure. I'll see you tomorrow then?"

"Definitely, and thanks again for the help, Red." She gave him a big hug. "It's nice to have good friends."

He pulled back and brushed a curl back from her cheek, resisting the urge to kiss her. "Anytime, Doc."

He pulled away from her place, feeling pretty damn good about the turn of events. Five minutes down the road, he silenced the radio in his truck to answer his phone. "Hello."

"McAllister."

That voice again. The one that had every *"Spidey"* sense he possessed tingling. It still sounded warbled, like he was using some kind of distorter to change the sound. Could that mean it was someone he knew? "Look, I don't know what your problem is, but I think you have the wrong guy."

The voice on the other end of the line chuckled sadistically. "You wish, but no. No chance of that."

"Did I do something to piss you off?" he asked, trying to glean as much information as he could from this guy.

The voice paused. "You could say that."

"Then tell me, what the hell did I do?"

The caller flicked his cigarette butt out of the truck window. "When I want you to know—you'll know," he growled. *You killed my brother you son of a bitch.*

"Maybe you have the wrong guy."

"Don't worry McAllister, I know what you did, even if you don't." He pulled a toothpick out of his pocket and placed one end in his mouth then hung up.

Red's was wall to wall people, packed to its legal limit, and starting to bubble with action by ten p.m. They'd been turning people away for an hour, always a great sign for a club, and so far, no sign of trouble. Red had just finished speaking to the head bartender when the unmistakably sexy voice with a thick Creole/Cajun accent reached his ears.

"Hey *beau*, you got a hug for me, *cher ami?*"

He turned to see a familiar pair of beautiful green eyes, sparkling from behind coal black lashes.

"Angelique! *Comment ca va?* How are you?" He smiled at the tall, voluptuous, dark haired beauty of Creole lineage. Her Spanish, French, Native American, and Caribbean ancestry showed in her olive complexion as well as dark, exotic eyes.

"*Ca va bien*, I am well, but horny as hell, how about you?"

"I'm fine, actually."

She stepped back to openly ogle him. *"Ca se bellesir,* Red. You are one handsome man, but damn if you don't get better looking every year!"

"Well thanks, Angel, but look who's talking. You're still as gorgeous as ever. What brings you back to Lafayette?"

The woman rolled her eyes. "Visiting *mon vieux monde*, my old folks, for the holidays."

"How are your parents?"

"They're good, but if I had to sit through one more minute of watching *ma pere* sleep in the recliner while *ma mere* watched another re-run of 'Everybody Loves Raymond', I'd lose my freaking mind." She grabbed his arm and jerked him toward the dance floor. "Come on Red, *allons danser!*"

Red took her into his arms and they swayed to one of the soft, bluesy ballads of Marc Broussard and his band.

Angelique's arms looped around his neck and she pulled herself closer, rubbing herself provocatively against him. "What do you say Red? Would you like to take me back to your place when we leave here?"

"I don't have a place in Lafayette anymore, Angel. I sold the house here and bought a ranch outside of Lake Coburn."

Her eyes widened with undisguised horror. "Why would you do that?"

"I have friends there, one whose wife is expecting my twin godchildren, and I'm opening up another club there."

She waved her finger in front of his face. "*Non, non, non*, Red baby, that's why you hire people to take care of things like that for you. And by the way, I *have* a godchild I see twice a year . . . for birthdays and Christmas. Unload that *ranch.*" She didn't bother hiding her disdain. "Move back to Lafayette where you belong. Meanwhile . . ." She practically purred as she rubbed against him suggestively. "We could go to your office down the hall and lock the door. What do you say, Red? *Allons piquer, oui?*"

"Angel." He couldn't say how truly disinterested he was by her suggestion without hurting her feelings. He removed her arms from his neck and took one step back. "We've been through this before, Sweetie. You know this. We both decided we're better as friends, remember?"

Her lower lip pushed out in a provocative pout. "That was before I realized that there are no more good men out there. Come on Red, one more for old time's sake. No other man has ever made me feel what you could," she breathed into his ear. "Work your magic on me one more time. Let's rent a hotel room for tonight. Just one more night of great sex for good measure," she said, pulling his face close for a kiss.

Red pulled away from her. "*Arrete ca*, Angel! Stop! We'd end up hurting each other, and I don't want that."

She pouted prettily again, but finally relented. "You don't know what you're missing out on. I haven't had it in a while, and I'd be a real wildcat for you tonight."

Red chuckled. "I appreciate the offer, but no."

She gazed at him suspiciously. "Have you met someone?"

"I've met plenty of people since you."

Angelique shook her head. "Are you in love with someone?"

He hesitated a split second before answering. "Of course I'm not."

Her eyes narrowed. "I believe you're lying."

"Look, Angelique, I'm not *with* anyone. I don't have the time to start anything new right now."

She tapped his chin with her long manicured nail. "I think you're keeping something from me, *monsieur beau.*"

It didn't take him long to get annoyed with her third degree. "Do you want to dance or not?"

"Okay, sha, we'll dance, but you know I don't like it when people keep things from me."

Red snorted. "People keep things from you? It wouldn't have anything to do with that hot temper of yours, would it?"

"*Moi?* Me? *Je connais pas.* I don't know. I haven't the foggiest idea what you're talking about."

Red cocked his head to one side. "Let me refresh your memory. How about the girl you attacked in the ladies room because I danced with her a full month after we broke off our relationship? Does that ring any bells?"

Angelique's brow furrowed. "Are you going to hold that against me for the rest of my life? I only pulled out a small patch of hair, and that '*tit putaine* had a headful. Besides—"She fluffed her own hair, "—I saw her two months later, and her bald patch was filling in nicely."

"I'm surprised she let you close enough to see," he said, snorting.

"It was tricky. I had to sneak up on her from behind and tap on her shoulder. When she turned around and saw it was me, she screamed like she'd seen a *gros betaille*, and ran in the opposite direction."

"Hmph. I can't imagine why." He gave her a stern look of warning. "I'm telling you now, Angel, if you ever pull anything like that in any of my places again, I will ban your ass. Do you understand me?"

She sulked, but remained silent.

"Answer me, Angelique."

"*Oui!* Yes, I understand! Just dance one more with me, Red."

Red complied, praying that Angelique would be gone by tomorrow night. The last thing he wanted was for her to be anywhere in the same vicinity as Tiffany.

Chapter Eight

Saturday Morning

Drake LeBlanc sat at his desk in his Houston high rise apartment trying to shake off his insomnia induced exhaustion with more coffee. Damn, but he'd give anything for a full night of restful sleep. He'd decided Tiffany was right about him needing a career change, but suspected his job was only the first in a long line of changes he'd need to make for some satisfaction.

His life, as it existed now, bored the hell out of him. Everything from the fancy restaurants and take-out food he survived on, to the company he kept. Finding the necessary diversions of the female persuasion without saddling himself with a wife and children had proven to be challenging of late. After the display of mind numbing lack of feeling he'd seen from his parents, the *last* thing he wanted was to get tied down to someone permanently. No way would he contribute to keep *that* particular dysfunctional family lifestyle alive and kicking. Especially when he found himself increasingly bored as hell with the usual parade of gorgeous, shallow, model-thin women that usually hung on his arm.

Mid-thirties seems kind of early for a mid-life crisis. He made more than enough money, already owned the vehicles he wanted. Should he buy a bike? He'd always had a hard on for Ducati bikes. He waved it off, knowing he wouldn't be able to enjoy it. Just because he could afford to drop twenty to thirty grand on a bike, didn't mean he could justify buying one for the fifteen minutes a month he may find to ride the damn thing.

He sighed, turned back to the contents of the file Dan had delivered to him first thing this morning. In seconds, he'd spread Scott McAllister's life neatly before him on the glossy surface of his desk. So far, he hadn't seen a damn thing out of line with the man. Valedictorian of his high school class, graduated with top honors from Louisiana State University, with a bachelor's in Business, worked himself through the Master's program and had several successful businesses in and around the Lafayette area since then, just as he'd said. The man was a self-made millionaire and Drake was thoroughly impressed with his credentials.

Even more impressive, in Drake's opinion, was the character references that Dan had collected. Everyone, without fail, said the same thing about Scott 'Red' McAllister. The man was hard-working, fair, honest, and possessed a level of integrity that most men strive for, but few actually attain. Although he didn't go looking for fights, he obviously didn't back down from any.

The one item on the sheet that jumped out at him was the fact that even the two people he'd managed to alienate over the years called him incorruptible. Apparently they'd tried to hold back services to his businesses, demanding kickbacks. Instead of complying, McAllister had come out swinging—exposing them both for their dishonesty, and causing serious repercussions for both men. It had resulted in one board member resigning his position, and another dropping out of a re-election campaign.

From what he could see, this guy was the polar opposite of Tanner Collins, and Drake figured Tiffany could do a hell of a lot worse. A bachelor with no children, he had no serious relationships to speak of, so he was definitely free to start up something with Tiffany when she was ready.

He held up a snapshot of the man in question and wondered if he was looking at a picture of his future brother-in-law. He hoped Tiffany could find a way to be happy now that she'd finally had enough of their parents' interference. They'd practically sold her at birth to the Collins family and no matter how hard he'd tried to convince them that pushing her to marry Tanner was unfair to her, they'd turned a deaf ear to his reasoning. It thrilled him to know she'd finally found the backbone to stand up to them, and he'd do what he could to support her.

Drake picked up the phone and dialed his father's mobile number. "Hey Dad," he said after his father answered the phone.

"Drake!" Daniel Drake LeBlanc's deep voice boomed over the phone. "How are you, Son?"

"I'm good, and how about you?"

"Oh, can't complain. You hardly ever call, so I know there must be something on your mind. Out with it."

"It's about Tiffany breaking it off with Tanner."

Daniel groaned. "Your mother called hotter than a habanero coated in cayenne pepper. She insists she'll never be able to hold her head up in her circle, and wants me to talk some sense into her."

"Well, don't even try. She's done with that piece of crap. You do know that, right? That he's not fit to lick the soles of her shoes?"

"I know Tanner doesn't have the spic and span persona that your sister admires in people, but she's living in a dream world. Let's face it, Son. Good husbands aren't that plentiful, and she's not getting any younger. If she's going to make a match, she needs to get on the ball."

"You know, Dad. You and Mother have only missed the age of arranged marriages by a century and a half."

"That's not funny, Drake."

"It wasn't meant to be. So, tell me, how'd your arranged marriage work out for you?" He heard his father's growl of disapproval.

"Your mother and I look at our marriage as a business arrangement. Marriage for any other reason is pure foolishness."

Drake shook his head, amazed at his father's stubbornness. "I've heard all this before, but the fact is, Tiffany doesn't love Tanner. Hell, I don't think she even likes him. I know I can't tolerate the bastard. He's weak-willed and arrogant, and those two qualities don't make for a good husband or father of your future grandchildren. Wouldn't you rather see her with a decent man? Wouldn't you want your grandchildren to have a better role model?"

"Women don't have the luxury of waiting as long as we can to have children. Her biological clock is ticking away as we speak."

"You should have thought of that before you coerced her into wasting five years with a man, and I use that term loosely, who wasn't suited to her. Besides, you act like she's a shriveled up old maid, when she could easily pass as a teenager to someone who didn't know her."

"Our families have known each other for years. She could tr—"

"You know, Dad," Drake cut in, his voice tight with irritation. "That horse you're beating? It died a good while back, so you might want to bury that son of a bitch, and soon."

"Is that what passes for parental respect at that fancy ivy league college?"

"If respect is what you're after you'd better start showing your daughter some support," Drake drawled. "At this rate, grandchildren won't do you a bit of good because I doubt she'd bring them around." For the first time in the conversation, his father answered with dead silence. "Dad, are you still there?" Finally, he heard his father's tentative reply.

"She wouldn't do that, would she?"

Drake rubbed his jaw in frustration. "Hell, I wouldn't blame her if she never set foot in Texas again. You do know that mother expected her to walk away from her career after marriage. Do you have any idea how insane that is?"

"Your mother has strange ideas about women who work."

"Hell, the only thing mother ever worked at was spending your money. Even then if Melinda hadn't been around, we wouldn't have gotten a 'hello, how are you', much less three square meals a day. Tiff and I knew early on that, as mothers go, ours sucked—bad."

His father gave a loud harrumph. "That woman never did have any kind of maternal instinct. She wasn't any better of a wife than she was a mother. The bed was a desolate place with your mother in it."

Drake cringed to himself. "I sure as hell don't need to hear any of that." His father chuckled, as Drake continued. "I want you to stay off Tiffany's ass about this, Dad. You know, if you do, she may find someone on her own who's more suited to her. God knows she deserves to be happy."

"All right son, I'll speak to you mother, as much as it pains me to do so."

Drake grinned, feeling he'd finally accomplished something worthwhile today. "Trust me, you won't be sorry."

Once the phone call with his father ended, he dialed his sister's home number. She answered on the third ring, sounding slightly winded.

"Hey Sis, how's it going?"

"Hey Drake, I just came in from my run."

"How far?"

"Um, three and a half miles. It helps me deal with Tanner calling twenty times a day telling me I need to reconsider. I'm sure he has the parental units' blessings."

"Not anymore, Tiff. I spoke to Dad and he's going to tell Mom to lay off."

"No kidding? If that's true you get the brother of the year award."

"Just for that?" Drake couldn't keep his laughter at bay. "I thought I'd at least have to whip Tanner's ass for that honor."

"That would get you brother of the decade, at least. The century, if you put him in traction for a while."

"Hmph. Don't tempt me, Sis. I've wanted to do that for years."

"Now, you sound like Red."

"Your hero, McAllister. Why would you say that?"

"Red broke Tanner's nose at a wedding a while back."

Drake snorted. "I knew I liked him. What was his motivation?"

"Oh, there was some old history there, but Tanner putting the moves on Annie, Red's youngest sister, was the last straw."

"Any chance his sister welcomed Tanner's attention?" Tiffany's sudden burst of laughter surprised him.

"If you knew Annie at all you wouldn't be asking that," she snorted. "Besides, Red walked in just in time to see her slap him and call him a jerk. She's a scrappy little thing."

Drake chuckled softly. "Well if anybody would know scrappy, it's you. I can still see you kicking Randy Johnson's ass when I was in first grade."

"Hey, that big bully had no right picking on you. He left you alone, didn't he?"

"Yeah, but he was never quite the same after that incident—I think you did permanent damage to his psyche."

Tiffany laughed. "The male ego is such a delicate thing."

Drake smiled at the sound he hadn't heard near enough lately. "Damn, it's good to hear you laugh. You know, I've been keeping track."

"Of what?"

"Your laughter, it's been at least three years since I've heard it or seen you smile like you really meant it." He heard her take a deep breath and release it slowly.

"I feel like I can breathe again. I wish I could see you little brother. Why don't you come for a visit?"

"I'm working on something right now, but I plan on wrapping up a couple of pending cases in the next two weeks."

"When's the last time you took any time off?"

"I went skiing in Colorado. Last year sometime."

"Was that the time you sprained your wrist?"

"Yeah."

"That was three years ago, Drake."

"Oh. I know—I went to Mardi Gras in New Orleans."

"That was before the ski trip."

"Oh, yeah. Well, hell. I guess it's been awhile."

"I'm holding you to Christmas, you know. Your butt had better be here. We've both been invited to Red's ranch, and his entire family will be there."

"I will. So, are you falling for this Scott McAllister? Because if you are, I want to meet him first."

"We're good friends, for right now, anyway. I'm not saying that I couldn't have some feelings for him in the future, but I need to be by myself for a while."

Not if McAllister has his way. "Whatever you say, Sis. Hey, I need to let you go, but I promise I'll be there for Christmas."

"While you're at it, plan to come back for New Year's Eve," she pleaded. "You could be my date for the opening of Red's new club."

He nodded, thinking that might not be such a bad idea. "Maybe I will," he said. "I love you Tiff."

"Love you too, little brother."

Drake ended the call and took a deep breath. For some reason, the heavy feeling in his chest seemed to dissipate. Maybe it was the fact that he'd just helped someone other than his own firm to screw someone over.

He sat back in the expensive leather executive chair, swiveled to stare out at the Houston skyline from his window.

"Maybe it is time for a change, Sis."

Tiffany groaned at the sound of her cell vibrating against the wooden surface of the table. She'd silenced it hours ago to stop its incessant ringing, but didn't want to miss any important calls—from someone other than her ex-fiancé. It was only noon, but she'd already been avoiding calls for two hours. Fed up with the inconvenience, she swept up the phone and pushed the talk button without bothering to check the screen. "Don't make me put a hit out on you, jack ass!" The answering deep chuckle told her she missed her mark.

"Is it that bad?"

A perusal of her screen showed Red's name flashing. "Sorry about that. I just assumed it was him again. He's been calling since ten a.m."

"Maybe you should get your number changed."

"Why should I go through that kind of trouble? It's time Tanner learns he can't always get his way."

"Listen to you going all 'girl power' on me. I'm so proud."

"I'm sure. What's up, McAllister?" She checked her watch. "I've got an appointment in fifteen minutes."

"You need a lift to my club tonight?"

"That depends on how long it takes my hair stylist," she said. "Can I let you know when I get back?"

"Absolutely."

They disconnected and Tiffany picked up her purse to leave for her 12:15 hair appointment. Stopping in front of the mirror, she took one last look at herself as a blonde. "Good riddance."

Drake LeBlanc parked his white Denali pick-up next to the candy apple red convertible. He unfolded his six foot two inch frame from the front seat and paused a moment to stretch his long legs. He, threw his bag over his shoulder, and made his way to the front door. The doorbell dinged, making itself heard over the classic rock ballad blaring from a sound system inside the house.

He waited with bated breath, anticipating his sister's reaction to seeing him, and wasn't disappointed. She squealed with delight and threw her arms around him.

"Oh my God, I can't believe you're here!" Tiffany gushed, breathless from excitement.

After a prolonged hug, he set her away from him to get a good look at her. "I couldn't stay away one more day, Tiff."

"Do you have a good reason for shocking the hell out of me? Is this a by-product of a twisted sense of humor?"

"Well," he drawled, "I wanted to surprise you, but I think it just backfired on me." Drake touched the soft brown curls and gave a nod of approval. "*That's* the Tiffany I know and love."

She patted her soft curls and beamed up at him. "Thanks little brother."

"Okay, seeing as how I'm nearly a foot taller than you are, do you think you could stop with the 'little brother' thing?"

"You may be bigger, but I'm older and you'll always be 'little brother' to me, so get over it." She pulled him inside.

Drake looked around the place and nodded appreciatively. "Nice place you got here, sis. Aren't you glad you have such a brilliant brother to convince you to hang on to it?"

"Every once in a while he proves his worth," Tiffany admitted. "How long can you stay?"

"This is a one night only appearance, so you'd better appreciate the trouble I went to for your sake."

She gave him another hug. "God, I needed to see you. Oh hold on," she said, picking up the phone. "I need to call Red and tell him not to pick me up."

"Hold up! I'm not keeping you from a date, am I?"

"No, I was just catching a ride with him to his club tonight in Lafayette. But, I can go there anytime." She waved her hand.

"I'd like to go, but only if I'm not a third wheel."

"Then we'll drive over together," Tiffany suggested. "It'll give us more time to visit."

Drake walked around while listening to his sister's phone call to Red. She asked for the address and told him she'd be there around eight, along with her brother.

She finished the call and met him in the kitchen, pouring himself a glass of water. "Are you sure you're up for this? After a two and a half hour drive, I hate to make you ride for another hour or so."

Drake brushed off her concern. "It's not a problem. I just hope I can find someone to dance with besides my sister. That would be pathetic."

"I'm kind of surprised you didn't bring along one of your *chick-ees* from the model of the month club."

"Come on, now, they weren't all models," he murmured.

"Every last one of them looked anemic and like they'd scratch my eyes out for one bite of my steak and baked potato."

"Oh please, quit exaggerating," he snorted.

"I'm not! What is it with guys and skinny women?"

"*You're* skinny."

Tiffany's jaw dropped. "I am not skinny. I'm athletic. Do you think any of your dates in the last five years could run three miles a day? I don't think so. Now, let me see what you brought to wear, because I don't think it's a tee shirt and faded jeans kind of place."

Drake lifted his bag by its strap. "I brought a set of decent clothes in case. I just didn't want to drive in them." He set the bag on her floor. "You let me worry about me and get yourself dressed to impress Mr. McAllister."

"I'm not doing anything to impress Red. I just wanted to have a little fun with a good friend."

"Yeah," he said, still unconvinced. "Whatever you say."

Around eight o'clock Red finished his discussion with one of the many bartenders on hand that night. He turned, to see his youngest sister approaching. "Hey Sis, you got your dancing shoes on?"

Annie nodded. "Yep, it's been a hell of a week. I'll have the usual, Bobby." The bartender handed her a light beer. "Where's Tiffany? I thought she was driving in with you?"

"Her brother came in unexpectedly and she decided they'd drive over together."

"She has a brother?"

"Yeah, Drake—younger by a couple of years."

"What does he look like?"

"I have no idea. We've only spoken once, and it was over the phone. He seemed pretty straight-up, like Doc."

"Is he a doctor too?"

"He's a lawyer."

"Ugh!" she said, unable to hide her cringe. "I hate him already."

"Give him a chance, Annie. If he's anything like Tiffany, he can't be that bad."

She spun on her heels, tossing back her auburn locks. "I don't have to give him a chance. *I'm* not in love with his sister."

He opened his mouth, but shut it, thinking it wouldn't do a damned bit of good to argue with the truth. After taking a call from a backer in his office he exited, scanning the club for Tiffany. He thought sure she would have been here by now. It was nice to have a packed club, but it sure as hell wasn't a substitute for the woman he cared for. He headed for Annie again, who stood in a group of women he didn't know. He reached out to place a hand on her shoulder. "Hey sis, you haven't seen Doc yet, have you?"

One woman turned abruptly and he found himself staring into a pair of familiar, soft brown eyes. He stood there, his mouth gaping open, knowing he must look like an idiot. He'd remember his first sight of Doc as a gorgeous brunette instead of a beautiful blonde forever.

Tiffany's eyes crinkled with laughter. "I won't hold it against you since I barely recognize my own reflection."

Somewhat recovered, but wanting nothing more than to get tangled up in those rich brown curls, he managed to close his mouth. He fought the urge to reach out for her, thinking he'd be helpless if she only knew the effect she had on him. "I can't believe the difference it's made."

Tiffany's left eyebrow rose in a delicate arch. "For the better, I hope."

"Absolutely," he said, nodding as he finally gave in and touched the silky softness of the curls shimmering with golden highlights. "Tanner is a fool. You are positively stunning."

"Thank you, Red."

"Hey," Annie said, waving a hand in front of Red's face. "I want to go meet Bailey, but judging from the heat you two are generating, I'm not sure it's safe to leave Tiffany alone with you."

"Okay sis," Red murmured, never breaking eye contact with Tiffany.

"Oh Lord," Annie grumbled, as she turned away. "Get a room, you two."

Chapter Nine

Drake rounded the corner after leaving the men's room and nearly knocked a tiny, though tightly-packed woman, clean off her feet. He reached out to keep her from flying backwards onto her diminutive derriere.

"Excuse me, little lady," he managed to drawl, just before his breath caught at the sight of the beautiful blue eyes, wide with surprise. He'd never been attracted to red heads, especially ones with curly hair.

Until now, anyway.

He gazed, transfixed by the silky auburn curls framing the delicate features of her face. Brows of the same hue lifted as her eyes widened.

"It's—it's okay." She took a moment to visibly compose herself. She sidestepped him and made her way toward the ladies room.

Drake couldn't help but stare at her tight little butt in the short brown skirt and body hugging sweater. The stiletto heels she wore accentuated shapely, toned legs—even though they fell far short of giving her the height she obviously longed for. He'd dated more than his fair share of women, but never had he been witness to a body as perfectly proportioned as that one. He watched her turn back, aiming a curious glance his direction, just before she ducked into the ladies room.

Hell to the yeah! Drake parked himself at the end of the hallway, where he'd be sure to see her when she exited. No way was he losing that one's coordinates tonight. Red McAllister would just have to wait.

She hoped Mr. Too Sexy for Words with the drawl to match was watching her, and chanced one last backward glance his way. He was watching, all right—with an intensity that nearly took her breath away. An unfamiliar shiver of excitement crept up her spine, making her wonder about the tall stranger. She forced herself to turn away and escape into the ladies room. *He's definitely not from here. Not with that accent. Texas or Oklahoma, maybe.*

There had been just enough light in the hallway to be certain about the color of his eyes. They were big and brown, the exact same color as her favorite candy, chocolate M & M's. His neatly trimmed hair was sandy brown and looked like it would curl if left to grow out. Big boy had the slightest hint of a cleft in his otherwise perfect chin, a straight nose, and lips perfectly shaped for kissing.

She knew he was in shape. She'd nearly broken her nose on his solid chest. Every physical trait on that man was perfectly suited to her tastes—except for one. He was too tall for her. Being just under five feet and a perfect size one, she was more comfortable with guys who didn't make her feel like one of Jeff Dunham's dummies. That being said, damned if she hadn't been craving the touch of a gorgeous hunk of man lately. And what would their difference in height matter when all she was interested in was a dance or two?

The fact that he waited a full five minutes for her reappearance proved his level of attraction. He didn't need to wait on a woman. Ever. Concealed by shadows, he watched as she cleared the hallway and stopped, scanning the area. He used the several seconds to study her delicate profile, thinking he'd never seen anything so lovely in his life.

"I sure as hell hope you're looking for me," he drawled. She whipped around to face him, her lovely face registering shock. "Because I need a dance partner and you look like a dancer to me."

She lifted her chin and extended her hand. "I never dance with anyone unless I know their name. I'm—Nicole."

He took it, filing away a vital piece of evidence, revealed by the slight hesitation in her voice. *Not her real name.* The redhead was either cautious, or cagey as hell. He could respect cautious, but cagey generally meant a husband or fiancé at home. "I'm Marcus." He chose to give her his first name only.

She gave him a pert nod. "I trust you can dance, Marcus. Don't disappoint me."

He led her onto the main floor, where they jumped into a quick paced Texas two-step. Drake held her, amazed at how good she felt in his arms. He felt larger than life, somehow, in a protective sort of way. He dismissed the thought, chalking it up to her being so vertically challenged. Besides, ideas like that were out of line when he didn't even know her real name. He pushed it aside—this was a world apart from his life, anyway.

The two-step ended and the live band stopped for break as the DJ went right into the Eli Young Band's Crazy Girl. Not bothering to ask if she wanted to continue dancing, he pulled her closer, feeling her respond with a slight tug on his shoulder.

An old feeling stirred in him. Something he hadn't felt in years with the women he'd dated in the past. Drake tried to act casual as he stole a glance at her, but what he saw blew that all to hell. As an attorney, he'd long perfected his ability to read people, their body language, speech patterns, and facial expressions. Nicole's body language couldn't be any easier to read if it was plastered in neon. He recognized the passion, accompanied by a desperate, though unsuccessful effort to hide it from him. He also saw surprise, mixed with a little terror. He suspected she was as unaccustomed to having this kind of reaction to a stranger as he was.

There was just enough of a pause between one song's end and the next track for her to thank him politely and step away. Halfway into her retreat, the introductory bars of a soulful piano ballad had every woman in the club moaning, including Nicole. Drake smiled to himself, thanking God for Adele as she belted out the first lyrics of *One and Only*.

He reached for her hand. "One more, Nicole?" He hoped like hell she'd accept the offer. "I've got a fondness for the piano."

She reached slowly for his hand and nodded. "I do too."

Pulling her close, he considered himself lucky. He'd felt her reluctance to accept the third dance and wondered if it was the thought of dancing with him again that made her uneasy—and if so, why? He brushed aside his curiosity, telling himself it didn't matter. This one last dance would be enough for him.

He believed it, too.

Right up until Nicole's head lolled back as though hopelessly lost in the music.

Reveling in the feel of her in his arms, he knew he wouldn't be satisfied without taking just a little more. Unable to resist the temptation, Drake defied his own conservative nature and leaned down to kiss her. If he was surprised at his own action, he was shocked all to hell with the intensity of her reaction. She kissed him as though they were well acquainted lovers instead of virtual strangers. As her arms looped around his neck he wrapped his arms around her, encompassing her tiny waist. He stood then, straightening, and lifter her until her legs dangled at least a foot above the floor.

Gasping, she pulled her lips from his. "Put me down, Marcus."

He set her down gently, watching her, sensing that if there had been more light he would have seen her fair skin stained pink from embarrassment. As it was, she wouldn't look him in the eye, and it flooded him with an unfamiliar, as well as overwhelming need to protect and comfort her.

"I'm sorry, Nicole. I couldn't help myself. I didn't hurt you, did I?"

"I'm fine." She spoke in a rushed, breathless voice, and then turned her crystal blue gaze upwards.

"I can see that." He lowered his head, unable to keep his lips from hers another second.

Nicole's arms returned to his neck, sending him into an all-encompassing sensual tailspin. Totally absorbed in her presence, he became aware of his hands nearly encircling her tiny waist. His fingers skimmed her silken, supple skin, bared to his touch as her sweater rode up with the lift of her arms.

Her lips, so unbelievably soft—who the hell was he kidding? Everything about her was feather soft. Nicole's hair—he suddenly didn't give a rat's ass what her name was or wasn't—her skin, even her scent was all soft, supple woman. He wanted to immerse himself in her essence, was just thinking how he wouldn't be satisfied until he knew everything about her, when she pulled free from his embrace. Her sudden disappearance left him with the strangest sense of loss, a void he was totally unfamiliar with until this moment.

Drake scanned the shadows, and found her hurrying to a table. She spoke to its occupants, grabbed her purse, and ran to the door. In a few short seconds, she's escaped to the parking lot. He followed—because how could he not? He caught up with her easily.

"Nicole, wait!"

"Don't you follow me," she said, never breaking her stride.

He hurried ahead, blocked her path. "Can't we talk?"

She pointed to the club, sent him a wild-eyed, terror-filled look. "*That* was not me. I don't do things like that—not—ever!" Her tone was just this side of hysterical.

"I know that. I could tell. Believe this or not, but neither do I. That's why we need to talk." His one step forward prompted her to back away.

She raised both hands, shielding herself. "Don't. You scare the hell out of me. You're too—it's—it's all too intense. I don't need this right now." Her voice trembled with nerves, or emotion, or both.

He reached for her, perplexed by his own desperate need to console this woman. "Can't we at least explore this? Let's exchange phone numbers. I'd like to talk to you again. Later. Without all the music and crowded dance floor. We could take it slow."

Her laughter, high and shrill from her state of near hysteria, rang out across the parking lot. "You're kidding, right?"

"Not at all." He tried to maintain a modicum of composure. "I'd like to see you again. We could take our time and get to know each other."

She shook her head wildly. "Can't do it. We both know there's no way in hell we could take anything slowly." She brushed her curls away from her face. "This is my time. My life. My career has just started." She walked around him, her steps quick, sharp, and determined. "Don't follow me."

She climbed into her vehicle, a black Ford Escape with a sunroof— barely gave the engine time to turn over before throwing it into drive. She drove off, but not before Drake got a good look at her Louisiana license plate. He ran inside, borrowed a pen from the bartender, and jotted down the series of numbers and letters on a napkin.

Annie waited until she was out of the parking lot to make a phone call. She took a deep breath when the other party answered. "Hey. I've got to go home. I have another one of my migraines. Yeah. I'm fine to drive. I'll call you tomorrow."

She barely had time to end the call before her tears started. She drove the entire way home, crying and cursing intermittently, completely confused by the rush of emotions, as well as her tears. By the time she made it to Kenton, she still hadn't decided if she'd narrowly escaped a major stumbling block, or missed out on a golden opportunity for happiness.

Chapter Ten

Drake searched for his sister and Red, hoping his possible future brother-in-law knew this *Nicole* or whatever her name was. He found them both at the other end of the bar.

Tiffany turned at his approach. "Here he is. What happened, Drake? Did you get lost?"

"I got side-tracked, sorry." Drake took a good look at the man standing beside her and reached out. "Drake LeBlanc."

Red gave him a firm handshake, exuding confidence and a straight-forward attitude. "Scott McAllister, but you can call me Red. It's nice to meet you, Drake."

Drake nodded. "I've heard good things about you."

Red aimed an unabashed gaze of admiration at Tiffany. "Likewise."

Oh yeah. He's crazy about her. Drake cleared his throat as he looked around. "You've got a nice place."

"Thanks man, it's been a few years coming."

"When's the one in Lake Coburn opening?"

"New Year's Eve; it should be a big party. I hope I can count on you to be there." He passed an ice cold beer to Drake.

Drake thanked him before taking a much appreciated drag on the long neck bottle. "It's possible. Tiffany tells me we got ourselves invited to Christmas dinner at your ranch. You dabble in livestock, too?"

Red gave his head an ardent shake. "Nah, the previous owner was a rancher, but I don't have time for it. I just got tired of living in the city, fighting the traffic every day. I'm sure you can relate."

Drake cringed. "Houston traffic is a bitch, man."

Red nodded and looked up. "Here are two more members of my clan. Drake, I'd like you to meet two of my sisters, Melissa and Bailey and their husbands."

Drake turned, doing a double take at the two beauties that joined them. Both had blue eyes like their brother, and both had red hair—not bright red, but a light auburn, burnished with golden highlights. They looked remarkably like . . . Nicole. He kept quiet about his suspicions during Red's introduction to the others.

"Where's Annie?" Red asked, scanning the area. "She came by here with a group of friends from St. Gabe's, but I haven't seen her in a while."

"She left because of a migraine," Bailey said.

Drake's excitement turned to worry when he saw the veil of concern pass over the club owner's face.

"Was she all right to drive?" Red asked. "Those things usually hit her hard and fast."

Bailey nodded. "She said she'd be fine. I told her to call me as soon as she made it back to Kenton."

"I'm gonna do a little genetic profiling by assuming she looks a lot like her sisters, am I right?" Drake asked, trying not to give anything away.

"Yep," Tiffany answered. "They all have the same gorgeous auburn hair and trademark McAllister blue eyes."

Drake nodded and fought to keep the grin off of his face. "I may have seen her. Was she wearing a brown skirt, with a tan sweater and some really tall heels? A little bitty thing—maybe about yay tall—with the heels?" He held up his hand to illustrate.

"That's Annie," Melissa said. "Did you meet her?"

"We didn't officially meet, but I did see her."

Tiffany frowned. "I guess you'll have to wait for Christmas. You think you can make it?"

"I promised I would, didn't I?" He glanced toward the door he'd recently followed Annie McAllister through. "As a matter of fact, a herd of wild ass buffalo couldn't keep me away from your place on Christmas Day, Red. Give me a time and an address and I'll be there."

Tiffany pulled her brother out on the dance floor to an old country favorite of hers. "I wish Annie could have stayed, I was counting on her to be your dance partner. She's the only sister of Red's not taken."

"Yeah," he said, with an over dramatic sigh. "Who wants to dance with her brother when she could be dancing with the guy that looks at her like a half-starved man staring at a bucket of hot-wings?"

"Oh please," Tiffany said, giving him a sisterly eye-roll. "I know how difficult it is for you, but could you at least *try* to keep the smart-ass comments to a minimum?" When he answered her with a slight nod and a grin, she cocked her head to the side to study him. "What's going on with you? You're kind of quiet tonight."

"I've got some things to think about, that's all." He led her back toward the table when the dance ended.

As soon as Tiffany was settled in her chair, she picked up the questioning. What kind of things?"

He twirled the long neck beer bottle between two fingers. "I'm considering a career change, as well as my state of residence."

"What kind of change, and where to exactly?" She frowned, hoping she wouldn't lose her brother to some location across the country.

"I was thinking Lake Coburn seems like a nice place to work—and live."

Tiffany clapped her hands and squealed. "I'd love that! Are you going to start your own practice?"

"I'm considering it. I can't do what I do anymore, Sis. My conscience won't allow it."

Tiffany beamed. "Good for you, Drake. Have you told Dad yet?"

"Nope, you're the first. Don't you feel special?"

"Ah, you know it," she said, as the D.J. kicked off an old favorite, "Two Dozen Roses". She saw Red cut his talk short with the bartender and make a bee-line for her, holding his hand out.

"This is my favorite song, Doc. How about it?"

Tiffany gladly took his hand and let him lead her to the edge of the dance floor. God, the man could move, and it was remarkable how good she felt in his arms. Maybe it had something to do with him making her feel like she was the only woman in the room. That song ended, jumping right into a slow country ballad that she adored. Before she could even hint that it was a favorite, Red thrilled her without a single word by pulling her closer for another dance.

She closed her eyes, letting her bones turn fluid, pliable in his arms. Her insides heated from the soul searing need produced by the nearness of the man. Not just a sexual need, though she couldn't deny *that* but also a rekindling of an urge she hadn't felt in years. Tanner had quelled her desire to settle down, marry, and have a house full of babies. But, in Red's arms, she found herself wondering what her child would look like if she had any with him.

Tiffany shook herself mentally. She wasn't some sixteen year old child. If she didn't rein herself in soon, she'd be scribbling pages of her new name as practice. She smiled at the thought of a page full of Tiffany McAllister, Mrs. Scott McAllister, and Mr. & Mrs. Scott McAllister signatures.

"What's got you smiling like that?"

She stifled her urge to laugh. "Just thinking what a good dancer you are." She attempted to redirect her line of thoughts—tried to think about Mrs. Lassiter's upcoming knee replacement and Mr. Bertrand's rotator cuff repair on Monday. Try as she might, soon her thoughts wandered back to what her and Red's children would look like and what it would be like to wake up in his arms every morning. She sighed, giving in to the fantasy for a brief moment, and rested her cheek against his rock hard chest.

From his spot at the bar, Tanner watched *his* fiancée dance with that red headed, white trash, and anything but blue-blooded asshole. He should have known McAllister would be behind this. Ever since Jackson's wedding last month, the bastard had been a royal pain in the ass, as well as other body parts. He gave his perfectly realigned nose a gentle brush with his surgeon's fingers. Walking over to the D.J., Tanner slipped him a fifty for an immediate play, and waited patiently for the current belly rubber to end.

The sight of Red's hand placed at the small of Tiffany's back had him bristling as he watched them leave the dance floor. He smiled to himself when Tiffany faltered at the opening notes of *What I Wouldn't Give* by Blake Shelton. He damned near crowed when she froze in place at the D.J's announcement of a special request, but he had to be careful. Tanner knew Tiffany well enough to sense that any sign of hostility toward McAllister would have her turning her back on him for good. He moved from the shadows to stand between them and their table, and held his hand out toward Tiffany.

"Tiffany. Would you honor me with one last dance?" He nodded a greeting at McAllister, forcing his facial features into a mask of calm composure.

Tiffany stood there, apparently shocked speechless, as well as immobilized by his presence.

"One last dance, Tiff—for old time's sake," he pleaded quietly while reaching out to her.

Scott stiffened as if he would step forward, but Tiffany stayed him with her hand before addressing Tanner. "One song, if you promise to leave afterwards."

Tanner nodded and pulled her to him, placing his own hand possessively on the small of her back. He walked her to the dance floor, angling his head slightly to see if McAllister felt confident enough to turn away. Nope. *Not even.* He struggled to conceal the smug grin he longed to throw his way. That troglodyte looked like he'd set his life savings on fire to have one more shot at his nose. *Not tonight, Scott, old buddy.* Tanner knew his song request was high on Tiff's favorites list, and this was his chance to make sure she didn't throw away five years on a loser like McAllister.

"How'd you know I was here, Tanner?" They began a slow, but perfectly synchronized waltz.

"I went to the hospital to look for you, and Sally acted surprised that I hadn't gone dancing with you at 'that club in Lafayette'. I took a chance it was here."

"Why are you here, Tanner?"

He brushed her hair back from her face. "I want another chance."

"I've given you five years of chances. Don't you think that's enough?"

"Just one more, Tiff. Don't you think five years is worth one more try?"

She shook her head. "You've slept with dozens of other women since we've been together."

"I was wrong and I know that now. If you take me back I would never do that to you again, but you need to be honest about one thing. You never did fully commit to me, did you? Don't you think I felt that?"

Tiffany stopped dancing and stared up at him, her irritation obvious as her eyes flashed with anger. "Are you trying to blame *me* for your affairs?"

Tanner put his hands on her face. "I'm saying I've always felt your reservations about our relationship. I'm saying give me one more chance, we set a wedding date, and I'll be faithful to you, I *swear* I will." He held his breath as she gave him a slow shake of her head.

"It's too late, Tanner. I could never trust you again. It's impossible. And I can't live without it."

"If we love each other we can get through it."

Tiffany closed her eyes, and took a deep breath as though to brace herself before returning her serious brown-eyed gaze to his face. "I don't want to get through it."

Tanner studied the tight, grim line of her mouth. "But, we've built a good life together." Her mouth curved in a smile, and for a second he thought he had a chance.

"Tanner, it may have been good for you, maybe, but it hasn't been so great for me."

"Look, I know you've been moody, but I thought you were happy most of the time."

Tiffany released a huff of nervous laughter as she pulled her hair back from her face. "Moody? I don't suppose the fact that I haven't looked like myself in five years has had anything to do with it. Or maybe it was the fact that I couldn't walk into a club, or sit down for a meal at my favorite restaurant without meeting up with one of your—side dishes."

He lowered his head, for once seeing it from her view point. She shook her head slowly and gave him a sad little half-smile. "At least you have the sense to look ashamed, whether you really are, or not."

"I am," he confessed.

"Look, Tanner, this isn't easy for me to say, but you were never *my* choice. You were my parents' choice for me. I don't love you, I never have— not the way I should, anyway."

"Tiff . . .don't do this."

The song ended and they stood facing each other at the far end of the dance floor. "Tanner, please just go. Find someone else, and learn to be happy."

"What if I can't be happy without you?"

"I can't be your reason for happiness, and you can't be my reason to be miserable anymore." She held up her hands as he started to reach for her. "I'm done with this, Tanner."

He'd learned to read her in the five years he'd been with this woman, and he knew she'd spoken from her heart. He lifted his gaze to clash with McAllister's. The guy stood several feet away, Tiffany's alert watchdog, bowed up and waiting for any sign of distress from her to pounce. What the hell did she see in that guy?

"Is it McAllister? Are you sleeping with him?"

She shook her head. "You have no right to ask me that."

He nodded with certainty. "I see. Not yet." He reached out and gently touched her face. "I'm not giving up, you know."

She pulled away from him. "Go, Tanner. You got your dance, now leave me be."

Tanner backed slowly away from her then turned without sparing another glance at McAllister before leaving the club.

Red watched Tiffany lower her head, looking heart sick as she headed slowly in his direction. He met her halfway and pulled her into an alcove where it was quieter. Placing his hands on her face, he gazed into her tear filled eyes. "Are you all right, Doc?"

She wiped her eyes and nodded. "I'm okay. It's just that he actually sounded sincere, and five years is a lot to walk away from."

Red felt the icy grip of an invisible hand over his heart. Was she taking him back? He gave her a brusque nod. "I understand," he said, and turned, not wanting to walk away, but not trusting himself to stick around. He felt her gentle touch on his arm and paused.

"But I am walking away from it, Red."

He turned and saw the truth of it in her eyes. Only then did the hold on his heart begin to loosen. The space around them grew heavy—thick and dense with the type of quiet that spoke volumes.

Tiffany finally shattered the weighty silence. "Dance with me, Red."

Red laced his fingers through hers and pulled her out to the dance floor with him. Alan Jackson's voice crooned *Like Red on a Rose* as they moved in unison to the sultry ballad. He pulled her tighter and folded her right hand close. Warmth enveloped him as she rested her head on his chest, filling him with the absolute certainty that she belonged there.

Towards the end of the song Tiffany lifted her gaze to his. He smiled down into her dark eyes, made darker by the shadows. "Hey Doc," he said softly. He saw the ghost of a smile on lips that looked soft and pliant, ready to be kissed. Unable to resist, he did just that. He'd meant it to be quick, but it turned into something more. A connection neither of them wanted to break until the end of the song forced the inevitable. He pulled away, studied her still closed eyes, as her long, silky lashes rested against smooth cheeks. Red threaded his fingers in her hair, giving her scalp a gentle massage. He watched as glossy curls looped over and around his long fingers, completely amazed at how he'd lived nearly thirty-nine years of his life without her in it.

Angelique watched from her spot at the opposite corner of the room, furious to have been passed over by Red for a piece of insignificant fluff like that. She'd known the man too many years to have missed the subtle clues of him holding back from her. Always too curious for her own good, she'd decided to come back and check out the reason for his evasiveness. Clearly, the competition was no competition at all. She knew Red liked his women with a little more meat on their bones and it was her understanding he'd always been a breast man.

What could she do? With last night's warning still fresh in her mind, she knew she'd have to tread carefully. She watched calmly as he led that woman into the second dance, this one an extremely slow one. Within a few short minutes, she'd formulated a plan and positioned herself to make her move at the earliest possible opportunity. Judging from Red's ridiculous show on the dance floor, there wasn't a moment to spare.

Tiffany made her way to the ladies room, a little lightheaded and a lot flushed from the last two dances. She still glowed from Red's reluctance to let her go. He'd slid his hand slowly down the length of her arm before releasing his hold on her. She'd finally walked away, fully conscious of his gaze on her backside.

She'd just finished washing her hands when the door opened and a buxom, dark-haired woman entered the room. Meeting the woman's gaze in the mirror, Tiffany was rather surprised when the beauty stopped just behind her.

"So, you're Red's latest lay of the day? Join the club," the woman said with undisguised disgust.

Tiffany turned to face her. "Excuse me?"

"I wish I could tell you that it's a very exclusive club, but unfortunately it's not. The membership must be in the hundreds by now."

Tiffany dried her hands, feeling sick to her stomach as the other woman stepped closer to the mirror and began to touch up her hair.

"You know he uses that music, don't you? He signals the D.J. or the band to play songs to help put you in the mood. Then he makes his move and kisses you, oh so gently, making you feel as if you're the only woman in the room." She released an exaggerated sigh before adding, "Or the world."

Tiffany's heart sank as the woman gave a soft chuckle and shook her head.

"Oh yeah, Red McAllister has had years to perfect his irresistible little act, and, trust me, *mon amie*, when I say I've seen many women fall to his charm, including *moi, et vous,* and you, *naturellement.* Obviously. My advice to you is to run like hell, honey. I almost decided to keep my mouth shut about it, but you seem like such a nice lady, and we girls have to stick together, *non*?"

Tiffany watched as the woman turned and walked out. Her gaze returned to the mirror. She stood watching the shameful red stain begin at the base of her neck and continue on up to her face.

Of course Red was a player—the man owned dance clubs. Just like that woman said; he'd had years to perfect his lines because he'd been playing his game for decades. It took a few minutes for her to calm enough for her coloring to return to normal. By the time she'd rejoined the group at the table. Her mind was sharp and clear on how to handle this situation. Damned if she'd be the one to cower off. Determined to let him know he wasn't playing with a child, she resumed her place at the table. She'd endured five years of Tanner's antics and she could damn well put Red McAllister in his place.

Red gave her a bright smile. "Hey, Doc, are you ready for another beer?"

Tiffany gave him a look, one she knew conveyed confidence and self-assuredness. "Make it a Crown and cola—just a splash of cola."

The request seemed to surprise him a bit, but he called the waitress over and ordered her drink. She felt her brother's gaze on her, recognized his burgeoning curiosity. Drake had always known Crown and Coke was her drink of choice when she was upset. He must have decided now was a good time to prepare for the drive home, because he ordered a bottled water for the next round.

When Red asked Tiffany to dance the next slow song, she smiled politely before taking his hand. He noticed the change in her immediately, the coolness to her demeanor that hadn't existed before. They made it through the entire song without her uttering a single word to him. She allowed him to pull her a little close at times, but for the most part she kept her distance, keeping her back board-straight and rigid. By the time she finally made eye contact with him, any sign of previous emotion she may have shown for him earlier was nowhere to be found.

Tense with frustration, he wondered what the hell he'd missed that produced the change in her. The prickling sensation at the back of his neck alerted him to what he'd find, and he began to search the room for someone in particular. He couldn't see her, but he damned-well knew she was here somewhere, watching, waiting, and totally responsible for this. Resigned to the fact that he couldn't do anything about it until later, he thought of the clubs hidden security cameras—particularly the one in the hallway outside of the restrooms. The cameras were there to protect both the patrons and the business, but tonight it would solve the mystery for him.

He finally caught sight of her standing on the opposite side of the room and swore under his breath. Damn, he hated to be a hard-ass, but that woman had used up her last chance with him. Their gazes clashed briefly and he nodded, acknowledging her presence. *I'll deal with you later, Angelique.*

Drake released an exasperated sigh as Tiffany ordered another Crown and Coke. "Sis."

She turned on him. "What?"

Red shot him a glance before leaning forward. "Why don't you just shoot tequila, Doc?"

She rounded on him, keeping her icy veil in place. Her voice was hard and low, but he heard her anyway. "Not with you around."

Red nodded, seeming to accept her answer, also seeming to sense how this night would end.

An hour later, Tiffany finished her fifth Crown and Coke and asked for another. Red sent Drake a look of disapproval.

"Don't you think you've had enough, Doc?"

Tiffany pointed at Red, stopping within inches of his face. "Are you my daddy?"

"No, but if I was—"

"Then I don't have to listen to you, do I?" She cut him off. "Besides, Drake's my designated driver, aren't you, little brother?"

Drake leaned forward. "Yeah, but I think Red is right. You've had enough." She turned on him, but before she could reply he closed the gap between them. "Look, I don't know what happened, Sis." He spoke in a volume only she could hear. "But you may want to get the facts before you tear this guy a new asshole."

She faced him, her gaze hard with anger. "That's the problem, Drake, I already got the facts." She blinked several times as her anger suddenly seemed transformed into deep hurt. Drake recognized the threat of tears and leaned in close to whisper in her ear. "Now isn't the time, Tiff. You're the one who taught me to control my emotion, to own it. Pull it together."

To her credit, he saw her do exactly that, even in her inebriated state. The veil came down over her face, effectively erasing all signs of hurt or anger. She gave him a tentative smile. "I think I'm ready to go home, how about you?"

Drake nodded, admiring his sister's gumption. "I am too, we have a long drive and I'm tired." He stood up and helped her to her feet. "Red . . . Everyone . . . it was nice meeting all of you. Tell Annie I'm sorry I missed her. Bailey, tell your husband I think his band is excellent."

Tiffany turned to the group at the table. "Good night all." She faced Red, who sat silently; wearing the same grim expression he'd worn for the last hour, and nodded before leaving the table without one word to him.

Drake asked for the keys as soon as they exited the club. After fumbling in her purse, she passed them over to him. He could see her struggling to keep her emotions under control. "Hang on, Sis. Wait until we're in the car."

As soon as Tiffany buckled herself in the seatbelt, she crumbled.

Drake let her cry for a minute before questioning her. "Okay, what the hell happened in there?"

Between sobs, hiccups and sniffles the story of the bathroom incident unfolded. "He's just a player, Drake, and I almost let him play me, too." She wiped her eyes and sniffed loudly. "I thought he was better than that."

"Maybe he is, and you don't have all the facts yet."

She answered groggily, "Maybe he's not, and I already do."

"Look, Tiff, it's understandable that you'd be leery after five years of Tanner, but I'm telling you now, Red is not the least bit like him."

When he didn't get an immediate answer from her he looked over, seeing she was already passed out in her seat. He sighed and smiled to himself. In her state of drunken sleepiness, she looked just like she did when she was sixteen years old. "Thank God you quit torturing your hair," he said, as he touched one of her curls and became flooded by memories. Memories of his protective big sister, punching a bully in the face, the day she got her braces and how he'd made fun of her, the day he got his own braces and how she'd comforted him and told him it was no big deal. She'd always been a better sister than he was a brother, and she deserved to be happy. He couldn't, for the life of him, understand why his parents treated her like a redheaded stepchild. The thought made him laugh out loud.

"Redheaded," he murmured. "Annie 'Nicole' McAllister, with your red hair and beautiful blue eyes—If you think I'm letting you off the hook that easily, you are so seriously wrong." He shook his head and laughed again, thinking this was the first Christmas in years he'd actually look forward to. He looked over at his sister again, thinking that if Red didn't find a way to get back into her good graces, neither of them would be at his place for Christmas. Tomorrow would be soon enough to call him.

Red waited until Tiffany was out of sight before pushing his chair back roughly. He stood, zeroing in on the brunette across the room.

"What the hell just happened, Red?" Bailey asked.

"Did you say or do something to hurt her feelings?" Melissa accused.

"I didn't, but I'm thinking someone else did, and I'm about to deal with her right now. Excuse me while I confirm my suspicions." He strode toward Angelique.

She was talking to a man on the other end of the bar when Red walked up behind her. "What the hell did you tell her?"

Angelique turned to him. *"Excuse-moi?"*

"Cut the crap, Angel. You know what I'm talking about. What did you tell her?"

"Oh, sweetie I don't know what you're talking about," she gushed. "Did your little friend leave you in a bad way, Red baby?" She rubbed up against him suggestively. "Maybe I can help you out."

He grabbed her by the elbow and marched her toward the opposite end of the club, then on down the hallway. He stopped in front of the restroom doors and pointed up toward the ceiling. "Do you see that? It's a camera. Do you understand what I'm saying?"

She rolled her eyes at him until he shook her by the elbow again. "Answer me!"

"*Mais oui*, yes, I understand!"

"The electronic video files are in my office right now. I'll see you follow her into the ladies room, won't I?" He shook her arm. "What did you do to her? Did you threaten her?"

"No!"

"Then what did you tell her?"

She pulled away from him angrily. "You are out of your mind Red! You turned me down for a skinny little thing like that? What is she, some silly little school girl? You need a woman, Red."

"She's a surgeon, Angelique." He saw the stubborn lift of her chin as her green eyes flashed angrily.

"She is *pas bon*—no good for you. She is nothing compared to me!"

Red stood nose to nose with her. "She is *everything* to me. She is the woman I love and you will never speak to her or go near her again. *Do* you hear me?" His voice rose to an angry crescendo.

Angelique's eyes grew wide at both his admission and the tone of his voice, but she remained stubbornly silent.

He pulled her out of the hallway, past his shocked family.

"Red, don't do this!" She struggled to keep up with him while he kept a firm grip on her wrist.

He stopped in front of the exit and pointed at the door. "Get the hell out of my club and don't come back."

She tried to touch his face. "Oh, come on, baby, don't be like this."

He turned her by the shoulders and opened the door to give her a much gentler than she deserved shove through the portal. He pointed a thumb at her while addressing his door man. "Take a good look at her Benji. She's no longer welcome in this, or *any* of my establishments. I'm holding you personally responsible if she gets by."

Benji tamped out his cigarette then took out his camera phone to snap a picture of her. "Got it, boss."

Red nodded and slammed the door in her face before storming back to his table. He addressed his sisters and brother in law, who had obviously watched the entire display in shock. "Sorry, but I need to attend to some business in my office," he ground out through jaws clenched tight with anger and frustration.

Red walked resolutely into the quiet seclusion of his office, and sat in front of his state of the art workstation with several large screen monitors. He stopped the digital video connected to the hidden camera so that he could watch it replay, starting from approximately one hour earlier. That was about the time Doc's demeanor toward him had changed from heated to decidedly icy. Just as he suspected, he saw Angelique enter the rest room while Tiffany was still inside. The vindictive Creole beauty came out grinning so big he expected her to break out with a victory dance. He continued watching, and growled when Tiffany walked out a few minutes later looking like ice water ran through her veins.

"Aw hell, Doc. What did she tell you?" He rubbed his face and sat back, sighing. Hoping for some kind of explanation, he pulled out his cell phone to call her. A deep voice answered on the fifth ring.

"Hey McAllister. It's Drake."

"How is she?"

"She passed out about five minutes after she got in the car. That's her 'screw it all' drink, you know. Did you figure out what happened?"

"All I know is an ex-girlfriend had something to do with it. She followed Doc into the restroom, but wouldn't admit to anything. She's a spiteful bitch when she wants to be," he seethed. Drake's low chuckle reverberated in his ear.

"She told her you were a player, and that she was only one of hundreds of women you've manipulated into sleeping with you. Something about you getting your DJ to play certain songs? She was slurring pretty bad during that, so I may not have caught all of it."

"Hundreds, huh? That's stretching it quite a bit. Now, I admit to having requested a couple of songs before, but only once, and only when I wanted to dance with Doc. I wanted to give her something to remember me by before sending her off with Tanner."

"Was that after you broke his nose?"

"Yep."

"Man, I've wanted to do that for years. How did that feel?"

"Pretty damn good. I came close to a repeat performance tonight," he said, as Drake laughed aloud.

"Hey, did anyone hear from your sister, the one with the migraine? Did she make it home?"

"Nobody's heard from her, but I'm sure she's okay," Red answered, wondering why he'd be that concerned.

"The traffic's kind of hairy tonight, that's all. It could be dangerous for somebody with bad migraines like you said she's prone to. Uh, what does Annie do, anyway?"

"She's a physical therapist in Kenton. She moved into a position there about three months ago."

"How old is she?"

"She's thirty; the spoiled rotten baby of the family, but she's something else. She was part of the reason for Tanner's broken nose, you know."

"Is she the sister her threw himself at during some wedding reception? I didn't know who Tiffany was talking about at the time. But now that I've seen her, I can't imagine her standing up to him; she's such a tiny little thing."

Red snorted. "Man, you don't ever want to tangle with Annie. Believe me, she's tougher than she looks."

"So, you two are the only ones who never married?"

"Yeah, but if I can straighten this thing out with your sister, I hope to rectify that."

"Well, if it's any consolation, I wish you luck. I want her to be happy."

"Thanks man, I appreciate that," he said before ending the call.

Red pulled a flash drive out of the top drawer of his desk to download the file. He'd bring it by her house tomorrow and pray she wouldn't slam the door in his face. He pocketed the drive, turned the camera back on, and left his office.

Chapter Eleven

Sunday Morning

Red sat in front of his computer with a cup of coffee, dressed and ready to go. He rotated his neck slowly, trying to get the stiffness out of it. After coming in around two o'clock in the morning he hadn't slept well—no surprise there. He planned to swing by Doc's after church to show her the surveillance video.

He plugged in the jump drive, deciding to watch the video from the beginning to check things out. There were cameras at three different locations in the club, and three screens appeared showing the different views. The camera near the dance floor also caught action at the entrance, so he was able to see the moment Tiffany and Drake entered the club. He'd just reached to fast forward the video when he witnessed the body slam between Annie and Drake. A particular look between them had him glued to the screen throughout their entire encounter. He watched until Drake re-entered the club after going after Annie.

"I'll be damned." He sat back in his chair then checked the time. He rubbed his chin, wondering what to do with this newly discovered revelation. He pocketed the jump drive and left the house.

Red exited the mission style church and pulled his cell phone from his pocket on the way to his truck. He pulled up Tiffany's number, let it ring several times—nearly gave up when a faint voice answered.

"Doc, is that you?"

"Yes."

"You don't sound well. Are you okay?"

"No."

"Is Drake there to help you?"

"I don't know. What do you want?"

"I wanted to tell you that the woman who spoke to you in the lad—"

She cut him off quickly. "I can't—talk—right now."

The phone clattered, as though she dropped it on the floor. Red heard her cough, and then cringed at the distinctive sound of dry heaving.

After a quick trip to the nearest grocery store, he stood at her door, waiting for her to answer the bell. Realizing she wouldn't, he took a chance and walked inside the unlocked door. He placed two grocery bags on her table and reached for the folded piece of paper with the word 'Sis' written on it. Curious, he opened it and read the brief note.

Tiff,

I know you won't feel like having company when you wake up so I'm going back to Houston. I have some loose ends to wrap up if I'm going to relocate to Lake Coburn.

Hope you're not feeling like death warmed over today, but, we did try to tell you. I'll call you tonight and let you know my plans.

Love you!
Drake

P.S. Try not to give old McAllister such a hard time. I think he's a good man. Give him a chance.

He re-folded the letter, placed it back on the table then walked quietly into the hallway. "Doc, I'm here to help." He heard a faint response from the last door on the right.

"Red?"

"Yeah, it's me, Doc. Are you okay?"

"No."

He stood outside her bedroom door. "Do you need help?"

"Yes."

"I'm coming in." Red opened the door and slowly made his way inside the semi-darkened room. Once his eyes became accustomed to the dim light, he was able to make out Tiffany's form in her bed. Upon closer inspection, he found her wrapped in sheets, as pale as the worm at the bottom of a bottle of Mexican tequila. Her curly hair was in wild disarray and she lay still as death, clutching a plastic bucket to her.

He sent her a piteous look and shook his head. "Doc, even if what she'd said had been true, it wouldn't be worth that."

After several attempts, her eyelids finally fluttered open. Tears rolled down her cheeks as she managed to speak. "I'm s-sick, Red."

"I know. Will you let me help?" Red waited for her nod before doling out a portion of thick, clear, sweet smelling liquid from a bottle he'd just purchased. He helped her to sit up and brought the dosage cup to her lips. "Here, this will help with the nausea."

She smelled it and turned her face away, gagging.

"I know, it smells sweet, but I promise it'll help."

She wrinkled her nose but drank it down with a shudder.

"Do you have a blender?" he asked.

"In the kitchen—somewhere," she groaned, covering her eyes with one hand.

Red placed a gentle kiss on the top of her head. "I'll find it and promise I'm going to make it all better, Doc."

After a quick search through her cabinets and several minutes of prep time, he poured a blended noxious looking concoction into a glass. He brought it to Tiffany, along with a couple of aspirins, some vitamins and a glass of water. Helping her to sit up again, he held the glass under her nose.

She looked at it warily. "You expect me to drink that?"

"Trust me, it works."

"What's in it?" she asked.

"I'll tell you later. Come on, it'll make you feel better."

She took a sip and shuddered.

"Don't sip, gulp it down. Hold your nose if you have to."

She did as she was told, gagging once in between gulps. When she'd finished about half of the large glass she pushed it away from her. "That's all I can take right now, I swear." She put both hands on her head. "Oh my head . . ."

He handed her a glass of water, two aspirins, and the vitamin tablets. "Take these now."

She took them and collapsed on the bed, holding her head.

"Do you have an ice pack, Doc?"

"No."

Red left her just long enough to scrounge through her freezer, came back with a bag of frozen peas wrapped in a clean, dry dish towel. "This will help." He placed the bag carefully on her head.

Tiffany covered his hand with her own. "Thank you," she said weakly, as a single tear rolled out of the corner of one eye.

Red brushed the tear away with his thumb. "Sleep now. You'll feel a lot better when you wake up. Call me when you do." He tried to stand but Tiffany gripped his hand tightly.

"Please. I don't want to die alone."

He gazed down at her, curled up on her side, facing the edge of the bed with her eyes closed. If he hadn't already been in love with her, the sight of her, so vulnerable but wanting him with her—that would have done it for him, for sure. "You're not going to die, Doc, but I'm not going anywhere." He walked around to the other side of her full sized bed, kicked his shoes off and crawled in with her. Scooting as close to her body as he dared, he covered her with his left arm. Red barely managed to smother his groan of satisfaction when she grabbed his forearm to pull it close while pulling his right arm under her head as a pillow.

He lay holding the woman he loved, overcome by a feeling of languid belonging, and eventually, blissful sleepiness.

Something cold and wet woke Tiffany. She lay surrounded by a luxurious warmth and struggled to remember what had led up to her being there. Nausea—awful nausea—and a debilitating headache from hell. Her stomach felt fine, but she rolled her eyes around under her lids, trying to determine if she'd need a pain reliever stronger than an OTC. Miraculously free from pain, she opened her eyes. She saw two glasses on her nightstand, one with water and one still half-filled with that awful stuff that Red made her drink.

Red. He'd come by, offering help.

The cold and wet made its presence known again by dripping on the bridge of her nose. That's when she remembered the bag of frozen something he'd put on her head.

She attempted to raise her arm to remove it, but something very warm and heavy pinned it down. Something so very strong and masculine that smelled wonderful.

Red. Again. He'd stayed with her, just as she'd asked him to.

She looked down, saw his left arm wrapped around her, and then realized her head rested on his right arm. She snuggled closer to him and felt him stir, moving his arm just enough to free hers. She lifted her hand to remove the cool, wet bag of—she stared at what *used* to be a bag of frozen peas. Now it was a soggy bag of room temperature peas soaking her head and pillow. It fell to the floor with a soft, squishy *shplat*. She used her hand to push her hair back from her damp forehead as Red spoke, his voice deep, raspy with sleep, and sounding sexy as hell.

"How do you feel?"

"Warm—and cozy, actually."

"Any residual nausea or headache?"

"Completely gone." It was amazing, but the total truth.

"I told you it would work."

"What was in that stuff?"

"Tomato juice, strawberries, banana, orange juice, honey, soy milk, salt, and a dash of nutmeg, all blended up."

"What did you give me besides aspirin? B12 and C?"

"B complex and C, I would have given you some Cysteine, but I would have had to make a trip across town and I didn't want to make you wait that long."

"Is that an old Scottish McAllister remedy, handed down from generation to generation?"

A chuckle rumbled deep in Red's chest. "Any old Scottish remedies would probably have killed you. The same goes for any old Cajun cures from my family, for that matter. Seriously, every bartender I've ever employed swears by it."

"I've only heard the old raw egg in orange juice thing."

"It won't hurt, but it won't rehydrate you like the tomato juice will. Nothing works as well as not allowing it to happen in the first place. You should know better, Doc."

She sighed and lowered her chin so that it rested on his arm. "I know, but that woman—"

"—was all over me as soon as you walked out. She couldn't wait for you to leave."

"Who is she?"

"An old friend—a girlfriend for a short—*very short* time—Angelique Baptiste. She's got Creole blood in her, and she's mean as all hell if she doesn't like you. It looks like she doesn't like you."

"But does she like you?"

"Not anymore. I threw her ass out and banned her from all of my clubs. I can't have her around upsetting my—clientele."

"Thank you, Red."

"You're welcome." He raised his arm, looked at his watch, and blew his breath out in a loud puff. "It's five o'clock."

"You're kidding," she gasped, glancing at her own watch.

"Man, I can barely get five hours of sleep in at night, much less during a nap."

"I can't either, and I feel so rested." She stretched lazily.

"It could be why I can't feel my right arm," Red commented.

She swung her legs over the side of the bed to sit up.

Red tried to move his arm and couldn't get it to budge.

"Is it completely asleep?"

He winced. "Yep."

"Sorry about that. I never moved, which is strange because I usually toss and turn all night."

He grabbed his temporarily dead appendage with his left hand and moved it down to his chest, cringing as he flexed his fingers. "No need to apologize."

She kneeled next to him and began to massage his shoulder joint and upper arm. "That's going to hurt like hell when the feeling starts to come back, you know."

He gave her a crooked grin. "It was worth it. I need to show you something, though."

"Okay," she said pushing her curls away from her face. "I need to go take a quick shower first, and do something with this hair. It's a mess, isn't it?"

He shrugged the one shoulder he could move. "I grew up in a house full of women with curly hair, Tiff. It looks perfectly normal to me. Go take your shower. I'll be here when you get out." He grunted as he tried to work his right shoulder and arm. "Most likely still in severe pain, but I'll be here."

She grabbed a clean pair of jeans, a long sleeve T-shirt, and some underclothes before padding into her bathroom.

As soon as she stepped into her running shower, her landline rang. "Red, that's probably Drake. Can you answer that for me, please?"

Red threw his legs over the side of the bed and picked up the telephone.

"Dr. LeBlanc's residence."

"Is Tiffany there?"

He immediately recognized the deep, Texas drawl. "Drake?"

"That you, McAllister?"

"Yep."

"How's my sister?"

"Better now, she had a hell of a hangover this morning."

"I figured she would. I didn't even try to wake her before I left. How long you been there?"

"I came in a little after eleven and made her a hangover cure. Then we both fell asleep. We just woke up a little while ago and she's taking a shower."

"Good, I'm glad she's feeling better. Did you straighten things out with her?"

"I haven't had a chance to yet. I have footage from a surveillance video that proves my point. I'll show it to her once she gets out." As he expected, he heard the unmistakable sound of horrified silence from the opposite end of the line.

Drake finally cleared his throat uncomfortably. "Uh huh. Where do you have this surveillance camera set up?"

"In the hallway by the restrooms and my office."

"Oh . . ."

Red chuckled, hearing the relief in Drake's reply. "But I have others."

"I never saw any cameras. Wh-where are they?"

"Well, they're called hidden cameras for a reason, and right about now, I'm thinking you sure *would* like to know." Drake's release of a long, drawn-out sigh, a sound of complete surrender, had Red holding back a laugh. Not surprisingly, Tiffany's brother detoured from the subject of hidden cameras and the secrets they might reveal.

"So, I guess we're still invited to your place for Christmas dinner?"

"If I were a betting man, I'd go for it."

"Good, I'm looking forward to it," Drake admitted.

"I bet you are," Red answered smugly.

"Well sheee-it . . ."

Red couldn't keep the laughter at bay any longer. "You poor bastard." He laughed again as Drake released another long sigh.

"Tell Tiff I'm glad she's feeling better. I'll be pretty busy for the next month or so."

"I'll tell her. Oh, and Drake?"

"Yes," he drawled, sounding as though he was waiting for the dig.

"Good luck, man. You are *so* going to need it." He ended the call with a hearty laugh and placed the cordless phone on Tiffany's nightstand.

Almost immediately, he heard the impatient ringing of Doc's doorbell. He walked to the door, hoping like hell it was her ex. He wasn't disappointed. He felt like crowing as the smug smile faded from Tanner's face. He settled for a grin and a bright greeting.

"Tanner! Just when I thought my day couldn't get any better."

"What the hell are you doing here, McAllister?"

Red stepped into the doorway, filling it with his bulk. "Replacing *you*. As it happens, it's not that difficult."

Tanner's face turned a shade darker. "She's been screwing around with you for months, hasn't she?"

"You would think that." Red gave his head a slow shake. "No, Tiffany has a lot more class than you do. It astounds me that you think you even have the right to ask after what you've done to her."

"Maybe you need to shut the hell up." Tanner's tone was tight with anger.

"Care to make me?" He jerked open the door, laughing as Tanner flinched from the nearness of the screen to his face. "You might want to get the hell out of here before you get that precious nose of yours broken— *again*."

Tanner didn't attempt to disguise his glare of seething hatred. "This is far from over, McAllister."

Red smiled broadly at him. "Oh, I think it is. You've had five years to make her happy, Collins. Now back the hell off and I'll show you how a real man gets it done."

Red had just closed the door on Tiffany's past when she joined him. He grinned at her attire: comfy jeans and a long sleeved tee with her freshly shampooed hair wrapped in a towel. "I swear, Doc, I still say without make-up you could pass for a fresh-faced teenager."

Tiffany shrugged as she dropped to her overstuffed couch, curling a leg under her. "Some women can't leave the house without make-up, but I hate wearing it. I always felt like I had to before. The hair, the make-up—had to look the part, you know."

"You're beautiful either way. I say make yourself happy."

"Thanks, Red. I plan to. Was that the doorbell I heard?"

"Yeah, it was your ex. It pays to go to church on Sunday. It kind of made my day to have him find me here."

She smiled. "It kind of made my day to find you here, too."

"I hope you don't mind, but I sort of threw it in his face. I couldn't help myself."

"I'm sure he said something to deserve it. But, you need to know that his father is a powerful man. He's always saying that his dad can 'make things happen' to ruin people's lives. I'd hate to see your life in turmoil just because Tanner can't stand to lose."

"Don't worry about me, Doc. I can take care of myself."

Tiffany picked up the note from the table and smiled as she read it. She folded it into a neat square and tucked it into the pocket of her jeans. "Who was on the phone earlier?"

"Drake called to see how you were. He said he'd be busy for the next month, but he'd be here for Christmas."

She nodded and stood up suddenly. "I'm starving and I feel like cooking. How do you feel about spaghetti?"

"I love it. Is that an invitation?"

"Sure is."

"Tell me what I can do to help."

Tiffany cooked down a pound of ground sirloin and added a jar of spaghetti sauce and some seasonings, while Red got the water boiling for the pasta.

Once the noodles were cooking and the sauce was simmering on the burners, Red pulled his flash drive from his pocket. "I'd like to show you something on here. Can I use your laptop?"

Tiffany logged in for him and he pulled up the video files. Her eyes flashed with anger as she saw Angelique's self-satisfied expression upon leaving the ladies room. "She obviously thinks you're worth it."

"I guess," he said. He reached for the flash drive then paused, giving her a curious glance.

"What?" she asked.

"I'm just debating on whether to show you something else."

"You don't use this thing to spy on people, do you?"

"I use it to protect myself, my clubs, and my customers. I only check it out when there's trouble, but I rarely have any trouble."

"Well, you have my curiosity peaked. Is it more video of that Angelique woman?"

"It's better than that. You know how Drake said he thought he'd seen Annie?"

"Yes."

"He did more than see her, and I've got it on video."

She turned and grabbed his arm. "Ooh, I want to see."

He looked down at her and kissed the tip of her nose. "Now how can I say no to anything when you look at me with those big, beautiful brown eyes?" He turned back to the computer. "You have to promise to keep this to yourself."

Tiffany held up three fingers. "I swear, scout's honor."

"You were never a Girl Scout," he snorted.

Tiffany gave him an eye roll then stood at attention, her right hand raised in the three fingered salute. She repeated the Girl Scout Promise, word for word.

He gave her a crooked grin. "That's quite impressive."

"Yeah, yeah, now show me this mysterious footage you have of my brother and your sister."

Within seconds, Red had the video at the spot where she and Drake entered the club. He watched her reaction as their siblings collided in the hallway.

"Is that it?" Her voice fell in disappointment.

"Nope. Keep watching," he said, satisfied at her next reaction.

"Oh, is he waiting for her?"

"Uh huh. Watch this." He fast forwarded the video.

"They danced."

He scanned quickly through the first dance and partially through the second one.

She inhaled sharply. "Look at how attracted they are to each other."

"You think? Keep watching," he said, grinning at her expected reaction to the footage.

"Oh my God! That is *so* not like Drake. I have never seen him lose his composure like that before."

"It's the same with Annie. She's said for years that she would never fall for a guy because it would screw up her plans. She's about to remember that—right—about—*now*." They watched until she left the club, with Drake in pursuit of her. Red shut off the video after he skipped to Drake re-entering the club, alone.

She turned her beautiful brown eyes on him. "What do you think happened?"

"I think it scared the hell out of her and she ran."

Tiffany frowned at him. "But they know each other now, I'm confused."

"Well, my guess is you're only half right. When Drake met the other girls, he must have noticed the resemblance. That's when he asked what Annie had been wearing, remember? Obviously they didn't exchange names."

"But they shook hands, remember? They must have exchanged names."

"Maybe they didn't give each other their full names—or their correct names."

"It sounds like you're saying *he* knows who she is, but she has no idea he's my brother."

"Uh huh," he said grinning down at her. "You know what that means don't you?"

Tiffany responded with her own impish grin. "Oh, God, I can't wait for Christmas."

They joked their way through cooking the meal, then eating the spaghetti. Afterwards, they cleaned the kitchen and sat down to watch some television. They'd slept through most of the Saints game, but satisfied their craving for football by watching their mutual second favorite NFL team, the Texans, instead.

He sat on her couch, his feet crossed at the ankles and resting on a rattan trunk. Tiffany sat beside him, her head resting on his chest as he curled one arm around her shoulders.

Red played with a silky loop of her hair. "You comfortable?" It'd been a long time since he was this relaxed with a woman.

"Yep. I've got the best spot in the house," she said, splaying her hand on his chest next to her face.

He tightened his hold around her shoulders, urging her stay where she was as he answered his vibrating cell phone.

"McAllister here."

He felt the color drain from his face as he listened to the call. "How bad is the fire?" He lifted his arm. Tiffany sat up, her eyes wide and alert as tension filled his body.

He sat up. "So, as far as you know there are no injuries, right?" He chanced a glance in Tiffany's direction, mouthed the word 'fire'. "Yes sir, I'm on my way. Thanks for the call." He ended the call and stood up. "That was someone with the Lafayette Fire Department. I need to go, Doc. My club is on fire."

"Oh no."

"Yes, as we speak. I need to find out what the hell happened. Hopefully they can put it out before it causes too much damage."

Tiffany placed her hand gently on his arm. "I'll never forgive myself if Tanner had anything to do with this."

"You'd have nothing to blame yourself for, but if he did, I'll damn sure find out. I have my own ways of tracking down information." He turned toward the door.

"Wait, Red. I'm going with you."

He turned back in time to see her grab her purse and coat. "You have an early surgery tomorrow morning?"

"Yes," she groaned, dropping her purse on the sofa.

"It's gonna be a hell of a long night for me, but it means a lot that you offered." He leaned in and gave her a quick kiss then turned to leave.

"Red."

He pivoted one last time to gaze into eyes filled with concern.

She wrapped her arms around him to give him a tight hug. "Be careful, McAllister."

"I will." He hugged her tightly. Tiffany took a step back then pulled him down to kiss him fully on the lips. The kiss deepened as he responded, wrapping her in a tight embrace. He finally pulled away to rest his forehead on hers. "Damn, Doc. You sure make it difficult for a guy to walk away."

She laughed, using one hand to push him gently back. "Just wanted you to know that I'll be here waiting for you, Red, and I won't be able to relax until I hear from you, so call me back as soon as it's convenient."

"I will." He kissed her again then sighed. "I have to go."

She nodded and stepped away from him with tears in her eyes. "I'm so sorry, Red."

He smiled sadly and nodded as he walked out the door.

Chapter Twelve

Red called Tiffany an hour and a half after he left her house. "Hey Doc." He attempted to sound more upbeat than he felt.

"Are you okay?"

"Yeah, but the club's gone. Nothing is salvageable."

"Aw Red. Your beautiful club. Do they know what happened yet?"

"No, the Fire Marshal will have to go in and investigate to see what started it. I've already spoken to him and the police but if they suspect arson I'll have to go in and give an official statement tomorrow."

"Why you?"

"In cases of arson, the owner is always the first suspect, whether they come out and say it or not. I guess the insurance money would be tempting if the business was losing money."

"But it was doing well, wasn't it?"

"It was, but they'll still have to clear me before they can start looking for other suspects."

"If it's arson, will you need me to give you an alibi?"

He sighed loudly. "I guess I would. I hope you don't mind."

"Of course not, you were with me the entire time. Will they take a statement over the phone or would I have to go in?"

"I imagine they'll call you and let you know. I'll have to give them your phone number if they ask for it. You want me to give them your landline number or your cell?"

"Give them both numbers, along with the clinic and the hospital numbers. Let me give them to you."

"They're all on your card, aren't they?"

"You have my card?"

"One of my sisters left it on the island for Thanksgiving and I took it."

"I'm in the book, you know," she said, laughing.

"I know, but—well, hell—I just wanted something of yours." She was silent for several seconds and he pictured her smiling at his confession.

"Will you be there all night?"

"I don't know yet, hon. I'm not too damn sure what can be done tonight, after all."

"Call me when you get home?"

"It may be too late, and I don't want to wake you. You have to get up early."

"I won't be able to sleep until I hear from you, Red."

"Okay, I'll call."

"Thank you."

"I better let you go. I need to call the investors and let them know their money just went up in smoke."

Red drug himself through his door around ten fifteen, his clothes and skin saturated with the stench of smoke. He punched the button for Tiffany's number, smiling when she answered on the first ring.

"Hey, are you on your way back?"

"I'm home, Doc."

"Oh, thank God. I've been bouncing off the walls over here. I'd much rather have gone with you than be stuck waiting to hear from you. Are you all right?"

"Yeah, I guess." *That was a lie. He was sick at heart.*

"Red?"

"Huh?"

"Why don't you come over here?"

"I can't do that Doc. You don't need to be missing out on any sleep."

"I function well on a few hours of sleep, just like you."

"I know, but I have to go over some things over here. I haven't showered yet, and I reek."

"If you change your mind, call me."

He smiled. "I won't. Try to get some sleep, okay Doc?"

"You too, Red. Good night."

Red took a hot shower, washing every trace of soot and smoke from his body. He changed into his lounge pants and a tee shirt and lay down in his bed. After tossing and turning for thirty minutes, he finally realized the futility of his effort. He got up, roamed the house for a few minutes, and even stepped out onto the back patio for some fresh air. He stared into the dark winter night. The stars even hid from him tonight under dense cloud coverage.

He stepped back inside, thinking for the first time that being alone didn't suit him anymore. After exchanging his flannel pants for comfortable jeans, he picked up the phone and hit redial. She answered within a second.

"Red?"

He swallowed, struggling to take the first step as anything but the dedicated bachelor he'd been for nearly thirty-nine years. "Doc . . ."

"I'm leaving the door unlocked for you. Lock it after you come in."

Red stared at his phone, the line already dead from her quick disconnect. He squeezed his eyes shut, hoped nothing ruined this chance for them. He threw a few things into a small duffle bag and grabbed his phone and keys on the way out.

Thoughts of her filled his mind during the entire drive over to her place. This was new territory for him. Unexplored, unknown terrain—he should step gingerly. By the time he arrived at her place, he'd decided they had to take things slow. Doc didn't deserve any less. She wouldn't want it any other way.

Red entered her place quietly, locking the door behind him, and kicked off his shoes. He placed his bag on the floor by the door, silently made his way into Tiffany's bedroom. She was snuggled under the covers in the cool room, illuminated only by a nightlight. Red crawled under the covers and tucked up behind her into the spoon position, soon realized it was his favorite new spot. He draped his arm over her waist and pulled her close to him. She grabbed hold of his hand and arm with her own and held him tightly.

After a few moments of silence, she scooted around to face him, reaching up to brush his hair back from his forehead.

"I don't want to be alone anymore, Doc."

"I know."

"And I'm kind of depressed."

"I am too. Your beautiful club."

He reached for her face, using his thumb to brush a tear from the corner of her eye. "I can rebuild. I just don't like having enemies."

"Do you think it was arson?"

"Yes, I do."

"Isn't there a chance it was faulty wiring or something?"

"The wiring in that building was top notch. I know because I went over every single inch of it myself when the electricians were done. The building inspector was very impressed with it."

"Do you think it was Tanner?"

"I don't know, it could have been Angelique or either of two men whom I've managed to piss off pretty good. It could have been an employee that I had to fire for stealing a couple of years ago. I've been getting some strange phone calls lately from some guy with a grudge. I have no idea who it is." He sighed and rolled over onto his back, frustrated at the situation. "It could be the competition. Hell, I don't know. It bugs the hell out of me that someone out there could hate me this much, you know?"

"Drake said if it turns out to be arson, he'd like to help. He keeps a private investigator on retainer who's very thorough and has connections in the Lafayette area. He could help you get to the bottom of this."

"I've got my own P.I., but tell him thanks for the offer."

She trailed a finger across his furrowed brow. "Red?"

"Hmmm?"

"You're not alone anymore."

His heart constricted at her confession, hoping that meant what he wanted it to mean. "How's that?"

"You've got me."

He turned to face her again, and reached for her hair, letting her curls form ringlets around his fingers, another new favorite. "Do I?"

"Did I not make myself clear before you left me earlier?"

He smiled in the quiet darkness of her bedroom. "Maybe you should refresh my mem—"

She interrupted his words with another kiss.

Red held onto her tightly as she pulled his head closer and deepened the kiss. He tangled his fingers in her hair, groaning at the silken softness.

"God, you feel so good to me," he said, after they finally broke free from the kiss, his voice deep and raspy with emotion.

"You feel like home to me," she groaned, curling her foot possessively around his calf.

"I've wanted to get my fingers all tangled up in this hair since the second I saw those curls," he gasped.

Tiffany nipped at his ear lobe. "What stopped you?"

The sensation had him growling deep in his throat. "I didn't want to take advantage. You'd had a bad night."

She whispered seductively in his ear. "Your mother raised a gentleman."

"She tried, but when you showed up at the club with it all golden brown like it is now I just about lost it, I swear."

She grinned and rubbed her nose to his. "If I'd have known that, I'd have done it months ago."

Red kissed the tip of her nose. "It feels like I've been waiting for you my whole life, Doc."

"I know exactly what you mean, Red, but it's you who's having the bad night this time. I'm wondering whether or not to take advantage of you."

"All the way over here I told myself to take this slow. You deserve that. I told myself you'd want that."

"You were wrong. I don't want to take anything slow."

You need to get up early," he said, as he slipped his hands under her the soft cotton Tee to take hold of her waist. "I should let you get some sleep."

"I'm good—five hour nap, remember?" She nuzzled his neck and placed soft kisses on the curve of his shoulder.

"When do you have to leave here?" He closed his eyes and reveled in the feel of her mouth on his skin.

"Around seven-thirty." She caught her breath as he drug his hands across the surface of her bare back.

"I'll have to go around the same time, I guess."

"Red." She slipped her hands under his shirt and lifted it to explore the sculpted planes of his chest and abs.

"Wha-what?" His breath caught at the contact of her cool hands on his hot skin.

"We're wasting precious time with all of this small talk." She curled her leg around his thick muscular thigh, dragging him closer.

"I know, but it's not what I had planned for us."

"Best laid plans . . ." She lifted his shirt and kissed his chest. "Take this off, Red."

He ripped off his shirt, amazed that his night had suddenly taken such a turn for the better. "Well, hell then, Doc. What are you waiting for? Take advantage of me." He heard her sigh as her fingers examined the sculpted lines of his upper body.

"God, you are such a beautiful man." She brushed her hands gently over him.

He smiled in the dimly lit room as he began to push his hands higher, lifting her shirt, exulting when she sat up abruptly to pull it over her head. He wrapped his hands around her waist and pulled her on top of him.

The harsh and unwelcomed ringtone of his mobile phone had them both groaning in frustration. Tiffany flipped on the bedside lamp. Red reached inside his jeans pocket to retrieve his phone, no easy feat considering the significant erection he was sporting. He sent Tiffany a heated gaze, a silent promise of what he'd do as soon as he could get back to what they'd started.

"McAllister here.....Hey Mike, what's up?.....*What*?.....Do they know who it is?....How the hell could that happen?....Aw hell, this is turning into a freaking nightmare." He sighed heavily. "I'm on my way. Thanks for calling, Mike."

He disconnected, and sat up. "I've got to go, Doc. That was a friend of mine at the police station. They found the body of a woman in the club."

"Oh my God!"

He stood, facing away as she slipped her T-shirt back on. He found his own shirt and pulled it over his head. She faced him wearing the same type of grim expression that he was sure was plastered all over his own face. "Best laid plans." Damn, he regretted the lousy situation.

She gave him a sad smile and walked into his embrace for a tight hug, before walking him to the door. Tiffany stilled his hand as he reached for the door knob. "Come back to me, Red."

"I will." He knew now—there was nowhere he'd rather be than by her side.

She reached up and smoothed his hair back from his brow. "Do you need me to call anyone for you?"

"No but thanks for asking." He kissed her. Pulled away and went in for another. He finally broke free from her. "God, I hate to leave you."

"I know, Red. I know."

"But thank you, Doc. I don't feel so alone now."

She nodded. "I'll be waiting for you when this is all over with. Call me when you can and leave me messages. I'll check them in between surgeries and I'll call you back when I can. And Red?"

"Yeah?"

"I want you here with me."

"Are you sure? I don't know what all of this is going to bring about."

"I can handle anything as long as I have you."

"Same here, Doc." He kissed her again and walked out.

Tiffany crawled back into bed, amazed at how empty it felt without Red in it. It couldn't be this easy to fall in love, could it? *Maybe it is if it's the right person.* There wasn't a doubt in her mind that she was well on her way to loving him. Thoughts of him already filled her mind. How would she function knowing she could actually go to him at the end of the day? She smiled, thinking this was one challenge she was ready for.

She'd never had this kind of reaction to a man before, not even in her younger, boy crazy, less experienced high school and early college days. Once she'd switched to pre-med, work or studying had taken up every spare moment of her time. She'd never had time for relationships, and until now, she'd never had anyone to compare with Tanner. Now that she did, she knew the only thing she'd ever felt for her ex-fiancé was an acceptance of her parents' choice for her.

Once again, she wondered how they could have been so inconsiderate of her own wishes. To hell with them. She'd discovered her own options and made her own choices. She chose college, a career in medicine, and now she would choose Red, no matter what.

Her heart ached for him—every bit as much as her body ached for him. The look on his face when he'd heard the latest horrific news told her how devastated he was. If only she could have gone with him. She tried to relax, feeling for the first time ever, like her career was a lead weight around her neck. She loved performing surgeries, and knew that when she walked into that hospital tomorrow morning she'd be able to leave everything behind her and be at her best, but right now, all she wanted was to be with Red.

Imagining him making the hour or so drive to where his club used to be, alone and disheartened, had her brushing at tears. If she could just do something to make it easier for him maybe this gnawing ache inside her would disappear. She closed her eyes and tried to rest but finally realized that sleep would not be her companion tonight. She looked at the clock on her nightstand and discovered that Red had only been gone from her for ten minutes. This was only the beginning of a long, unbearable night.

Red glanced once more at the clock on his truck and discovered he'd only been gone from Tiffany's for five minutes. He wondered if time would always drag when he wasn't with her. Suddenly the thought of rebuilding the club in Lafayette didn't sound as appealing to him. Maybe he'd just keep the one in Lake Coburn so he wouldn't have to be away from her as much. If not for the dead woman they'd found in his club, he may have found some humor in his change of attitude since falling in love with Tiffany.

He had a sudden epiphany as to why his parents hadn't been as excited over his various business ventures as he thought they should be. Any time he'd tell them of his proposals or plans, they'd always come back with the standard, "That sounds nice, Son." His mom always gave him this sad little smile that told him she was holding back her honest opinion. Once he'd asked her what was wrong.

She'd shaken her head. I'm glad you're doing what makes you happy now, Scott, but I can't help but want more than that for you."

Suddenly, he couldn't wait another minute to tell her.

He'd been in contact with his folks several times since he'd heard about the club. It wasn't quite midnight but somehow he knew his mom would be awake. He opened his phone and called her cell phone number, hoping she had it near her.

Vivienne picked up in the middle of the first ring. "Scott, are you alright?"

He smiled. "How do you do that, Mom?"

"Caller I.D.," she said.

"No, I mean know that I would call. You must have had your phone in your hand."

"I did, I admit. I know you're upset. Your father and I are praying for you."

"I know you are, and thank you. Listen, I called you for two reasons. The first is not good news—they found the body of a woman in the club, no ID on her yet. I have no idea who it could be. No clue to what's going on, why someone, anyone would have been in there."

"Oh, I'm so sorry. I'll pray for her when I pray for you."

"I didn't want you and Dad to have to hear about it on the news. But, there's another reason I called. I wanted to let you know that I finally understand what you meant when you said you wanted more for me. I finally want more too." He smiled at his mother's quiet laughter.

"Falling in love has its own way of changing things."

"I guess it does." He laughed nervously.

"Does she feel the same way?"

"She wants me with her, Mom. I don't know what I did to get so damn lucky."

"I'm ecstatic for you, Son. Tiffany is a wonderful young lady."

"Wait until you see her again. She's got this head full of gorgeous golden brown curls. Her ex made her keep it straight and blonde, can you believe that?"

"Tell her I'm proud of her when you talk to her again."

"I will. I'm seriously thinking of not rebuilding the club in Lafayette."

"Oh? Why not?"

"It would take too much time away from her."

She laughed. "There are two sure things that always have a way of rearranging your priorities. One of them is love."

"What's the other?"

"Why, babies, of course."

Red's phone beeped and he looked at the caller I.D. "Hey Mom, that's Doc calling me. I'll call you and Dad tomorrow morning, okay? I love y'all."

He hit the answer call button. "Doc? What's wrong?"

"I've got a serious problem, Red."

"What is it?" He took his foot off the gas, already seeking an exit.

"My bed is entirely too big without you in it."

He smiled, feeling the tension ease from his body. "Oh, I see."

"It feels like you've been gone forever."

"It'll be a hell of a long day without you."

"Nights won't be any easier. Now that I know how I sleep with you in my bed, I don't know if I can sleep without you."

He laughed. "How is it that you can make me go from miserable to laughing in under a minute, Doc?"

"It'd be funnier if it wasn't so close to the truth."

His smile faded. "I know, and I feel the same."

"After that nap, I don't know if I'll sleep again."

Red sucked in air through his teeth. "That depends on you, and whether or not you plan on swilling Crown like a freaking Marine anytime soon."

"Call me naïve, but I never imagined you'd have evil women scheming to get rid of your future prospects."

"Fair enough, Doc. Regardless, I hate that you can't sleep but I sure love that you called me."

"I got to thinking how you must be feeling on that long drive all by yourself and I couldn't stand it. I needed you to know how I feel before you went to face all of that."

He swallowed, sensing this would be big. Really big. "How you feel?" His heart pumped wildly in his chest.

"I've never felt this way about anyone before. Every night since Thanksgiving I've been thinking that when I wake up tomorrow morning, I'll feel normal again, and you won't mean that much to me. But every morning when I wake up you're the first thought in my mind. Yours is the first face I want to see. And—there's one other thing."

"What's that?"

"I can't stand being away from you."

He was quiet on his end of the phone. Finally he got the nerve to speak. "I just told my mom I'm considering not rebuilding the club in Lafayette."

"I don't understand. Why wouldn't you?"

"Because Doc. I can't stand being away from you either." He heard her quiet gasp and wished she were there in front of him.

"Next time I say I want to go with you, you won't be able to stop me."

"Next time I won't try. If our situations were reversed and I was home, I wouldn't be able to sleep either."

"Which home? Your home or my home?"

"I don't care, but my bed is bigger."

She laughed. "What difference does it make when we'll never use up all of that space anyway?"

"Not sleeping, but it may come in handy for other things."

She sucked in her breath sharply. "Let's not discuss other things unless you're standing in front of me. I can't take it."

He chuckled lowly. "Okay then how about the fact that it's a lot longer and my feet won't hang off?"

"I'm sorry, I hadn't even thought about how awkward my bed might be for a man of your height. How tall are you, anyway?"

"I'm a hair under six five. Too tall for you?"

"Nope, you're just right. But, um…"

"What's on your mind, Goldie Locks?"

"Oh, it's just that I find myself wondering if the rest of you is . . . in proportion?"

"Really Doc? I'm shocked." He smiled as she laughed openly.

"I guess we need to change the subject again," she said.

Red laughed nervously. "I have a feeling no matter what we talk about we'll end up right back where we started."

"Or where we ended. You have no idea how much I regret that you had to leave when you did."

"Want to make a bet?"

Tiffany emitted a half-sob." God, I wish you were here in front of me. I have all of these feelings—and there's no outlet when you aren't here."

He groaned, wishing he'd let her drive over with him. "I know what you mean. I feel the same way." The long slow sigh she released had him searching for something to put a smile back on that beautiful face of hers. "Hey Doc?"

"Yeah?"

"I'm pretty damned proportional."

By the time Red drove up to the ruins of his club, they'd been on the phone nearly an hour. He turned off the ignition and sat there in the silence of his truck, surrounded by flashing lights and yellow tape in a parking lot full of fire trucks, police cars, and other assorted emergency vehicles.

"I'm here, Doc. Guess I need to find out who's in charge."

"You're probably right. You know, Red," she paused, as though choosing her words carefully, "It's easier than I thought it would be."

"What's that?"

"Falling in love with you."

He was quiet for a moment, letting her words sink in. "You don't have to be afraid, Doc. I'll never hurt you and I promise not to step on your toes."

"I'm smiling," she said.

"I am too." He ended the call and stepped out of his truck—and into his own personal hell.

Chapter Thirteen

It was noon before Tiffany pushed through the double doors leading back to the area designated for staff only. She'd just completed her second surgery of the morning, making her hospital rounds in between, and hadn't had a chance to breathe, much less check her phone for messages until now. She turned on her cell phone, seeing that she had six missed calls—all from Red. She smiled when she saw that there were three messages from him also.

"What are *you* grinning about?" Tanner asked, walking up alongside her. "Your new boyfriend's club just burnt down and they found the body of a woman in it, didn't they?"

"Unfortunately, that's true."

"Maybe there's a chance he did it," he added.

"That's funny. I was just thinking the same about you."

"Why would you think that?" He seemed generally shocked at her accusation.

"How about all those comments about how your father is a very powerful man and has his ways of making things happen to ruin people's lives? I'm sure one phone call from his whiny, spoiled son about how I left you and took up with Red would have him plotting all kinds of things."

"Oh come on, Tiff, you know me better than that."

"Oh, I know you all right, and I wouldn't put a damn thing past you. But if you had anything to do with it, *he'll* find out." She sent him a look that promised trouble.

"Look, I didn't! I admit I was tempted to try to pull a few strings to slow down the opening of his new club but that's all I was thinking about doing," he insisted.

She glared at him. "And are you still?"

"Of course not. I wouldn't kick a man when he's down."

Tiffany tossed her curls back. "Yeah? Since when?"

Tanner closed his eyes as his head drooped forward. "Alright Tiff, I have that coming, I know I do. But, I swear, I would never get my father involved in anything like that. I didn't have a damn thing to do with it."

"We'll see." She pushed the side door open to go outside into the fresh chilly air, throwing a glance back at him. "Don't follow me," she said. She assumed her spot against the brick wall and proceeded to play back the first message.

"Hey Doc, I just gave a statement to the police. I had to give them your numbers; I hate that. No identification on the poor woman yet. They asked me to hang around, but I told them I don't live here and have another club opening up in a month. I've worked with a few of those people before and they know I have nothing to hide. They checked my record and it's clean, so they said I could go home later. I don't have any more info for you right now. I'll call you again if I hear anything else." He paused before finally continuing. "I hope you're having a decent day, Doc. I miss you. I'd be better if I could just hear your voice . . ."

Tiffany pulled up the second message.

"Hey, Doc. I miss you like crazy. I wish—Well, hell, there's no use saying what I wish right now. The place is a mess. I reek like—like a piece of smoked meat. I can't wait to go home and get cleaned up. I can't wait to hold you."

She smiled and pulled up the final message.

"I feel so alone, Doc." The sadness in his voice was overwhelming and Tiffany had to fight back the tears just hearing him. She heard him sigh deeply then he said, "Call me please." He paused to clear his throat as his voice broke slightly. "I just—I just need to hear your voice."

She wiped the tears from her eyes and hit the last number dialed button. She heard his voice asking to leave a message.

She took a deep breath and tried to sound positive for him. "Hey Red, it's noon and I just listened to the three voice messages you left for me. I've either been in surgery or making rounds all morning and this is the first chance I get to call. I miss you too—I guess it's a good thing I'm so busy or I'd be crazy from worrying. I need to grab some lunch in the cafeteria and I have another surgery at one. I can't wait to see you. Call me back and hang in there, babe."

She grabbed a turkey sandwich and an apple in the cafeteria along with a small container of milk and a bottle of water. She'd just sat down at the table in the atrium to eat when her phone rang. She pushed the talk button.

"Hello?"

"Hey Sis, how's it going?"

"Oh—Drake," she said, unable to conceal the disappointment from her voice.

He laughed. "I guess you were hoping to hear from Red."

"Yeah, I was. Sorry little brother. I haven't had a chance to speak to him all morning, and it's killing me. He was so upset that someone could hate him enough to burn his place down, but since hearing a woman died in the fire, he's really depressed. I need so badly to hear the sound of his voice."

"I've got my man working on it whether he likes it or not."

"Thanks Drake. Speaking of which, I had a little talk with Tanner. I asked him if he had anything to do with it."

"Well, hell, Sis, even if he did he wouldn't come out and admit to it, now, would he?"

"No, but I've heard Tanner lying enough to know when he's not. He didn't have anything to do with it and neither did his father."

"If you believe him, that's good enough for me."

Her phone beeped. "Drake I have to go, I have another call. Love you." She hit the button, and answered, praying it was Red on the other line.

"I'm trying to reach Dr. Tiffany LeBlanc."

"Yes, this is Dr. LeBlanc."

"Dr. LeBlanc this is Detective Michael Harper from the Lafayette Police department."

"Yes sir, Detective Harper, what can I do for you?"

"Are you aware of the investigation surrounding the burning of Mr. Scott McAllister's club?"

"Yes sir, I am."

"Mr. McAllister has said that you can provide him with an alibi for the day of the fire, is that correct?"

"Yes sir. Red . . . Scott . . . was with me from a little before eleven-thirty on Sunday morning until he got the call around seven-thirty that evening."

"We need you to come in and give a sworn statement establishing that, as soon as you can."

"How soon? I'm a surgeon, Detective Harper. I won't be finished here at the hospital until at least five o'clock this evening, maybe even later. I couldn't possibly get there until six thirty or so. Is that acceptable?"

"Yes ma'am, the sooner we can get his alibi established, the sooner we can eliminate him as a suspect."

"Then I'll be there tonight, detective. Ask anyone who knows Scott McAllister and they'll tell you that he is simply not capable of anything like that."

"I do know him, ma'am and I was hoping you'd have exactly that attitude."

Tiffany could have cried with relief at the idea of Red having at least one supporter on the police force.

"Do you need directions here, ma'am?"

"I just need an address. What section of the city is it?"

"We're east of Johnson Street by the university—the address is 555 College Avenue."

"That's all I need. Will you still be there, Detective?"

"If I know for sure that you're coming, I'll make it a point to be here." He gave her the number to call when she was on her way.

"Is Red with you right now?"

"No ma'am, he left here about an hour ago to go speak with the fire marshal."

"Is he okay?"

"He seemed upset. Kind of . . ." His voice trailed off.

"Depressed?"

"Yes ma'am. He was okay this morning, but now that we've got an I.D. on the body, well I guess it's just sunk in."

"He doesn't deserve something like this to happen to him."

"In my line of work, I see bad things happen to good people every day. If it's any consolation, I have great respect for him. A lot of us do in here," he said.

"Thank you, Detective. I'll be leaving straight from the hospital, so I'll be in my scrubs."

"That'll be fine, ma'am just bring some kind of picture ID for verification."

"I will." She tapped her phone on her teeth, hit redial and waited. Again she had to leave a message.

"Hey, Red. I wanted to let you know that as soon as I get off of work I'm driving to the Lafayette PD to give a statement. I spoke to Detective Mike Harper—it sounds like he's in your corner and that makes me feel better. I will definitely see you tonight. I should be leaving the hospital anywhere from five to six, depending on how my rounds go. I may not be back on this end before nine o'clock tonight or later. I'll call you, though. Keep trying to reach me. Everything will work out, but I need to hear your voice."

Tiffany was about to walk through the doors to go scrub for surgery when she finally got the call she longed for. "Red! Thank God you called when you did. Another few seconds and I'd have missed you again."

"Hey, Babe. It's good to hear your voice. I really needed it."

"Me too, Red."

"I got your message. I should get home an hour or so before you do. Can I go meet you?"

"I have a better idea. You go home and relax. When I get back into town I'll go meet you at your place."

His low chuckle reverberated over the air space. "This time I'll leave the door unlocked for you. I'll see you later Doc."

"Bye." She disconnected and pushed through the door, finally able to relax.

Just before seven o'clock Detective Mike Harper sat at his desk and glanced at his watch one more time. Tiffany LeBlanc had called him when she was leaving Lake Coburn at five forty-five and he expected her to walk in any minute now. Seconds later the door swung open and a woman in green scrubs walked into the office area. As she got closer, it was easy to see why Red was so ate up over her. He'd known him for several years and had never seen him lose his composure over a woman before. When Red had checked his phone and saw a second missed call from this "Doc" person, his first reaction had been to cuss loud enough and long enough to make a roughneck proud. Once he'd regained his composure, Red had looked like he wanted to either kick something or cry. He'd felt sorry as hell for the poor bastard.

He stood and extended his hand. "I'm Mike Harper."

Tiffany reached out for his hand as she stared up at him. "I'm Tiffany LeBlanc, Detective Harper. How tall are you, if you don't mind my asking?"

"I'm six foot seven, ma'am. I know. I hear I'm somewhat of a rarity. I guess people around here don't see many half-breed Native Americans my height. I have my grandfather from San Antonio to thank for that."

"Sheesh! I thought Red was tall." She grinned at him.

He nodded and laughed. "So you're the little lady that has Red all in a tailspin. I can see why."

Tiffany blushed at the compliment and thanked him. "Oh, you need these." She pulled her two I.D. badges from the hospital out of her purse. "I used to wear my hair like this until just a couple of days ago." She showed him the badge with her straight blonde hair. "I figured I needed to take another one after I colored and quit straightening it."

He looked at the blonde in the picture. "You look good as a blonde but the way you wear it now is even more becoming."

"Thank you," she said.

"Let's get this over with, Dr. LeBlanc. You must be tired, and you still have to drive home." Within ten minutes, he had his report printed out for Tiffany's signature. He scanned her driver's license, along with her two hospital badges and handed them back to her. "Thank you for your cooperation, Dr. LeBlanc. You're free to go."

"Thank you, Detective. That was quick. I hope you catch whoever's behind all this."

"We will." He shook her hand and sat back in his chair as she practically ran out of the office. "Going home to Red, no doubt, the lucky son of a bitch," he murmured. Mike ran both hands through his coal black, straight as iron hair, cut slightly longer than the military style he'd grown accustomed to throughout his ten year stint in the Corp. "I wonder if she has a sister."

Tiffany got home around eight fifteen that night. She showered quickly using her favorite scented body wash, washed and blow dried her hair. After applying the tiniest bit of eyeliner to her lids to accent her eyes, she dressed in a comfortable pair of old jeans and a shirt. She threw some things she'd need for work the next day into a bag and headed for Red's.

She entered the cozy, warm house as silently as she could and locked up behind herself. She slipped off her shoes and treaded silently down the carpeted hallway toward the soft sounds of Red's acoustical guitar playing *Stairway to Heaven*. She found him in his bedroom, slightly illuminated by the lamp on his nightstand—in bed, and leaning against the headboard, with head back and eyes closed. His long legs stretched out forever on the bed, crossed at the ankles and covered by flannel sleep pants. The sight of his upper torso, gloriously bare, made her mouth water and her fingers itch to touch the sculpted mass of muscle and still tanned skin.

Tiffany approached silently—watching—listening as the haunting melody drifted throughout the room, infusing her with a melancholy that made her want to cry. Better to speak before she did.

"Red," she whispered, wanting so much to be a part of this man's life, she ached with it.

He opened his eyes slowly and focused on her, but continued to play.

She unbuttoned her jeans, easing them slowly down her hips until she stepped out of them. Tiffany reached out and covered his hand, stilling his fingers on the strings of the guitar. The last chord echoed eerily, replaced by a silence, dense and thick with emotion. She took his guitar, laid it gently aside—reached for his hand to help her up onto the massive bed. Straddling him, she allowed him to pull her into a tight embrace, then sat back to study him. Tiffany placed a gentle touch upon his brow, wishing she could remove the lines of worry from his face.

Red wove his fingers into her curls then pulled her close for the kiss she'd craved all day. Afterward, he buried his face in the crook of her neck and hugged her so tightly she could barely breathe.

"Hey," she whispered, urging him to loosen his grip. "It's okay, Red. I'm not going anywhere."

He shook his head slowly. "Maybe you should. Maybe you should run like hell."

She curled her fingers into his thick hair and smiled down at him. "Not on your life, buddy."

"I'm telling you now, Doc, I don't have a good feeling about this."

"About you and me?" She leaned forward to place a gentle kiss on his furrowed brow.

He shook his head. "About the fire—and the rest of it. Someone out there—I don't know who—is determined to see me ruined, at the very least."

She kissed the tip of his nose, then either cheek, ending with a soft caress of his lips. "We'll have to stop them, won't we?"

He held her gaze for a moment before letting his head fall forward. "People will start ugly rumors about me, and I don't want you to feel trapped if you start believing them."

"Look at me, Red." He lifted his chin, revealing a look of total despair. "I know you, and I know what a good man you are. I know that nobody who came from a family like yours could be capable of doing anything that could make me lose faith in you. I'm here for you, and so is Drake. That detective I spoke to, Mike Harper—he believes in you, too. You have friends in that department who respect you enough not to let you get railroaded into paying for something you didn't do. *That* is what comes from being a good man. *That* is what comes from being the best man I know." She prayed he found comfort in her words, hoped they acted as a healing balm to soothe his wounded soul.

He closed his eyes and let the weight of his head fall forward into her hands as she began to gently massage his scalp.

"They've identified the body as a woman from New Orleans. Someone I've never even seen or heard of," he murmured.

"How do they know?"

"The dental records match with the ID found in a purse near her body. Poor girl was only twenty-five." His voice cracked as he pressed an open palm to his forehead. "God, this is a nightmare—I still can't believe it happened."

"I know, Red."

He grabbed her shoulders, touching his forehead to hers. "I need you, Doc."

"I'd be lost without you," she said before his kiss clouded her mind completely. She pulled away, flushed with the heat of a soul-searing need. Their gazes locked and she gave him an encouraging nod. Wordlessly, they slipped out of their remaining clothes.

Tiffany resumed her position, straddling him, knowing he was ready for this also. She braced her hands on his shoulders and slowly lowered herself, releasing a long, appreciative sigh as the length and breadth of him filled her completely.

"Wait—" His voice came out in a hoarse whisper. "We need a c-condom."

She didn't budge. "I'm healthy. Are you?"

"Absolutely. But—"

She placed a finger across his lips. "Hush, Red. Make love to me."

He stared at her a long while then drew her to him for a deep kiss.

They made love quietly, as if they were afraid to disturb the haven they'd created for themselves. Maybe later they could allow their passions to find a voice, but for the moment—just for tonight—they needed to bond with each other in the silence of this room, letting the peacefulness of their time together fill any voids in their hearts—heal all their hurts.

Tiffany's head fell back as the wave built, slowly beginning to overtake her. Red gently pulled her head forward.

"I want to see you come, Doc."

His blue eyes, bright with passion, burned into hers and she barely managed a nod. He lifted her, filled her once more, one stroke, a second, and another, filling her completely. She gave in to the wave, letting it crash down on her. "Red!"

"I love you, Doc." Her eyes flew open at his confession, barely a moment before she began to shudder against him.

When she could focus again, she looked down to see that Red was on the verge of his own release. His eyes were closed tightly in concentration, she suspected in an effort to hold back until she finished. She placed her hands on his face and he opened his eyes, gazed lovingly up at her.

"Let go Red. I love you too." She covered his mouth with her own.

He released a low primal groan, and did as she asked. He did more than that—he let himself believe she could love him, despite the threat of impending disaster.

The strength of his release left him trembling, unprepared for its ferocity. She kissed him once more before leaning back to settle her gorgeous brown eyes on him. She smiled, obviously pleased with what she saw.

"Hey," she murmured.

It took some effort and several blinks to keep his eyes from rolling blissfully back into his never-more-satisfied-than-this-moment skull of his. "Hey." He pulled her close to his chest then rolled over until she was completely under him.

"I have a confession, Doc," he murmured, brushing her curls away from her face.

"Hmmm?"

"That was my first time without a condom. Ever."

She grinned, nipping playfully at his chin with her teeth. "How was it?"

"It was—It was fantastic."

"If you marry me you'll never have to wear a condom again," she said, nipping at his lip.

"Hell, I'd marry you tomorrow if I could."

"I'd marry you tomorrow if you'd ask."

"Marry me, Doc."

"All right."

"Really?"

"Yes, Red."

He pulled back to look at her. "Are we crazy?"

"I'm crazy about you. Does that count?"

"I love you, Tiffany." He began to move inside of her.

She smiled, thinking how wonderfully strange her given name sounded coming from his lips. "I love you too, Scott. Are you ready again this soon?" She sounded shocked, but in a good way.

"Apparently so." He placed several soft kisses at the base of her throat. "Is that a problem?"

"Not at all." She closed her eyes in what he hoped was bliss. "I just thought you'd need some time."

"Apparently not . . ."

Red blinked the grogginess from his eyes and stretched his free arm and leg hard enough to hear the bones pop and crack in the room's silence. He lifted his head, squinting at the bright blue digital numbers of his alarm clock. He did a double take, then dropped his head back on the pillow and smiled.

Sleep. Heavenly sleep.

He couldn't remember the last time he'd slept this many uninterrupted hours. Then again, he'd never experienced a night like he'd just had.

He stared down at her, still asleep in his arms. He assumed she needed to get up soon to get ready for work, and decided he'd better let her know how unbelievably late they'd slept. He reached down and began to trace the outline of her face with one fingertip, smiling at the unconscious twitching and scrunching of her facial muscles. He brushed his fingers through her soft curls, wondering again at the miracle of them finding each other at this time in their lives.

After a minute more of touching and tickling, Tiffany's beautiful eyes finally opened, and gazed lovingly up at him. She smiled and he returned it.

"Good morning Red," she whispered.

"Good morning Doc."

"I'd be a very happy woman if I could hear those three words first thing every morning."

"Let's take care of that. Let's get a license, a J.P., and a couple of courthouse workers to sign as witnesses so you can be my wife."

"Don't you think your family might be a little upset if we deprive them of a wedding? Especially since your poor mother has waited so many years for this?"

"We could always do what Jackson and Giselle did, have another ceremony later and invite everyone we know."

Tiffany beamed at him. "I like that idea. I'll meet you at the courthouse on my lunch break."

He gazed down at her, as the heaviness of his troubles came flooding back to him again. "Maybe we should wait and see how all of this mess with the club turns out first."

"I've got faith in you, Red. I know that whatever happened, you had nothing to do with it. That's good enough for me."

He pulled her close for a hug. "I don't know what I'd do without you."

"Probably live another thirty-eight lonely years as a bachelor. Your poor mom would die without seeing a grandchild from you and she'd haunt you for the rest of your life."

"Lucky I have you to save me from that miserable existence." He kissed her nose.

"Very lucky—could you do me a favor?"

He nibbled at her neck. "Anything for you, baby."

"Would you let me be the one to tell your mother?"

He chuckled. "Are you sucking up to the mother in law already?"

"I'm not sucking up! I just know how much it would mean to her," she said, punching him playfully on the chin.

He pinned her to the bed and kissed her again. "You don't need to suck up," he breathed into her ear afterwards, rejoicing at her shiver of pleasure. "I got the feeling if I had let you get away, she would have disowned me."

Tiffany pinched his cheeks. "Only for a little while, McAllister. There's no way she'd stay angry at you for long, not with *those* genes!"

He grinned. "Ah, yes—it'd be such a waste if they weren't passed on, or so I've been told hundreds of times over the years. This will make her day, especially coming from you. It's a little after six now. What time do you have to be at the hospital?"

"My first surgery isn't scheduled until ten this morning but I normally start my rounds by eight."

Red crawled over her to get out of the bed. "We need to get you showered and fed. I'll cook breakfast for you."

She gazed at his gorgeous body as he stood there and immediately felt the need for him again. "I've seen your shower you know, and it seems spacious enough for two." Her tone was more than suggestive.

"That's what the previous owner, Bill Broussard, told me," he grinned. "Care to find out?"

"Go on in and get that water all warm for me and I'll join you in a bit. I'm going to call your mom, first. Do you think they're up yet?"

"Absolutely, and use my phone." He brought up a speed dial entry. Here's their number, Doc. Knock yourself out."

"Thanks, I'll try not to keep you waiting too long." She gave him a quick kiss before he walked to the bathroom.

Tiffany supported herself on one elbow to gaze at Red's retreating figure, a hair under six feet and five inches of scrumptiously lean muscle with broad shoulders that tapered down to a narrow waist and hips. She watched him, amazed at the gracefulness of his movements for a man of his size. And yes, true to his word, *all* parts of him were built in perfect proportion to his body size. She flushed at the memory of how completely he'd filled her.

The door closed and she shook herself mentally to clear her head before reaching over the bed to pull her phone from the pocket of her jeans. Once she heard the water start in the shower, she called Drake.

"Hey, ya Tiff, what's going on over there with McAllister?"

She filled him in quickly with the current happenings then paused. "That's not actually why I've called this morning, Drake. I was wondering if there's any way you could get here for noon today. It's very important to me."

"I can have a friend of mine fly me over there in his private plane if it's important enough. What's up?"

"Red and I are getting married at the Lake Coburn courthouse today around noon, and I really want you there."

"Well hell, Sis, I'd be happy to."

"Really?" She was slightly shocked at his reaction. "You're not going to tell me I'm crazy and try to talk me out of it?"

"Nope, McAllister's Grade A, in my opinion."

Tiffany beamed at her reflection in the mirror. "He is, isn't he?"

"I can't think of a better husband for you, and I know he loves you. You don't nurse a woman back from a hangover unless you're in love with her."

"I love him so much, Drake."

"I know you do. I'll be there. What about the folks?"

"No," she said, tight lipped.

"All right, I won't mention it to them."

"Thanks. Love you little brother."

"Love you, too."

Tiffany disconnected, and walked into the hallway before calling Red's parents.

"Hello?"

"Mrs. McAllister? Vivienne? This is Tiffany LeBlanc."

"Tiffany! Is everything all right?" Red's mother sounded a little panicked.

"Yes, ma'am, everything is fine. I'm calling to tell you that Red has asked me to marry him and I've said yes. Would you mind terribly having me for a daughter-in-law?"

Vivienne laughed in delight. "I would absolutely love it! You two were made for each other, you know. Pete and I could tell at Thanksgiving."

"Thank you so much Vivienne. Now I'd like to ask a favor of you. Red and I are getting married at the courthouse today to make it legal. We're planning on having another celebration later on so everyone can be there. But, I'd really love it if you and Mr. Pete could be there as witnesses for us today. My brother is coming in from Houston also. I didn't want to do this with no family around."

"We would love to, and I feel honored that you asked us."

"Thank you so much. Could you not let on to Red that you're coming if he calls you? I want to surprise him."

"I promise I won't, dear."

"Thank you so much. I want you to know that I love him and I'll be here for him."

"I know you do Tiffany. Welcome to the family."

"Thank you, Vivienne." Tiffany ended the call and walked back into the bedroom. She smiled as she heard Red's deep, resonating voice singing something by James Otto. She opened the door quietly and stepped into the shower with the man she loved. "There's plenty of room in here, isn't there?"

"Sure is," he replied, pulling her into his arms. "What did mom have to say?"

She grinned. "That they could tell we were made for each other at Thanksgiving, and welcome to the family."

"It sure will be nice coming home to you every night."

"I'm kind of looking forward to waking up with you every morning," she countered.

"Mm. That sounds pretty damn good, too."

He soaped up the rag, letting it glide softly over her skin, her breasts, her belly, and lower. In moments, he'd awakened new desires in her.

"Now," he growled. "Let's see how many ways we can break in this shower."

It was seven fifteen before Tiffany walked into the kitchen, dressed and ready for the hospital. She walked up behind Red, who stood at the stove taking the last of the bacon out of the pan. She put her arms around his waist and hugged him tightly. "Is there anything I can do?"

"You can hand me those two plates." He stirred the scrambled eggs one last time before distributing them and the bacon into each plate.

Tiffany placed them on the breakfast table while Red poured two cups of coffee for them.

"Do you want juice this morning?" he asked her.

"Just coffee, please. I need to leave here early enough to go by my place to get my birth certificate and pick up something to wear to the courthouse. I know it's informal, but I refuse to marry the love of my life in scrubs."

"Just so you know, I'd marry you in scrubs—or barefoot in a pair of daisy dukes—or in jogging attire—or better yet, wearing nothing at all."

"I bet you would—but I'm not sure how the JP would feel about that," she laughed, accepting an eager kiss from him.

"I have a ring to buy this morning," he said. "Any style in particular you'd like?"

"I do not want a solitaire engagement ring. I wore one of those for two years and it left a bad taste in my mouth. Besides, it got caught on everything. I want an old fashioned wedding band."

"Just a band? No engagement ring?"

"That's right—matching bands—and I trust you to pick them out."

He walked her to the door after breakfast, making it difficult for Tiffany to tear herself away from him. "I have to go," she said, going back for one more kiss before turning away from him. She heard him call out and glanced in his direction.

"Check your phone messages often, Babe," he said, sending her a wink that had her wishing it was "take your fiancé to work" day.

Chapter Fourteen

Red unlocked his house and walked inside, loaded down with the purchases he'd made that morning. He made his way to the master bedroom and hung the garment bag containing the *Scala* gown he'd chosen to surprise his intended bride. He placed the bag bearing his other purchases on the bed: a pair of size seven ivory pumps to match the dress, and two boxes from a top of the line jewelry store. One containing the set of matching bands Tiffany had requested, the other holding the diamond dinner ring he hoped she'd accept in lieu of the solitaire engagement ring she did not want.

Red was primed for this. He could feel in his bones that he and Tiffany were meant to be together. He knew how much he adored her and could only hope she felt the same way about him.

He suddenly laughed out loud at the picture he must have made. Confirmed bachelor, club owner and entrepreneur, Red McAllister—damned near infamous for wanting to remain single and unattached. Here he was, surprising his bride to be with wedding gowns, shoes, and rings, and he was happy as hell to do it. He didn't care how many clubs of his were burned down. As long as he had Tiffany by his side, he knew it wouldn't matter one iota.

He pulled out his Armani suit, chose one of his many tailored shirts and silk ties, and laid out a pair of dress shoes and socks. He walked into the bathroom, whistling, as he turned on the shower jets. He was picking up Tiffany in two hours and he had to be ready for her. Life was good.

As he reached for a towel, his phone began to ring.

"McAllister here!"

"Well, aren't you the happy camper this morning?" the mysterious voice snarled.

"What's wrong, asshole? Couldn't get your rocks off this morning, so you decided to get your jolly's by trying to ruin my day? It ain't happening buddy. I'm too pumped up to let a punk like you piss on my parade today."

The deep, raspy chuckle crackled from his phone's earpiece. "Wrong again, McAllister. Life, as you know it, is about to end. Wait for the call you pompous bastard."

Red stared at the dead phone in his hand and pushed aside the sudden feeling of dread. He put the phone down and waited for the feeling to pass, but it only got stronger.

"Shit," he muttered as his land line began to ring. He walked into his bedroom and sat on the edge of the bed, still unmade and rumpled from his and Tiffany's hours of love-making.

He saw Mike Harper's name and number on the caller ID window and answered with trepidation. "McAllister here and before you say a word, the asshole just called and basically told me the shit was about to hit the fan."

"We've got trouble, buddy—big trouble," Mike said.

"Lay it out, Mike."

"Can you come to the police station so I can fill you in?"

Red put his free hand on the back of his neck. "Come on Harper, don't make me wait. Just tell me what the hell's going on." He heard the man that he respected take a deep breath and release it slowly. Red closed his eyes and waited for the next link in his chain to weigh him down.

"They found some kind of timing device and a detonator at the origin of the fire, bro. It was in your office. And, that means—"

"That means my alibi is useless, and I'm still the number one suspect," Red finished for him.

"Uh, yeah—along with a few other things."

"What other things?

"We got two phone calls this morning, Red. One from the parents of Angelique Baptiste saying their daughter has been missing since Saturday night. The second was from an anonymous caller, a man saying he knows the woman who was killed in the club. He claims she told him she was pregnant—with your child." Mike released a sigh. "The coroner's report came in not five minutes ago confirming the pregnancy."

Red was too shocked to speak. He sat there, feeling as though the earth were crumbling beneath his feet. He vaguely heard Mike calling his name and finally got the presence of mind to speak. "It's not true, Mike. I never met her."

"I believe you, Red, but that phone call, along with the fact that everyone in the club saw you good and pissed at Ms. Baptiste. Well, I'm sorry, but we have to bring you in."

Red rubbed his face roughly. "I know," he said. "I'll be there in an hour and a half or so." More to himself than anyone else, he added, "But I have to tell Doc, first."

Tiffany came out of surgery at ten forty-five, feeling pleased with the routine arthroscopic cartilage repair. She turned as she heard a technician call her name.

"Dr. LeBlanc, someone is waiting to see you at the nurse's station."

"Thanks Shawna," she said, walking quickly in that direction.

She beamed when she saw Red leaning up against the wall, but as she got closer, she could see the glum expression on his face. He pushed off from the wall and walked toward her.

"Hey Tiff, is there some place we can go to talk?"

She pointed toward the doctor's lounge. "Sure Babe, this way. What's up?"

He grabbed on to her upper arm and pulled her in the direction she'd pointed to, but remained silent.

"Red, you're scaring me." Tiffany gasped, trying to keep up with his long strides.

"Where are we going?" he asked brusquely.

"Through those doors."

Red pushed through the double doors of the lounge. As soon as they entered the room he released her and walked to the window.

"What's happened?"

"Everything's a bust, Doc. They found a detonator in my office, rigged with a timer, and that means the alibi is useless."

"That doesn't mean anything. What else has happened?"

"I can't marry you."

"Are you going to tell me what's happened?"

He spun away from her and ran his hands through his hair. "We moved too fast, that's what happened."

She pulled her hair from its ponytail prison, frustrated at not getting any answers. "Damn it, Red, stop being stupid and tell me what happened."

He turned to face her. "I don't want to marry you."

The message didn't affect Tiffany nearly as much as the dead pan tone he used to deliver it—cold as ice. She felt as if he'd slapped her in the face. "Red, we'll work through whatev—"

"Nobody has seen Angelique since Saturday night, and everyone in the club saw me angry enough to kill her that night. It doesn't look good."

"I *know* you didn't have anything to do with that. Don't do this, Red. Let me be there for you," she pleaded.

"There's more. The woman who died in the club was pregnant and an anonymous caller said the baby was mine."

Tiffany could feel the blood leaving her face. "Was it?"

"No, but that won't stop people from believing it."

"It stops me from believing it, and that's all that matters, Red." She watched him carefully, knowing he was doing this to protect her, praying he'd stop and instead accept the support she offered. He took a deep breath and she tensed, knowing in her gut he wouldn't do that.

"I don't want you, Tiffany. It was fun, but that's all it was. I'm sorry if I made you feel otherwi—"

"Cut the crap, Red!" she barked. "You weren't the only one to graduate Summa Cum Laude. Only difference is that I didn't have a mother who was proud enough to shout it from the mountain tops. So don't think you can pull off that pitifully lacking performance with me. I know the tru—"

"You don't know a damn thing."

"I know the two most important things in this world—in my world. I *know* you're crazy in love with me, and I *know* you're incapable of murder." She saw the battle raging within him and felt a sudden urge to slap some sense into him, knowing he only did this for her, *the selfless bastard*. She watched his jaw work furiously as he prepared himself to speak.

"Yeah, Doc—and the jails are full of innocent men." He pressed his palms over his eyes. "Look, I can't worry about myself and you too. I've got to go turn myself in if I want to avoid the humiliation of being arrested in a public place." He turned toward the door. "It was nice knowing you, Doc."

"Nice knowing you?" Her voice rose with hysteria. "Red, you've *known* me, biblically speaking, three times in the last twelve hours—without a condom—remember?"

He strengthened his resolve and turned to her, knowing what he had to do. "It was good, too. Thanks for that, by the way." He turned, thinking how ashamed his parents would be if they knew how he was treating her. *Thank God they didn't have to find out.* He'd only called Jackson and Giselle to be witnesses for the civil ceremony and had already informed them both that it couldn't happen. He walked to the door, stopped dead in his tracks at her next statement.

"You need to call your parents before they leave Gardiner."

He turned slowly toward her. "What do you mean?"

"I wanted to surprise you, so I invited them to the ceremony. I wanted us both to have family there," she said, lamely.

Both? "Who else did you invite to the ceremony?" He dreaded the answer.

"Drake."

He let his head fall forward, heavy with defeat. "I'll call my family—you call yours. I'm sorry, Doc. I've got to go." He turned and left, leaving Tiffany alone in the room.

Red climbed into his truck and called his parents, thanking God they hadn't left Gardiner yet. He filled them in on recent developments, and his mother seemed to understand his reasons for calling off the wedding. The fact that he'd put an end to his relationship with Tiffany drew immediate disapproval from his tiny matriarch.

"Oh Red, that's just stupid. That girl cherishes you. Don't toss her willingness to be there for you like last week's paper."

"I'm sorry, Mom, but it has to be this way. Tiffany has had to jump obstacles all her life to get where she is. I'll be damned if a relationship with me is going to be the one thing to trip her up now."

"I still don't agree but you know we both love you and we're here for you, Son."

Red spoke to his dad for a bit before disconnecting. He pressed his hand to his chest, recalling one of his grandmother's old sayings when she felt sad about something. *I feel ti peu, a little, sick to my stomach, but beaucoup, a lot, sick at heart.*

He gave himself several minutes to get over feeling like a scumbag before calling Mike Harper. "Hey buddy, I just wanted to let you know that I'm on my way in to the station."

"Thanks Red, I'll be here. Oh, I ran a trace on your phone lines. Those calls have all been made from cheap cell phones. All disposable, all untraceable. We're trying to track down who bought them, but I don't have much faith that we'll find anything. He probably picked them up from different places like 7-Elevens and Quick Shops and paid cash."

"Yeah, I figured that would be a dead end. That son of a bitch was right about one thing. Life, as I knew it, is over."

"Hey, don't give up on us. You have friends over here."

Red grunted low in his throat. "That doesn't mean you won't throw my ass in jail if you have to."

"Well, yeah, if it comes down to that, we will. We'll also bust our ass trying to catch the SOB that's setting you up. Have a little faith, Red. That girl of yours is worth it, don't you think?"

Red's silence must have spoken volumes to the seasoned detective.

"You didn't do anything stupid like break it off with Dr. LeBlanc, did you?"

Red kept his mouth shut.

"Oh man, for somebody so smart, you sure are a dumb bastard. Are you out of your mind? Women like that don't come along every day, you dumb Scottish prick."

"Hey, watch the name calling," Red growled. "Do I call you a stupid Half Breed? Besides, what the hell was I supposed to do? Let her pine away for me while I rot in jail? That's worse than the shit she had before."

"You can start by not being so damned dramatic. We'll catch this guy, Red. Then you can sail off into the sunset with the good doctor."

Red wiped his face with one hand. "Hmph. After the way I just left her, she may never speak to me again."

"Really? Well if that's the case, maybe I need to buy myself a big old boat."

"Shut up, you half-breed, scum bag, son of a bitch!" He frowned at his friend's guffaw of laughter.

"See ya, McAllister."

Tiffany shuffled into the doctor's lounge after her last surgery and collapsed on the sofa, feeling bone tired, despite the fantastic night of sleep she'd experienced in Red's arms. Or had that been a dream? So much had happened since then. Last night seemed too far away, or removed, as though the memory of it was like watching a scene in a movie about someone else's life. When she thought her day couldn't get any worse, Tanner sauntered in the room. She groaned and stretched out on the couch, all while thanking God she hadn't spoken of the wedding plans to anyone here at the hospital.

Tanner stood over her. "You feeling all right, Tiff?"

"I'm great. What do you want?"

"I—uh—heard the news."

Tiffany tensed. "What news?" She shifted her gaze to the back of the couch.

"They're holding Scott McAllister for suspicion of murder, arson, and possible involvement in the disappearance of someone named Angelique Baptiste."

She turned to face him again. "So, you came here to gloat?"

He sat next to her on the edge of the couch. "No, and despite my dislike of Red, I know he's incapable of doing any of those things."

Tiffany remained silent, knowing if she opened her mouth now, the flood gates would open. She would not humiliate herself by crying in front of Tanner or any other member of this staff.

"I want you to know I'm here for you. If there's anything at all you need, just ask."

"Thank you, but I'm fine."

"Seriously. You don't look fine. You look like you're miserable."

"Well, you ought to know what that looks like. I spent five years that way with you."

"But you're with McAllister now, and you're still miserable. Go figure."

She pinned him with an icy glare. "Is there a point to this conversation?"

"Frankly, I'm a little surprised that you're not with him at the police station to show the world you're standing by your man."

"Shut up, Tanner," she seethed. "I'm in no mood for any of your crap."

"Tiffany. I didn't mean it like that."

She pushed him off the couch and stood up suddenly, angry that her ex had the *cajones* to confront her about this. "How the hell *did* you mean it? You said you weren't here to gloat, but here you are, doing just that!"

He stepped closer. "Tiff, I'm sorry. I'm so sorry. Please let me help you," he said. "What can I do to help? Is there someone I can call for you? Drake, maybe?"

"You want to help, Tanner? Be a friend."

He placed his hands on her shoulders. "I am. I will be."

Slowly, she relaxed. Maybe they could be friends. "He didn't do this."

"Shh . . . Don't think about that right now." He pulled her gently to him. "Even if they prove otherwise, I still love you. I'll always love you."

She stiffened, seeing this for what it was and pushed away from him. "Get away from me," she hissed. "You know, even if I don't end up with Red, I still won't go crawling back to you. I'm done with that life and I'm done with men who don't want me." She turned her back, leaving him alone in the lounge.

She waited anxiously for the internet browser screen to appear then pulled up the website of one of the Lafayette news stations. Every day she'd kept tabs on the story of the burning of Red's club. The first day they'd reported the club owner was not a suspect in any investigation of arson. It relieved her, hearing he had an alibi. The second day she read about the woman's body found in the rubble, and despite turning her skin cold and clammy, it still gave no word of him being a suspect.

The real horror had begun the day she'd about the timing device that negated his alibi, the pregnant woman, her cause of death being a broken neck, as well as the tip from the anonymous caller claiming Red was the father.

"Anonymous, my ass." She knew damn well who the caller had been. Every day for a week, she'd pulled up the station's website, praying to read they'd found the real murderer/arsonist. Here it was, seven days later, and the police were still no closer to the truth.

Angelique released an exhausted sigh and sat back against the chair, wondering how she'd gotten herself involved in something like this. Her anger and humiliation at being thrown out of the club, rejected by the only decent man she knew other than her father, and she'd let it happen. *He* had met her at her car. *He* had said all the right things to soothe her, to repair her damaged ego: *"Of course you aren't to blame. After all these years you had every right to think there should be something more...Red used you then threw you aside for another woman. A beautiful woman like you doesn't deserve to be treated that way. What you need is a real man."*

Cher bon Dieu! She'd thought she'd found herself one that night.

Just thinking about the things she'd done with him, things she'd never done before in her life, made her skin heat. She'd had sex with him out at the back of the building, up against the rough exterior surface of the club. She was tall, nearly six foot, and by no means skinny, but he'd handled her as easily as if she were a rag doll. The man had definitely been talented in the area of pleasing a woman and he was most definitely well equipped. She had never had pleasure like that before.

Looking back on it now, she knew she'd been played, that every word he'd spoken was done with the sole purpose of taking advantage of her emotional insecurity at the time. That alone, was enough to shame her.

What she'd discovered about him later did more than shame her. It terrified her, enough to disappear without a trace. That man had skills above and beyond the norm of the average Joe, she was sure of it. She'd seen several tattoos on him, some of them military in nature, she was sure of that, too. She also remembered seeing one in particular, out of the ordinary and somehow familiar. Try as she might, she'd failed at recalling where she'd seen it.

After their sexual encounter in back of the building, he'd held her close, asked her if she wanted to get back at Red, and her pride had overtaken good sense.

Once she'd agreed to meet him at the club after closing time, she'd driven around to clear her head and eventually reason had prevailed. She realized it was her own fault Red had thrown her out of the club.

After closing time, she'd gone back there, but only to tell the man she'd changed her mind. She entered the quiet club through the unlocked side door and heard an angry confrontation between him and a woman—his girlfriend as it turned out. The things she'd heard him say had made her blood run cold and scared her enough to make her leave town without a word to anyone—especially her parents.

Angelique laid her head on the desk, wondering what she could do to help Red out of this mess. She picked up the phone and dialed his cell number, but it was turned off. She called information for his new listing in Lake Coburn and jotted down the number given to her. She dialed it carefully and waited for someone to answer. Again, with no luck. She thought about calling the Lafayette Police Department, but what if *he* had friends there? She couldn't risk it, not yet, anyway.

Chapter Fifteen

Tiffany moved mechanically through her surgeries during the next week. She was a perfectionist when it came to her skills, and as far as the situation with Red was concerned, that changed nothing. Every cut, every suture was performed with precision. Every patient seen to with her usual care and expertise, but the harder she tried to act like nothing was wrong, the worse her heart ached. She overheard the nurses whispering that something was missing, her usual spark was gone.

Again, Tanner walked in on her while she was seated in the doctor's lounge sipping a cup of hot chamomile tea. He walked over and stood in front of her, effectively blocking her view of the wall hung television screen.

"Move," she said.

"I want to talk to you about something, Tiff."

"Does it pertain to work?"

"No."

"Then I don't want to talk about it with you."

"You look like you're miserable and need to talk."

"I've grown accustomed to misery, Tanner, thanks to you." She threw back the last sip of tea and tossed the empty cup in the trash. "Now that I think of it, the five years I spent being miserable with you was like a training camp for the big game." She spread her arms wide. "It's game time."

Tanner sighed and sat down next to her. "What's going on with Red's case?"

She shrugged. "You watch television. I'm sure you know as much as I do. I'm not in that loop, anymore."

"Tiffany, this isn't like you."

She stood suddenly and looked down at him. "How the hell would you know what I'm *like*? You tried to mold me into something I wasn't for five years because you didn't like the real me."

He stood up. "Is that what you think?"

"What else would I think?"

"That's not why—I was—I was trying to help you."

"How? By making me feel like I wasn't good enough for you?" She shook her head. "Way to help, Tanner."

"It was because of your mother. I thought maybe she'd accept you if you looked . . ." His voice trailed off.

"Like her clone? Like seeing a reflection of the woman who's hated me all my life staring back in my own reflection would be an *improvement*? You can't be serious."

"I was only trying to improve your relationship with your mother,

Tiffany. That's all, I swear."

She stood, emptied the remainder of her tea and disposed of the cup. "You failed—miserably."

He nodded. "I know that, and I'm sorry. For what it's worth, you're even more beautiful this way."

She stared out the window, ignoring his compliment.

"Have you spoken to Red recently?"

"That's none of your business."

"I just want to know because I care."

She turned toward the door. "Sure you do. I've got to prep for surgery."

He grabbed her arm as she passed him. "Whether you believe it or not, I do care about you. If you need to talk, I'm here."

Tiffany glared at his hand on her arm until he released her and left the room without a word.

By noon she'd checked on her last patient and she was ready to jump out of her skin.

She went to speak to her administrator and thirty minutes later, walked out with his blessing to take a week and a half off of work. A travel guide friend of hers had called her the night before and told her she could get her on a five day Caribbean cruise because of someone's last minute cancellation. Five days on a ship drinking tropical drinks was just what she needed, and God help any man who tried to hone in on her alone time. She'd come back tanned, relaxed, and hopefully free of this ache and emptiness in her chest.

After stopping for a few supplies she went home and began to pull her suitcases out of closets to pack. That's when she realized she'd left her Louis Vuitton carry on at Red's house. She needed that bag. She pulled out her phone and dialed Red's number. As usual, he didn't answer. A fresh stab of pain hit her at his willingness to throw everything away.

Determined, she sent him a text:

I need my bag. I left it at your place

Within moments he'd replied. *You left with it*

No. It's n ur BR. R u home?

Lafayette PD

Locked up?

Sort of. House arrest at Melissa's when not here. U takin a trip?

Yes

Where to?

NOYB

Alone?

Surely NOYB

A short pause, then he followed up with: *I know...*

U shut me out

Won't drag u down with me

I need my bag

Not there. Bye Doc

Frustrated, she threw her phone on the sofa and poured herself a glass of wine while she packed. She'd only taken two sips when her home phone rang.

"Hello."

"Tiffany, is this you?"

"Yes, it is. Mrs. Vivienne?"

"Yes. How are you, dear?"

"I'm-I'm . . ." Just like at Red's place for Thanksgiving, something about the woman's voice made her want to bare her soul to her. "Not good, actually."

"Oh, sweetie, I know. Red is just as miserable as you are, and I don't know why he's being so stubborn."

"I don't either, Mrs. Vivienne. I wanted to be there for him, but he's shut me out."

"He's trying to protect you, Tiffany, but I knew you wouldn't see it that way. Men don't think as we do."

"I'm so hurt."

Vivienne began to cry softly on the other end of the phone. "I know you are, sweetie. But please don't give up on him. This will all be over one day."

"Will it?" She fought to hold back tears.

"It has to. My child serving a prison sentence for something he didn't do—that can't happen."

"Oh God, I hope not, Mrs. Vivienne. I—I ache for him—I feel like I'm dying inside. I can't function anymore. I need to get away but I left my carry-on bag at Red's. He says no, but I know it's there and I need it. If I can just distance myself from this pain—this *rejection*—for a while." She worked at the tension in her neck with one hand. "I think I might have a chance at getting back to normal."

"I understand, Tiffany. Red keeps a key hidden in a ceramic lighthouse on his back patio. It unlocks the kitchen door. Go get your bag, sweetie. Take that trip, wherever it is you're going. It'll do you some good to get away for a while."

"Thank you."

"Maybe by the time you get back, Red will have come to his senses or they'll have caught the person responsible for this mess."

"Maybe. I just—love him—so much."

"He loves you too, Tiffany. He's trying his best to protect you, right now. This is all he can do. He feels like there's no other choice, do you understand?"

"I don't. I just want to be with him."

Just as Vivienne had said, she found a key hidden in the ceramic light house. She entered Red's home, seeing everything as it had been the last morning she'd left from there, except for some receipts on the kitchen island.

Tiffany made her way to Red's bedroom and found her bag, exactly where she'd left it. She stared at the bed with still tangled sheets and couldn't help but think of their night of lovemaking. Catching sight of a full length garment bag hanging from a door hook, she walked closer seeing it was from an exclusive dress shop. She approached the bag, her curiosity on maximum overload, as she lowered the zipper.

Tiffany gasped at the contents, a gorgeous designer gown in ivory silk with exquisite lace and beadwork in a size six—her size. She glanced at the bag hanging next to it, opened it to reveal a pair of matching ivory pumps in size seven—her size. She tried them on, feeling like Cinderella when they both slid on for a perfect fit. She saw Red's beautifully tailored Armani suit hanging on another hook, along with a gorgeous shirt and coordinating silk tie. His dress shoes and socks were laid out on the floor beneath the clothes.

She raised trembling fingers to her mouth, realizing this must have been their wedding clothes. Tears flooded her eyes when she thought of Red picking out the dress and shoes for her.

She scanned the room and her gaze settled on three boxes from a high end jeweler in Lake Coburn. She opened the first box and gasped at the lovely diamond earrings nestled in blue velvet. The second box contained the most gorgeous dinner ring she'd ever seen in her life. She'd told him no solitaire. Sobbing openly now, she opened the third box containing a matching set of platinum bands with inlaid diamonds and exquisite braiding around the edges. *He did want to marry me.* If Vivienne was to be believed, he still wanted to marry her.

Tiffany didn't know whether to laugh or cry. The joy in her heart vied frantically with the unfairness of the situation. She did both, laughing through her tears until a calmness returned to her. She rinsed her face in his bathroom. The huge shower brought to mind their last bout of lovemaking. When Red's land line began to ring she only hesitated a moment before answering it from his bedroom.

"McAllister residence."

"Oh, thank God someone is there. I need to speak with Red."

Tiffany would never forget the heavily accented voice of the woman from the ladies room. "Where the hell are you, Angelique? They suspect Red for being involved in your disappearance."

"Where is he?"

"He's back and forth between the Lafayette PD and being under house arrest at his sister's place. He can't leave the area. We suspect he's being set up."

"He is."

"Who?"

"I don't know who to trust."

"Trust me, Angelique. I love him."

"Yes, but do you know who can be trusted? It's someone very close to him."

"Tell me."

"I'm not saying anything until I know both of my parents are safe and I'm making an official statement to the police."

"Angelique, you could be putting Red in danger by keeping it from him. The police will make sure both you and your parents are safe."

"I don't know."

"You can't let him be blamed for this!" Tiffany pleaded.

"I don't want to see him blamed, but I'm afraid for my parent's lives, can you understand that? They're all I have and I love them very much. I'm dying over here, knowing they don't know if I'm alive or dead. I'm afraid he'll hurt them if I call," she sobbed.

This was no act. This woman's fears were real. She took a deep breath and tried to stay calm. "Look, you shouldn't be in this alone and you don't have to be. Would it help if your parents were in protective custody at the police station?" She sent Red a text from her cell: *Angelique on your phone...call me NOW!*

"Can you make sure that happens?"

"Of course." Within seconds her phone rang. "That's Red calling me now on my cell. Don't hang up!" She answered her phone and put it on speaker so Angelique could hear the conversation. "Red, she's on your home phone right now. She knows who's setting you up but is worried for her parents."

"Her parents are here with me at the police station. They came in to see if anyone had heard from her."

"Did you hear that, Angelique? Your parents are at the station with Red."

"Thank God! I want to speak to them," Angelique said. "Please tell my mother to call me on my phone."

Tiffany repeated her request to Red and he disconnected to let them use his phone to call her. "How soon can you make it back to the station to clear Red?" Tiffany asked Angelique.

"I'm only thirty minutes away, but I'm terrified to drive back alone."

"Ask Detective Mike Harper to send you a police escort," Tiffany suggested. "That should make you feel safer."

"Definitely. My mother is calling now, but thank you."

Tiffany didn't waste time waiting on Red to call her back. With phone in hand, she loaded every one of his purchases into her car, including the birth certificate he'd left beside the rings. Hers was tucked away inside the glove compartment of her car. She fully expected to get some use out of them before this day ended.

She was ten minutes from the police station when her phone finally rang. Her heart leapt with excitement as she saw Red's name flash across the screen.

"Red?"

"Doc! I'm free and clear. Angelique has been picked up and is giving her statement to the police right now. It was Benji, my doorman."

"I know! I just heard on the radio that there's an APB out on him for the fire and the woman's murder. What the hell happened, Red?"

"He was going to murder Angelique and leave her in the club to burn. Everyone saw me throw her out so I'd have motive. She went to meet him at the club after it closed and overheard him telling his girlfriend. She said they were arguing and the girl told him she was pregnant. That's when she got the hell out of there. She knew Benji had friends with the department and didn't know who she could trust. We know everything but why, Doc. I can't figure out what kind of beef he has with me."

"I guess we'll have to wait until they catch him to find out."

"God, I want to see you. Where are you?"

"I'm a few minutes from the station."

"Here, in Lafayette?"

"Yes, and you may as well know that I picked up my suitcase from your place." She waited for his response.

"You did?" His voice cracked slightly.

"Yes, I did. It was in your bedroom, right where I'd left it. You'd done some shopping."

"I wanted to surprise you."

"You certainly did."

"Did you—see everything I bought?"

"I believe so."

"And what did you think?"

"You have excellent taste, Mr. McAllister, in both clothes and jewelry."

"Of course I do. I chose you, didn't I?"

"You also pushed me away when you needed me most." She ignored his groan. "You hurt me, Red."

"I didn't want to subject you to anything that may put you in danger. Hell, I'm terrified right now because you're not here, and Benji is still out there."

"I'm just driving up to the station," she said. "And Red?"

"What?"

"Don't push me away again. If we have problems, we'll face them together. You got that?"

"I got it, Doc."

Tiffany got out of her car and headed toward the entrance. As she rounded the corner she froze, horrified at the sight before her.

"Well damned if the devil isn't smiling on me today." Benji practically crowed as Vivienne McAllister, the queen bee herself, pulled into the parking spot at the end on the same row as his truck. She took her time getting out of the car and locking her doors. She didn't even assess her surroundings, completely lured by the false security that all police property, even the precinct parking lot, was a safe zone. He opened his truck door and headed stealthily in her direction, his gun pocketed and ready. Once he'd realized that all his plans for revenge were shot to hell, he'd headed to the station, hoping to catch Red alone, or not. He knew damn well he wouldn't be spending a single day in prison, so he didn't give a rat's ass how the situation turned out, as long as Red lost his own life, or that of a loved one.

He caught up with Vivienne and shoved the gun in her side. "If you want to live, you'll come quietly, *Mom*."

⚜

Tiffany froze, seeing Benji walk with Vivienne's arm tightly in his grip. She couldn't see clearly, but judging from the look on Vivienne's face, she suspected he had a gun her.

"He's here outside of the police station and he has your mom. I think he has a gun on her, Red. I can't let him take her."

She heard Red shout to everyone what she'd just told him and heard scuffling sounds coming from the phone.

"Tiffany, don't you do anything stupid!"

"If anyone comes barging out here he'll kill her Red. You must know he just wants to make you suffer. I have to do something!"

"Tiffany . . ."

"I'm putting the phone in my pocket so you can hear." She ignored his pleas to wait and pocketed her phone.

She forced herself to stay calm. "Benji!"

He swung around, jerking Vivienne so roughly she nearly fell. The bulk of a man dwarfed the tiny woman, and although she was trying to be brave, Tiffany could see the terror in her eyes. "She'll only slow you down. Take me, instead. I'm his fiancée."

He leered evilly at her. "Why don't I take both of you and we can all have some fun?"

Tiffany walked calmly up to him. "You can't keep an eye on both of us, and she's older—she *will* slow you down."

His eyes narrowed to two evil slits before he shoved Vivienne roughly away, causing her to fall on her knees. Tiffany tried to help, but was stopped short by Benji's violent jerk on her hair.

"I like the curls, Doc. You're much easier to hang onto." He pulled her along by her hair, turned to glare at Vivienne. "If you move from this spot, she's dead, do you hear me?"

Tiffany exchanged a look with Vivienne as the woman nodded in understanding.

"I won't, but please Benji, don't hurt her."

"Not right away," he scoffed. "Tell that baby boy of yours I intend to have some fun with her before I snap her pretty little neck." He pulled Tiffany's face closer and gave her a long, slow lick from her jaw line to her ear.

Tiffany squeezed her eyes shut and shuddered in revulsion, swallowing the bile that threatened at his invasive act.

Benji caught Vivienne's horrified expression and laughed sadistically. "Let's go have some fun, sweetness."

"So what exactly is your plan, or do you have one?" Tiffany was amazed at the sense of calm washing through her.

"I plan to blow your head off if I see even one uniform."

"My car is over there," Tiffany added.

"And no doubt loaded with GPS so they can track us? No thanks—everything I need is in my truck." He jerked her roughly along with him, turning often to make sure they weren't being followed.

"Do you want me to drive?" she asked.

"So you can drive us into a ditch or a tree, or something equally imaginative? I don't think so." He jerked her around to his side of the truck, opened the door, and shoved her inside before climbing in after her. He took the gun from her long enough to start the engine, but as soon as it roared to life he aimed it at her and threw the truck into drive, activating the automatic door locks.

Tiffany scooted all the way over to the door, putting as much space between them as she could. The truck was a fairly new Chevy Silverado with electric everything, and she made a mental note of where the unlock button for the door was. The gleam of something metal between the handle and the door panel caught her attention. A metal letter opener, the decorative, heavy stainless steel type and very pointed on one end. Using her body as a shield, she eased it from the space, barely having time to conceal it under her leg before he jerked her back over to his side of the truck.

"You get your pretty little ass back over here so I can keep an eye on you, Curly Q," he said, grabbing her by the hair again.

Tiffany sucked in her breath as she felt some of the hair rip from the base of her skull. She clenched her teeth against the pain, using the opportunity to place her phone on the seat beside her, out of Benji's line of sight.

Tiffany forced herself to think, to be aware of every movement he made, and everything going on around them. If the chance to escape presented itself, she had to be ready. As long as he had that gun pressed to her side she was pretty damn helpless to do a thing. If only he'd move it for a second or two, she could make her move. She knew that the further from the police station she got, the less chance she had of ever seeing Red, or anyone else, again. He'd never let her live.

She cast a sidelong look at her captor. "What did Red do to make you hate him so much?"

Benji shrugged. "Not a damn thing to me personally, but he fired my little brother a couple of years ago. McAllister accused him of stealing from the door. He got in with the wrong crowd after that and was shot in a drug deal that went bad."

"So, you're thinking he didn't steal?"

Benji laughed loudly. "Hell yeah he stole. That little son of a bitch came off his mama's tit wanting whatever wasn't his."

"Then why blame Red?"

"Because I *can*, that's why," he sneered. "Bobby was the only family I had, and he's dead because of McAllister. If he'd given him another chance and kept him on, he'd be alive today. It's not right that he should get everything he wants out of life when others have nothing."

Tiffany forced herself to remain calm in light of this new information, and tried to put herself in his frame of mind. She knew he'd stop at nothing to make Red pay, even though he wasn't responsible. Benji's failed attempt at framing Red for murder left him no choice but to take away someone he cared for. She suddenly knew with certainty that he would be more than willing to die, as long as she did, too. *Oh God, help me.*

She forced herself to keep the fear out of her voice as she continued to talk, trying to glean as much information as she could. "It's not like it was handed to him on a silver platter, Benji. He's had to work hard for it. That club was his dream and you burnt it down. Isn't that enough?"

"Hell no! He would have rebuilt with the insurance money and it would have been bigger and better. People like him keep coming back financially. I have to let him know what it's like to lose someone he really cares about." He sent her an evil glare. "I saw the look on his face when he threw Angelique out of the club. You don't throw away a dish like that over nothing. She was good too, I almost regretted the plan to kill her but it was the golden opportunity to set him up. I don't know why she never showed up."

"She did. She went through the side door and overheard you talking to your girlfriend. Your *pregnant* girlfriend—you killed your own child."

He laughed maniacally. "The hell I did. I know for a fact that my loads are all blanks. Once that bitch said she was pregnant and tried to pawn it off as mine, I knew she'd been screwing around. That was the easiest kill I ever made. Walked up behind her while she was bitching and moaning and snapped her neck like a twig."

An icy chill went down Tiffany's spine at his confession. God, she hoped Red hadn't heard. She had no doubt that everyone knew her exact location. Her phone had a built in GPS, and she suspected they were being followed very closely. All she could do was stay alert, and wait for her opportunity to escape.

They were a few miles from the station when she got the chance she'd been praying for. Just as they crested the overpass that led to one of the busiest intersections of Lafayette, she saw at least a quarter mile of brake lights ahead of them, clear down to the intersection.

Benji swore when he saw the bottle necked traffic due to the accident at the light. He slammed on his brakes and grabbed the wheel with both hands to avoid hitting the car in front of him.

Tiffany took a deep breath and gripped the letter opener tightly in her right hand. Channeling every ounce of strength she had, she jabbed the opener just above Benji's right knee where she knew it would do the most damage.

His furious, pain-filled roar resounded throughout the truck a second before he dropped the gun. It hit the truck's floor board, sliding over to the passenger side. Tiffany lunged for the door and hit the unlock button. She threw it open and slid out, grabbing the pistol in one fluid movement before she hit the pavement running.

Panic closed in on Red as he watched Benji's truck approach the crest of the overpass. They weren't more than thirty car lengths behind them and the three passengers of the Jeep had been keeping a close eye on the pick-up with binoculars. "Can't we drive any faster?" he groaned. "We're about to lose sight of them." He caught Mike's reflection in the rearview mirror.

"Just hold on, Red. He doesn't know it yet, but the intersection ahead of him is gridlocked because of a wreck. We can use the opportunity to get closer but we'll have to be careful with all these people around." Just as he predicted, as soon as the truck disappeared behind the overpass, vehicles behind it began hitting their brake lights. The instant traffic stopped around them, the officers exited their vehicles and began to run up between the lanes of traffic toward the crest.

Red got out and stood next to Mike and the two accompanying officers. He strained his eyes at something up ahead. "What the hell is that?" He pointed in the direction of the overpass then raised his binoculars to focus on the sight. It only took a second before he realized what he was seeing. "It's Doc!" Before the other officers could stop him, Red bolted toward Tiffany, who looked like she was trying to break her own personal record for speed. Recognition dawned on her face as he approached.

Benji howled with equal parts of psychopathic rage and pain as he pulled the letter opener out of his knee. *I'll kill that bitch for this.* He hobbled out of the truck then pulled his rifle with the scope out from under the seat. He ignored the people in the cars around him, several on their phones. Let them call the cops. By the time they got here it would be finished. He was ready to die to avenge his brother's death, as long as McAllister's whore died too.

He hobbled to the top of the overpass with some difficulty, cursing her the entire time. He switched off the loaded rifle's safety, and brought it to his shoulder. Just as he'd brought her into focus, Red reached her. He swore again when Red grabbed her hand and pull her in front of him as they headed the opposite direction.

"That's okay, Red. This son of a bitch is powerful enough to go right through the both of you. Two for the price of one." He applied smooth and steady pressure on the trigger until the shot fired.

The captain raised his binoculars. "Do you have a clear shot, Hobbs?"

"I will as soon as McAllister and his lady get out of my way."

Red had already reached Tiffany, pulled her in front of him as they both ran back to the Cherokee. They passed at least a half dozen officers positioned along the roadway at regular intervals to insure that no passengers exited their cars.

"Hobbs, you got it?" the chief asked.

"Yes sir."

"Take it."

Ken Hobbs fired just as the couple dove inside the Jeep. The single shot explosion filled the air and Benjamin Bradford crumbled to the ground before pulling his own trigger. "It's done."

The captain lowered his binoculars. "Good job. Let's go pick him up and see what we can do about this FUBAR of a traffic situation."

Red and Tiffany returned to the station twenty minutes after the shooting. As they entered the precinct's central office, Vivienne threw her arms around Tiffany.

"Please tell me he didn't hurt you. Sweetie, you risked your life for me."

"I'm okay, Vivienne. Did he hurt you when he knocked you down?" She looked down at Vivienne's scuffed slacks.

"I'm fine! I felt so helpless watching him take you away like that." She began to cry as she placed her hand softly on Tiffany's curls.

"It's all over with and he can't hurt us anymore."

"Is he . . ."

Red and Tiffany both nodded.

She covered her mouth with one hand. "I can't believe something like this happened to one of *my* children."

Red hugged both women tightly. He caught a slight movement in the doorway and grinned. "Mom, where's dad, anyway?"

Vivienne pushed away from her son. "Your father's at home, fighting the flu. He wanted to come with me, but he was burning up. I had to sneak out while he was in the bathroom." She covered her eyes with one hand and groaned. "He'll be furious with me. After this, I'll *never* be able to win an argument with him again."

"You didn't win that one, Vivi. You cheated."

Vivi jumped at the sound of her husband's deep baritone. She turned to see Pete McAllister's massive bulk filling the doorway.

"It just took me awhile to get cleaned up to get here."

Vivienne rushed into her husband's bear hug.

"You should have waited for me, hon," Pete scolded.

"I know, but you've been so sick." Vivienne touched her husband's face then reached up to feel his forehead. "You've still got a fever, Pete."

He pulled out a bottle of aspirin and downed two tablets with a cup of water from the cooler. "Satisfied?"

Vivienne smiled at him and nodded. "Melissa called me a few minutes ago. She said one of the local networks had a helicopter view out there because of that accident and they preempted regular programming to show the entire thing. She wants a 'family gathering' at her place to make sure everyone's okay. They live in a subdivision across town, Tiffany, but it's on your way back to I-10."

"Let me find out what we need to do before we can leave." Red left in search of someone in charge. He returned in less than a minute, accompanied by an officer. "Doc, you need to give your statement to Officer Tate before we can go."

Tiffany held up one finger to the officer. "I need a minute first," she explained before pulling Red off to the side for a private consult.

"Hey, McAllister," she said, placing her hands around the back of his neck and beaming up at him. "You feel like getting married today?"

"Don't tease me, Doc. Not after I came so close to losing you."

"I'm not. Everything we need to seal the deal is in my car. Think you can find us a judge that can take care of what we need to do to get this done before we leave Lafayette?"

"Are you serious? After everything you've been through today?"

She nodded. "I can't wait to be Mrs. Scott McAllister. Our birth certificates are in the glove compartment of my car. Here's my set of keys. There's a Scala design I'm dying to wear and a sexy as hell suit for you with all the trimmings. You think you can handle this?"

Red beamed at her. "You bet your beautiful ass I can. I know just who to call." He wrapped her in his arms for a mutually mind blowing kiss as the station erupted in a chorus of 'atta-boys', cat calls, and whistles.

Chapter Sixteen

The ceremony had been short and simple, starting with a quick run to the courthouse for a waiver from a judge who was a close friend of Red's, as well as an agreement to perform the ceremony. Two hours later, they faced each other on Melissa's back patio, surrounded by Red's family, as well as Jackson and Giselle.

Tiffany had glowed with happiness in the Scala gown he'd chosen for her. Red, dressed in Armani, beamed with pride as he stood before friends and family and vowed to love, honor, and cherish her until death. They'd stayed for a little over an hour to visit with everyone before the need to be alone overwhelmed them both. They'd said their goodbyes and left for the ranch, each driving their own vehicle.

Red closed and locked the door behind him and turned to his new wife, starved for her touch after being separated during the hour long drive home. "Oh God, come here." He pulled her into his arms for a scorching kiss. She jerked frantically at the buttons of his shirt, finally tore the damn thing off, baring his chest to her palms. He pulled her sweater from her in one fluid motion, his fingers flying to the button of her jeans. They stumbled down the hallway to the master bedroom, leaving a trail of discarded clothing. Gloriously naked, they fell into Red's king size bed.

Within seconds, Tiffany had him flat on his back and had straddled him. "I need you. *Now.*" Her low, demanding growl turned to a gasp as he entered her quickly. She rode him fast and hard with a sense of desperate, needy recklessness. As Tiffany neared her moment of release, she threw her head back, but bit back anything more than a whimper.

"No, Doc . . . Hell, no." Red tangled his hands in her hair and pulled her face down to his. "Don't hold out on me. I want to hear you."

She needed no other encouragement to release the sharp cries she'd been holding back from him. She finished, and Red bellowed with his own release, as though to prove his point.

He rolled them both onto his side without releasing her. Red lay there, holding his wife, and waiting for his rhythm to return to normal.

Tiffany wiped at a stray tear, then another, until they were coming non-stop.

Red recognized a simple release of stress when he saw one. He kissed her tears away, comforting her, speaking in low, soothing tones until she could speak.

She sniffed and snuggled closer to him. "I'm so relieved it's all over."

"I know, Babe. I know." He held her, one hand moving softly in her hair, the other clutched around her back and shoulders. Her breathing evened out.

He continued to hold her as she slept, and eventually, he joined her.

Red waited until Tiffany stepped into the shower that evening before dialing he'd acquired from his new brother-in-law. Within seconds, a deep voice barked out a greeting.

"Daniel LeBlanc here."

"Mr. LeBlanc, this is Scott McAllister. I wonder if you have a few minutes to speak to me, Sir."

"Scott McAllister. The same man someone tried to set up for arson and murder? The man I just saw on the evening news running to my daughter on an overpass in Lafayette—*that* Scott McAllister?"

"Yes Sir, the one and the same."

"I'd be more upset about this call if my son hadn't already been singing your praises to me, and why the hell hasn't Tiffany been answering her phone?"

"Well, I wasn't aware Drake had done that, Sir, but tell him thanks for me when you see him next. As for Tiffany's phone, she lost it at some point during the incident."

"Hmm," he grunted. "Drake had his P.I. check you out, you know. If he hadn't, I would have."

"Not surprising. I had my own check out the both of you, also."

"How did that bouncer get past your investigator, Mr. McAllister?"

"He was half-brother to a man I fired two years ago—same mother, different fathers, different last names, no family resemblance. He was the perfect employee for two years, and extremely patient."

"I see. I assume you called for a reason. Is my daughter all right?"

"She's fine, but I did call for a reason. I was wondering if you had a little time in your schedule to meet with me tomorrow."

"Just you, or will Tiffany be accompanying you?"

"Just me; I thought I'd speak to you man to man before dragging her into this. She's been hurt enough by you and your wife. I don't want it happening again."

"Excuse me, boy? Just who the hell do you think you are?"

"I'm a thirty-eight year old man, Sir, so *don't* call me boy. I'm her husband, and I'll do whatever I can to keep her from being hurt."

"Her husband!" Daniel bellowed. "What the hell are you talking about?"

"We got married this afternoon in Lafayette."

"Why weren't we told about this?"

"Ask Tiffany. We'd planned to do it several days ago and it fell through. She'd wanted Drake there, but not you or her mother."

"Well, why the hell not?" Daniel sounded more perturbed by the second.

"I don't know, Sir, but she's been your daughter for thirty six years. I bet if you try hard enough, you could think of several reasons."

Red waited through an awkward silence before taking control of the conversation again. "Okay, let's start off with the most recent and work our way back, shall we?" He cleared his throat and began. "How about the fact that you both tried to force her to marry a man she didn't love, and who obviously had mistreated her for five long years? Your wife went so far as telling her she'd be responsible for making her a social outcast." He heard Daniel's long drawn out sigh.

"Monica always did have a flair for drama."

"Tiffany feels like you both tried to sell her to the highest bidder to bring money into the family."

"That's ludicrous—we don't need any more money."

Red stared at the phone in disbelief. "Sir, excuse me for asking, but do you and your wife ever communicate at all?"

"Not if I can help it."

Red thought he was beginning to see the problem. "How long has it been like this between you two?"

"At least thirty years."

"My God," he murmured in disbelief. "Are you aware that you didn't pay for Tiffany's college education?"

"That's ridiculous!" Daniel exploded. "Tiffany went to a very fine college—L.S.U. is my old alma mater, as a matter of fact."

"Yes, but did you know that you didn't *pay* for it? Her school counselor had to help her fill out applications for academic scholarships. *Someone* told her that if she didn't go to law school, you wouldn't pay for it. She had to hold down jobs all through college and med school to make ends meet, and she still graduated at the top of her class."

"You're a fool if you think I'd let something like that happen to one of my children."

"It *happened*, sir. So who's the fool here, me or you?"

"You can't be serious."

"Don't take my word for it, Mr. LeBlanc. Ask Drake, or better yet, ask Tiffany."

"How could I not know that?" Daniel asked, obviously in shock.

Red replied in a cold, dry tone. "I don't know. How could you not know that your daughter has been neglected all her life by her own parents?"

He heard a deep sigh on the other end of the phone. "Well, it seems as though I've got a lot to be held accountable for. I've made a lot of mistakes in my life but the biggest one, by far, was marrying Monica Reed. For the past thirty-eight years, she's made my life a living hell."

Red's jaw worked in agitation. "You could have made a difference in their lives, you know. You could have shown them a little affection instead of letting the hired help provide the only love they ever saw at home."

"I always assumed Monica took care of that. I should have known."

"Yes sir, you should have," Red growled in anger.

Daniel cleared his throat noisily. "It's obvious that we do indeed need to talk, Mr. McAllister. I admire you for wanting to talk man to man. I'll make time to see you at any point during the day tomorrow."

"That's fine, sir. Tiffany has decided to go into the hospital tomorrow, so I won't leave until after she does. I'll be there around ten. Oh, and Tiffany doesn't know about this."

"I'll be waiting for you. Do you want this to be just you and me, or would you like to meet with her mother, also?"

Red paced the floor with his phone to his ear. "I'll leave that up to you. It doesn't matter to me one way or the other."

"You know, my son is quitting the law firm and opening his own practice in Lake Coburn. Is any of that your doing?"

"No sir, I believe he wants to be close to his sister."

"I believe it's more than that."

"It may well be, but I assure you, I had nothing to do with it. You've had over three decades with both of your children, Mr. LeBlanc. If they don't feel any kind of bond to you by now, you and your wife have no one to blame but yourselves."

Daniel cleared his throat uneasily. "I suppose you're right about that."

"You can reach me at this number. You let me know if you want to meet at your home tomorrow or your office—either is fine with me," Red told him.

"I'll call you after I've spoken to my *wife*," Daniel sneered before they ended the call.

By the time Tiffany got out of the shower Red was showered, dressed and waiting for her. She walked into the kitchen dressed in comfortable jeans and a dark green sweater. She reached into the cabinet for a glass.

"You know, babe, if you want to remodel this place, we can do that. Or even sell it. Maybe you'd like to build one day?"

She looked horrified at the last suggestion. "Are you kidding? I love it here. When I came out here for Jackson and Giselle's wedding, I fell in love with the place. My being able to come home to this ranch *and* you...well, that's damn near perfection."

"Only *near* perfection?" he asked, pulling her into his arms. "What's missing?"

She reached her arms up around his neck and pulled him close for a kiss. "Babies, Mr. McAllister. Lots and lots of babies."

Chapter Seventeen

Red was halfway to his destination the next day when Daniel LeBlanc called to tell him to meet him at his office in downtown Houston. He arrived on time and walked confidently into the high rise reception area of the law firm at ten a.m. sharp.

A secretary showed him into Daniel LeBlanc's plush inner office and he stood, calm and straight backed as the large man behind the desk rose and walked over to meet him. They surveyed each other carefully; the older man in his western cut business suit, and Red, cool and confidant in a pair of dark blue jeans, long sleeve shirt, tie, and sport coat.

"You're taller than I thought you'd be, sir," Red told his new father-in-law.

"I guess I could say the same for you, young man."

"I see where Tiffany and Drake get their brown eyes and curly hair," Red told the man who looked to be about the same height and build as his father.

They both reached out their hands at the same time and clasped in a firm hand shake. "Daniel LeBlanc, it's nice to meet you."

Red cocked his head slightly. "Scott McAllister, Sir. That remains to be seen."

Daniel jerked back in surprise. "You shoot straight from the hip, don't you, Son?"

Red nodded. "Yes Sir, I do. The fact of the matter is that your daughter is far too important to me not to take this seriously. I won't allow her to be hurt by you or your wife anymore. I'm here to tell you that if you have any intentions whatsoever of trying to interfere in our marriage, she will cut you out of her life like the two of you never existed. Tiffany is happy with me, and my parents already love her like a daughter. I have seven siblings who adore her like another sister. I promise you, Sir, if you and your wife interfere, you won't be missed."

Red shook his head before continuing. "Now, personally, I'd prefer not to see that happen. I've always imagined that I'd have a good relationship with my in-laws, but I can live without it if she doesn't want anything to do with you."

His father-in-law listened quietly while Red laid out the ground rules regarding Tiffany.

Once he'd finished speaking, the older man nodded. "Drake's right, Tiffany's chosen well by you. My son is an excellent judge of character."

"If you ask me, I'd say your daughter is."

Daniel nodded. "Point taken, Scott. I know this isn't a good excuse, but I grew up in a family with no sisters and a hard man for a father. He was hard on me and my brothers, and a real son of a bitch to our mom. When I got married, I didn't know how to relate to women—either wives or daughters."

"Was it arranged by your parents?" Red asked, his tone slightly more bitter than he intended.

Daniel shook his head vehemently. "Not by *my* parents. I came from working class people. I did find out later that Monica's parents pushed her to marry me. I'd made my fortune early in the oil fields, before attending law school. Monica's mother, like her mother before her, always emphasized the importance of marrying into money. I thought we would grow to love each other over the years." He pointed for Red to sit in the leather chair and made his way back behind his desk. "Not since then have I been so monumentally wrong," he said, shaking his head. "It didn't take me long to figure out what a cold hearted bitch I'd married. By then Tiffany and Drake were born, and my wife said I could do whatever I wanted to on the side, but that if I divorced her she'd take me to the cleaners. I worked too damned hard for my money to lose it to her and her money grubbing mother. The women in that family can be terrifying, if you want to know the truth."

"That's still no excuse for you neglecting your children."

"Look, I told you, I had no idea how to relate to a daughter. Monica hired nannies to raise Tiffany, and believe me, some of them were harsh. The one time I did put my foot down was when I went over Monica's head and hired Melinda Dawson. I dared my wife to fire her."

Red nodded in quiet approval. "Tiffany loves Melinda. She said she's the nearest thing to a mother they ever had."

"I know that. My mom recommended her because she knew she would be good to them. Monica hated Melinda because she was my mom's choice, and mine. After a while, my wife just distanced herself completely from them. I, like a fool, trusted her to do what was best for them. That's my shame."

"Have you spoken to your wife about any of this yet?"

The older man clenched his jaw. "No. I wanted to cool down awhile before seeing her, and I decided I wanted to meet you first. But you can bet your ass I will. I'm not happy about that college thing. Tiffany never complained."

"Who would she have gone to, sir? The nanny?"

"If she'd come to me I'd have corrected the situation, you know. I'd have made sure she went to whatever college she wanted to attend."

"I'm sure if she felt that was an option she'd have done so. Eighteen years of indifference has got to be difficult to overcome."

Daniel sighed in defeat. "You're right, of course."

Red decided to cut him some slack. "She ended up where she wanted to be and did what she wanted to do. I'm proud she did it all on her own."

"Just as you did," Daniel told him.

"I had both academic and sports scholarships for grades and baseball, but my parents made sure that none of us had to work through school. They thought it was important we were able to concentrate on school work. It must have been difficult for Tiffany. She made it through medical school on student loans and odd jobs."

Daniel shook his head in exasperation. "I'm sorry as hell for that, I really am. But, I've always been proud that she chose to go to LSU. I thought maybe she went because she knew I'd gone there. Now I find out that she really didn't have a choice at all, did she?"

"That's one choice she'll never regret, if it's any consolation. She told me once she bleeds LSU purple and gold."

Daniel's face broke out in a broad smile. "I hear she's the best orthopedic surgeon around."

Red puffed up with pride. "She is, but I need to know, sir, are you going to interfere in our marriage?"

Daniel shook his head. "I wouldn't dare. I truly hope she can find the happiness she never had in our house."

"Then, call me Scott, please. Or Red, if you prefer. All my friends call me Red."

Daniel guffawed and slapped him on the back. "I like you, Red. Tell me, how's my daughter doing since her escape yesterday?"

"She's fine. She spent enough time in the truck with that lunatic to know she had to get out of there as quickly as possible. Do you know that she convinced him to take her instead of my mother?"

"No! How did that happen?"

Red related the entire story to him and watched as Daniel had to sit down at one point. It almost seemed as if he was going to be sick.

"My God, she could have been killed."

"She could have, yes."

Daniel's eyes narrowed. "Did he die quickly?"

Red nodded. "My dad said too quickly, and it was a much kinder fate than he would have chosen for him, but it's done, none the less."

"I have to agree with your father on that one. Where is Tiffany right now?"

"She's at the hospital, working. She had asked for some time off, but now that everything is all cleared up, she decided to go back. She would prefer to take some time off for our honeymoon. By the way, we'll be having our marriage blessed on the day after Christmas and will have a big reception at my new club in Lake Coburn. I'll leave it up to you as to whether or not you'll attend. We don't know the details, but I'll make sure to send an invitation to your home."

"Send it to my office or my country home. If you send it to my wife's home in Houston, I'm sure I'd never see it."

"I'll send it to your office then." Red stood up to leave and suddenly remembered something. He reached into his pocket and pulled out a small flash drive. "I brought this for you."

"What the hell is that?" the elder man asked.

"This contains a file showing my assets. I wanted to prove to you that I can be a good provider to Tiffany. I can download this to any computer so that you can look at it at your convenience. Or you can keep it."

Daniel grimaced and shook his head. "I wouldn't know what to do with that. They give me a new computer every year but damned if I can do much with them."

Red laughed. "You sound just like my dad. Maybe I could print out the report for you?"

"If you feel it's necessary. I already know everything I need to know about you."

Red shook his head and sat down at the man's computer. He transferred the files and printed them out. Five minutes later, he handed him the stack of neatly printed sheets.

"Now, that's more like it," Daniel told him. "Drake keeps telling me I need to learn how to work that damn thing but I'm too old to start learning anything new."

"You're never too old to learn."

Daniel smiled and nodded. "Red, is there anything I can do for the wedding? It's traditionally the bride's parents who pay for everything, isn't it?"

"Don't worry about that, sir, I've got it under control."

"How about the honeymoon? Have you two planned anything, yet?"

"No sir, we haven't had a chance to think about it yet."

"Why don't you let me pay for it? It would mean a lot to me if you did. You two can go anywhere in the world. I'd pay first class for everything."

"We don't need your money, Sir. It might be a good idea if you called her first before offering. I didn't tell her I was coming here today, but regardless of her answer, I thank you for the offer." He walked to the doorway. "I've got a club opening coming up, and I've been neglecting it." He gripped the older man's hand firmly. "It turned out to be nice meeting you, after all, Sir."

Daniel's face broke out in a wide grin. "Thank you, Red. That means a lot."

Tiffany walked in around five fifteen that afternoon. She dropped her bag at the door and walked straight into Red's waiting arms.

"Mm, it feels good to hold you," he groaned, holding his wife close while wondering how to broach the subject of this morning's visit.

"It feels good coming home to you," she said, reaching up to kiss him.

"Makes me happy hearing you say that, Babe. Are you hungry?"

"Starving. What'cha cooking?"

"Chicken gumbo."

"Perfect weather for it, the temp is dropping fast out there."

"I just got home around four. It won't be done for another hour or so. Can you wait that long?"

She nibbled on his earlobe. "I can think of something to pass the time while we wait."

He grinned and turned to lead her to the bedroom.

Forty-five satisfying minutes later, Tiffany lay curled up against her husband, one ankle wrapped possessively around his leg. "I tried calling you to meet me for lunch today, but you never answered. Was your phone turned off?"

"Yeah, I was in the middle of something." He cleared his throat. "I went to see your father today." Her reaction was a wall of icy silence as she pulled away from him.

"Let me explain."

She turned on him. "*Why* would you do that without talking to me about it first?" Her tone was as stiff and unwelcoming as her posture.

"I wanted to get it out of the way without concerning you with it."

"Concerning me? You don't think you talking to *my* father is my concern?" She climbed out of the bed, wrapping herself in her robe and looking for her slippers.

"Doc, what's the problem?"

"I don't like anyone sneaking around behind my back, Red. If I wanted that I could have stayed with Tanner."

"Babe, I told you I wanted to contact him."

Tiffany pulled a set of clothes from the tall boy chest of drawers, clothes she'd just unpacked the night before. "And I told you I didn't want him to be a part of my life anymore." She swung around to face Red. "Why the hell would you do this now?"

Red swung his legs over the bed and sat up. "Don't you want to know what he had to say?"

"I don't even want to hear what you have to say," she said, her tone flat and hard.

The slam of the bathroom door echoed throughout the spacious room. Still somewhat dazed from her actions, Red stared in shock at the closed door. The shower started and he forced himself to rise from the bed, wondering how the hell to fix this situation he'd gotten himself into. He grabbed his clothes, and stopped to stare at his reflection in the mirror. "You were warned, dumb ass, but you didn't listen."

Tension, thick and heavy, pressed down on Tiffany's chest as she tried to eat her supper. Red sat across from her at the snack bar with a bowl of gumbo in front of him. He pushed the spoon around, looking like he had no more of an appetite than she did. Married a little over twenty-four hours, and they'd already had their first argument. She would have expected this with Tanner but sure as hell not Red. She pulled her gaze away quickly as Red looked up.

"How's the gumbo?" he asked.

"Good."

"Need anything? More tea?"

"No."

"Doc, I'm sorry."

"You should be."

"I thought I was help—"

"I didn't ask for your help," she blurted, whipping around to face him. "I specifically told you I didn't want anything to do with him. Didn't I?"

Red nodded. "You did. I'm an ass."

"You won't get any arguments from me," she said, with an adamant shake of her curls. Tiffany's mobile phone rang and she cursed lowly while reading the caller I.D. "Great. Just. Flipping. Great." She pushed her stool back from the counter and put her phone to her ear, all the while glaring at Red. Taking a deep breath, she braced herself, both mentally and physically, before answering. "Hello Father."

"Hello, Tiffany. How are you?"

"I'm fine." She didn't bother removing the iciness from her tone.

"Do you have time to talk?"

"I'm in the middle of supper."

"Oh, I'm sorry. I'll call back."

"No, we may as well get this over with. I seem to have lost my appetite, anyway."

"Aw—hell—"

"Talk, Dad. I have things to do." When she began to load the dishwasher, Red placed his hands on her shoulders and attempted to guide her gently toward the hallway, presumably to the master bedroom. She pulled away angrily and sat instead at the island, giving him a brusque shake of her head as he shrugged, then took over cleaning the kitchen.

The ensuing phone silence grew heavier. It seemed neither she nor her father knew what to say next.

Daniel LeBlanc took a deep breath and released it slowly. "I'm sure your husband told you he came to visit me today."

"Yes, he did. Not terribly long ago, actually."

"He's a fine man. You've chosen well for yourself."

"He can be, when he listens." She saw the obvious stiffening of Red's shoulders at her comment.

"Have I called at a bad time?"

"Honestly, there will never be a good time, so shoot. Why the call?" Her father took yet another deep breath. Funny, he almost sounded terrified.

"Tiffany, I'm sorry for any part I've played in trying to get you to marry Tanner. That was wrong of us, I know that now. I spoke to your mother today and told her she's not to interfere in your marriage, and you have my promise that I won't either."

"Thank you." *If there's even a marriage after tonight.*

"I also spoke to her about a few other things, like her refusing to pay your college tuition. I swear to you, I had no idea. I was a fool for leaving the raising of you and Drake to her. I always assumed she was doing what was best for both of you. I never dreamed she would do such a thing."

Tiffany froze at his confession, anger suffusing her mind and body. "Are you trying to make me believe you had nothing to do with that?"

"I'm not making excuses, I know I dropped the ball and I know I have some heavy-duty atoning to do. It's my fault that you didn't feel comfortable enough to come to me. Please believe me when I tell you that I am so terribly sorry."

"Wait. Are you saying you didn't know?"

"It's God's honest truth, Tiffany. Whether or not you believe me is the issue."

She remained silent long enough for him to ask if she was still on the line.

"Yes, I'm still here." She bit her lower lip as Red turned in an agonizingly slow movement to lean against the sink and cross his arms. "How could you not know that?" Her gaze locked on Red's, trying to hold back tears that threatened.

"I had a law firm to run, Tiffany. I left the family finances to your mother, who probably paid some accountant to do them for her. Honestly, I assumed you chose LSU because you knew I'd gone there. I was proud you were going to my alma mater. Now I see how stupid I was to assume that."

"I—I didn't find out until years later that you went to LSU," she turned her back to Red, biting back tears. Her new husband walked up behind her and wrapped his arms loosely around her waist. She didn't pull away, almost hated the fact that she took strength from his presence. "I guess I have no choice but to believe you. It doesn't matter anyway, it's done."

"It matters plenty, Tiffany. Is there anything I can do now to make up for it?"

"No."

"I've told Red that I'd like to pay for your honeymoon if that's okay. Anywhere in the world the two of you would like to go—all expenses paid and first-class everything."

Tiffany's jaw clenched at her father's offer. Her first instinct was to hang up on him, but she forced herself to be civil. "Red and I both make plenty of money. We don't need you to pay for anything."

"I know that Tiff, I just wanted to do something. I'd really like to do this for you."

Stiffening, she pulled out of Red's embrace to pace the kitchen floor. Tiffany caught her husband's eye, could tell by his grim expression that he was waiting for the explosion. She continued to pace silently, seething inside, until her father asked again if she was on the phone.

"Yes, I'm still here. I'm just thinking about your offer."

"I hope you accept."

She stopped pacing and her voice rose sharply. "Do you think that would make everything better?"

"Well, no—but I was hop—"

"Surely, Dad—you can't possibly think that after thirty-six years you can buy me off like I'm one of your business acquisitions."

"No Honey, it's not like tha—"

"Don't call me Honey!" Tiffany's voice shook with anger. "You don't know me well enough to call me by any pet names."

"I—I'm sorry Tiffany. You're my daughter and I didn't mean to insult you."

"But you did! You *do* insult me by thinking I would even consider taking a dime from you after all these years! You insult me by thinking you can waltz back into my life after not giving a damn all this time. You and that woman who were both supposed to be caring for me and Drake. You ignored us the entire time we lived in that house and now you want to suddenly make it right? It doesn't work that way, and I'll be damned if I'm going to let you off that easily!"

She caught Red's eye again, could see him swell with pride for her. He had no idea how difficult it was for her to stand up for herself against her father. Her new husband was clueless to the fact that the only reason she could now was because of his strength and support, whether or not she liked that fact. Even if she didn't like it, she had to admit it was the truth.

"Tiffany—I—I am so deeply sorry," Daniel sputtered. "That was not my intention at all. I have no excuse. I've been a lousy father and I know it's late to just be learning this dad thing, but I sure would be grateful to you if you'd let me have a shot at it. I want to change for you and Drake. I want to be a better man. Please, give me the chance to do that."

Tiffany turned her back on Red, finding it more difficult to be angry with him beaming down at her like she'd just won best in show. "I don't know, Dad. If you suck at it, it won't be good. I don't think I need that kind of aggravation in my life." She whipped around to cast a narrow-eyed glare at Red. "Believe me, I have enough here at home." Her husband had the good sense to give her a nod of concession without cracking a grin. She frowned at the sound of her father's heavy sigh of frustration, thinking this was it. He'd give up and hang up, in that order and she'd never hear from him again.

"I'm obviously not good at making myself understood over the phone. Would you mind if I paid you a visit? I could go over this weekend. Please, I sincerely want to change."

Tiffany's legs nearly buckled at his offer. She pivoted back and forth a few times, trying to comprehend what she was hearing from him, before stopping. "Look, I'm warning you now—unless you intend to keep up this new relationship you seem to want with me, don't bother putting us through this. I don't want to put forth an effort on someone who's going to forget about us as soon as he's out of range. I want our children to know their grandparents, but if you neglect them like you did Drake and me, I'll make sure you never see them. They'll already have one set of wonderful grandparents in Gardiner, and they won't miss you. Do you understand what I'm saying?"

"I do, and I don't blame you one bit. I deserve everything you throw at me and I understand that I've got a lot to live up to next to your new in-laws. They must be wonderful people to have raised a son like Red."

"Vivi and Mr. Pete are wonderful. They're like the parents I never had."

She couldn't help but smile when Red snorted and muttered a low "burn" comment from behind her.

Daniel groaned. "I know I deserved that, both your mother and I do, but it's still difficult to hear it. So, can we meet somewhere to talk in person?" He suddenly sounded much older and completely exhausted.

Tiffany pulled away and paced the floor for several moments thinking about his request. Finally she spoke. "You can come over on Sunday."

"Sunday is fine. I could take you both to lunch."

"You can come as early as you want but be here no later than eleven a.m. We'll cook and eat here. The Saints will play at noon so you're welcomed to stay and watch the game with us."

"I'm an early riser, so I can leave here by six thirty and be there by nine. Is that okay?"

"That's fine. Do you need the address?"

"I've got it. Thank you, Tiffany, I won't disappoint you."

"If you do, you won't get another chance." Her voice cracked slightly with emotion.

"I won't—I promise."

"We'll see, Dad." She ended the call and stood staring out the window into the darkness. The pane reflected her husband's image as he walked up behind her. She felt his arms slip around her waist.

"Are you okay?"

She nodded and wiped the barest trace of moisture from her eyes. "Did he tell you he wasn't aware he hadn't paid for my tuition?"

"That's what he said. Apparently your parents haven't communicated with each other for some time. Who was it that said if you didn't go to law school, he wouldn't pay?"

Unfortunately, Tiffany could recall the conversation, nearly word for word. God knows she'd replayed it enough times in her mind, holding down sometimes two jobs during college. "Mother told me. I never discussed anything with my father." She turned to face him. "What else do you know about my father that I don't?" she asked, still a little perturbed at him for going against her wishes.

He backed off, raising his hands as a barrier between them. "I'm not going to tell you a damn thing if you're going to use it against me for the next fifty years."

She took a step closer and poked her index finger into his chest several times to emphasize the severe repercussions of his actions. "If you. Don't tell me now, McAllister. There won't *be*. A next fifty years."

Tiffany sat at the snack bar next to her husband, still shocked at all he'd revealed to her. "So my father is the one responsible for hiring Melinda?"

"Yes, he and your paternal grandmother—and he dared your mother to fire her. He said she hated Melinda because of it."

"I knew she hated Melin, but mother hates everyone. I always wondered what kind of power Melin had over mother. If mother threatened her in any way, she seemed to take it with a grain of salt."

"Now you know she had your dad's support. Your nanny was the last link between you, your father, and your grandmother."

She shook her head. "I'm amazed that I never knew."

Red reached out to her but pulled his hands back when she put her hand up to stop him. "I have a feeling there's a lot you never knew," he said, his voice tinged with disappointment.

"Yeah, well whose fault is that? I don't trust him to do the right thing. He might start off okay, but I doubt he's got the stamina for the long haul."

"That may be, Doc, but you'll never know unless you give him a chance."

"Maybe." He cracked his knuckles nervously, with good reason, since he wasn't out of the woods yet. "And you. Do you have any idea how I feel about you going behind my back to set this up?"

He wiped his mouth and sat back in his chair, looking dejected. "I do now, but I swear I was only trying to help the situation."

"You interfered, and you kept something from me, Red. I can't have that."

He nodded. "I know that now, and I can promise you it won't happen again. You're right; I should have told you."

She twisted her lips and squinted in concentration. What was she supposed to do now? She'd never heard Tanner admit he was wrong in the five years they'd dated, and longer than that, if she counted their childhood squabbles.

"Doc. Forgive me. Please?" He pulled her gently to him.

She saw sincerity in his eyes, knew he meant it—for now, anyway. Was there a chance he was a man who actually learned from his mistakes, or would he eventually revert to a Tanner? Her heart told her to let it go, that he was nothing like her ex. But her mind—ah—her mind told her otherwise. She pulled out of his arms, determined to show him she wasn't a pushover for his blue eyes, soft words, and hard body. "Don't let it happen again, McAllister." She turned away from him. "I'm going to the room to call Drake."

"Hey," he said, grabbing one of her hands. "It won't, but I want you to know how proud I was of you for standing up to your father like that."

She paused, turning her head slightly toward him. "Tell me the truth, Red. Did I sound too bitchy with him?"

"You sounded like you wouldn't put up with any crap from him, and you shouldn't have to." He whistled and rubbed one side of his face. "Hell, I could even feel the sting of that slap again. I think he was very smart calling you first."

"I'm sure *you* had something to do with that."

He squeezed her hand tightly. "Maybe—But I sure as hell am proud of you, Doc."

She forced herself to turn away from the sexy as hell grin, not to mention those pheromones rolling off of him in waves. She'd have plenty of time to deal with him later. She walked toward the master bedroom, turning at the door to throw him one last look. He still watched her like a parched man ogling a glass of water. Yeah, she could definitely get some use out of that later tonight.

Tiffany threw herself on the massive bed and punched in the code for her brother's mobile.

"Hey Tiff," Drake answered.

"Hey, little bro. Dad is coming here Sunday to talk. I wondered if you wanted to come, too."

"Aw, hell no. I've already had that talk with him, it's your turn."

"When?"

"This morning. It seems my new brother-in-law paid him a visit. After he left, dad came into my office and got all sentimental on me. He apologized for not being there for us then asked me if it was true about your college tuition. It blows my mind that he didn't know about it. He asked if there was anything else that he needed to know before calling mother. He also asked if I thought you would be receptive to reconciliation."

"What did you tell him?"

"It was up to you. He asked mother for a divorce."

"He did?"

"Yes, he told her he'd hurt enough people because of her and it was time he started living his life the way he should have been all these years."

"He told you this?"

"No, she did. She called me to ask if I'd represent her."

Tiffany's jaw dropped in surprise. "You're joking, right?"

Drake chuckled. "I wish I were."

"What did you say?"

"Hell no! I'm not getting caught in the middle of that shit storm."

"Good for you."

"Even if I wanted to, I couldn't, but she doesn't need to know that. Tiff, did you know that dad's had the same mistress for twenty-eight years?"

"Really? Mother always implied he had a bevy of lovers."

"No, that was more her style than his all these years, it turns out. He's been with Leah Hanson forever. He bought a nice home for the two of them out in the country. She breaks horses and trains them. They keep a few for themselves out there. It's a nice little set up."

"Have you met her?"

"Several times over the years, but I don't know if she knew who I was. She's nice, but always seems a little sad."

"Did they have any children together?"

"No, I don't think she could. I think he wants to marry her. I don't know how he could stand being married to mother knowing how happy he was with Leah all those years."

"Everything revolved around money, Drake. He didn't want to lose his precious business."

"Well, Sis, he started with nothing."

"So did I. I would have given it all up for Red if it stood in the way of us being together."

"And he knows he's got a job ahead of him when it comes to you. Were you rough on him?"

"Red told me I was."

Drake's booming laugh carried over the lines. "Good, he'll respect you more for it. I'm wrapping up a few cases and by the beginning of next week I should be able to start looking for two places in Lake Coburn, one to live in and one to operate a business out of."

"You can stay in my rent house—it's mine until May. I wish you luck with everything, and I can't wait to have you nearby."

"Thanks, Sis. Is Christmas still set for your house?"

"Absolutely. Are you still coming?"

"You bet your ass I am. I guess you know what happened with your sister-in-law."

"Uh uh, I don't know a damn thing." She smiled as his deep chuckle filtered through.

"Yeah, sure you don't. I'll talk to you later. Love you sis."

Chapter Eighteen

The week flew by for the newly married couple. By the time they returned from eight o'clock mass on Sunday, Daniel LeBlanc was waiting in the driveway for them. Once Daniel and Red shook hands, Tiffany and her father shared several tension filled moments of silence. Red couldn't help but hold his breath when her dad reached out to touch Tiffany's shoulder length curls. He saw his wife's barely noticeable flinch, even if Daniel didn't. It made him want to wrap his arms around her. But he didn't. She had to do this on her own terms, even if he'd been the one to set things in motion.

"I haven't seen your hair like this for years. You look just like you did in high school." He smiled down at her and shook his head. "My God, I'd forgotten how much you resembled your grandmother." At Tiffany's frown, he began to explain further. "You look like *my* mom—not that deplorable woman who gave birth to your mother."

"She must have died before I was born, I'm sure I've never met her." Her father's laughter rang out, sounding unfamiliar—nearly alien to her ears.

"Sure you did. She died when you were a little over a year old, but you two were very close during that time. I've got pictures of you together somewhere—if your mother didn't destroy them. I'll try to find some for you," he said, as Red ushered them both inside.

Daniel's smile broadened as he surveyed their surroundings. "This is a beautiful place you've got here. I've always loved log cabins."

"It's comfortable," Red told him.

"I noticed the barns and stables earlier. No horses?"

"No, the previous owner had quite a menagerie of animals. I only moved in here from Lafayette about a month ago. We had a horse when I was young that I rode mostly to work my uncle's cattle, but we've already discussed buying a couple once we get the chance to breathe. We're looking forward to riding together."

Daniel nodded, smiling down at Tiffany. "From what I can remember, you handled yourself pretty well on the back of a horse."

"That's right, both Drake and I rode," Tiffany said. "We did anything we could to get out of that house every day for a while. To tell you the truth, I'm surprised you were even aware of that." She made her way to the kitchen to start a fresh pot of coffee.

Red passed his father in law a look of apprehension. "I hope you weren't expecting to waltz in here to an easy fix. This could take some time, as well as commitment."

"I heard she wasn't pleased that you called me."

"No, she wasn't—and I'm *still* sensing a hint of reservation, like sometimes she wonders if she made a mistake in marrying me." He nudged his father in law. "You'd better be serious about this, because I sure as hell don't want to lose her because of it."

Daniel stared after his daughter. "If I wasn't serious, I wouldn't be here." He shook his head. "She's really lovely with her hair that way."

"She's always been beautiful to me, but I have to admit, I love it like this." Red watched his wife move comfortably around the kitchen until he heard Daniel clear his throat. He turned, somewhat surprised to see the older man wearing an unexpectedly tender expression.

"Do you really love her, Red?"

He nodded. "I can't imagine my life without her."

Daniel's face split in a wide grin. "That's excellent," he said, before returning his gaze to his daughter.

"Do *you* love her, Sir?" Red asked him.

"I sure do."

"Then it shouldn't be that difficult to find a way to show her. That's all she's ever wanted from either of her parents."

"Coffee will be ready in a few minutes," Tiffany announced as the two men joined her in the kitchen.

"Coffee sounds good," Daniel said.

Tiffany got three mugs down from the cabinet. "Have you eaten breakfast?"

"Yes, I have."

"I hope you eat chicken. I'm roasting a hen for lunch." She turned back to gauge his reaction.

"The entire bird?" His eyes gleamed with delight. "I eat a lot of baked or broiled poultry, but I'm not allowed to eat anything but the breast. Ugh, I *hate* white meat."

"It's too dry," Tiffany interjected, before recalling she was supposed to be making him work for today.

"Finally, someone who agrees with me! Would it be rude to call dibs on a big, juicy leg quarter?"

Tiffany frowned at her father. "I guess that would depend on *why* you're not allowed to eat anything but the breast."

He looked down, scuffing the heel of one expensive western boot on the floor tile. "My doctor says I need to lower my cholesterol level and my blood pressure."

"Do you get regular check-ups?" she asked.

"Every six months, if not more."

"Have you had a colonoscopy and a PSA test done?"

"Several times already, and my results are always good."

Tiffany nodded, satisfied with his answer.

"Does this mean I can have that leg quarter?"

She pursed her lips. "We'll see."

"If it helps, I've just come up with a sure fire way to lower my blood pressure," he volunteered.

Tiffany placed the carafe of coffee in front of her father as they seated themselves around the island. "Oh yeah? How's that?" She pushed a mug toward him.

Daniel poured himself a cup of the steaming brew and took a sip. "Mm...good, strong coffee," he said, adjusting his position on the bar stool. "I've asked your mother for a divorce. I don't know if you're aware of this, but I've been in a relationship with another woman for twenty-eight years. I realize now how unfair I've been to all of you. If I'd divorced Monica years ago, I could have taken you and Drake to live with Leah and me." He took another sip of coffee and set the mug down on the granite countertop. "Your mother would have taken me to the bank, of course, so we wouldn't have been as well off, but we could have been a family. Leah couldn't have children of her own, but she would have been a wonderful mother to you and Drake. More importantly, I would have been a better father to the two of you. I was such a fool."

"Mother would have put up a fight for the check book, that's for sure."

"Of course," he grunted. "And she'd have dragged us all through the mud, while playing the poor, pitiful housewife—"

"All the while sleeping with the pool boy—" Tiffany said.

"—and the horse groomer—" he added.

"—don't forget the gardener."

"—and several of my friends at the Gold Club."

Tiffany shook her head, thinking it would have been much funnier if it wasn't all so true. "Drake says Leah's a nice lady."

"She is, Tiffany. This whole situation, her regret over not being able to be a part of your lives, it's always made her so sad."

Tiffany studied this virtual stranger standing before her, not quite ready to let him off the hook. "You'd think if she cared that much she would have convinced you to take a more active role in my and Drake's life."

"Oh, she tried, believe me. She almost left me a couple of times because of it. But she stayed, thank God." He took a deep breath. "I'm sorry again for upsetting you over the phone last night. Leah reamed me out pretty good for offering to pay for your honeymoon. She said it was tacky, considering how neglectful I've been all these years."

"Leah sounds like a smart lady," Tiffany said.

Daniel chuckled. "She is. Is there anything I could do? Besides being an active part of your lives, because I still intend to do that."

"We don't need your money."

"I know you don't, but Leah did make one suggestion that you may possibly find more agreeable."

Tiffany sighed, already tired of the subject. "What is it?"

"A college fund for any future grandchildren. She said the only thing that could replace an education would be another education. Do you find that offensive?"

She looked at Red, who smiled and gave her a nod of encouragement.

"I guess that would be okay," she said.

Daniel beamed at his daughter. "Good. At least that's something. Now, have you spoken to your mother lately?"

"Not since she called me after I broke off my engagement to Tanner. She said she had no need for ungrateful children." Tiffany shook her head, still amazed at her mother's nerve. "Did she *ever* want Drake or me? Did she ever even *try* to care for us? I mean, change a diaper or give either of us a bottle in the middle of the night? Something—anything?"

Daniel LeBlanc shook his head. "In all fairness, she raised you the same way she was raised. She had the first nanny hired before we even brought you home from the hospital. My mom was still alive then, and when she came to see you for the first time and saw how that woman was handling you, she begged me to get rid of her and find someone decent. I can't remember what the woman's real name was, but she was German. My mom called her *Fraulein Frankenstein*, and said you wouldn't have lasted a month in her care. After that, we went through three more, and your grandmother and I vetoed every one of them. Then mom met Melinda and talked her into taking over your care. She said Melinda needed you as much as you needed her. It really irked your mother, and she even tried to fire her once. I told her unless she wanted to take over the diaper changing and two o'clock feedings, she'd better leave Melinda the hell alone. That was the end of it. So, as much as I'd like to take all the credit for hiring Melin, you can thank your grandmother for finding her."

"I wish I'd have known her long enough to remember her. Any fond memories of my childhood only include Melinda and Drake," she said, as an uncomfortable silence filled the room.

Finally her father cleared his throat. "Like I said, I'll try to find some photographs of you two together."

"I'd appreciate that. I'm going to change into something more comfortable before starting lunch." She walked down the hallway into her and Red's bedroom.

Daniel McAllister let out a low whistle. "She wasn't kidding, was she? She's not going to make this easy on me at all."

"Do you blame her?" Red asked him.

"Not one bit."

"About those photographs, I need to get my hands on a couple dozen photos of Tiffany from infancy through college. My mom wants to have an album made for Tiffany for Christmas. It's a surprise, so don't say anything to her."

"I doubt seriously if Monica has anything, but I'll bet Melinda has plenty."

"Do you have a number where she could be reached?"

He shook his head. "I don't, but I'm fairly certain Drake does. She's married and lives in Washington state now."

"That's what Tiffany said. Listen, Daniel, this is a time sensitive issue, so I'm going to get this rolling right now. I don't want Tiff to hear me, so I'll step out for a minute, if it's okay with you."

Tiffany rejoined her father, dressed in comfortable jeans and a sweater. "Where's Red?" She didn't particularly cherish the idea of being alone in a room with her father.

"He had to step outside to make a business call."

"Oh," she said, as she programmed the oven then pulled the pan containing the hen out of the refrigerator. She added a few more seasonings to the bird she'd prepared the night before, feeling her father's gaze on her.

"Tiffany," he said, finally breaking the silence. "I was wondering if you would like to pursue a relationship with Leah. If you say no, I won't push you. I won't blame you a bit, but she told me that nothing would make her happier than to become a part of your lives. She's hoping to become a doting step-grandmother one of these days."

Tiffany stopped in her tracks, trying to imagine what it would be like to have another mother figure besides Melinda. "Does she really?" She was still somewhat leery of accepting his word on faith.

Daniel nodded enthusiastically. "Absolutely. She wanted children so badly. She stayed on the pill for years to avoid getting pregnant, and when I finally told her that we could try for a baby she developed uterine cancer and had to have a complete hysterectomy. She had chemo for a year and it almost killed her. I came so close to losing her."

She turned to face him, curious about this new information. "How long ago did that happen?"

"That was fifteen years ago."

Tiffany stared at her father in disbelief. "And *still* you didn't divorce mother for her. That must have made her feel really special."

He sighed. "Okay, Tiffany, we've established the fact that I've been a fool for a lot of years now. Could we move on?"

"I wouldn't necessarily call you a fool, Dad."

"Well, then what would you call me?"

"How about an asshole?" she accused bitterly. "You tell me you love this woman but she nearly dies of cancer after you decide to allow her to have an *illegitimate* child of yours and still you can't make an honest woman of her!" She jerked open the oven door and sent the roaster containing the hen skidding over the wire rack. She slammed the door closed and turned on him. "What else would you call a man like that? You don't like asshole? How about selfish, self-centered, or insensitive? Any one of those would fit!"

Red chose that moment to re-enter the tension filled room. He cleared his throat quietly and walked over to his wife. "I leave you two alone for a minute and look what happens," he said, apparently trying to make light of the situation.

Tiffany stalked to the refrigerator, searching the contents for absolutely nothing then slammed it shut to turn on her father again. "I have to know. Why the hell didn't you leave mother then? Why didn't you marry Leah after that, if you loved her so much?"

"Because of you and Drake," he said quietly.

She couldn't stop the burst of hysterical laughter. "I cannot *believe* you're going to blame Drake and me for that."

"It's always been about you and Drake, Tiffany. You kids were only eight and six when Leah and I got together. She refused to do anything that would hurt the two of you. Your mother would have made all our lives a living hell. So she stayed on the pill until you were older. When you were both in college we decided to try for a baby. She was thirty four at the time and I was forty-nine. I planned to divorce Monica and marry Leah, but one day she began to hemorrhage and had to be rushed in for emergency surgery. That's when they found the cancer—already in stage 2. It's a miracle she's even alive. She had to have a complete hysterectomy with several rounds of chemo. After she knew she couldn't have kids, she said there was no point in me divorcing Monica to marry her. She said it would only have hurt the two of you and it would have been for nothing."

Tiffany stood there astonished, not knowing what to say. She finally shook her head. "My God, you must have resented Drake and me horribly."

"I *never* resented you or Drake. I resented your mother, and now I'm beginning to see how ridiculous that was. I was stupid, Tiffany. I was a coward for not taking the chance when I should have. It would have been worth losing every dime I had to have you and Drake brought up in a home filled with love. Leah could have given you that. With her around I could have been a better father. I'm a far better man with her."

Tears streamed down Tiffany's face as her father continued.

"I will live the rest of my life knowing that, not only did I waste years of my life and Leah's, but also yours and your brother's childhoods. I could have made it better for all of us if I'd just been—better. I'm so sorry Tiffany. Can you ever forgive me?"

The icy grip around Tiffany's heart suddenly broke loose as her father spoke the words she'd longed to hear for so many years. She began to sob openly as her father reached his arms out to her. She stood there crying, but still unable to move toward him. She felt a gentle touch on her shoulders as her husband whispered softly to her.

"It's all right to let it go now, Doc. It's time to open a new door." He gently pushed her so that after one step she walked into her father's open arms.

Red stood and watched his wife and her father as they mended thirty-six years of broken bridges—broken by lack of communication, poor judgment, and selfishness. He left them to themselves, giving them the privacy this situation called for, hoping Daniel didn't say anything stupid to ruin the moment. After fifteen minutes he thought it might be safe to venture out. He opened the door and immediately heard Tiffany giggling, accompanied by Daniel's hearty laughter. He approached cautiously, leaning against the wall at the end of the hallway to watch his wife interact with her father. They spoke comfortably, as though the years of difficult feelings had never existed.

Tiffany saw him and went to him, smiling as she walked into his open arms. "Thank you, baby," she said. "This happened because of you."

"All brides need their daddy to walk them down the aisle. That is if you're still willing to marry me," he whispered in her ear.

"Of course I will." She gave him a gentle kiss. "And I'm sorry for being so harsh."

He pulled her tight for a hug. "I deserved it."

She hugged him back before pulling away to face her father. "So, how about it, Dad? I need someone to walk me down the aisle the day after Christmas. Think you can handle it?"

He nodded, his eyes glistening with tears. "Definitely."

"Thank you," she said.

"I do have one question, and you can say no if you want to, but can Leah come to the wedding? She's dying to meet both of you."

"I'd love to meet her. As a matter of fact, I'd like the four of us and Red's parents to meet before the wedding. Can we try to plan something for next weekend?"

Daniel beamed at his daughter. "Tiffany, you pick the dates and times, and we'll be here, I promise. My God, I feel ten years younger," he said, throwing his head back and bellowing with laughter. "I feel like the weight of the world has been lifted from my shoulders. I can't wait to tell Leah, she's wanted this for so long."

"Would you mind if I called her right now and spoke to her first?" Tiffany asked.

Daniel was quick to give her his home and cell number, along with Leah's cell number, in case she was outside with the horses. Tiffany walked out to the pool house to call her while Red and Daniel remained in the kitchen.

Daniel stared after his daughter, wearing a look that could only be described as unadulterated joy. His father-in-law turned to him, beaming once more, and extended his hand to him. He grabbed it and gave it a hearty shake.

"I can't believe how good I feel. You're a Godsend for this family, Red, and I am truly grateful."

"I'd do anything to make her happy, Sir. She's the most important thing to me."

"Just wait until you have children of your own. There's not a doubt in my mind you'll do a hell of a lot better job at raising my grandchildren than I did at raising my own." He leaned over and spoke in a conspiratorial whisper. "Forgive me for prying, but Leah wanted me to ask if I got the chance. When exactly can we expect some of those?"

Red gave him a satisfied grin. "We're already trying."

Daniel's face practically glowed with happiness. "I tell you what, Red. This must be how ole Charlie Dickens' Scrooge felt on Christmas mornin'. I've visited all my ghosts and thrown off all those damn chains." He put his head back as another burst of laughter erupted. "And by damn it, I can't wait to start those college funds!"

One week later, Tiffany and Red hosted a Sunday dinner with Red's parents, Tiffany's father, and Leah Hanson. She'd tried to get Drake to come but he'd begged off, saying he was trying to wrap things up with his firm by New Year.

"Besides," he'd told her in their last phone call, "I've already seen them twice this week. You've really opened up the flood gates as far as Dad is concerned. He can't seem to get enough of 'family' now."

From the instant the two older couples were introduced, they took an instant liking to each other. Tiffany stood at the doorway of her kitchen staring out at the three men on the patio, near to bursting with pride for her husband and satisfaction at the turn her life had taken since meeting him four short months ago. Their fathers lounged on the furniture as Red tended to what he'd dubbed the 'Absolute kick-ass DeLorean of Grills'. Her husband had decided to take advantage of the unusually crisp, clear weather they were experiencing this last weekend before Christmas by breaking in his latest acquisition.

"Ah, the mystery of men and their attraction to cooking anything over an open fire." Leah's comment was accompanied by a light touch to Tiffany's shoulder.

"I've always believed it's stemmed from prehistoric man," Vivienne added.

Tiffany turned and began an animated dance around the kitchen. "Ehhh…Look what I have created!" she said, in a guttural imitation of Tom Hanks in the movie *Castaway*. "I have made fire. I—" She slapped her chest. "Have made fire!"

The three women broke into laughter before going back to preparing the mandatory potato salad and baked beans, along with a green salad. Tiffany had baked a lemon meringue pie, knowing it was her father's favorite, as well as the banana pudding pie that she wanted reviews on as a possible replacement of the requested banana pudding.

"So, Tiffany, do you have your dress for the wedding?" Leah asked her.

"I was thinking if you wanted to come and meet me one day, there are some nice shops in Houston."

"That sounds like a wonderful idea. It'll be difficult to find something prettier than the dress Red picked out for our civil ceremony."

"Red chose your dress?" Leah's eyes widened.

"Uh huh, along with my shoes, earrings, the matching wedding bands, and my gorgeous dinner ring," she admitted, thrusting her hands out to show off her rings.

"Oh Tiff, you have to show her the dress," Vivienne urged her daughter in law. "She was gorgeous, Leah."

Tiffany brought the two women into the huge master bedroom's walk in closet. She pulled the dress reverently from its storage bag and hung it on a hook. "I love my dress," she crooned, over Leah's gasp of admiration. "I'm bringing it on the honeymoon. I am absolutely determined to get more wear out of it."

"That *is* beautiful," Leah agreed. "What was Red wearing?"

Tiffany pulled out Red's Armani suit, allowing memories of that afternoon to wash over her. "Oh God, he looked so good in this thing," she said, closing her eyes and picturing him in it. "I could have just..." Tiffany stopped short, suddenly realizing who she was talking to, as heat infused her face.

The two older women looked at each other and burst into laughter before attempting to assuage her embarrassment.

Vivienne hugged her shoulder. "You know Tiffany, I *still* look at my husband sometimes, and could *just* . . . Especially now that we finally have the house to ourselves. Just because we're older doesn't mean we're dead."

"Amen to that, sister," Leah agreed.

Tiffany giggled. "That's right. You two just got rid of Annie a few months ago, didn't you?"

Vivienne nodded. "I love my daughter, but *no one* should have to live with a child until they're thirty years old."

Tiffany held up her hands. "Hey, I was out at eighteen!"

"I was too," Leah said. "I was holding down two jobs and sharing an apartment with a friend of mine."

"No college, Leah?" Tiffany asked.

"No, I never was that great of a student, unfortunately. The only thing I would have been interested in would have been animal husbandry, and there's no way I could have made it through those college courses. We're not all born brilliant, so I just train horses, instead of treating them."

"Train them for what?" Vivienne asked.

"For rodeos mostly; you know, roping, barrel racing, and pole racing. Some I train for cutting cattle. Some I just break, or gentle, I call it. I love it, and it pays the bills. Daniel bought the house we live in, but my business pays for everything else."

"Drake said you and Dad live on a ranch outside Houston."

"Yes, it's about the size of this one, but the house is smaller. I love this home of yours Tiffany—this is fantastic."

Vivienne grinned at Tiffany. "Let's show her the pool."

"You have a pool in the back yard? I haven't had a chance to look around yet," Leah said.

Tiffany smiled as they walked back into the kitchen. She covered the potato salad and checked on the baked beans. "Are we done in here, ladies?"

"Yep, the salad is ready to go," Vivienne said, as she placed the bowl in the fridge.

"Does anyone want a refill before we go out there?" Tiffany held up the bottle of wine.

"I do," Vivienne said, holding out her glass.

"I could use some too," Leah answered. "You girls have me curious about this pool thing."

Tiffany smiled as she refilled both ladies wine glasses then grabbed a bottle of water for herself. "Let's not keep you in suspense." Tiffany followed them outside, feeling Red's hungry gaze on her as she played hostess. She opened the door to the pool house to let the two other women inside, using the opportunity to send her husband a wink. The heated look he sent in return had her immediately moist with need, and imagining what she could do to the man if they didn't have company.

Chapter Nineteen

Christmas morning started early for Red and Tiffany. By nine a.m. their home was filled with the aromas of roasting turkey, breads, and other delicious treats. Thanking God for the extra wall oven, she'd just taken the last two pies out when the doorbell signaled the first of their guests. Within seconds, Red walked in with Annie.

"Hey sister-in-law," Annie called out jovially. "I'm not the first one here, am I?"

"Yep. But it's not a problem…somebody had to be," Tiffany said, giving her a hug. "Hey, go check out our new acquisition in the living room. We figure if anybody would appreciate it, you and my brother Drake would."

"Close your eyes first," Red commanded while leading her slowly into the corner of the living room.

Tiffany followed closely, anxious to see her reaction. "Now, look!" she said, clapping gleefully as Annie screamed with delight at the Steinway grand piano.

"It's beautiful!" Annie said, dropping onto the plush bench and placing her fingers reverently on the keys. "Where'd it come from?"

"It was my parents," Tiffany said. "It's been sitting in my mother's music room for three decades. Nobody's touched it since Drake left for college so dad had it delivered here. He always called it 'the overpriced dust collector'."

Annie played a scale or two and beamed at Tiffany. "Perfectly tuned," she said before stretching her fingers. "Any requests?"

"Do you know Pachelbel's Canon in D Major?" Tiffany said, hoping she did. "It's always been my favorite to relax to, and I sure could use some relaxing right now."

"Any pianist worth her salt knows Canon from memory," Annie said.

"Well, I would appreciate it if you'd play for me while I finish up the meal," Tiffany pleaded.

"It'll be a pleasure on this instrument." Annie closed her eyes and positioned her fingers on the keyboard.

Tiffany relaxed her shoulders and sighed, as the notes floated throughout the vaulted ceilings of the living area and kitchen of their home. "Beautiful." She and Red returned to the meal preparation in the kitchen.

"Hey," Annie called out several minutes later, as she played the last haunting notes of the song. "I thought Drake was coming early so we could practice the duet together. I'm a little nervous about it."

Tiffany's gaze clashed with Red's. "Uh, yeah, he *should* be here any minute." She sidled up close to her husband. "She's going to hate us when she sees him," she whispered.

Red shrugged. "Maybe at first, but she'll get over it." He pulled his wife into his arms. "Besides, if he's as ate up over her as I think he is he'll find a way to make her listen to him. I mean, hell, Doc, I got you to marry me and we didn't exactly get off to a glorious start."

"Well, that was your fault. I was just trying to do my damn job." Tiffany looped her arms around his waist and stood on tiptoes to nibble on his neck.

"Mm," he growled into her ear. "I was just trying to help."

She slid her hands down onto his butt and pulled him close. "If you hadn't been so insulting, maybe I would have been more willing to listen to you. I mistook you for a dumb jock." Annie's groan had them both facing the doorway.

"Oh my God, would you two stop that? You're preparing food, for chrissake!"

The shrill ringing of the phone cut through the air. "Annie, could you catch that, please?" Tiffany placed her hands back on her husband's firm butt. "My hands are sooo full right now."

Annie pivoted at the doorway of the kitchen and grunted in disgust. "If you stop now maybe I'll have my appetite back by lunchtime." She picked up the cordless. "Merry Christmas from the McAllisters! Who are you calling for—the doc or the jock?"

"Is—Tiffany there?"

"*Tiffany's* hands are a little full right now." She turned her back on the smooching couple. "This is Annie McAllister, the jock's sister. Who may I say is calling?"

"Oh. Annie." A long pause followed.

"Are you there?"

"Yeah. Um. This is Drake, her brother."

"Oh *Drake!* The lawyer *slash* composer of that beautiful piano piece. Will you be here soon so we can practice together?" Why did his voice sound so familiar to her?

"I'm stuck in traffic on I-10 just east of the state line. A tanker overturned in the median and both sides of the roadway are shut down."

"I hope no one was hurt," Annie said. "Put the radio station on FM 96.5, and you should be able to hear the most updated traffic reports. Hang on, Drake." She carried the phone over to Tiffany. "You think you could unhand *my* brother long enough to speak to *yours*? He's stuck on I-10."

Tiffany grinned, and lifted one hand to grab the phone while keeping a tight hold on her husband's right butt cheek. "Hey, what's up brother mine?"

"Tanker overturned, Sis. Haz-mat's here already but it could still be awhile. Does Annie suspect anything?"

"Doesn't seem like it," she said, her voice sounding muffled as a giggle escaped.

Drake craned his neck, trying to see further ahead of him. "This is just my damned luck. I wanted to get there early and clear the air before anyone else arrived."

"I know you did,

but it can't be helped. If you get here too late, we'll have to send Vivienne and Pete outside later so that you two can have at least one practice session when you get here."

"I don't know when they'll let us through. It could take hours."

"It'll all work out. Hey, I need to tend to some things but I'll let you talk to Annie again. Maybe you could discuss the piano music—or something else, maybe. Here she is."

He waited for Annie to come back on the line.

"Hey, it's me again. It's pretty bad, huh?"

Drake chuckled. "Bad enough to put a damper on Christmas day for a lot of people, including me," he added below his breath. "This is disappointing, Annie. I wanted to get there early—to, ah, practice with you."

"Aw, don't worry about it. I'm sure it'll be fine. I hope you don't get mad but I have to ask this. Why did you write it as a piano duet?"

"Red sent me the .wav file of the way he and Tiff sang it with each their own parts and—I don't know—I thought it would be nice to have the same his and her piano parts." He attempted to massage the tension from the back of his neck with one hand. "If I can't make it there soon, you'll have to play it solo."

"We didn't plan to perform it until the afternoon, so you've got plenty of time."

"Maybe there is hope, then. Think you could stay on the line with me awhile longer to help the time pass?"

"Not a problem. So, I heard you showed up at Red's club last month. How'd you like it? Not that it matters anymore since the damn thing burned to the ground and won't be rebuilt."

"What I saw of it was very nice."

"It's probably not as nice as what you're used to in Houston."

"Actually, it's a lot nicer than most of them. And speaking of Red's club, where'd you go that night I was there. Everyone said you had to leave."

"Oh. Um—I get migraines that come on suddenly."

"That's too bad, I hope you weren't too incapacitated." He'd have spotted that lie even if he hadn't known he was the real reason she left.

"No, it—it turned out to be nothing, but—I couldn't—take the chance."

"I guess you did what you felt was necessary at the time." *It sure as hell didn't feel like nothing to him.* He decided a change of subject may be the safest course of action. "So, did you have any trouble with the piano piece?"

"Not at all. It's beautiful. I can play anything that's put in front of me, but I could never compose like that. What about you?"

"I'm passable."

Annie snorted. "Oh please, Tiffany says you could have been a professional. Maybe I should play for you so you can judge whether or not you need to make any adjustments. You know, dumb it down a little so you don't show me up too badly?"

The last comment took him off guard and he laughed. "I doubt seriously that will be necessary, but if you want to play for me, I'd like that." After a minute or so of hearing her situate her sheet music and herself at the piano, she came back to the phone.

"Okay, here it goes. Oh, and by the way, I believe this is your old piano."

Drake closed his eyes, visualizing her in front of the piano he'd played for years, seated on the bench he'd used throughout those same years. He smiled as she played for him. He'd heard her in his mind so many times, sounding exactly this way. He imagined her delicate fingers passing lightly over the keys, turning the notes on the page into the haunting melody that would forever remind him of Annie McAllister. That was for certain, because although he'd written it for her parents' anniversary, the only approval he cared about had been Annie's.

He'd agonized over the piece, working on it every spare minute and losing more sleep than usual over it. It didn't matter what time he woke up during the night, once he opened his eyes, he had to get up and work on it. It was the first thing he thought of—that, and the way she'd felt in his arms as they'd danced, the way she'd tasted on his lips.

He opened his eyes as the last notes rang out through the earpiece, feeling cheated out of seeing the look on her face the first time she'd played for him.

"Well?" she asked.

"That was beautiful, Annie. I knew you'd do it justice."

"No adjustments necessary, 'Mr. Could Have Been a Professional'?"

"You played it perfectly, Annie." *Just as I imagined you would.*

"You know how it is when you really connect with a piece? Well, I must have played this a hundred times since Red gave it to me. Each time I play it feels like the first time. There's something about it that—I don't know—it speaks to me."

A flood of mixed emotions washed over Drake. Thrilled with her reaction to the music, he felt like a giant heel. He could have done this dozens of different ways, and now it was too late. He couldn't tell her who he was over the phone. If he did, she'd run like hell. He knew she would, and he'd be to blame for her missing the chance to perform. Any chance of her discovering his identity without being witnessed by a live audience was rapidly evaporating. No way in hell this day wouldn't end up as a major drama fest.

"Annie . . ." He stopped himself.

"What is it?"

He tapped his hand several times on the steering wheel, agonizing over what to tell her, how much to tell her. Finally he released a long sigh and spoke. "I'm glad you like it." He couldn't do a thing until they were face to face. "What do you do for a living?"

"Physical therapist—I just joined a practice in Kenton."

"Kenton, huh? Do you like it there?"

"Yes, I do."

"No boyfriend or fiancé?" he drawled.

"Nope, there is absolutely no place for that in my life right now. This is my time to do what I want to do. Work, work, work—put some money aside, and when I can get time off, I want to travel, either alone or with friends, but at my convenience."

"That's very independent of you."

"That's me—little Miss born on the Fourth of July."

"You were not."

"Yep."

"That's my birthday too—July 4th."

"Seriously?"

"I swear, ask Tiffany," he insisted. He heard her cover the phone and yell the question out to his sister.

Once Tiffany confirmed his statement, Annie returned to the conversation. "I'll be damned! I was born at 4:05 pm."

"I was born around 4 am. What are the odds?" he murmured. "Hey, I think something is happening. It looks like they're going to let us through soon."

"Well, just be careful and get here when you can. Like I said, we'll wait for you."

He smiled to himself. "Okay, thanks. Annie?"

"Yes?"

"I'm sorry I couldn't get there early. Please remember—I—I really wanted it to be different." He ended the call before she had a chance to respond.

By the time Drake arrived at Red and Tiffany's, it was noon and the home's driveway was already packed with vehicles. Even his dad and Leah had arrived before he did, he noted, seeing his father's Navigator parked in front of the ranch house. He parked at the end and grabbed his keyboard out of the back seat of his Denali pick up, along with the bag of gifts he'd been collecting all week.

Drake paused to look around, thinking his father's description of the place as 'a real nice spread...perfect for raising horses and grandkids," seemed to fit. He made his way to the door and rang the bell several times. When it became obvious there was too much commotion going on inside for anyone to hear, he opened the door and entered the small foyer. He put down the keyboard and bag of gifts, scanning the living room full of children, all dressed in their Christmas finery. Every child in the room had various shades of red hair, from strawberry blonde to dark auburn, and from what he could see they all had what Tiffany called McAllister blue eyes. He glanced toward the hallway as one more Annie look alike walked into the room carrying an infant wrapped in pink. She greeted him with a bright smile and walked over to meet him.

"You must be Drake. I'm Red's sister, Kathleen." She held out her hand.

Drake shook her offered hand. "It's nice to meet you Kathleen—and who's this?" He pulled back a corner of the blanket to reveal a beautiful baby girl who happened to be staring up at him with her big, wide opened, dark blue eyes.

"This is Brynn, and she's a week old today."

He gazed at the exquisite features of the child, clearly destined to be a beauty. "Tiffany said all the children in this family are beautiful and she wasn't exaggerating. She's gorgeous."

"Thank you." Kathleen beamed up at him then held up the baby to plant a kiss on her forehead. "I'm in love with her already."

"Merry Christmas, by the way," he said.

"Merry Christmas, Drake. Come on in, the kids took over the living room, and all the adults are spread out in the kitchen and dining room. We were waiting on you to eat lunch."

"Oh, that wasn't necessary. Y'all should have started without me."

"No way." She pulled him toward the kitchen. "You're part of the family now, whether you like it or not." She stopped in the doorway. "Hey everybody, look who I just found," she announced.

"There he is," Tiffany walked up to him and threw her arms around him. "Merry Christmas, little brother, I was starting to worry," she murmured into his ear.

"Merry Christmas to you too, Sis—where is she?"

"In the dining room, she can't see you from here."

He pulled away and shook his head. "This isn't how I wanted this played out. She'll be hurt."

Tiffany gave him a sympathetic smile. "You always say you thrive on challenges."

Drake grunted as he followed her into the kitchen and exchanged Christmas greetings with those he knew already, and introduced himself to the ones he was meeting for the first time. His father hugged him tightly.

"Hey Son, glad you could finally make it. Merry Christmas!"

"You too, Dad—Leah," he added, giving her a big hug.

Daniel beamed as Tiffany and Red joined their circle. "It's good to be here together, isn't it? My God, I feel like we're a part of a real family."

"Yep, it's a whole new life, now come on in and meet everyone else," Tiffany gently urged him.

Annie's presence drew Drake's gaze like a starving man to a bowl of spicy Texas chili. He spotted her immediately, seated at the far end of the table, absorbed in a conversation with Bailey and Melissa. He tried to keep his gaze from gravitating to her while being introduced to Red's other siblings— Rebecca and Kenneth, along with their spouses, then Chad. He stopped in his tracks and held his breath when Bailey turned to address him.

"Hey Drake, it's good to see you again. Merry Christmas!"

Annie's gaze finally landed on him. He watched as the laughter in her eyes faded, her smile transformed into a look of shock as recognition dawned. Finally, her eyes widened with horror as she was hit with the full impact of the situation.

He barely noticed Melissa's approach, barely acknowledged her greeting and somehow managed to return it with a feeble one of his own. He struggled to keep his gaze from Annie while simultaneously craving the sight of her.

With only Annie left to 'meet' he approached her slowly, wishing for a moment of privacy that would be impossible to achieve in this household at the moment. "And you must be Annie." He held his hand out to her. "I'm Drake, and it's nice to finally meet you."

She stared silently at him for several seconds, surely as aware as he was of them being the center of attention. "Same here . . . Drake." She spoke quietly, ignoring his hand.

Drake could see that her calm exterior was nothing more than a mask she'd perfected to hide her feelings. He smiled at her and for one brief moment the mask lifted, revealing a hurt she'd probably carried for years, long before he'd been in the picture. At least that's what he'd surmised from their one and only meeting. Why else would she be so afraid of a commitment? The one thing he knew for sure was that he felt like a monumental ass for helping to pile on more hurt in her haunted eyes.

Red stepped forward, breaking the awkward silence. "Everyone! It's time to eat, now that my brother-in-law has finally decided to grace us with his presence."

"I didn't expect all of you to wait on me. It was plain old rotten luck that kept me from getting here early, like I planned to." He glanced over at Annie. He'd hoped to see something other than anger, and what he saw was total indifference toward him. She'd completely tuned him out, continuing her conversation with everyone around her. He caught Red's eye, and they exchanged grim expressions. At some point during the day he'd need to attempt some kind of damage control. What could he possibly say that wouldn't make her loathe him more than she did at this moment?

The room suddenly turned into a hive of activity as everyone prepared to set the table for Christmas dinner. Drake caught Annie pulling Red down to her level to speak to him briefly before she spun away, leaving her brother sputtering for an explanation.

Drake sidled up to him. "What'd she say?"

"Oh, she just thanked me for ruining her day."

"Damn, I feel bad for not doing something about this situation sooner, but I thought I'd have time. I'm sorry Red."

"Don't feel sorry for me, buddy. If she's that pissed at me, just wait till you see what she's got in store for you."

Drake cocked one eyebrow. "I'll take a little abuse from her for today, but she's just as much to blame as I am for the rest of it."

Red shook his head slowly. "I'm glad to see you so determined and unbendable on this, Drake, old boy." His tone was rife with sarcasm. "You should have, at the very least, called to warn her before now."

Drake shrugged. "I've brought down multi-million dollar companies before, I think I can handle little old Annie McAllister." His entire body tensed at the feminine clearing of a throat just behind him. The smirk on Red's face verified that Annie had heard his comment.

He aimed an accusing glare at Red, who wore an expression that screamed "Better you than me, Pal".

"Excuse me, but *little old Annie McAllister* needs to set the table."

Drake took a slow, deep breath and strengthened his resolve before turning to face her. "Is there anything I can do to help you?"

She raised one brow. "You want to help? I've got an even better idea. Here." She thrust the stack of plates she was holding into his chest, forcing him to take hold of them. "A man like you—a man who brings down *multi-million dollar companies*, no doubt putting hundreds of people out of work—why, a man such as *you* should have no trouble setting this table all by yourself." She turned and announced that Tiffany's baby brother had graciously offered to set the table.

Drake smiled tightly at the round of applause her little announcement had garnered. After being virtually abandoned by Red, he circled the table, placing a plate before each chair at the huge table. Pleased with the completion of his assigned task, he walked into the kitchen to tell Annie he'd finished. She pointed to the storage unit, telling him that's where he'd find the silverware and glassware for the place settings, before leaving him standing there like a gullible child. Rather than waste the given opportunity, he paused a few seconds to get a good look at her shapely, though retreating, little butt.

Tiffany met her brother at the cabinet. "She's upset right now. I wouldn't try to start up a friendly conversation just yet. Here, we need these goblets and all of this silverware, just bring the tray in with you. Do you want me to do it for you?"

"After that announcement? Hell, no. She'd love to see me back out of it."

Tiffany chuckled. "She hates lawyers you know—she's got this real *aversion* to them."

Drake sighed, letting his head drop back. "Why should I expect anything else at this point?" He got the glassware from the cabinet and brought it to the tables. After several trips, he figured he was finished and walked over to where Annie stood.

"Would you like to inspect my work?" he asked.

Occupied with the napkin folding, she spoke without facing him. "There are at least two dozen other people in this house right now who *don't* detest being in the same room as you. Why don't you go ask one of them?"

He leaned in close, trying to keep his voice lowered. "Look, I tried like hell to get here earlier. I didn't *want* you to find out like this."

"You could have picked up a phone at any time. I'm assuming you figured out who I was as soon as you met my sisters that night. And let's not forget that fifteen minute phone conversation we had this very morning," she said, as her voice rose in anger.

"Annie—"

"Marcus!" she snapped.

"Nicole!" he snapped right back. Her eyes widened, focusing on something behind him. He turned to discover every occupant in the room had stopped to tune in to their discussion.

"Uh, we've met before—obviously. We just didn't know at the time who we were—or rather—who the other was—or something like that," he finished lamely.

A voice from the back of the room piped up. "I think I'm having a déjà vu flashback from Thanksgiving."

Another added. "It's Red and Tiffany all over again." Several giggles followed.

"Not so funny now, huh, Sis?" someone else volunteered.

"Welcome to the McAllister family, Drake. Or as we like to call it, life in the fishbowl." A chorus of chuckles broke out.

He heard Annie swear mildly under her breath and turned in time to see her escape out to the patio, slamming the door behind her. "Don't hold dinner for us, this could take a while," he said, heading for the same doorway.

"You may want to let her cool off awhile," one of the brothers-in-law suggested.

Drake paused at the door. "Thanks, but I'd better do this now while my litigation skills are still sharp." He couldn't help but grin at the chuckles, snorts, and a couple of 'Good luck with that, buddy!' comments from the crowd.

He exited out to the patio. A quick perusal of the area and back yard got no results. Thinking the pool house he'd heard so much about would be an acceptable escape, he entered quietly through the door. He walked toward the center of the room and whistled under his breath at the huge indoor pool. Continuing around to the other side of the large double lounge chair, he found Annie sitting with her feet tucked under her, trying to look invisible, but failing miserably.

"Can I sit here?" he asked, pointing to the spot beside her.

"Sure you can," she said in a tight voice as she rose from the chair. "I'll go back inside."

"Please stay, Annie." He grabbed her arm gently.

"I don't think so, Mar—Drake. I told you in the parking lot of Red's club, I'm not interested in anything you have to say or offer."

He leaned in, wanting to get his fill of her delicate scent. "Aren't you even curious? I mean, I've never come across anyone who's had that kind of effect on me before. Doesn't it make you wonder?"

She looked straight past him. "No it doesn't."

"Really? I haven't been able to stop thinking about you since that happened between us."

"Nothing happened between us." She tried to pry his hand off of her arm.

"Bullshit," he murmured. "I've thought about you every day—and, God help me, every damned night, too."

"I didn't." She tried, again, to extricate her arm from his strong hand.

"Stop fidgeting, Annie. *Look* at me and tell me that."

She did then, and Drake was mesmerized by the large, crystal blue eyes staring up at him. He pulled her closer until she was near enough so that he could see her hair stir with every breath he took. Her perfume, a warm, spicy, floral combination, blended with her own soft scent to leave him in a state of heady intoxication. His eyes drifted shut of their own accord as he inhaled, attempting to permanently install this moment in his memory bank for future reference. He opened his eyes—saw her watching him with eyes widened and filled with the desire she so strongly denied. He leaned in closer, wanting...*needing* to taste her again, to feel her sweet lips on his.

Annie pulled out of his hold and backed away from him. "I believe I've already said I don't want this. Or are you one of *those* guys?"

"Don't go there, Annie. You know we both felt something extraordinary that night."

"Maybe *you* did. Maybe it wasn't so extraordinary for me."

"I don't believe that. What if it's good between us? What if we miss out on the chance of a lifetime?"

"It's not."

"How do you know? I told you I'm not usually this attracted to someone and I don't think you are either. Maybe it's a sign."

Annie placed a finger to her temple. "Let's see, what is it you do for a living again? Oh yes, now I remember, you're a lawyer—a corporate lawyer. Maybe *that's* a sign too, you know, since I hate lawyers and all."

He gave her a crooked grin. "Ah, but I'm quitting my dad's firm, and opening up my own family law practice."

"Good for you. I'm sure those Houston socialites can always use one more high profile divorce lawyer." She headed for the door.

"Not in Houston, here in Lake Coburn."

She stopped suddenly, spun around to face him. "What? Why here?"

He gave her a casual shrug. "I miss my sister."

"If your relocation has anything at all to do with me, you'd be making such a colossal mistake."

"It's something I'd been pondering for a while, but I'll admit that our first—meeting—well, let's just say it definitely pushed me over the edge." Her subtle lift of brow, the hitch in her breathing, and the slight widening of her eyes told him everything he wanted to know. He wasn't the only one kept up at night thinking about that night. He'd woken up tangled in sheets more times than he'd care to admit, especially to her.

"B-but, your parents are there," she stammered.

"I'm not close to my mother at all. Dad and I are okay, but it's Tiff I really miss. Besides I have a feeling when she and Red start rolling out babies, Dad and Leah will want to be closer to them and move here, also."

"Maybe Red and Tiffany will want to move to Houston." She didn't sound convinced of her own words.

"No way, Annie. Tiff loves it here. It's her home, and Louisiana will be my home as well. Deal with it. I'm family now."

"Tiffany is family. You're nothing but an unfortunate by-product," she insisted.

He took a few steps closer. "It's the same thing, Hon."

"I despise pet names."

"Every birthday, holiday, anniversary, or grand opening in the family, I'll be there. I plan on becoming a permanent fixture in your life—*Hon*."

"I doubt that."

"But we have time for all that. Why don't we just agree to be friends for now?"

"Oh, let's not."

He sighed then smiled seductively at her. "You're only prolonging the inevitable."

She shook her head and opened the door. "Arrogance is such a turn off, and you positively reek of it."

"You weren't turned off the first time we met."

She cast him a sidelong glance. "You weren't arrogant that night. If you had been, I wouldn't have wasted a dance on you."

"You wasted a lot more than a dance, as you well remember, and there's a difference between arrogance and knowing what you want, Annie," he drawled as she made her escape through the door.

Drake leaned casually against the door jamb to watch her walk off. "And I sure as hell know what I want!" he called after her.

Chapter Twenty

By the time Annie got back inside, both tables and the island were nearly all occupied. She leaned inside the wide door opening of the room while her father prepared to say grace. The noticeable disturbance in her air space told her Drake was near. She couldn't help but wonder what the hell it was about the man that made her want to scratch his eyes out and tear his clothes off at the same time.

Annie closed her eyes as her father began the blessing. She bowed her head, feeling Drake's overpowering presence as he moved beside her, his arm a hairsbreadth away from her own. She resisted the urge to fan her face, suffocated by the heat his body produced.

Pete recited a standard blessing, ending with heartfelt message. "We're especially thankful for the addition of five new family members, one being newborn Bryn, along with Tiffany, Leah, Daniel, and Drake."

A not so subtle nudge from Drake had Annie glaring up into his smiling, smug face as everyone else ended with a hearty 'Amen'.

"Told you so," he drawled, sending her a sexy as hell wink.

"Arrogant ass!" she hissed.

"Watch your mouth, Hon. It's the Christ child's birthday." His eyes sparkled with mischief.

Annie's ire peaked, furious at herself for letting him get to her. "Yeah, well—every nativity I've ever seen includes a donkey. Baby Jesus had *his* ass and I have you. I guess I'm stuck with you until this duet's over with. I'm done with you after that."

He leaned close to whisper in her ear. "It'll be sleeting in hell the day you're done with me."

She pulled away, ignoring the frisson of awareness his nearness caused. "In your dreams."

"Yours too, I'd wager."

She turned haughtily and went to find a chair at the huge table where two extra chairs had been placed to accommodate all of the adults. When Red motioned for Drake to sit next to her, she grabbed her plate, filled it with her favorites and stood up. "I'll sit with the kids today. It's not as *stuffy* in there."

"Annie." Vivienne spoke quietly.

She locked gazes with her mother, who gestured with a single hand motion for her to sit and remain seated. Obediently, she obeyed, knowing her mom would not tolerate any such form of rudeness at the Christmas meal. Unable to resist, she cast a look at her neighbor.

Drake winked at her and gave her that crooked grin that made her want to attack him on the spot.

"Stuck with me," he whispered.

She did her best to ignore him as the conversations became decidedly more animated. Drake joined in the joviality, as well as his father and Leah, all three obviously delighted at being included in this festive occasion. She fidgeted nervously, nibbling occasionally at her food. Suddenly tired of pretending to eat, she gave up and shoved her plate away.

Drake leaned in close. "What's wrong?"

"I seem to have lost my appetite."

"Are you ill?"

"No, I'm sure it's only the close proximity to you."

"Maybe you're nervous about the duet."

"Should I be? Can you even play?"

"I can."

"How well?"

Thankfully, Drake spoke low enough to keep his response private. "Oh, about as well as I can make out on a dance floor with you."

Annie watched as his lips curled up into a smirk that made her want to slap it right off of his face. She narrowed her eyes at him. "I'm glad you find this so amusing, *Marcus.*"

He put another slice of turkey breast in his plate. "I have to admit that I do, *Nicole,* but we really do need to practice together. I know I won't have a problem. I mean, I wrote the damn thing. I just don't know if you can handle a duet, since you're so insistent on spending the rest of your life solo."

"Bite me."

His lips curved upward in a lazy smile as his voice lowered to a tantalizing decibel. "Now *that's* the best suggestion you've given me all day. Do I get to choose the spot?"

Annie turned away from his sexy brown eyes, but not before a shiver ran through her. "Arrogance," she snarled quietly, before leaving the table.

Once the scrumptious meal was over with, the younger adults pitched in to clean the kitchen. When Daniel and Leah asked if someone would show them the barns and stables on the ranch, Pete and Vivienne were more than happy to oblige.

With the two couples out of sight, the musicians made quick work of setting up their instruments. Drake placed his keyboard next to Red's piano and warmed up, feeling Annie's gaze on him.

Annie warmed up a little, flexed her fingers, and waited.

The piece began with Drake's piano part and Red singing his stanza in his soulful baritone, while everyone else sang harmony in the background. When he was done, Tiffany sang her part in a strong, clear voice accompanied by Annie on the piano as well as the other instruments. The last verse and final repeat of the chorus culminated in the merging of all singers as well as the instruments. The result was such that those who weren't participating remained motionless, obviously captivated by the piece. As the last notes played out, the room was filled with an overpowering silence.

Finally Sienna sniffed loudly. "That was amazing."

Miranda, who was hearing it for the first time, nodded. "They are so going to love this performance."

"Did anyone hear anything that needs adjusting?" Red asked.

"Nope, it's perfect the way it is. That piano duet is truly breathtaking." Miranda looked out the side window. "Hey, they're coming back everyone."

"Are we good, then?" Red asked. "Annie, Drake—do you need another practice run?"

"I'm good," she said quietly.

"Me too," Drake agreed.

"All right then, everyone stay where you are and we can get this thing over with as soon as they come back in." He looked over at his wife. "Hey Doc, you were wonderful."

"Thanks Babe." Tiffany leaned over to accept his tender kiss then pulled him closer to deepen the kiss right in front of Annie and Drake.

Drake watched her reaction, a rolling of the eyes. She opened her mouth to speak but caught sight of Drake and closed her mouth, seeming to think better of it.

"What, no comment?" Red asked.

She shrugged as if it didn't have any effect on her. "I guess I'm getting desensitized."

Red grinned at his sister. "Yeah, I'm sure that's it."

"I thought Jackson and Giselle were going to be here today," she said, desperate to change the subject.

"They went to Carrie and Sam's for lunch, but they said they would be here around three o'clock to see everyone. We might have to perform this one more time."

"Good, Julia and Jacob should be here by then," Chad added, speaking of his estranged wife and their son. "I'm sure they'd like to hear this."

When the two older couples re-entered the house, Chad's daughter, Miranda, escorted her grandparents into the living room. They sat, front and center, waiting and wearing curious expressions.

Red approached his parents. "Mom and Dad, we know you don't like us to do anything special for your anniversary, but we thought it's time we showed you how special it was for all of us to grow up with your wonderful influence in our lives. We were fortunate to have parents who truly love each other and weren't afraid to express it. My beautiful wife and I wrote this song for you and my talented brother-in-law, Drake, composed the parts for the pianos. This is from all of us, to you."

Vivienne snuggled close to her husband as he placed his arm around her. After several moments, the ensemble began to play and sing the beautiful song that had been composed in their honor. Sienna handed Vivienne some tissues when she began to cry silently. There was no other noise in the room as every man, woman, and child who wasn't part of the musical group listened attentively. By the time it was over, there wasn't a dry eye left in the room among the adults and older grandchildren.

Vivienne, who had struggled to keep control over her emotions, began to cry openly. Pete held her closely and pulled out his handkerchief to wipe his own eyes and try his best to comfort his wife. Vivienne finally scanned the room, seeking out her children and anyone else who'd participated in the song. "This is absolutely the best gift you've ever given us. That was beautiful, and we love you all so much." She turned and buried her face in her husband's broad chest.

Pete smiled as he held his wife. "Your mother's right. It was wonderful, and we couldn't ask for a better group of children. I know you're all adults now, but to your mother and me, you'll always be our babies. Just wait," he said, giving them a hearty laugh. "You'll see one day."

Vivienne wiped her eyes with a tissue. "Oh, wait until the Garden Club hears about this. I know none of them have *ever* had a song written and performed for them." She placed a hand over her heart. "You kids are the best."

Annie hugged her mother. "If we are, it's all thanks to you and Daddy. And, and as much as it pains me to admit this, I'm beginning to enjoy seeing you two act all *'lovey- dovey'*." She glared at the astonished faces of her siblings. "As long as you don't overdo it," she added.

Daniel approached Drake and slapped his shoulder. "That was played beautifully, Son. I knew you played, but I had no idea you composed. And you," he said, turning to his daughter. "I had no idea you had such a gorgeous singing voice. You get that from my side of the family, you know." He beamed with pride.

"Do you sing, Dad?" she asked him.

"Well, sure. I sang in a band to earn extra money when I was in college, but nothing close to what I heard from you just now. That was beautiful. You sound just like my mother." Tiffany gave her father a big hug as Drake watched in approval.

⚜

Around three, Tiffany made a huge pot of coffee and asked who was ready for dessert. "We have banana pudding pies, lemon meringue, and pecan pies." She turned to Drake. "Wait until you taste Vivienne's goodies, Drake. Pecan pralines, fudge, and divinity like Melinda's. She could sell it and make a killing, I'm not kidding."

Drake's eyes widened. "Yeah, I remember you flaunting that in my face for Thanksgiving. Lead me to the good stuff."

As soon as everyone had been served dessert and coffee, the doorbell rang. Giselle burst through the door with her family. "Are we in time for dessert?"

"Absolutely, and Merry Christmas." Tiffany hugged her friends.

Within moments, the doorbell rang again and Red walked in with Julia and Jacob in tow.

Chad and Miranda met them and Julia hugged her daughter tightly, while Chad did the same with his son.

Red watched as Julia's gaze settled briefly on her husband's, but just long to make her eyes blur with tears as she turned away.

"Merry Christmas Julia," Chad spoke quietly while offering to take her coat.

Julia relinquished her jacket, somehow managing to avoid further eye contact with him. "You too, Chad."

She stepped into the living room and walked straight into Vivienne's open arms.

Vivienne held her daughter in law tightly. "I've missed you so much, Jules."

Julia stood holding her as if she wouldn't let go. "I've missed you too, Vivi. Tea and crumpets don't compare to your good coffee and banana nut bread, or your company."

Julia felt a firm hand on her shoulder and turned to see Pete standing there. "Mr. Pete," she said, letting the big man wrap her in his strong arms. "God, I've missed all of you," she sobbed.

"We feel the same way," Pete told her. He finally let her go, so her sisters-in-law could close in on her.

She beamed when Kathleen walked in the room carrying newborn Brynn. She hugged Kenneth, and finally turned to Red, who'd stood watching it all, waiting patiently to introduce her to Tiffany.

"And Red. Oh, my God. I'm finally getting to meet the woman who has brought this confirmed bachelor to his knees," she said, laughing. "Tiffany, it is such a pleasure to meet you. I've heard fabulous things about you."

Tiffany nodded and smiled. "I've heard pretty much the same about you, Julia." She looked around at her new family. "From everyone here."

The little ones allowed several more minutes of catching up, coffee, and dessert before complaining they'd waited long enough for gift opening. The four oldest grandchildren were the designated Santa's helpers and charged with distributing the mountain of gaily wrapped packages to everyone present.

Tiffany cried when she opened a gift from her new mother-in-law; a leather-bound book with *Tiffany Danielle LeBlanc McAllister* and her birthday, *February 12th,* stamped in gold on the cover. Vivienne had contacted Melinda Dawson Hart, the LeBlanc's nanny, through Red, and the woman had come through for her, sending dozens of digital files to Vivienne, who'd organized two more books and sent them off as a rush order.

Tiffany stopped at a picture of an infant with a woman who seemed to be about fifty years old. The woman had curly brown hair, large brown eyes, and looked remarkably like Tiffany. "Daddy, who is this?"

Daniel's eyes filled with tears. "That's you and your grandmother, my Mom."

"I look just like her," she said. "Why weren't there ever any pictures of her around the house?"

Daniel smiled sadly and patted his daughter's hand. "I'll tell you all about it later."

She nodded, continued for now to flip through the pages to see a few other photos of her with her grandmother and snapshots of her and Drake that she hadn't seen in years.

"I remember seeing some of these when we were kids. I never realized they were Melinda's photo albums, but I guess I should have." She wiped her eyes. "I miss her so much. We invited her to the wedding, but they can't make it. Greg's the mayor of the city, and Melin's got a bakery to run." Tiffany smiled through her tears and looked up at her brother's approach. "Drake, you need to take a look at this book."

"Oh, I almost forgot!" Vivienne said. She walked to the foyer, then back into the room with another large, square, flat box and handed it to Drake. "This one's for you, Drake. It was delivered late yesterday and I didn't have a chance to wrap it."

Drake ripped open the tab and pulled out the leather bound album, identical to Tiffany's but with the words *Marcus Drake LeBlanc* and the date *July 4th* embossed in gold lettering.

He flipped through the first couple of pages and turned to her. "Ms. Vivienne-I-I don't know what to say. I can't believe you went through this much trouble for me," he said, obviously touched by her actions.

"You're family now, too." She laid a hand on his shoulder.

He skimmed through the rest of the book then closed it. He gave Vivienne a big bear hug. "I want you to know how much this means to me, but I want to check it out later, when I won't make a fool of myself," he whispered.

Vivienne laughed and gave his face a gentle pat. "I understand, Drake. That's what my boys did, too."

He straightened up and caught his sister watching the display of affection with tears in her eyes. "I have my own book," he said with attitude, trying to lighten the mood.

"I see that. There's no need to get all cocky," she said, making anyone within hearing distance chuckle.

An hour later, with gift opening behind them and the wrapping paper mess cleaned up, Tiffany turned to her husband and thanked him again for the gorgeous diamond necklace.

"You're welcome, and I can't wait to see my gift from you." He looked at the picture of the beautiful pair of quarter horses she'd asked Leah to acquire for them, along with new saddles and everything they'd need to care for them.

"They won't be delivered until after we get back from the honeymoon," she said. "That way we won't have to have anyone tend to them while we're gone."

He pulled her into his arms. "That sounds good. Have I mentioned how much I'm looking forward to our honeymoon?" he murmured into her ear.

Tiffany gave her husband a sexy little smile and kissed him before pulling away. She turned to her father and picked up the receipt for the savings account he'd opened with the name *McAllister Grandchild Number One* written on the outside of the envelope. "Thanks Dad, this is really generous of you," she said of the $50,000.00 deposit showing in the book.

Daniel beamed at his only daughter. "It's just the beginning. My grandchildren will be able to go to any college they want to and not have to worry about it," he told her. "I just hope they start coming soon."

"Ah, Dad, be careful what you wish for," she whispered.

His eyes lit up. "Are you?"

Tiffany shook her head. "Not that I know of, but we're trying."

Daniel put his head back and laughed. "Hell, I like the sound of that. I think I should warn you that I plan on being a doting grandfather, you know." He paused. "When you have time, I'd like to explain something to you about your mother, Tiff."

She pulled the corners of her mouth down. "Will it make me happy or sad?"

He shrugged. "Maybe both, but it may help you to understand some things."

"I think I have the time right now, Dad." She tucked her photo album under one arm, and took his hand. "Let's go out to the pool house where we can talk."

Once inside the pool house, he took the album from her and found the page with the snapshot of Tiffany with her grandmother. "You do see the resemblance between the two of you, don't you, Tiff?"

Tiffany looked closely at the photo. "Yes, definitely…the hair…the eyes…the mouth…as an adult, I'm even shaped like her."

Daniel smiled and nodded. "From the day you were born, you resembled her. It gave me great satisfaction that you looked like my mom, but your *mother*—God, it really ate her up." He shook his head sadly. "She hated Mom. I mean, really *loathed* her, because she was everything that Monica wasn't. She was a wonderful mother, a wonderful wife, even though my bully of a father didn't appreciate her, and treated her badly until the day he died. Mom spent a lot of time with us the first two years of my marriage."

"Did she live with you?"

"No, I'd purchased a small, but comfortable, home for her not too far from us. We already had Monica's mother living with us, and she and my mom were like oil and water. Those two clashed something fierce, and my mother never backed down from an argument. Between Monica and her mother, they never gave poor Mom a moment of peace when she was around. But, after you came, she put up with them so she could see you. I've already told you how she was responsible for me hiring Melinda. Had she lived longer, you and Drake would have known more happiness as children. She doted on you for a year."

"Dad, why haven't we seen pictures of her before now?"

"Monica wouldn't allow it. She hated when my mother came around. She hated that every day you grew more to look like her while Mom celebrated the fact. You had her big brown eyes, when Monica's were ice blue. You had a head full of beautiful golden brown curls, when Monica's hair was blonde and straight as a board. It ate at her, Tiff—infuriated both her and her mother."

Tiffany gave her head a curious shake. "Why would they care when they obviously felt so little for me? Why would they begrudge an infant someone, *anyone* who would show it tenderness and love?"

"They couldn't relate to someone like her. Neither of those women had ever been capable of loving anyone but themselves. Hell, they didn't even like each other, Tiff. The only time they ever got along was when my mother was around to give them a common enemy. They joined forces just so they could hate her together, because she forced them to see everything they weren't."

Tiffany nodded, thinking she could understand that. "What happened to her?"

"One morning she didn't show up. I called, and didn't get an answer. I waited until late that afternoon, thinking she had a doctor's appointment or something, and called again. I went over to her place and found her dead on her kitchen floor. She'd had a massive heart attack."

Tiffany took her father's hand and gave it a tight squeeze. "I'm sorry, Dad. That must have been horrible for you."

"Oh, I won't sugar coat it—it was a bad time for me. All I had to turn to was a shrew of a wife, and a mother-in-law who reminded me at every turn how thrilled she was *that woman* was out of her life for good. That's what she called her...*that woman.* Monica never allowed photos of my mother to be displayed in our home, but Melinda and I had always taken plenty of snapshots of her holding you, giving you a bath, washing your hair, with you sitting up for the first time, crawling for the first time, taking your first steps—my mother was in every one of them. We had an entire photo album full of snapshots of her with you. Mom and Melinda are the ones who took you for your studio portraits."

"Where are they? Are they at mothers put up somewhere?"

"No honey, I'm sorry. After my mom died, Monica found the album and tried to burn it—threw it in the fireplace."

"Why would she do such a thing?" Tiffany asked, horrified. "All she had to do was put it away and never look at it again."

"That's not Monica's style."

"Where did these photos come from?" she asked.

"Melinda pulled the album from the fireplace as soon as your mother left the room. She even burned her hand badly. Your mother actually fired her when she found out, but Melin knew what would happen to you if she wasn't around, so she came to me. I told Monica she couldn't fire Melin. I also threatened to kick her mother out of the house."

He shifted uncomfortably in his chair. "I could barely stand to be in the same house with her after that. I guess Monica started getting worried that I'd boot her out, or leave. We had a party one night, some society thing that she was so fond of. Monica cozied up to me all night and made sure my drink was constantly refreshed. As a result, Drake was conceived that night. Once she gave me a son to carry on the family name, she felt like she'd done her duty. We never slept with each other again after that night. Once I met Leah that was it for me."

Tiffany put her hand on her father's shoulder. "I'm sorry Dad. I wish I'd known growing up."

"I wish I'd had enough gumption to tell you, but the whole point of this story is Monica couldn't stand to treat you like a daughter because every time she looked at you, she saw my mother. She seemed to transfer her hatred for my mother to you. I'm so sorry I didn't do what I could to get you out of that place, but you did have Melinda. She loved both you and Drake like her own. It's a real shame she never had any children."

Tiffany shook her head in confusion. "But Drake and I look so much alike, the same curly hair, brown eyes, the same mouth. Why didn't she hate him as much as she hated me?"

"My guess is because my mother wasn't around to fall in love with him like she did you. Monica didn't resent Drake the way she did you. She was— indifferent to him. She wasn't capable of showing him any more love than she was you, or me, or anyone else, for that matter. She's a cold, heartless woman—just like her mother."

Daniel paused to check out the screen of his ringing cell phone and grinned. He hit the answer button and after a brief conversation with the caller, he disconnected.

His immediate rise from the lounger and big grin had her curious. "Who was that?"

"*That* is the second half of your Christmas gift. It's actually the best part of it." He grabbed her hand and pulled her back into her home. "Hey, Drake!"

Drake looked up from the snack bar, where he was talking to Red and Chad. "Yes Sir?"

"Come here, Son. You have an interest in this, too." He pulled them both to the front entrance and threw open the door. A woman stepped into the doorway a second before Tiffany's squeal of excitement ripped the air.

"Melin!" Tiffany threw herself at Melin. "How did you get here? Why didn't you call and tell us?" She stepped back and stared through tears of joy at the woman who'd raised her and Drake as her own. "I've missed you so much!"

"Daniel wouldn't let me call. He wanted to surprise the two of you." The pretty, green-eyed woman stroked Tiffany's soft curls and beamed at her. "I've missed you so much. How are you, baby girl?"

"I'm wonderful, especially now that you're here. How long can you stay?"

"We're staying for the entire week through next weekend." Melinda caught Drake's eye. "Marcus Drake, get over here and give me a hug."

Drake wrapped her tightly in his arms and spun around with her before planting a big kiss on her cheek. "It's good to see you, Melin. You're as beautiful as ever, and you look happy."

Her husband's deep voice answered unexpectedly from the doorway. "I'd like to think that's my doing."

Drake put Melinda down and reached out to the man. "It's good to see you, Greg. You must be taking excellent care of her."

Greg Hart nodded. "We take care of each other, Drake. It's good to see you both." He hugged Tiffany as well.

Tiffany placed one hand on her chest. "You can't know how much it means to me to have you here for both Christmas and our wedding."

"We never would have been able to make it here on time if it hadn't been for Daniel," Melinda admitted. "We were supposed to come in early tomorrow morning. Your father called me two days ago, begging us to come in for Christmas and stay the entire week to be with you for the opening of the club. By then every flight was booked solid, so he arranged for a private plane."

Daniel stepped forward to greet the couple. "And how was the flight?"

Melinda gave him an appreciative sigh. "Wonderful, but I believe it's ruined me. I don't know if I'll ever be able to fly commercial again after being so pampered on that flight."

Tiffany pulled Red forward and introduced him to the Harts.

Melinda gave him a hug. "Have we heard some stories about you, Red McAllister." She pointed a finger at him. "You keep my baby girl happy, you hear? Or you'll have to deal with me."

Red hugged his wife and nodded. "I'll do whatever it takes to make sure she is, Melinda. I promise you."

Greg cleared his throat. "Good, because this lady will go ballistic if she feels either of her "kids" is being mistreated.

After a bevy of introductions, Tiffany settled her new guests at the table for coffee and conversation. She'd just shown off the photo album Melinda had contributed the photos for when she turned to her. "Okay, Melinda," Tiffany began, "I know you and Greg were high school sweethearts. I never heard the story of why you broke up in the first place." She looked at Greg and winked. "What happened? Did you catch him with a cheerleader behind the school bleachers, or something like that?"

Melinda's gaze clashed with her husband's. Greg gave his head a slow shake and turned to Tiffany. "It was more serious than that. We had our parents to blame for our separation."

"And we were too young to stop them," Melinda added. "In December, of my senior year, I finally got the nerve to tell my mom I thought I was pregnant. She was devastated, and I was terrified. I hadn't told anyone yet, not even Greg. I didn't want him to worry until I knew for sure. My mother told me to stay in my room while she spoke to my dad. They never raised their voices, and by the time the two of them came back up to my room, they had everything all planned out. McCray is a very small town, still under 1,500 people, and they didn't want anyone to know the *situation* I'd gotten myself into."

"But, you eventually told Greg, right?"

"Honey, I never got the chance. My parents made one or two phone calls, then came to my room with a large suitcase. My mom threw some of my things inside and within an hour we were in the car. We drove non-stop, except for bathroom breaks and to eat. A day and a half later, we arrived at a home for unwed mothers in Dallas, Texas. And that's where I stayed until my baby was born. I had no phone privileges—only weekly calls from my parents. No letters in or out, no privacy, and no way to run away. I had it all planned—I was going to grab my baby when it was born and run out of there then call Greg to pick me up." She gazed at her husband, her eyes sad and tearful. "That's not what happened."

Tiffany sniffed and wiped her eyes. "Melinda…I had no idea. All these years I thought you couldn't have children."

Melinda swallowed with some effort and looked as if she were lost in the past as a memory took hold of her. "I only got to hold my baby girl once, just long enough to see that she had my nose and her daddy's chin. I couldn't see her eyes because they were closed, but I always thought they would be green. For years I looked for little girls with curly hair, green eyes, my nose, and Greg's chin."

Tiffany finally found the ability to speak. Even then, it was with a voice thick with tears. "Why didn't you tell us, Melin?"

"Your grandmother Mary knew, and so did your dad. It was too painful to talk about it. I ended up hemorrhaging. I remember passing out just after that awful nurse ripped my baby from my arms. By the time I woke up, my uterus was removed and my baby was gone." Greg grasped her hand as she wiped the tears from her eyes.

Drake shook his head. "You went through all of that alone?"

"My parents had planned to drive down a week before my due date to be there with me, but I went into labor two weeks early. They were called early on, but even with fifteen hours of labor, they still didn't make it in time." She smiled sadly at her husband. "When I left that place I had no baby, and no hope of ever having another child. All I had was the diploma I'd received while in the home, the name of the orphanage they'd sent my baby to, and the air fare my parents had left for me to fly back to McCray once the doctor released me to fly. The hemorrhage had been so severe he wouldn't do that for two weeks. When I walked out of there, I went straight to a pay phone. I called Greg's home and they told me he'd moved on and joined the Marines."

Tiffany turned on Greg. "You left without trying to find her?"

His mouth tightened in a frown. "I was in college when all of this went down—studying for mid-terms. But, this is where the real deceit from our parents comes in. Hers told me she'd gone to live with a relative in California. They said she didn't know how to tell me to my face that she didn't want to see me anymore. I didn't believe them, of course. I sat back and waited for her to contact me—a phone call, a letter, or something. After six months I accepted it, dropped out of college, quit my part time job, and joined the Marines."

Melinda placed her hand softly on the side of her husband's cheek. "Years later, I learned his mother had never told him I'd called or forwarded any of my letters I sent to his house. Of course, the orphanage wouldn't give me any information without a lawyer. I knew she could have been anywhere, but I felt this need to stay near the home. So I stayed in Texas, and went to work—in cafes, at restaurants, in fast food joints, and as a cashier. I ended up around Houston eventually, and met Ms. Mary, Daniel's mother. She talked Daniel into hiring me as a live-in babysitter for you, Tiff."

"Mary spent a lot of time with me at first, to make sure I could handle you. Once Drake came along, I had enough money saved up to start the search for my baby, but when I tried to contact the orphanage again, it had burned down and all the records were destroyed. By then I was so attached to you and Drake that I couldn't leave you. Mary was already gone, and Daniel, well he was too busy working to watch out for you two. I wasn't about to leave you kids with your mother and grandmother—ugh, those horrible women!" She shivered visibly, as though repulsed by the thought. She turned back to Tiffany.

"And you'll remember my mom passed away just after Drake left for college. My dad was sick and needed me to take care of him."

Tiffany's mouth opened in shock. "I can't believe you still kept in touch with your parents after what they did to you and Greg."

Melinda's eyes misted over. "Time has a way of lessening the anger and hurt. Good or bad, they were my parents. They made a bad decision, but it didn't mean they didn't love me. They both regretted it later."

Giselle had been leaning against the doorway, mesmerized by the story. Suddenly, she cleared her throat and spoke a single word, sounding hesitant to say anything. "Melinda?"

Melinda turned to face her. "Yes?"

Tiffany frowned, noticing Giselle's flushed face. "Giselle, are you feeling all right?" She rose from her chair to check her friend's pulse. "Your heart rate is sky high, are you feeling any pressure?"

Giselle waved off Tiffany's concern. "Stop being a doctor, Tif. I'm fine." She turned back to Melinda and Greg. "Did you say the orphanage they'd brought your daughter to was destroyed by fire?"

"Yes, along with all the records and files," Melinda said. "Why?"

"Was it in June of 1977?"

Melinda nodded. "Y-yes."

Jackson appeared beside his wife. Giselle clutched at his arm for support. "Was your daughter born in 1975?"

Greg aimed a curious look at his wife, before turning back to Giselle and nodding. "April 24th, 1975."

Tiffany gasped as her friend's knees buckled out from under her. Jackson scooped up his wife and sat her on one of the dining room chairs. He looked at Melinda. "That's her birthday. She's adopted, and we've been trying to find her birth parents, but the orphanage burned down, along with all the records. All we have is her birth certificate."

Melinda crouched to her knees in front of Giselle and stared into her eyes. "Your eyes—green, but dotted with specks of gold. Like Greg's," she said.

Giselle blinked. "Wh-what?"

Tiffany crouched down between Giselle and Melinda, sensing this was something big—wanting to support them both.

Melinda shook her head. "It's just that the gold specks in your eyes—Greg has those."

"Their chins are very similar—they're both cleft," Vivienne added.

Greg looked back and forth between the two women. "You have the same hair and noses." Greg kneeled down next to his wife as their gazes locked. "Is it possible?"

With Jackson's help, Giselle rose slowly from the chair. She took Melinda's arm and brought her to the mirror in the foyer. They stood there, the two of them, each being supported by their husbands.

"My God," Melinda breathed, "Can this be possible?"

Jackson pointed out the freckles across Giselle's nose. "Melinda has the same spattering of freckles."

"She does have my chin," Greg said.

"My hair," Melinda added.

"Our faces are shaped the same," Giselle sniffed, and rubbed her belly.

"Is everything going well with the pregnancy?" Melinda asked.

Giselle nodded. "Very well."

Jackson turned to Melinda. "We discovered last month that we're having twins."

"Every third generation woman in my family has had twins for the last 75 years." Melinda's gaze latched on to Giselle's in the mirror. "You'd be third generation if you're my daughter. And those babies will be identical, not fraternal."

"Excuse me, do you mind?" Vivienne pushed gently through the two men to the women standing in front of the mirror. "I noticed something earlier," she said, moving next to Giselle.

"What is it, Mrs. Vivi?" Jackson asked.

"Giselle's ears." Vivi checked the shape of the cartilage. "Look at that little projection she has on both ears, and the shape of the lobe." She looked up as Jackson nodded. "Now look at Greg's ears." She pointed out the similarity. "Those are both very unique genetic traits. I have eight children and I've always been amazed how certain features get passed down from parent to child." She stood back and crossed her arms while smiling at the two couples. "You'd need to have DNA tests done right away, to confirm it, of course. But I'd bet my last cent, even without it, that Giselle is your daughter."

Giselle's hand flew up to her mouth as she began to sob openly.

Drake listened to the exchange, but couldn't seem to pull his gaze from Annie, who'd become increasingly more emotional as Melin's story unfolded. She finally broke away from the crowd that had gathered around the two couples and rushed out to the patio. He wasted no time in following her out.

"Are you okay?"

She jumped at the sound of his voice. "Damn it, Drake! *Must* you follow me wherever I go?"

"Well, you ran out of there like a thoroughbred draggin' a tail full of barbed wire. I was concerned."

"You don't need to be." She turned her back on him. "Now, go away. You're annoying me."

Drake ignored her and walked closer. "That's some story, isn't it?" He waited for a response from Annie, who remained silent, a distinct rarity. He crept nearer and realized she was crying quietly. Without saying a word, he wrapped her in his arms, determined to comfort her. Damn, it felt good holding her again. It felt so right, and just for a moment, he thought she'd give in to it—accept that they could be good together. She pulled away from him, suddenly.

"Let go of me, Drake."

Drake smiled as she turned away, obviously struggling with her emotions. "I only want to help, Annie. I didn't realize you were so soft-hearted."

"Well, I am—I get it from my mom, so there." She sounded as upset with herself as she was with him. "Things like that," she waved her hand at the house, "it's *sad*—what their parents did to them."

"But Melinda and Greg got back together. And if your mother is to be believed, and personally I think she knows what she's talking about, it looks like they may have found their daughter."

"But look at all the time they lost. They've missed out on a lifetime of seeing their child grow." She swiped uselessly at the tears running down her face. "It's just so sad."

He couldn't help but smile as he watched her sniff and dab at her tears with the cuff of her sweater. "Yeah, it's a sad thing when people miss out on a chance for happiness. At least Melin and Greg have the excuse that it was out of their control. It wasn't because of his or *her* stubbornness." He spoke quietly, hoping his words sunk in.

She turned her back on him again. "Give it a rest, would you?"

He laid his hands softly on her shoulders. "Not as long as there's the slightest chance of wearing you down."

"It's not going to happen, Drake." She turned on him, her voice hard with impatience. "You need to face that—and stop tormenting me."

"What are you so damned afraid of Annie?"

"I'm not afraid."

"That's not what you said at the club that night in the parking lot. You said I scared the hell out of you." He slipped his hands on her waist and pulled her closer. "So what is it? Are you afraid of being happy?"

"I *am* happy." She twisted out of his hold. "I've got a wonderful career just starting and a full life ahead of me. I don't need to be side-tracked."

"But we could at least be friends." He was willing to take that—for now.

She snorted. "We couldn't just be friends if our lives depended on it, and you damn well know it. This is how it has to be. I'm not putting my life on hold for you, or anybody." She walked back inside, leaving Drake to stare after her.

Inside the emotional tear-fest of the house, Red rushed to his wife's side to console her. "Babe, what's wrong?"

"Red—they've been separated for so long. First, Melinda and Greg, then from the baby wh-who-co-could be Giselle." She wiped at her eyes, continuing with her emotional babbling. "Your mom thinks she is and I bet she's *never* wrong. I just feel so—oh, I don't know!"

"Aw, Doc," Red groaned, holding his sobbing wife in his arms. He looked to his parents', caught the knowing look they exchanged.

Vivienne left her husband's side to collect her daughter-in-law. "Come on dear, let's go have some girl talk." Within seconds, the majority of the women had disappeared down the hall into the master bedroom.

Red furrowed his brow, torn between wanting to comfort his wife and distance himself from the emotional turmoil and tears. His father's reassuring hand on his shoulder had him looking toward him, his brow furrowed in concern. "Is that a normal reaction?"

Pete McAllister's face spread with a knowing grin. "Oh, it may be normal for a while, but believe me, it'll pass, Son."

He turned away, still wearing the grin, but not soon enough to keep Red from hearing his low chuckle and comment.

"It always passes."

Chapter Twenty-One

Red stood at the front of the church, fidgeting in his classic black tux, anxious for the first glimpse of Tiffany. He scanned the church full of family and friends, thankful the two of them were blessed with so many, while waiting for his bride to appear. At her request, the church wedding was a simple affair. The only items they'd added to the traditional Christmas decor gracing the apse and altar were several more poinsettia plants.

Red had been right when he said every girl needed her father to walk her down the aisle. It turned out, that's all Tiffany needed. She'd requested no bridesmaids or groomsmen—only her father.

The doors opened at the far end of the nave, revealing Daniel LeBlanc, dressed in his own black tuxedo, and the center of Red's world. His breath caught at the first sight of his beautiful bride, stunning in a simple, but elegantly cut gown of ivory satin.

As they approached, he noticed more details—how she wore her hair pulled up, her golden brown curls strategically escaping from their loose binding of crystal adorned combs. She was perfection. Her beautiful brown eyes sparkled with happiness—no sign of a tear or trace of nervousness. Daniel hugged his daughter tightly, took a moment to whisper something in her ear. Whatever it was, had her prolonging the hug she gave him.

Daniel finally handed her over to him and gave his hand a firm shake.

"Thank you, Sir."

Daniel's eyes grew misty for a second, and he blinked several times to clear them. "Thank you, Red—for opening my eyes. You brought my daughter back to me."

"You're welcome."

Daniel nodded. "I don't have to ask if you love my daughter; it's obvious that you do. You two will be fine." He turned and left them alone at the altar. Red's gaze locked onto his beautiful bride and for several moments, everything else, everyone else in the building faded away.

"You take my breath away, Doc."

"Thank you, Red." Her right brow quirked as she passed an appreciative gaze over him.

He grinned. "Like what you see?"

She leaned close to whisper. "I'll show you how much I like it when we get home tonight." She gave him one last wink before they turned and took two steps up to where Father Mitch waited to join them in holy matrimony.

Red's new club, again thanks to Tiffany's simple, but elegant tastes, was beautifully decorated, even though it lacked the usual fuss and fluff of so many weddings he'd attended. The food, provided by a catering service, was delicious and artfully displayed, the champagne, high quality, and the music was Red's D.J., playing every song from the couple's carefully created playlist. Brandon had offered the services of his band, but Tiffany flatly refused, insisting this night was for family to *enjoy*. He was under strict orders to dance the night away with his wife. The couple had each chosen a song to dedicate to their spouses. Red smiled when the D.J. announced the bride's choice for her husband, "This Love," by LeAnn Rimes.

"Do you recognize this song?"

"Mmmm…our first time in the shower," Red said mischievously. "You made an excellent choice, as usual. Have I told you how breathtaking you are today?"

She smiled. "I believe you have. It's quite a change from me walking around the house with no make-up, jeans, or scrubs, and sneakers, isn't it?"

"You always take my breath away—even in your no-frills running gear." He nuzzled her neck. "Sing to me, Mrs. McAllister."

She lifted her mouth to his ear, filled their personal air space with the voice that had captivated him a month earlier. He waltzed her around the floor, enjoying the feel of her in his arms, the way they moved together as Tiffany sang sweetly into his ear. Red stopped in the middle of the floor as the melody ended and closed out the song with a tender kiss for his wife.

They stood toe to toe, and motionless as the D.J. interrupted with an announcement.

"Okay folks, I have to admit, I'm not quite sure what this is all about, but the groom has dedicated this one to his lovely bride."

All was quiet in the room when the sharp military tap of a single snare drum filled the air. Tiffany's brow initially furrowed in confusion. But when the sprightly notes of a flute and piccolo joined to form the opening notes of *The Yellow Rose of Texas*, Tiffany's eyes widened. Her mouth flew open in a show of semi-serious horror. "Red McAllister. Tell me you didn't!"

He took two giant steps away from her—spread his arms wide, a huge grin plastered on his face. "Baby, I couldn't pass up the opportunity."

Excited screeches from Melissa and Bailey cut through the air as they approached the edge of the dance floor.

Bailey pointed toward Tiffany. "The tattoo!"

"Spring break in Panama City!" Melissa called out.

Bailey acted like she was pouring something from a bottle. "Somebody break out the te-qui-la!"

Both women turned and touched a finger to a spot just above their right butt cheeks. The crowd erupted in laughter as the newly married couple played along. Tiffany leaned over, presenting her backside to the crowd as Red pointed out the exact spot of her tattoo. He looked up at the spectators, winked, and gave the crowd a big thumbs-up. The room exploded with more cheers, laughter, and finally applause. Tiffany straightened, her cheeks flushed slightly with embarrassment.

Having teased her enough for one day, he motioned to the man in charge.

The DJ cut the song. "Yellow rose tattoos aside," he announced, "here's the *real* dedication song from the groom to his bride." The familiar opening notes of Van Morrison's *Brown Eyed Girl* blasted from the speakers.

Red gave her a dramatic bow at the waist. "Is this more to your liking, my lady?"

Tiffany pointed to her husband then crooked her finger at him. "Now, *that's* more like it, mister!"

Red took his wife's hand, and delighted the crowd with a lively dance with her.

Later in the evening, Tiffany felt a pair of strong hands at her waist. She turned from Carrie and Giselle to look into her husband's gaze.

"Excuse me ladies, but could I steal my wife for a dance?"

Red whisked her off in a waltz to a song she couldn't help but link to this man. She let her head fall back and hummed along to Hold On To Me. She opened her eyes, catching her husband gazing at her, wearing his trademark sexy grin. "What are you thinking about, McAllister?"

Red nuzzled her neck. "Our last dance at Jackson and Giselle's wedding reception. It was all good, right up until that slap." He pulled back and rubbed his face.

She kissed the cheek that had once worn her handprint for several minutes. "That too, but I was talking about the first time I spent the night at the ranch, when neither of us could sleep. I walked into your office, and you were sitting there, all shirtless and buff…looking so damn sexy and playing this on your guitar. I was mesmerized."

"You thought I looked sexy?" He kissed the tip of her nose.

"Like you didn't know." She slid her hands seductively up his torso. Her husband released a deep rumble of a groan and had her mind returning to the last time they'd made love, and wishing they were home—alone.

"If I'd known that's what you were thinking, I'd have left the damn thing off a little longer. There I was, trying not to offend you."

She scrunched up her face. "I was so disappointed when you put your shirt back on."

He chuckled. "Every time I closed my eyes that night, all I could see was an image of you in that whirlpool tub. Every time I dozed off, I woke up in a pool of sweat and wanting you."

"Wanting me?" She traced a nail softly over his lips and chin.

"Why the hell did you think I had my shirt off? It was freezing that night, but I was on fire. There you were, in my *home*, and I couldn't tell you how crazy I was about you." He shook his head, wearing a pained expression. "If you'd only agreed to go skinny dipping with me." Her low chuckle had him smiling again.

He moved her gracefully around the floor then finished by pulling her close to him. "I can't wait to get you home."

She nibbled at his lower lip, smiling at the low growl it produced. "I'm ready, but we have a few gifts to open first."

He dropped his head back in frustration. "We have to open those *here*? I thought we'd get to take them home and open them all later."

"No, we have to do it here, babe. Your mom insists it's a McAllister family tradition."

"Aw man, why can't we start our own family tradition?"

"Stop whining, Red. Come on, it won't take that long. There are just a couple of dozen actual gifts. Most are gift cards." She pulled him over to the gift table and enlisted Melissa and Bailey's help to make a list of gifts and who brought them for thank you cards. As promised, they went through them quickly. Tiffany handed him the last gift on the table. "This one says 'To be opened by Red', so here you go." She handed him the box and stepped away.

Red studied the square, flat box, wrapped in white ribbons. He removed the ribbons, then the lid, revealing several layers of tissue paper. Pulling the paper aside, he stared at the contents, gently nudging one, then a second, then the third of the three items inside. He covered the box and looked to his left, and then his right for Tiffany. A light tap on his shoulder had him spinning around to see his wife standing behind him, wearing an ear to ear grin.

He placed his hands gently on her shoulders. "Are you serious? Can it happen this quickly?"

She looped her arms around his waist, snuggled close for a kiss. "I think I've married into a very virile family."

"What is it?" The call from the crowd had Red reluctant to release his wife. He finally did and turned to their wedding guests. Lifting the lid from the box, he removed the three different test sticks from three different pregnancy tests. Each one showed the same result in different ways—whether it was a blue dot, a pink plus, or simply the word PREGNANT.

He couldn't keep the smile from his face as he made his announcement to the crowd.

"We're having a baby!"

Whistles, applause and cheers ringing in his ears, he lifted his wife and spun her around before setting her down. He kissed her until she pulled back, breathless and flushed with excitement.

"I can't wait to see our baby, Red. I'm so looking forward to bringing another beautiful McAllister child into this world. And I'm praying he'll have that same gorgeous, strawberry-blonde hair and his daddy's blue eyes."

He gave her a seductive grin. "Not me. I'm hoping we break the cycle. Let's inject a little curly haired cutie with huge brown eyes like her beautiful mama." He nodded decisively. "Yeah, that's what I'm putting on my wish list."

"Oh, but I adore my red-haired, blue-eyed devil."

He kissed the pretty pout from her lips. "Not any more than I love my brown eyed girl."

ABOUT THE AUTHOR

Lori Leger is a wife, mother, doting grandmother, and Mistress of Procrastination. She lives in Louisiana with the love of her life, her very own Studley-do-Right. He's earned his spot in the Keeper Husband's Hall of Fame by allowing her to walk away from an eighteen year career as an Engineering Technician in Road Design to stay home and write.

She adores writing stories set in her beloved south Louisiana, where good Cajun cooking, helping your neighbors, and saying y'all is as normal as hurricanes, heat, and humidity. She figures as long as she's not tunneling through ten feet of snow to get to her car, it's a perfectly acceptable trade-off.

Lori has nine novels published in two series: La Fleur de Love and its spin-off, Halos & Horns series. She has also contributed to, as well as published, short stories in each of the five Seasons of Love anthologies, an author collaboration series. She's contributed to the Sweet & Savory Cookbook of Amazon Authors, published by Top Ten Press. Lori also has an article published in the non-fiction book Writing After Retirement: Tips From Retired Writers, published by Rowman and Littlefield Publishers, and edited and compiled by Carol Smallwood and Christine Redman-Waldeyer.

Her latest book, Running Out of Rain is the first book in her Prime of Love Series, novels dedicated to mature characters finding love and laughter through the everyday twists and turns of growing older. She has a second planned for a fall 2015 release date, and a third set for the summer of 2016.

Lori Leger
P.O. Box 641
Kinder, LA 70648
cajunflair@lorilegerauthor.com
www.lorilegerauthor.com
www.facebook.com/lorilegerauthor
www.facebook.com/llegerauthor
www.facebook.com/CajunflairPublishing
Twitter: @LoriLegerAuthor

OTHER WORK BY LORI LEGER

Fleur de Love
(Series set in southwest Louisiana)
Book 1: SOME DAY SOMEBODY
Book 2: LAST FIRST KISS
Book 2.5: HART'S DESIRE - A Novella
Book 3: BROWN EYED GIRL
Book 4: HEAVEN IN YOUR EYES

Halos & Horns
(Spinoff series: Where residents of Louisiana and Texas cross the state line to find romance.)
Book 1: GREEN EYED TEMPTATION
Book 2: SARAH SMILE
Book 3: MEAGAN'S MARINE
Book 4: ONE YEAR TO FOREVER

Seasons of Love
(Multi-authored Seasonal series by Cajunflair Publishing)
Book 1: HEARTS, HEARTHS & HOLIDAYS
("Bells Will be Ringing" by Lori Leger)
Book 2: SPRING PROMISE
("Loving Cat" by Lori Leger)
Book 3: SWEET SUMMERTIME LOVE
("Still Loving Cat" by Lori Leger)
Book 4: CHRISTMAS BY CANDLELIGHT
("Baby Blues Christmas" by Lori Leger)
Book 5: IT'S A SUMMER THING
("Full Circle Summer" by Lori Leger)

FULL CIRCLE LOVE
Cat & Zach Stories
(The last four stories from the Seasons of Love Series in one book)

Prime of Love
(A Mature Love Series)
Book1: RUNNING OUT OF RAIN

Non-Fiction article in the book:
WRITING AFTER RETIREMENT
Published by: Rowman and Littlefield Publishers